JESSICA GRACE

Cover design: The Pretty Little Design Co.

Editor: Mackenzie (Nice Girl, Naughty Edits)

Authors Note

*The book confronts very real issues that could be potential triggers.
These include, but are not limited to, mental health, alcohol abuse,
sexual content, and explicit language.*

Dedication

To anyone who's ever said a bad word about me—
thank you from the bottom of my middle finger, all the way to the top.

the songs
that inspired

Two Feet *Tell Me The Truth*
Sam Fischer *Hopeless Romantic*
The Neighbourhood *Daddy Issues*
Tones And Eyes *Don't Lie (Acoustic)*
Jacob Banks *Chainsmoking*
Gracie Abrams *Mean It*
Billie Eilish *No Time To Die*
Noel Gallagher's High Flying Birds *Dead In The Water*
The Neighbourhood *Sweater Weather*
Rhodes, Birdy *Let It All Go*
Christy *When We Get Old*

Prologue

"WHERE HAVE YOU BEEN?"

I expected it—the interrogation. The question protruded from her lips like a terrier snapping at my ankles. Fuck, I wasn't one foot through the door and into our home before the words had completely escaped her mouth.

My wife stood in the middle of the room, wearing only a thin white camisole. Her brown hair laid across her chest, barely covering the peachy skin that led to her breasts. She was beautiful—when she wasn't being a bitch.

With her eyes wide, she stuck her chin out, trying to bait me into giving her an answer. She seared her head back when I didn't respond straight away, rolling it with unequal motion as her impatience grew. Then the frown came, disapproval and accusation wedged between the lines of her forehead. I fucking hated it when she did that. When she looked like that.

The red wine swished around the glass she held as she waltzed towards me. Despite her need to be closer, I decided we needed more space, so I headed to the kitchen sink.

"I went for a run," I said, staring at the tiled wall in front of me. She could see I was dressed in my workout gear. But no, perhaps that was too blatantly obvious for her. She needed words. The why, where, and was I alone? Shit, the fucking coordinates, probably.

"A run?" she asked, but it wasn't a question. Not really.

I felt her presence move closer, heard her wine glass clink on the counter, and then her arms were wrapping around my waist from behind. Her cheek pressed against my back, holding me tight to her. Her breasts pushed into me, causing the dampness of my sweaty T-shirt to mould onto my skin.

"Sophia," I grunted, pouring myself a glass of water. I knew what came next. She wouldn't stop until she got what she believed to be her version of the truth.

I took a gulp of water and then attempted to shake her away. Except she held on too tightly. I wasn't the only one at fault here, but she had a habit of making me feel like I was to blame. Like it was solely my fault our marriage was dying.

The rhythm of her heart accelerated between us as she moved up on her tiptoes, her nose skimming the bottom of my neck as she inhaled my scent.

"You smell like her," she whispered.

"I went for a run," I repeated. "I smell like sweat." I slammed my glass against the kitchen counter. It cracked with my strength, but it didn't break.

"Don't lie to me, Walker."

My knuckles whitened as I clenched the cracked glass still in my grip. "Go back to bed, Sophia. You're drunk and deluded," I added after a beat. "This shit–it's another fake scenario you've made up in your head."

My patience for her, for what was left of our relationship, was barely held together by a fray. What more was there to say to a woman who always thought the worst of me?

"It's our wedding anniversary. You should have been here with me. Not her."

I sucked my teeth. "You're projecting your guilt onto me, throwing accusation after accusation at *me*. When it was you who went against our arrangement. It was you who made that choice."

"It was a one-time thing. I've said I'm sorry. Why do you have to call it an arrangement? It's a marriage, Walker. Our marriage."

"Shit, I don't want to keep doing this," I said, setting my glass into the sink before turning it into shards. "I can't keep having this conversation with you."

I turned in her hold to face her, and she allowed her hands to drop between us. She pursed her lips, tilting her face up towards mine.

A second passed, and then, "Who is she?"

My frustration wallowed in my blood like cancer. I knew better than to continue the same argument we'd been having for the past however many months now. But I couldn't help myself.

"When are you going to get it into your pretty fucking skull that I've been nothing but loyal, despite the farce of the last eleven years?"

"I don't believe you," she said, her fingernails digging into my chest. "You're lying."

"No," I sighed. "You're just deaf to the truth."

My nostrils flared as her hand travelled down to the waist-band of my shorts, and then she slid her hand underneath them and into my boxers. Her nails scratched my skin as she moved to wrap her hand around my flaccid cock.

"For fuck's sake, Sophia, what are you doing?"

"I'm checking for signs of your infidelity," she said simply, as if it was normal.

And I guess it was for us. This wasn't the first time she sought answers to the bullshit she had created in her head. I'd caught her checking my phone on numerous occasions.

Our relationship was past the point of return. I was exhausted fighting it. There was nothing left to hold on to. And I'd only have to be smiled at by another woman before the inter-rogation began.

"Do you know her?"

"Why did you smile back if you don't know her?"

"Shit, Sophia, stop this. If this were a real marriage, it would be me seeking answers after what you did."

Of course, it stung when she first told me she'd cheated, when she described how good it felt to be wanted by someone because she wasn't wanted by me. How she thought she'd over-served her purpose. Though once that hurt subsided and I gave way to the anger, it seemed I no longer gave a single fuck. A part of me wondered if anything we ever had was real or whether the bigger picture had clouded my judgement. The sole reason we got together in the first place.

Still, somewhere, somehow, our relationship had diminished. And the apparent *love* I once held for my wife was long gone.

That's if it ever truly existed at all.

I supposed I couldn't blame her entirely. The intimacy she shared with a stranger really did feel like the least of our problems.

"I just need to know." She pushed her head into my chest. "Who is she? Tell me. I'll stop if you tell me. Are you paying her? What is she giving you that I can't?"

She squeezed my cock in her hand, enough that I couldn't help but become hard. It was human nature, I guess. We hadn't been intimate for months. And amidst the atmosphere, the fighting, she was still my wife. My beautiful bitch of a wife.

"We made fucking vows, didn't we? For better, for worse. As fake as they were, there's no one else." Yet, things were always getting worse, and I didn't want to stay married for the sake of it any longer. I couldn't love her–not the way she wanted–no matter how hard she fought me to.

Her warm breaths seeped through the material of my shirt as her hand began to stroke up and down my shaft, bringing out the masochist in me. I was probably harder now than I'd been in the past twelve months, when our marriage really began to splinter.

It was primarily mundane things to begin with.

Petty shit.

Things I couldn't name while she was stroking my cock in our kitchen.

But those things grew into unhappiness that was tough to tunnel out from, which ultimately led to her infidelity, which of course, brought us to the here and now.

"Have you found what it is you're looking for, Sophia? Is my cock hard enough for you?"

She groaned. "You're lying, Walker. Do I know her? Is she employed at the club?" Her hand stroked from the base of my cock to the top, her fingers wiping a bead of pre-cum over its tip.

There was a time when I'd have fucked her on the kitchen counter, had my fingers in her ass and my tongue down her throat, but what was the point of any of it anymore? If it weren't for the legal document which bound us together, we wouldn't be together at all.

"Do I?" she asked again as her hand squeezed around my length.

"No," I grit. "Because there's no one but you."

"Is this for her or for me?" She slowly ran her hand back and forth, squeezing every time she reached the top of my cock. She knew what I liked, knew what got me off.

"Fuck," I rasped, and then I told her what she wanted to hear, just to get her off my back. "It's for you, Soph."

My words seemed to satisfy her, and then her hand began moving swiftly up and down. I felt my balls draw up with every pinch. Every tug.

I couldn't tell her the truth—that I was only hard because it had been months since a hand that wasn't my own had touched my cock. How was someone supposed to tell their wife that they could barely get it up for them anymore? That the constant accusations, the misunderstandings, and the confessions of her love only retained them fucking soft?

"Good, that's good," she whispered, speaking the words into my chest.

It was as if my denial was finally submerging. But I was past caring. I'd already decided I wanted out before I stepped through the door. It's all I'd thought about when I was running laps around Hyde Park in the dark of the night. It was the penthouse I noticed for lease that cemented it. I needed out. And we needed time away from each other so we could both gain some clarity–not for our marriage, but for ourselves. I didn't voice any of this, though. I decided I'd tell her once everything was in motion. Once I'd leased the property, with no time for her to attempt talking me out of it. Not that she'd succeed. My mind was made up.

My balls and spine tingled with satisfaction as my release took flight, and strings of my jizz covered her hand. Despite the moment of euphoria, I knew the arrangement we made all those years ago was stale. This would be the last time we shared even a resemblance of intimacy. Nothing between us would ever get back to the way things once were.

The euphoria was fleeting.

Our reality spoke the loudest.

For the last twelve months, or maybe even the last eleven years, I'd tried to convince myself the love I held for my wife was just warped. Bent and twisted out of shape, moulded that way because of the people we were. I often asked myself how was a man to know the difference if he'd only ever experienced one side of the coin? But that was then, and this was now.

Heads or tails, it didn't make our outcome any different.

You couldn't force a cat to bark.

I was confident I'd never been in love with my wife, but that created an issue–because irrespective of her infidelity, my wife just happened to be psychotically in love with me.

CHAPTER ONE

Blue

I COULDN'T BELIEVE my eyes as I scanned the email in front of me for the third time. My lips parted, but no sound came out. My fingers dragged the cursor over the email address it was sent from, worried one of my so-called friends was trying to ruse me. But it was all there. The email was completely legit.

"Holy shit."

"Are you talking to yourself?" Ebony walked into my bedroom, startling me. She tossed her long, straight, glossy black hair over her shoulder and pointed a freshly varnished fingernail in my direction.

I dropped my head to the side and studied her over my laptop. My friend's hair held a similar resemblance to mine up until two days ago. Her dirty blonde was now pitch black, and I was still getting used to her dramatic change of appearance. "Who let you up?"

She scoffed and threw her Louis Vuitton bag onto my bed, spilling its contents over my quilt. "Your new maid."

"Right, number twelve. I forgot about her." My eyes rolled. I'd lost count of the number of maids my father had been through. They rarely lasted longer than a few months. Learning their names used to be easy, but recently it felt more like trying to complete a Rubik's cube. There was Patricia. Tricia. Sarah, and Sia. Who the hell cared? Eventually, their names all merged into one I could remember. Maid.

"How long do you think this one will last?" Ebony asked, walking around my four-poster bed to the window. She used her fingers to open the white shutters covering them, peeping through the gap she created. I half expected her to turn to dust, but my father said I always did have an overactive imagination.

"Your dad didn't bat an eye as I swanned up your driveway. He's shirtless. He's got bimbos naked in the pool like he's Hugh Hefner or something. It's not even midday."

"He dates them," I said casually.

Me and Ebony had been friends for years, but up until today, it had been easy enough to swerve the rumours of my father's bachelor lifestyle. Now it seemed it was no longer possible when there was evidence to back it up right outside my window. It looked like last night's naked parade continued through the night.

My eyes were still on my laptop screen, re-reading the email for the fourth time just to be sure I'd understood it right.

"Dates them?" she queried. "Plural? As in, he's dating multiple women at a time, and they don't care? All those media tales are true, then? How have we not discussed this before now?"

"*I* don't care. Which means I don't care if they care."

She groaned, flicking the shutters closed as she moved her hand away. "But your dad is so old, and they are so–"

"Young." I finished for her. "I know. Don't remind me."

She settled on my bed amongst the contents of her bag, eyes still on the closed shutters. "Are they as young as us?"

"Ebony," I groaned, dropping my laptop from my lap and onto the yellow velvet ottoman beside me.

I glanced over at her. She looked so out of place in my room. All dark and edgy, while my room looked like a rainbow had thrown up inside it. A leap from how I felt on the inside, but I had a habit of purchasing colourful things. Call it a guise.

"What? You can't blame me for being curious. I've never seen your dad shirtless, let alone all over naked girls that look to be in the same age bracket as us. You know I'd never judge you for who your father is or *what* he is."

"What are you insinuating, Eb? Because gross. I can assure you my father isn't a predator. They're in their twenties, at least."

"Not too far from our seventeen, then." She stuck a finger in her throat and feigned sickness, though it lacked her usual carefree enthusiasm. "Your dad has to be thirty, maybe forty years older than them. Who likes wrinkly dick?"

"Are you asking me that question because you want to know, or trying to convince yourself you don't?"

Everyone had heard the rumour she'd slept with our school principal a few years back, but she was always the first to deny it. He was a married man with kids only a little older than us. If it were true, he'd lose everything and likely end up behind bars. He had a duty of care, and in the state of Florida, Ebony was a minor.

I didn't care who it was. I did not want to think, let alone talk about another older man's genitals or private life.

Ebony rolled her eyes, and a shiver ran through my body at the image of being one of those girls, hanging off a man old enough to be my father. Even so, I dropped my head to my shoulder, feeling the need to defend him and his actions.

"My father throws money about like confetti. At them. With them. Without them. Some girls... like that sort of thing. It's his coping mechanism, I guess. He closed off the compartment of his heart that loves like a regular person. You've just never stayed over long enough to witness what goes on here."

"Not through lack of trying," she said, raising a perfectly shaded black eyebrow at me. "He has you locked up like Rapunzel." Her eyes dipped to my laptop and then back to my face. "What's got you 'holy shitting' anyway?"

I wrapped my arms around myself and stared into her dark brown eyes. "I got in."

"You got in?" she questioned. Seconds passed between us that felt more like minutes, but I knew the moment realisation dawned on her because her eyes widened as she shot off the bed and hurried towards me. "Holy shit. To Duke?"

An awkward splutter of laughter bubbled up my throat, but before it had left my mouth, Ebony grabbed me by the hands and pulled me to my feet. Her arms went around me, squeezing so tight I had to swallow everything back down before it somehow choked me to death.

"Holy shit, Blue!"

My eyes filled with tears as I clutched her back. "You know what this means, right?"

Her grip loosened momentarily before growing tighter. "Uh, I think it means you're moving to London and finally getting out of this place you call a prison."

"It's not that simple, is it?" I pulled back and tugged on a strand of her black hair that had fallen into her face. "This is the easy part."

She regained her composure, her eyes becoming as wet as my own, though neither of us would spill our tears. That's not something we did together, knowing if we started, neither of us could stop.

And what good would crying do?

It wouldn't solve anything.

Tears wouldn't force a miracle.

We made some space between us, our hands gripping one another's inner elbows. "I take it you haven't told your dad yet?"

I shook my head. "How am I supposed to persuade him to let me go? He wants me to live the life he set out for me. That doesn't involve anything but my trust fund and these four walls. Sometimes I think he's right, you know. That I wasn't made for more than this–a hot girl summer three hundred and sixty-five days of the year."

"Shut. Up. You were made for so much more than this. Besides, you're eighteen soon. He can't keep you locked up in his cotton candied globe forever. He has to let you go someday."

She studied my facial expression, looking for something I wasn't sure I was capable of giving, but I smiled for her anyway.

"Yeah," I sighed. No way anyone could understand why my father was the way he was without growing up with him. The persona he wore for the people around him was often much different to the persona he reserved for me. Overprotective daddy and sugar daddy were two entirely different roles to play after all. I'd always been the princess in his less than ivory tower, and he still treated me as such. It didn't matter that I was verging on adulthood–he endeavoured his best to stop me from growing up like he could hold on to the essence of my mother through me.

He couldn't.

I didn't even know my mother.

I didn't want to *remember* my mother.

And other than my looks, how was it possible to be anything remotely like her?

She was a ghost–often haunting my life.

Ebony's phone began buzzing from my bed. The sound of some heavy metal playing through its speakers. I raised a questionable brow. This phase she was going through was so bizarre. But that was Ebony, always trying to draw attention to herself. She'd make herself out to be something she wasn't to impress someone she desired to be.

She grinned and spun on her heels. "I'm late."

"You're leaving?" I asked. "Already? You've been here less than ten minutes."

She picked up her phone, staring at it while it rang out. "I wasn't expecting to waltz in here so easily and be able to *stay*. Your dad detests me."

"He doesn't detest you. He just doesn't believe you're genuine."

Some days, I questioned what he saw that I didn't. But maybe that was me, always seeing the good in people even if those people weren't good people.

"Whatever. He's grotesque. And hardly daddy of the year. Besides, I made plans to finally Skype with banks262."

I frowned.

"What?" She shrugged, mimicking my expression.

"Finally Skype with *banks262*? You're telling me you've been speaking for weeks and haven't skyped yet? Have you ever seen his picture? Do you even know his real name?"

She pursed her lips and began shoving her things back into her bag that had previously spilt onto my bed, pausing briefly to shoot me a death glare before becoming serious. "Sorry, but are you a relationship guru now?" Her phone began ringing again as she finished packing everything into her bag. "I really gotta go."

I stood there in a daze, wrapping my arms around my shoulders while she sauntered backwards towards my door, blowing kisses. "Good luck with your dad. Text me later, 'kay? I want all the details. Every single one."

"You got it," I said, throwing my palm in the air to catch her kisses. "Doubt there'll be much to tell. There's no way he'll allow me to move across the state, let alone to another country."

"What's the worst that could happen?" she asked, leaving my room with a sympathetic smile.

I fell backwards onto my ottoman, her question hitting me with force. I didn't want to think about the worst because the worst would mean staying exactly where I was–with a bleak future with no prospects.

My eyes darted to my darkened laptop screen beside me as I held on to what little hope I had left. I promised myself I'd get out of this place. Duke was out of reach, but my lips still twitched with a smile at the probability of change.

———

IT WASN'T until after I graduated and until the end of summer that I decided to speak with my father about my future.

It was late in the evening when I cornered him in his office. He sat at his expensive pedestal desk, a stream of paperwork spread out under his palms. Strands of his recently coloured brown hair fell over his forehead, and I couldn't tell whether he was trying to convince him or his hook-ups that he wasn't nearing sixty. Not that a box of dye could hide it. A quick Wikipedia search was all you needed to learn the A to Z of James Sterling. Everything but an insight into me or my mother, anyway. I thanked my lucky stars for that.

His brows pinched when I sat down in the leather chair opposite him. "What's wrong?" he asked.

"What makes you think something's wrong?"

He placed his elbows on the wood and steepled his hands

under his chin. The antique signet rings on his fingers openly showcasing every bit of our wealth. "The only time you ever come to see me in my office is if something is wrong. Is it Anna? Has she done something to upset you?"

"Who's Anna? Another one of your throwaways?" I winced at my own judgement. But 'throwaways' did appear much kinder than fuck friends or sugar babies, and I'd never dared to curse in front of my father purely out of respect, though I felt he held little for me.

He gave me a stern look before he frowned. "The new maid. Anna."

"Oh. Well then, no. Anna is fine. I hope she's not put off by your indecencies and decides to stick around."

"Blue," he scolded, rubbing a finger over my mother's initials tattooed onto his finger, where he no longer wore his wedding ring. "What I do in my time is up to me. It's not harming anyone, and it's unquestionably not harming the bank account of any maid I hire."

Gnawing the inside of my cheek, I chose not to reply to his statement. The chances of him accepting my proposal were already slim. The chances of him accepting my proposal when he was angry and defensive would be zero.

"So..." He raised an eyebrow, allowing a moment of silence to linger between us. "What's the issue, princess? What brings you to my office at this hour?" He looked over my shoulder at the grandfather clock in his office's corner. I knew it was close to chiming on the tenth hour. My curfew–where I was assigned to my bedroom until the next morning–was almost up. All so he could invite yet another woman around without having to bear the guilt of me witnessing his obvious use for the female anatomy. I didn't always stick to it, of course. But it beat listening to the slapping of body parts and moans travelling down the corridors and through the walls. Sometimes I imagined a neon

BLUE

arrow stuck at the end of our expansive driveway, with the words
"ORGY THIS WAY!" just to make it feel more like a joke than the
reality. I wasn't sure what was worse–my actual reality of not
having a mother or him treating women like whores.

I took a breath, wrapped the fringe of my denim shorts
around my finger, and watched as he dropped his elbows from
his desk.

"I applied for college."

An awkward smile framed his lips as he shuffled the papers
in front of him into a pile. "Why?" he asked, not meeting my
eyes. He probably wouldn't have liked what he saw, anyway. "You
won't ever need to work a day in your life."

Sighing, I looked down at my finger wrapped around the
fraying cotton of my shorts and pulled it tighter. "I qualified for a
place at the University of Duke."

A rumble vibrated from his throat as he sat back in his chair,
crossing his arms over the chest of his shirt. "The University of
Duke... Well, that's in London."

I looked up at him from under my eyelashes and nodded.

"No." One simple word held a tone full of certainty.

"Dad," I said calmly, even though I was beyond agitated.

"London is halfway across the world. Where would you
stay?"

"They have shared accommodation available on campus. It's
already been arranged."

"No daughter of mine is living in halls. Do you know how
many young girls end up sexually assaulted at university? More
than half." He scoffed. "And the amount of knife crime? London
recently reported its worst-ever death toll from teenage
homicides."

The fringe of my shorts snapped off when I pulled on it too
tightly. With the cotton between my fingers, I looked up at my
father's solemn expression. "How do you know all of this?"

"A lot of The Lagoon's fighters come from the streets. It's my job to stay in the know when it comes to these things."

"Come on, dad, *please*? There's nothing for me here. Almost all my friends are off to Ivy League schools. I hardly leave our house without an escort. Let me do this. I can't stay cooped up in this house any longer, and you can't keep treating me like a child."

He ground his molars and ran a hand back through his hair. "But why? I don't like it. The thoughts of you in a city you barely know, with no one to look after you. No one to protect you. Halfway across the world." He shook his head. "No. It's insanity."

"Nobody said you had to like it." I hiked my shoulders and etched forward in my seat. "Please, dad. I'm a Sterling. Why on earth would I need protection? I can take care of myself. I won't be the first person to attend college in a foreign country. I'm hardly the type to get mixed up in any gang wars or find myself alone in a rough part of the city. I'm not as fragile as you think I am."

He observed my face, and I knew what he would say before he said it. He always brought her up in times like these, which was next to never. "You have the same blue glint in your eyes your mother used to get when she was excited about something. It lessens the green."

My shoulders slumped. "I don't want to talk about her."

He rubbed his knuckles over his heart, then moved them to his jaw, brushing over the short stubble on his cheeks with a roughness that often came with the mention of my mother. "It would make you feel better if we did."

"It makes me feel better when we don't speak about her at all."

"You're lucky, Blue," he said. "You're lucky you survived the accident."

"Lucky?" I scrunched up my nose. "I'm not *lucky*."

"I have to disagree. You're incredibly lucky a stranger pulled you from the car when they did."

"I have nightmares," I stated, swallowing roughly. "I hear her screams. I remember the warmth of the flames. Do you honestly believe that by telling me I'm lucky, you'll somehow convince me? That if we talk about it, over and over, one day I'll wake up and just be *normal?*"

Exasperated, he let out a heavy breath. "Princess, I am not trying to convince you of anything. All I'm doing is trying to explain. A three-year-old shouldn't have to relive such a horrific event. I don't think it's a good idea for you to move across the world when even now, years later, you're still so... so...."

"Dad–"

"Fragile."

He placed a fist onto the papers he'd piled on his desk and pinned me with a glare, ending our conversation.

"But, dad–"

"No," he said. "Now go to bed."

"But–"

The grandfather clock in the corner of the room chimed, signalling the start of my curfew. I stood from my chair and pushed it back with force. My mouth opened to say something else but closed again when I thought better of it. As much as I wanted to protest, was there any point in fighting a losing battle? I'd have to find another way to escape the horror of a life he created around me. Even if it meant waiting until the day I turned eighteen and not a day later.

He lifted his chin upon seeing the wheels turning in my head that told him exactly what I was thinking. How I was beginning to resent him for the way he treated me. As if I was always one step away from a mental breakdown.

That's right, dad, you can't force me to stay.

"You really want this?"

I didn't hesitate. "More than anything."

His eyes searched my own, but the thin line of his mouth stayed sealed. He held his arm out without another word, directing me towards the door. The second my foot was over the threshold, I heard his sigh sound through the room, and then I listened to his office phone being removed from its hook. Resisting the urge to listen to his conversation like I'd done countless times before, I decided not to stick around.

If he was revoking my place from Duke, I didn't want to hear it.

CHAPTER TWO

Walker

A VIBRATION from my bedside table stirred me awake. Groaning, I peeled open my eyes, just making out Sophia's arm as she reached over my head for my phone.

"Is that *her?*" she asked, moving her body haphazardly across mine when she realised she wasn't within reach. There was an irony to be found in her movements. She was so far from reach of the truth. We'd already established there was no other woman. But I knew one of my wife's worst habits was not learning when to draw her losses. It's why we lived the same day, over and fucking over. Day in and day out, like a revolving fucking door. Only the door was broken.

"No," I said, catching her wrist in my grip and halting her.

The buzzing continued from beside me, my phone the only light in the room's darkness. I pushed her away with force as I sat up. I didn't know who the hell was ringing me at this hour. Or what they could possibly want.

Noah had his own unique ringtone, so it wasn't him. And if there'd been an emergency at the club, I'd have had a different type of alert come through on my phone.

"It is, isn't it?" she spat. "Does she know you're married, or do you take off your ring when you're with her?"

My head throbbed, threatening a headache. "Is that what you did the night you cheated?" I asked, giving myself a moment's pause. Her mouth opened and closed like a fish out of water. Never had I rendered my wife speechless until now. The woman usually had an answer for everything, often coming across as unintellectual just to have her voice heard. Though I never married her for her brains or lack thereof.

It was her face.

Her pussy.

Her willingness to help in return for financial security.

Damn, maybe even her loyalty.

Her fucking friendship.

Only time taught me what a brilliant actress she was. I knew as well as she did, eleven years was too long a time to not let your mask slip. We were both guilty of our circumstance.

"Nothing to say? Just a second ago, you seemed to be so fucking sure of yourself. Do you have any idea how absurd you sound? Please, Sophia. Just... give it a rest."

Ignoring her scowl, I moved to the edge of the bed, planting my feet on the floor to balance the sway of the room as I picked up my phone.

James Sterling, my partner (more like my boss), was likely a second away from reaching my voicemail before I hit the little green button.

"James."

"Walker. Did I wake you?"

"It's fine. Everything alright?" I asked, dropping my elbows to my knees and fisting a hand into each of my eyes, attempting to dull their ache. The alcohol in my system didn't feel as good as it did not so many hours ago.

"I'm not too sure yet."

The covers draped around Sophia as she moved onto her knees, closing in on me. Then she leant forward, moving her ear near my own, listening in on my conversation with no shame. "What does he want?"

My lip curled as I covered the speaker with my palm. "You don't have the right to violate my privacy just because you're my wife."

James said something else through the line. I could barely contemplate what he asked of me with Sophia breathing down my neck and my head pulsating. I considered hanging up, but he didn't often call my personal number. Our business musings were usually allocated to email with the five-hour time difference between us. And Miami was too far away for a casual face-to-face.

"Walker."

"I'm sorry, what?"

"Did you hear me?"

I hesitated. "No." Then, because I felt the ridiculous need to defend myself and my joke of a marriage, I told him what I considered a white lie. "My signal must have dipped out."

"Hmm. How is business at the club? Noah doing as he's told?"

My brows pinched. "Everything seems to be on the up. We've been given the go-ahead for fight night. Hudson's looking strong. And my brother does whatever the fuck I tell him to do."

James Sterling founded Blue Lagoon from scratch, and alongside his name it was regularly in the spotlight for being controversial, operating as a multi-functional business. A night-club, a mixed martial arts gym, and events arena.

It had been years since he'd moved to Miami and taken a backseat. After working my way up to the top at the tender age of twenty-three and seeing something in me my deadbeat parents failed to recognise, he gave me a thirty percent partnership. At the same time, he established something he considered a more sophisticated business–Blue Lake Airlines.

Granted, I worked myself to the bone to get where I was today. To try and give back what I took. I even sacrificed my happiness for Noah's, marrying Sophia to aid my case in getting him out of foster care. And since the business and myself had grown, James now only checked in every quarter instead of once a fortnight, which was why his phone call felt entirely out of scope.

"Something tells me that's not why you're calling," I stated more than asked.

"Always so perspective, Walker. No, I suppose it's not." He was silent for a moment, and then, "Blue has secured a place at The University of Duke without consulting me first."

At the mention of her name, my interest was piqued. "Go on." I leant into my phone and away from Sophia as she shifted somewhat closer. So fucking thirsty for a taste of nothing that concerned her.

"I don't like it. Not one bit. But she wants this. I'd like her to stay with you and Sophia, if that's okay." He paused. "Just until she gets settled. I trust that she'd be better accommodated with you than in halls. I don't want her living with a bunch of unruly teenagers. She'd stand out like a sore thumb. I can email you all the important details in the next few days if you figure it's something you can do for me. You'll be paid accordingly, of course."

"Sure," I said too quickly. I wasn't thinking through the logistics. Now wasn't the time to divulge information on the problematic relationship with my wife. There was no simple explanation to confess. And like she knew just what I was thinking, she dragged her fingernails down my back, wanting to remind me of her presence. However, it was impossible to forget with her a hair's width away. "Is that everything?"

"Do you need to be somewhere? Are you in a rush?"

"No rush, boss."

Except for the opening and closing of a drawer through the line, he remained silent. After a heavy sigh, he finally continued, "No," he said, with what I could only assume to be a cigar in the side of his mouth with the way his accent faltered. His next words were clearer. "That's not everything. I'd prefer it if you could fly out and accommodate her on the plane. The idea of her by herself doesn't sit well with me, regardless of owning the aircraft. I'm not going to tell her what I've planned—she'll undoubtedly go against my wishes and purchase a flight with a competitor just to spite me. If she did that, I'd have no one to supervise her. No one to tell me all there is for me to know, while at the same time keeping her safe from any foreseeable harm."

I heard the click of a lighter, and then he sucked in a breath.

He meant no one to supervise her that wouldn't look like the typical help he usually hired to take care of his assets; black suits and stoic faces. He wanted someone discreet. Not a wolf in sheep's clothing. I gnawed on my cheek, hiding the smirk that ached to pull at my lips. Images of James's seventeen-year-old daughter giving him a hard time amused me more than it should have. No one else had that type of pull on him. No one would dare try.

"She's... fragile. And I need to know she's safe," he reiterated. "I trust she'll be that with you."

It made me wince, but I promised him anyway.

"I'll take care of her," I murmured.

I had once already–and how much more fragile could she be compared to then?

At my words, Sophia's eyebrows pulled together, repeating her earlier question through gritted teeth. "What does he want?"

I shoved her aside and stood from the bed, my free hand rising to grip the back of my neck. Something occurred to me. "Does she know?"

"No, and let's keep it that way. If she wants to move to London badly enough, she'll do as I ask one way or another. Can you have your brother handle the club while you're away?"

I nodded in agreement, though he couldn't see. I had every faith that Noah could handle The Lagoon without me. I'd taught him everything he knew. I just liked to keep him on his toes by bossing him around the way an older brother should and could.

The two of us had a lot of respect for James. He was the man who made it all happen. The reason we had no financial burdens. The man who got us out of the rubble, despite the part I had to play in his own. In a way, he was more of a father than my own flesh and blood. That was enough for me to accept his proposition without asking questions.

The next words from his mouth were what really made it worthwhile.

"You do this for me, and I'll see that you're rewarded highly for everything you've done for me over the years."

"You've done enough," I said sincerely. If anything, I owed him. There were more zeros on my bank balance than I knew what to do with. I already owned the expansive townhouse me and Sophia lived in. Four holiday homes–one in Barcelona with a private beach and its own marina. Another on an island in the Maldives. One in the states and the fourth in the French Alps.

Not that I ever made time to go on vacation. I couldn't remember the last time I'd spent time at either one. As sad as it seemed to anyone who wasn't me, work was my lifeline.

I heard James blow out smoke through the side of his mouth. "No. I've been thinking about it for a long while now, son. Because of you, the Club is thriving, and I'm not getting any younger. It's an excruciating business. There's no time like the present to let you lead. I'll have my solicitor draw up the negotiations for a generous sum, and then if you're happy, we can go ahead with a buyout."

I was silent on the other end of the line as I allowed his words to sink in. It wasn't until he said, "If you must, you can consider it gratitude for the past," that I realised he was being deadly fucking serious.

"Well, shit." My hand dropped from my neck, and my lips curled with ease. It seemed a lot for a thank you. But when you compared his club to his daughter's life, I supposed there was no comparison.

"What?" Sophia questioned. Her eyes grew wide, though her lips remained downturned. Wasn't she bored of asking the same question, knowing I wouldn't give her any answers? Or did she hear the word sum, and the reason behind her wide eyes was because they'd lit up with pound signs?

James chuckled, seemingly at ease when compared to the organ in my chest. "Don't let me down."

"Never. If that's everything, I'll organise a flight over as soon as you give me the go-ahead."

Once I'd hung up, I placed my phone back onto my bedside table and flicked on the lamp beside it. Adrenaline flowed through my veins. There wasn't a chance in hell I'd be able to fall back to sleep with the way I felt. I'm not sure how much Sophia heard, but she was grinding her jaw against her teeth. By the ugly look in her eyes, I knew that she was gathering words of spite to throw at me. And like clockwork–predictable as fuck– she raised her voice and began hurling abuse in my direction.

"You're leaving? To fly some teenage girl back here?"

With a nod of my head, she jumped from the bed and got in my face. I expected her to lash out. And I knew it didn't matter to her why I was leaving–not when it came to work–but because I wasn't putting her first, and she'd grown tired of it. Tired of not being able to mould us into a real-life *it* couple, like her Z lister friends assumed us to be.

"Tell me why the hell I agreed to marry you?" she accused.

She hadn't forgotten, but I wouldn't pass up the opportunity to remind her.

"You married me for the weight of my wallet and the size of my cock."

It was nasty, but it was the truth.

"God, Walker, why are you acting like such a cunt?"

Not wanting to have the same mundane fight we often had, I stepped away from her and into our walk-in closet, holding my tongue between my teeth before I said something I couldn't take back. Inside, the white lights came to life by motion. There was no saying when James would expect me in Miami, but I took my suitcase and my rucksack from their place beside my shelves and began packing. I imagined it wouldn't be long before I got his email. In my head, it made sense to be prepared. Besides, everything I was packing wasn't solely for the flight there. Me leaving was inevitable. The timing of the trip just worked out in my favour.

"How long will you be gone for?" Sophia asked, eyes darting from me to my luggage.

"I'm not sure. However long it takes."

My response would have been the same if she'd asked, *"How long will we be separated?"*

I hadn't told her about the penthouse I'd spotted on my run all those weeks ago. That I'd been in touch with the estate agent and signed a six-month lease. Call me a coward, but it was all about finding the right time–choosing the right moment. So far, no moment had been particularly appropriate. Especially this one. It wasn't the right time to tell her I wasn't coming back here, with or without Blue. Fuck, Blue Sterling had absolutely nothing to do with this, but I'm certain Sophia would've found a way to use it against me. The truth was, I had no idea why it had taken me so long. It's not like we had children to think about. I made sure of that. And Noah was grown now. An adult. Sophia had served her purpose in making me look like a responsible guardian all those years ago when I was finally able to give my brother a stable home. Something he never had with our parents.

If anything, I did Sophia a favour as much as she had me. I gave her comfort. Security. I took care of her emotionally, financially, and sexually. Why did she always expect more? It was never promised.

I gave it my best shot.

I'd stuck it out for this long.

And I hadn't fucked anyone else, despite being tempted. Despite every offer.

All I knew was what James asked of me served as the perfect diversion from the bumpy road I didn't wish to travel. His request had come at the ideal time. It was a classic distraction, and with any luck, the distance between Sophia and me would perhaps knock some fucking sense into her. Maybe she'd realise how much better things could be if we were free of one another. Find a man who could give her what I didn't have inside of me. Maybe not in her head, but in mine, I knew we were done. And ironically, though I still cared, my heart knew there wasn't a way to save whatever it was we'd lost.

I was so set on what I was going to do, I could barely concentrate on what it was I was doing. I threw shirt after shirt, trousers, sweats, and underwear into my suitcase without a second thought.

Then, contradicting her earlier tone, Sophia tried to ease herself back into the bravado of being the perfect fake wife, only pissing me off further. "Do you need that many outfits? You'll crease your shirts."

Jesus fuck.

Refusing to answer, because the only answer I had on the tip of my tongue was a bitter no, her features began to show her panic. With barely any warning, her bleak tone turned into a yell. "You aren't going across the country for the sake of some girl you don't know. I'm your wife. You married *me.*"

My muscles tensed as she took a step closer to me, her eyes never flinching from my face. Still, I ignored her and continued my packing. I didn't need all the clothes I was piling into the suitcase, that was true. I could afford a whole new wardrobe and leave these right here for her to burn if she wished. But it was for the best I kept my hands busy as not to throw my fist into the fucking wall.

I was losing my mind.

Sophia was making me lose my mind.

She pulled things from my suitcase in her haste and threw them on the floor. "Answer me!"

"She's not just some girl. Jesus, Soph. It's my job." My patience was on the offset. I wasn't sure how to handle this any better than I already was. Violence wasn't the answer, but that didn't stop my blood pressure from rising and my fists clenching whatever scrap of material I gathered in my hands.

"It's not your fucking job. You're allowed to say no."

I dropped the shirt I held and grabbed hold of her forearms, pulling her against me and forcing her arms to wrap around my waist. She screamed muffled obscenities into my chest, and her words slowly shifted into sobs. She hadn't cried in my arms since her parents died. Which I supposed was another reason I felt so tied to us. While work was my lifeline, I was hers.

Though maybe this was it.

Maybe she finally realised just how wrong we'd gotten all this.

She couldn't love me.

How could she?

I gave her nothing to love.

"What the fuck were we thinking?" I sighed against her hair. It was a loaded question. She knew as much. But with nothing to say, she just held me tighter. All I could do was brush my fingers through her tendrils of dark hair. I might not have ever been in love with her, but I still cared about her. Fuck, some part of me still fucking cared. Despite everything, eleven years was a long time to remain in a relationship with someone and not feel a thing. It was only natural I felt some type of way. I just wasn't able to give her what she truly wanted.

I could give her the white picket fence, the picture-perfect Christmas card, but none of it would ever be real. We would never be real.

"When I used to envision our future, this was never what I had in mind," I muttered.

"I'm sorry," she said. "I'm sorry for what I did to us."

I'm sorry, I thought. For thinking I could marry her first and fall in love second.

Regardless of her apology, I knew better. We'd been through this, time after time. Accepting her apology was no better for me than inhaling toxic waste. Admitting mine would only hurt us further.

"It's fine," I said, trying to settle her. When I loosened my grip and put a little space between us, her hazel eyes fought to hold my own. There was a spark of something between us, but nothing I believed was worth igniting for a temporary truce. Nothing worth igniting at all.

"Come back to bed," she said. "Please."

She tried to close the space between us, her lips kissing the corner of my mouth as I turned my head away from her.

"I can't." *I won't.* "I need to finish packing. I'm wide awake–I may as well pull an all-nighter and get things in order for Noah before I go."

Her features morphed back into anger, and then she pulled at her hair. "I don't get it. Why won't you just kiss me if there's no one else? Why won't you fuck me?"

I reared back at the outburst, my lips curling into a sneer. She had no right to demand anything of me after what she did. For someone who claimed so hard to love me, it made zero fucking sense. And if I couldn't make sense of it, she sure couldn't. Just because I never married her out of love didn't disguise the fact she was mine, that she carried my last name, that we agreed to remain loyal.

It wasn't just about what she did, but the feeling of betrayal after everything I'd given her. Everything I continued to give to her. I grieved for the life I never had. I suffered for the life I never knew.

My jaw ticked.

I was over it.

So fucking done.

I caught her eyes, knowing they'd convey everything I refused to voice. We'd been through it plenty of times before, there was no reason to keep the merry-go-round running. I wanted to get off.

"Don't look at me like that," she seethed. "You pushed me to it. You might have married me, but Noah always came first."

Not being able to help it, I shook my head on a laugh. Noah was the reason I'd married her; it was only right he came first.

"You knew what you were getting yourself into when you stood at the altar and said I do," I snapped.

"I just wanted you to see me, Walker."

She wanted me to see her.

"I wanted you to get angry. I wanted you to fight for me."

Fight for what?

She stepped into me, stealing my last shred of patience. "When it wasn't Noah, it was the club. It was never me."

She just didn't know when to fucking stop.

"Out of curiosity, where do you think my money comes from, huh, Soph? Who the fuck pays for all this?" I spread my arms out wide to elaborate my point. "You knew love was never in the cards. And you wouldn't have any of this if it wasn't for the hours I put in to get us here. Your designer clothes, your social lunches. That five-carat diamond ring on your finger–the one you bought yourself while the one I proposed with sits in a fucking jewellery box on whichever one of these thirty fucking shelves. You can't say I didn't try to love you. You've never made it fucking easy."

Her eyes lit up with fury, and her palm collided with my cheek hard and fast. My jaw tightened, and I watched her take a step back into the coat rail as I stepped forward.

Her hand covered her mouth, and then she was speaking between her fingers. "Walker, no, I'm so sorry."

My skin burnt with the aftermath of her slap, and my head pounded with rage. So much that I struggled to control my clenched fists. Despite feeling so angry that I wanted to punch her, remove her from my life forever and throw her to the fucking sharks, my fist drove past her, hammering into the wall behind her instead. Her synthetic apologies ran laps around my head rent-free, only contributing to the consequences of her actions and the consequences of me drinking too much alcohol hours before.

I should've known marrying for convenience would have long-term side effects. Sophia was a parasite. She infected my body, my life, and now... now she was making me sick.

CHAPTER THREE

Blue

I CLUTCHED my bag to my chest and shuffled myself down the thin aisle of the plane. I tried not to make a scene, but everyone else was already seated, their eyes rolling into the backs of their heads as I passed.

We were running thirty minutes behind schedule, and I was entirely at fault. Unfortunately, a panic attack had greeted me like an old acquaintance in the departure lounge. I wasn't sure if the pilot made a habit of allowing his passengers the lenience that I took or whether he caught on to my last name and feared for his job. Probably the latter, considering my father owned the airline. But the passengers on board the aircraft hadn't known about my situation. Row after row of accusation and judgement stared back at me. What they saw versus what they knew were vastly different. It was easy to assume I was a spoiled brat living out of daddy's pocket with my blonde hair, made-up face, and designer clothes. And they were right, to an extent. A normal seventeen-year-old wouldn't be wearing the latest Givenchy on an economy flight. Maybe I shouldn't have fought with the iconic James Sterling over flying first class and instead given him his one final hurrah.

I continued down the aisle and pulled my oversized black sunglasses over my eyes, allowing them to serve as my armour. Halfway, I spotted a pink bunny on the floor and a little girl with pigtails attempting to reach for it from her seat. Her arms weren't quite long enough, and the harder she tried, the more she seemed to blush in frustration.

Once I neared, I crouched down to retrieve it, careful not to show too much skin in my short black dress. She beamed a big toothy grin when I handed it to her. By instinct, I smiled back. Innocence was hard to come by and only much harder to grasp as you grew up because life's lessons stole it away from you, replacing it only with guilt and bitterness. I'd know because I was her once–the little girl clutching her bunny to her chest. The little girl that left her bunny behind.

Beside her, a woman bounced a crying baby on her lap and offered me her thanks, looking moments away from a breakdown.

"Sorry," I mumbled, not entirely sure why I was apologising instead of offering back a simple "no problem." I supposed being an empath was both a blessing and a curse. I could resonate with people on a level that not everyone understood, but it also magnified my issues. Cue my panic attack–sudden but predicted.

In my crouched position, I picked a piece of lint from my dress, then looked at the little girl one last time as I stood, gently tugging at one of her pigtails. "I had a bunny just like that once,"

I said, sharing something I would usually keep to myself. "Keep it safe, or you might lose him for good."

Her features pulled together, but she nodded in understanding, clutching her bunny tight to her chest like it was precious cargo.

My nerves re-emerged as I continued down the aisle with each step. Being on this plane meant I was leaving behind what I'd once considered my future. Just the fear of that alone was overwhelming. Little did I know what my future had really entailed. I'd likely spend my youth lounging by our pool, drinking stolen champagne flutes from passing waiters while my father hosted some lavish party, full of females walking around in their minuscule bathing suits. It was contradictory, but I loved my father as much as I loathed him for being so overbearing and overprotective. Which was why leaving that lifestyle behind was so important to me.

Something about the unknown terrified me as much as it excited me. And something about doing this on my own felt like it freed me from who I was expected to be. Even if I had no idea who I was going to become.

Sometimes I wondered why I couldn't just be an ordinary seventeen-year-old girl without these heavy thoughts residing in my head, making me feel like an outcast.

I checked my ticket for my seat number while both my heart and head wheezed with uncertainty—and that's when I realised I was still at least a quarter of the plane away from my seat. I tried not to think about how many more dirty looks I'd endure as I continued down the aisle, although I should have been used to it. Being brought up in a life where money overpowered everything, people often made assumptions based on what I looked like and who my father was, without knowing who or what was under the surface.

My father called it jealousy.

I called it stupidity.

The artificial blonde weaved into my brown hair may have been fake, but nothing else was when it came to my looks. I'd lost count of the number of times someone had asked me if my lips were natural. Or where I'd found a plastic surgeon who had happily risked his reputation to offer surgery to someone my age. They hadn't known I was the image of my mother. And I only knew so because of the photographs my father often put in my room right before I threw them out.

I couldn't help but want to erase her very existence.

I couldn't stand to remember her happy after the way I repeatedly watched her die in my nightmares.

Catching the eye of a flight attendant standing near the back of the plane, I snapped out of my trance. She'd be pretty if it weren't for the look of annoyance she wore, aimed right at me. There was no disguising the displeasure that shone in her overly made-up eyes. But as I got closer, she smiled all the same. I tried hard to control my own eyes from rolling, but it was deemed impossible. I'd finally reached my limit, I guess.

What could I say?

Nobody's perfect, even the girl wearing Givenchy.

I didn't return the fake smile she gave me, but I did say, "Thank you," as she held out her arm, pointing in the direction of my seat. Because against being raised spoilt, I still knew right from wrong. I learned how a simple hello, a please, and a thank you could easily alter someone's day. Manners didn't cost a thing, yet there were people in the world too selfish to endorse them.

Finally, I located my seat—the middle in a row of three. Except the lady on the outer chair, closest to me, was asleep and considerably large, which meant I'd struggle to pass her.

Before I attempted to wake her, I raised on my tiptoes in my suede boots and opened the overhead compartment to squeeze in my bag. A floral beach bag and a large backpack already occupied the space, not leaving much room for anything else, but after pushing the bags to either side, I managed to fit mine between them.

I pursed my lips in satisfaction as I sank back on my heels. Then, I gently tapped the lady's shoulder, hoping to wake her. When she didn't flinch, my eyes searched out the air hostess, requiring some assistance. Only she refused to acknowledge me and instead made her way down the aisle on the opposite side of the plane.

"Seriously?" I murmured. She clearly didn't care for my name, not that I'd use it to gain an advantage. That wasn't who I was, contrary to what others might've believed.

I tapped the lady's shoulder again, a little harder this time, and gave it a sort of shake. At the sounds of a snigger, I looked over my shoulder to see a little boy with curly auburn hair picking his nose. "My granny could sleep through a hurricane. You'll probably have to climb her."

He had a weak London accent. It was quite like my own, adopted from my father, only with a touch of... American, I suppose. I'd never really thought about my accent. Not the same way I did about other things. Like why were there spaces between the stars? Why was my life spared instead of my mother's? And why was it I suffered for something I had no control over?

I wondered if other seventeen-year-olds thought the same way I did. By choice, my thoughts weren't something I discussed with my friends over lunch in the school canteen. We'd chat about which member of the football team Kourtney Jacobs had dropped her panties for over the weekend, or how Marco had been caught injecting himself with who knows what before practice by the school janitor. Sometimes I wondered if they knew me–I mean, really knew me–what kind of things would they say?

Would they consider me as fragile as my father did?

Would they accept me for being as fucked up as I was?

I sighed.

"Climb her?"

The boy grinned at me, showing a gap between his two front teeth, and I turned my attention back to the task at hand.

Suddenly, another air hostess, blonde and slightly older, called to me with a bite to her tone. "Miss, you need to sit down as we prepare for take-off."

It was safe to say the cabin crew's patience for me was thinning by the second. There was no disguising my huff of frustration or the "fuck my life" that fell from my mouth. I wanted to raise my middle finger and wave it through the air to convince myself that I was like my peers. But I didn't.

I turned, dropping my chin to wink at the little boy over the rim of my sunglasses. "Looks like I'm climbing your granny, kiddo. Close your eyes; else you might see my ass."

The gapless toothed kid grinned wider and pinched his eyes closed tight. And I was happy to discover his parents were raising a gentleman. So then, without any other option, I raised my leg, wedged my foot on the chair's armrest of the row in front, and placed my arm on the back of the headrest, scaling myself across to my allocated seat. I felt like some damn spider monkey. My laced underwear barely covered my ass. All I could think was if my friends could have witnessed this, they'd have pissed themselves. I'd never live it down. And if we were still in school, *I'd* be the topic of canteen gossip.

As I moved across the back of the chair, I noticed a guy seated on the far side with his hoodie pulled down over his face. He hadn't bothered acknowledging me, so I could only assume he was asleep or perhaps didn't give a shit for the whole charade. At the very least, I was saved from even more embarrassment. Until I fell into my chair, accidentally elbowing him.

"Fuck," we both cursed.

At the same time, my sunglasses dropped from my face, landing somewhere on the floor with a clatter. "I'm so sorry," I mumbled, not sparing the guy beside me a second glance as I bent down to pick them up.

As my hands blindly searched the floor, my head practically rested on the stranger's cotton clad thigh due to the limited space riding economy. Coincidentally, it only made me more flustered. Once I caught my sunglasses in my grip, I sat back up in my chair, dropping them to my lap. Then I positioned my elbows forward, careful not to touch either passenger beside me as I smoothed my hair back into place.

I jumped when the small dashboard above my head chimed, ordering me to fasten my seatbelt. Just as quick, the lights inside the plane flickered off. Somehow, I'd missed the whole 'this is what to do in case of an emergency' talk, as if there was an inch of possibility you could survive plummeting to your death. Obviously, you couldn't. My father drilled that into me from a young age. How death can happen in the blink of an eye. You could be here one minute, gone the next. It's always better to be safe than sorry. Blah blah blah. He coddled and cosseted me throughout my childhood, worried he'd lose me as he lost my mother. He didn't need to program it into my head when I'd been there to witness first-hand how fast things could change.

My whole life had been a bit of a cliche.

Poor little rich girl.

I stroked a finger across the small scar on my collarbone, on edge with the reminder. That's when I felt eyes burning into the side of my head from the seat beside me. Maybe the guy *had* seen me make an ass of myself. Or was he trying to figure me out? Or did I think that because my guard was up, and my anxiety was screaming to be heard? No one could blame me, could they? I'd had enough of people's judgement today.

Lifting my chin, I turned my head to face the nameless dude to my side, dropping my hand as he dropped his hood.

The first thing I noticed was his eyes. One brown, one green, as they drank me in like a shot of my father's finest whiskey.

"Huh," I murmured. I hadn't intended to say anything, yet it was my lips' first and only response.

The corners of his mouth tipped up with a hint of a smirk, and ever so slowly, his tongue came out to lick his full bottom lip. He had the perfect amount of stubble covering his defined jawline, and his chocolate brown hair was neatly tapered on the sides with just enough length on top to run my fingers through. It was more wavy than curly. With the way it laid, I could tell it was previously styled with precision, only flattened by his hood.

I diverted my attention to his eyes, staring at him through my own greenish-blue.

He said one word, and immediately I pulled my attention from his eyes to his mouth as I watched each syllable sound through his lips.

"Heterochromia."

My eyebrows pinched together, and my lips formed a pout, not understanding the word or what it meant.

"I was born with a genetic mutation, and nope," he said exasperatedly, "there's nowt wrong with my quality of vision."

I bit my bottom lip to hold back a shy smile, not missing the undercurrent of his statement. "And I didn't ask," I responded, taken aback at his need to clarify.

"You didn't have to."

He had an accent I couldn't place–something British, dampened by the same London accent as my father's.

"You look familiar," I said with a hint of uncertainty. My eyes squinted as I took him in for the second time. Was he famous? A social media influencer? A model for Calvin Klein? Moments passed in silence as my brain tried to place him. And then it clicked–my recognition falling like dominoes.

"Wait. *Wait.*"

His head was off-kilter on the headrest of his seat when he drawled out, "Waiting," in a lazy pillow talk kind of way.

"I know you."

It was subtle, but he nodded.

"Oh my God. My father sent you, didn't he?" Although I couldn't recall when we'd met, my mind attempted to connect the dots. Noticing my struggle, he took out a black metallic card from the pocket of his hoodie and showed me his ID. It was the same ID as my father's. One he shared with all members of his staff. Like they were all privy to Sterling business, and I was not.

I pulled at the material against my thighs. I knew that not much ever happened by coincidence when it came to my life.

"You're all grown up," he said when I said nothing.

It felt more like an observation than a statement with the way his eyes began to move across every tittle of my face. His voice was low but rough, as if he smoked ten a day. But a small inhale through my nose told me he didn't smell like cigarettes. He smelt like expensive cologne and pheromones. His sleeves were pushed a small distance up his arms, showcasing strong veins. He had a tan, his skin a touch lighter on his arm where he'd usually wear a watch. And that's when I first noticed his knuckles.

Red, blue, and bruised.

"What happened to your hand?"

He clenched his reddened fist and clucked his tongue, never moving his eyes from mine. They were intense and full of severity, like he had something to say but wouldn't. But whatever the reason for his bloody hand, he didn't feel like talking about it. He remained quiet.

I'm not sure why, but not understanding something was always harder to cope with than not knowing, even if the thing in question had no relevance to me.

I turned away and faced forward, trying to breathe through the anxiety that was beginning to rework its way into my chest. The pressure only magnified once the plane started to gain speed down the runway. Tremors shot through me like waves, so I knotted my fingers together on my lap, hoping it would calm my shaking hands.

Somehow, the handsome sort of stranger had served as a temporary distraction to my fear of *flying*. But there was no backing out now, and definitely no time for regrets.

"Flying makes you nervous," he practically whispered against my ear. He hadn't changed his position once, giving him the vantage point. He was able to read me easily, and it seemed I couldn't have been any more transparent when a shiver floated from my neck and down the length of my body.

"Something like that."

He held his palm out to me, and I eyed it sceptically.

"Hold it if you want."

One hand went to my throat as my voice shook not only with nerves but with the vibration of the aircraft. "I don't hold hands with strangers."

Despite my words, I felt an unfamiliar sensation in my stomach. A feeling that somehow convinced me that though he was somewhat a stranger, and although his knuckles were bloody and bruised, there was something about him that was safe.

Before I could think any deeper about what the stranger beside me had asked, he sighed as if I was acting obnoxious. Then without giving me time to engage, he pushed his palm underneath mine and linked our fingers together, squeezing to keep my hand locked in his as the plane inclined towards the sky.

Walker

I ALL BUT pulled my gaze from her face and to her hand. "Fear is a survival instinct," I said, squeezing her fingers between mine.

"I'm not afraid of anything," she replied. But there was something in her tone that didn't convince me. She tried to pull her hand away, but that only made me hold it tighter.

"Are you sure about that? We're all afraid of something." One of the reasons I sat on this plane was because I was afraid. Afraid of what would have become of me if I decided against what James had asked. Afraid of continuing the mundane normality of my last eleven years, and not taking the plunge to do what I've wanted since the day Noah moved out. Though it seemed I was full of shit, because I'd already leased the penthouse. I'd already made my choice. It was the guilt sitting in my stomach that had me second-guessing myself. It had never been my intention to hurt Sophia, but it didn't matter if I left or stayed, I'd hurt her either way.

I knew taking Blue's hand was unethical. That contact of this kind wasn't asked of me whatsoever. But she was young and under distress–at least that's what I told myself. It was nothing to do with the annoyance I felt with my wife, or the annoyance I felt with my fucking life. It had absolutely nothing to do with the alcohol swimming in my veins. Alcohol that I'd disguised in a throwaway bottle of water before boarding the flight, all for the lie of sobriety. Perhaps it was all that and more. The least I could do was fuck with her to humour myself. It's how little Sophia thought of me after all.

My attention recoiled when Blue made a noise in her throat that could only be described as frustration, and her nails bit into the top of my hand. "I knew my father letting me leave quietly was too good to be true. He couldn't just let me go without having the last say, could he?" She attempted to remove her hand from mine again but failed. "This is a joke, right?"

I sighed. I had more credentials than to serve as Blue Sterling's babysitter, but it was all for a worthy cause.

"I could think of better things to do with my time," I told her. "I wish it were a joke."

She let out a breath that signified defeat as she searched my eyes for answers. In the end, she chose not to argue with me on the matter.

"So what, you're like, my chauffeur? Are you going to be reporting my every move?"

"Depends." I shrugged a shoulder and rolled my head back in her direction. "Does every move of yours warrant reporting?"

There was a glint of something in her eyes. It read sugar, spice, and all things fucking nice. But the shrug of her shoulder and the up-turn tilt of her lips was the only response I needed.

"You and I both know this is out of your hands," I said. Having me in her life temporarily was the lesser of two evils. She'd have never left Miami if her father hadn't given her his permission. Besides, this wasn't anything like a marriage, so I counted that a win. And thank fuck for that, because I already had one of those. A wildly fucked up marriage, nonetheless. With this, either of us could tap out at any time if shit got too much. We wouldn't have to worry about a piece of paper tying us together. Except I knew there was only one thing that would have me tapping out of what was essentially the most significant move of my career. And I had no plans to die anytime soon.

"Whatever. You can let go now," she said, trying to pry her hand from mine.

I looked down at our entwined fingers and noticed how I was possibly holding her small hand a fraction too tight. Strangely, I liked the way her skin felt against my own, how the warmth of her palm distracted me from the coldness in mine. In spite of all that, in spite of how much I craved something to make up for what I'd... lost, I loosened my grip. She was barely an adult compared to my age of thirty-four. I had years on her. She was still just a kid, and this wasn't adequate behaviour. It wasn't at all the behaviour her father expected of me. Regardless of how I'd watched him treat women in the past, he'd wear my balls as cuff-links if he knew just how reckless I was being.

She slipped her hand away, wiping both her palms against the hem of her short black dress. Designer, of course. Over-priced sunglasses and Louboutin suede boots made up the rest of her attire, which begged me to ask, "Why wouldn't you go to college back home when you have everything there at your disposal?"

"How well do you actually know my father?"

Unamused, I raised a brow. It was on the tip of my tongue to tell her I probably knew him better than she did. "Well enough."

"So your question was rhetorical, then?"

I chose not to respond to her question the way she probably expected, much as she decided not to respond to mine. It was apparent that her father's money had turned her into a brat. A lot like mine had Sophia. Though, I wasn't blind. Not only did I believe that it was her last name that helped solve her first world problems, but she was a beautiful girl, albeit much younger than me and totally forbidden. In normal circumstances–one where I wasn't in close business with her father–perhaps one where I was casually strolling down Bond Street, it's plausible I would have looked twice. Of course, I would have never acted on it. And undoubtedly, Blue's age factored into it too. She didn't look like most seventeen-year-olds. At least none that I'd ever known.

She was well dressed, with shiny brown and blonde hair. Petite, but with curves in all the appropriate places. Every teenage boy's wet dream, I'm sure. Yet, it wasn't those assets I found most appealing. I couldn't help but admire her face–the fullness of her pink lips and thick dark lashes surrounding eyes the colour of sea glass. I could always appreciate something beautiful when I saw it.

Marriage didn't blind me–it just drove me to drink.

She breathed a sigh and returned to her previous position, facing forward. Her eyes were on the back of the chair in front of her when she spoke again. "My father has wanted me to stay within the lines he'd mapped out for me since I was old enough to know better. Old enough to want more than a safe and wealthy lifestyle. He'd prefer it if I lived in the bubble he created, kept out of harm's way."

"Because of your mother's death?" I knew it was the most probable reason, but found myself asking the question anyway.

She snapped her head back in my direction. "Wow," she drawled. "You're going there, really?"

Taken aback by her reaction, my eyebrows pinched together. "What?"

"I don't like to talk about it. I don't want to talk about it. You're not a shrink, are you?"

"No, I'm not a shrink," I said with a frown. I ran my fingers over my knuckles, not feeling the need to disclose anything else if she didn't like talking about it–to explain that I'd witnessed the car accident–as none of it held much relevance to my present. At least it didn't until today. James said she was fragile. The question was *how* fragile?

After a few minutes of loaded silence, she decided to speak again. And what she shared had me understanding her a little better. "He worries about me way more than he should. And because of that, he controls everything. He tries to puppeteer every aspect of my life because he thinks he's doing the right thing. It's almost as if he overcompensates for the parent not here. Do you know how suffocating that feels?"

Keeping my gaze firmly on hers, I gnawed the inside of my cheek as a way to stop myself from saying something that might get me into trouble. We, too, didn't speak of the accident that took her mother. But none of that stopped me from noticing the resentment Blue held for her father in her eyes. If only she realised how fortunate she was to have one parent that gave a fuck rather than two who didn't. Not all of us were so lucky.

"I'm trying to say that I'm done living in his bubble. We don't have much of a relationship outside of his controlling ways. And if you know him as well as you say you do, for him to trust you anyway, then you must have some understanding of what I'm telling you. He likes to take charge. I'm sure you're not stupid. Come on; it's why you're sitting next to me right now. Tell me it's not."

I continued to frown, choosing to avoid her heavy stare by keeping my eyes down. "I'm sure he has his reasons. Not every person deals with grief the same," I said. "It can be different for everyone. Perhaps it's not right–the way he cares about you–but it's not wrong."

She scoffed. "Isn't it?"

I understood what she was trying to say. I understood how it felt to be under the control of someone else, or something else, for whatever reason. I understood how hard the fight could be to get out of something that felt so set in its ways. But fuck being soft just because I felt a touch of sympathy for her.

"It's not my job to chat shit, and neither is it my duty to attend your pity party for one."

Regardless of what I could have said, I had to act like I had it together if I wanted to keep James happy. I wasn't her friend. I was barely an acquaintance. And I sure as fuck wasn't going to lose a chance as big as the one James offered me so early in my career. Work was the only thing in my life that was faithful, and although this wasn't my usual way of business, ultimately, it was still business. It was much more than that in actuality because it meant my name above the fucking door of a club I'd worked myself to the bone for.

Blue didn't answer me. And though she didn't strike me as a dull girl, I wanted to be certain. I couldn't have her bad-mouthing her father or burrowing her way under my skin.

"Surely you're not naive enough to misinterpret that your father has your best intentions at heart?"

"No," she hummed, surprising me. "I know he does, but that doesn't mean I want him to control my entire life. I need to experience things on my own—make my own mistakes. Experience my own happiness. My first heartbreak. If my choices become my downfall, then I'll handle them. I don't need him to pick me up every time I fall over."

"He'd never allow such a downfall to happen to you, kid." I remained nonchalant but spoke in a tone that was anything but. Fuck, I'd easily trade her heartbreak for anything she had to offer Monday through Sunday. I still battled with my own, often thinking of the day Noah was taken into foster care. The guilt went hand in hand with the tragedy.

No one deserved to feel as though their heart was being pulled every which way from their chest while their head battled with the why.

She rolled her eyes, then casually pushed her hand down through the top of her dress and presumably into her bra before pulling out a small orange pill. "They help me sleep." And then she popped one into her mouth like it was nowt more than a mint. My eyes lingered on her lips until I pulled them back to her eyes.

"Prescribed?" I asked. "I take it your father knows."

I had to be sure. If James required my assistance, then I needed to know everything about the girl to accommodate her the way I was expected. The last thing I wanted to do was explain to James that his daughter had a drug addiction, and I'd sent her in a taxi to a rehabilitation clinic as soon as she stepped a heeled foot off the plane. The Lagoon had only just recovered from a drug raid, forced by the tabloids with their constant publication of lies. They found nothing, but I couldn't imagine James would still want to sign over his seventy percent if it turned out Blue did have a habit. In fact, he'd probably take it away.

I waited for Blue to speak, my eyes on the gentle movement of her throat as she swallowed.

She frowned, and for a moment she seemed confused, but then she said, "Duh, how else would I have gotten them through security?"

That attitude was as defensive as it was sassy. I couldn't hide my smirk even if I wanted to. "What the fuck have I gotten myself into?"

Her cheeks blushed a light shade of pink, but she didn't offer me a reply. As much as I wanted to ask more. More about her–more about her wants and needs, her likes and dislikes, all to keep James happy and the ball in my court–I remained tight-lipped, willing myself to think more rationally. I couldn't bombard her. She likely wouldn't give more than she could get, already backed into a corner like a feral kitten.

It took her forty minutes to drift off to sleep after taking her medication. To my surprise, and in the pretence of what looked like a tender moment, her head fell to the side and laid on my shoulder, where I had a strange sense it would remain for the entire flight.

It had been a long time since I'd been so close to another female who wasn't my wife. The saddest thing was how much more relaxed I felt knowing it *wasn't* Sophia's head on my shoulder.

What the fuck did that say about me?

It said a lot about my marriage, but not a whole lot about this goddamn situation I'd fallen victim to.

I was grateful Blue hadn't argued with me over her father's wishes. But I was confident she would throw a tantrum once the plane touched down at Heathrow. I was expecting to be faced with a less appealing version of her once she realised I wasn't her chauffeur but much more than that. I was giving her a roof over her head. Somewhere to eat, sleep, and piss.

However, with her asleep on my shoulder, it did give me time to process the information she had shared before.

She said she wasn't afraid of anything, but her tremor told me otherwise. It didn't matter how many times I went around in circles; the truth was, I kept coming back to the same conclusion. Her fear of flying was likely just the tip of one giant iceberg, encouraged by her father's unhealthy obsession to wrap her in cotton wool.

Though I couldn't say I blamed him.

Not after witnessing what he'd lost.

Not after throwing my fist through the window of his wife's car and hurling his three-year-old daughter into the safety of my arms.

CHAPTER FOUR

Walker

WITH THE END of the flight nearing, I nursed the disguised bottle of Vodka in my left hand, pondering how it wouldn't look good for word to get back to James and have him point a finger in my direction. I could only imagine the things he would say to me if he knew I wasn't at the top of my game. He trusted me to babysit his daughter, while little did he know, I was nursing somewhat of my own broken heart. Or as much of a heart that could be broken for a man *not* in love.

Bringing the bottle to my lips, I pried the cap open with my teeth and tossed back the last of its contents. The liquid burnt as it hit the lining of my throat–a welcome pain, unlike the one in my chest. I'd never experienced a feeling, or a circumstance, sad and satisfying both at once.

I squeezed the air from the bottle and hid it behind my back, turning back to face Blue beside me, who was beginning to wake as the plane made its descent. She still had her head on my shoulder. As I expected, she hadn't woken up once. Not for some food. Not to use the bathroom. And not to sass me with her pretty mouth.

Feeling my eyes on her, her own opened, glancing up at me under her eyelashes with a look of contemplation on her face. My brows lowered because I wasn't sure what she was contemplating.

Did she know?

Nah, she couldn't.

She raised her head from my shoulder, and then, as if had never been there, the moment was lost. Perhaps it wasn't the past but I'd let my mask slip when thinking of my future and where it was headed, giving her a moment's glimpse into my state of mind.

"That was fast," she said, surprising me. Then she shook her head and covered her mouth with a yawn, prompting a chain reaction from me.

I rubbed my eyes. "You almost slept the whole ten-hour flight."

"That was the plan. I hadn't slept for over twenty-four hours before this in preparation. I've had so much caffeine in the last two days that I'm surprised I slept at all."

I only wished I had the option of the same luxury. Sleep was hard to come by these days, even with liquor in my veins. Pills, on the other hand, weren't worth the daytime drowsiness.

The plane hit the runway, and not five minutes later we were unfastening our seatbelts and standing from our seats. My eyes were on the large lady on the end seat as she shuffled into the aisle, but my words were intended for Blue. "Your father cancelled your accommodation at the university halls a few weeks back. You'll be living with me for a while."

"Living with you?" Her voice raised an octave, which earned her some strange looks from other passengers. Then she turned to face me. "He cancelled my accommodation? What the fuck? I don't want to live with you." She rushed out the last bit in a whisper, but seemed to be shouting.

"Well, you don't have a choice."

"The whole point of me moving here was for the sole reason I could do things on my own without him coddling me," she groaned. "I'm perfectly capable of taking care of myself, despite what he might think. Despite what it is he's arranged."

She turned away from me with a roll of her eyes, then stepped out into the aisle where the passengers from the back of the plane had already made their descent. I followed after her, standing tall behind her petite frame as she stood on her tiptoes, reaching into the overhead compartment to seek out her bag.

Her rebellious attitude was edging closer to pissing me off more than it had previously amused me. I was too tired for this shit. Although perhaps her lack of understanding and the vodka strumming through my veins had only intensified the situation.

I had one job. One job that happened to be more intricate than I was comfortable with. And I didn't have a fucking clue how I was supposed to handle it.

My hand came down to her hip, grounding her, and then I let go, my front touching her back as I reached for her bag myself. Pulling it from the compartment, I pushed it against her chest and watched over her shoulder as her hands came up to take it from me.

The alcohol I'd consumed wasn't doing anything to control the aggravated energy coursing through me. And with that, I didn't let go. Not when she tried to pull it from my grasp. Not when she huffed in frustration. Not even when the flight attendant told us we were the last on the back of the aircraft and they were waiting for us.

I leant down and placed my lips against her ear as though I was sharing a secret. "Like I already said, kid, you don't have a choice."

She probably wasn't used to people telling her no in a way that was so hands-on. She might not have known it, but whatever she hoped for in London was likely nothing she'd expected. Suddenly, I didn't give a shit how fragile she was. She'd have no choice but to harden up pretty quick if she wanted to survive in the world I lived in.

"I know women like you. I'm sure you have people kiss your feet back home; cater to your every want and need just because you know how to pull someone's strings. But it won't be like that with me. Do as your fucking told, and we won't have any problems."

I'd been walked over enough for the last twelve months. Fuck, the last eleven years. Nothing I did was ever good enough. Sophia never stopped wanting more. I didn't need another woman, let alone a fucking kid, testing the boundaries on top of everything else in my life.

She yanked her bag from my grip and turned around to face me, our bodies a fraction apart, her bag barely keeping us at a distance. Eyes were on us. The staff on the plane were quite possibly on the brink of calling security. However, James may have paid them a hefty paycheck too. Who was I kidding? Of course he had.

It was his fucking plane.

They were his fucking staff.

Fuck them, I thought. They didn't have to put her up in their homes. They didn't have to force her self-indulgent attitude into submission. He asked me to take care of Blue for a reason.

He'd put his trust specifically in me because he *could* trust me, even if it didn't make sense to anyone but him. Even if it made no sense to me.

Blue looked up at me, more awake than she was five minutes ago, only now with anger in her eyes and an ugly scowl on her otherwise pretty face. A contrast to the timid smile from ten hours ago.

"You don't know me," she said.

"I don't."

We stood there quietly, bathing in each other's features until she raised her chin a fraction higher to sass me. "For someone who's been hired to look after me, chauffeur me, be my maid, or whatever else you've been paid to do, I think you're a total dick, FYI."

She dropped her bag with one hand and pushed the other against my chest. I didn't move an inch. I leant into her, forcing her backwards. "Say what you want about me," I grit, reaching over her shoulder for my rucksack. "But your father asked this of me, so if you want to take it out on anyone, take it out on him."

Even with one arm caged between us and her fingers brushing my abs through the material of my hoody, there was no mistaking the frustrated exhale that came from her mouth or the warmth of her breath against my collar. It was equally as pleasurable as it was uncomfortable. We were in too close proximity, given our current state of affairs. I mentally shook myself. She wasn't Sophia. She was my boss's juvenile daughter, for fuck's sake.

Before I could lower my rucksack and step back, she'd squeezed herself under my arm and took off down the aisle, looking so smug that she'd gotten away from me. I did the only thing I could do and followed after her, though it didn't take me many strides to catch up. She was still nearly a foot shorter than me in those heels, even with her toned sun-kissed legs looking a mile long in her dress.

With us being the last to leave the aeroplane, we were also the last to go through passport control. And after Blue's far from quick trip to the bathroom, we were also the last to collect her luggage. She didn't have just one suitcase, but two. After watching her struggle to pull them along, I snatched both handles from her and pulled them alongside me instead.

"I was managing just fine," she said, keeping up with my strides as her red-bottomed boots hit the floor in small bursts behind me.

"Sure you were."

I wouldn't see her struggle just to be a prick. There were other ways to abolish her fragility without allowing her to sprain her ankle. Still, irritation loomed over me like a rain cloud, and my knuckles whitened as I clenched the handles of the suitcases.

As soon as my vodka buzz had worn off, I'd be on the blower to her father.

This wasn't my forte.

No amount of money was worth this shit.

The booze was talking more than it was me. Because it was worth it. I knew it was all worth it. Every single detested second. It wasn't a rain cloud above my head; it was a rainbow. And unlike most rainbows that folks said led to a pot of gold, mine led to a goldmine. And that goldmine was The Lagoon.

Still, I couldn't fathom explaining to James why I was in such a shit state of mind. And why Sophia wasn't currently in the picture, helping me out while we, what, *parented* his fucking daughter?

"Thank you, I suppose," she mumbled, barely loud enough for me to hear.

"So you do have manners hiding under all that brat."

She scoffed. "Except I'm not a brat. Not even close."

Choosing to ignore her, I walked through the airport's automatic doors and into the dark, glacial British weather. And immediately, the noxious smell of London assaulted my senses.

Blue followed in tandem, almost bumping into me when I slowed to a stop in search of Finley, my driver. I spotted him outside the arrival hall of our terminal as requested, which happened to be just across from where we stood. His tired eyes met mine, and the wrinkles on his face stood out under the orange streetlight he'd parked under.

"Get in the car," I said to Blue as I walked across the road. "And don't fight me on this with all that yolo juvenile shit you preached on the plane."

"This is so fucked up. I don't even know your name," she squealed. "And please, none of that shit was juvenile."

My eyebrows dipped. "You know my name." But when I stopped in the road and reflected, I realised she didn't. Why would she? James had decided to keep me from her. I meant no more than any other man who worked for her father in her eyes.

"Nate–*Walker*," I corrected quickly, glancing over my shoulder to check she was still following me.

"Nate Walker," she repeated.

"Walker to everyone that knows me. Only my brother calls me Nate." I felt the need to clarify. Not James, not even Sophia, called me by my first name. So I wasn't entirely sure why I'd given it to her–another thing I could perhaps blame on my current mindset.

I led the small distance across the road and handed our luggage over to Finley with a nod, who placed it in the car. When Blue appeared beside me, I opened the vehicle's back door for her to slide in. She was a little hesitant, so I placed a hand on her head and gently pushed her down.

"Quit fucking about," I said, closing her door to muffle her response before rounding the car to slip in beside her.

Finley fell into his seat a second later. "Where to, boss?"

Blue was looking out the window when I met Finley's eyes in the mirror, giving him a subtle lift of my chin. "Kensington."

It was a thirty-minute drive to my penthouse. Blue sat in silence, but I could tell how her mind was racing by the stiffness in her body. The soft hum of the engine and the swish of passing traffic were barely a distraction from her presence. I wasn't used to sharing a car with anyone but my driver. Even Sophia had her own means of transport. Guess our relationship could have been read from that alone to anyone who cared to look outside the lines of our marriage.

My vision was recognisably fuzzy, but even in the fucking dark, I couldn't seem to tear my gaze away from the girl beside me. The last time I'd seen her in a car was when she was a child. Her sitting beside me now brought an uncomfortable memory of that night.

My eyes observed every detail I could make out with whatever light hit her through the window. Like the small scar on her collarbone and the dusting of freckles over her nose. I hadn't realised how intensely I was staring until she turned to face me.

When her voice finally broke through the silence, moulding the tension into something less than it was, I practically bathed in the sound of her voice. I had no idea how to handle a situation as unique as ours. I wasn't sure what I thought of her not knowing who I was–that I saved her. That I saved her yet harmed her.

What a head fuck.

"I'm not going to jump out of the car or anything ridiculous, so you can quit gawping."

"I'm not gawping," I replied. Except I was, just not in the way she understood. Perhaps not even in a way I did.

I relaxed my elbow against the car door and leant my chin on my fist. "Tell me, what's London got that Miami doesn't?"

"Haven't we already been through this?"

My eyes didn't leave hers. "Talk me through it again."

"Now you're starting to sound like *him*."

Him as in James.

It was dark in the car, but her eyes were still vivid even in the minimal light. I doubt I could ever forget them, even if I'd wanted to. Everything about her was different now, except for them.

"I was a dick on the plane," I stated.

"I said you were," she bit back, no hesitation in insulting me. I wondered if that was something she did often or if it was purely just her father and me that she had an issue with.

Something possessed me to reach up to the roof and click on the interior light. She looked from the light to me with intrigue, her eyes floating across my face.

The tension in her body was more noticeable with the light on. She'd knotted her fingers together on her lap, showing off their lack of blood supply. Her shoulders hunched up like she was on the edge of her seat.

"You're a lot different from what I imagined you to be," I said, my eyes moving from her hands back to her face. Up until today, I still had this image of her in my head. One of her as a child, her big Bambi eyes full of suffering.

"People tend to build a perception of me before getting to know me."

There was something flawed with the way she said it. Something equally offended as it was sad.

"And that offends you?"

"Wouldn't it offend you? People judge me," she said matter-of-factly.

"That's the way we're wired, isn't it? We're all guilty of barring judgement on others."

She turned to face the window, pressing her forehead against it as she looked out. Her breath fogged up the glass pane as she spoke. "If you want the truth, I never expected to hear back from The University of Duke. Especially with me living in Miami."

"Then why did you apply?" I wondered. "If you wanted to go to college, why not choose something closer to home?"

"I'm afraid you'll think my answer is *juvenile*."

I could see the subtle roll of her eyes as she threw my word choice back at me. "Is it another 'you only live once, so fuck the world and be damned response,' or does this one hold more merit?"

She glanced a look at me over her shoulder. "I thought about it. All summer, I thought about not leaving Miami. But I guess... I guess I had a point to prove, okay? I wanted to piss off my father as much as I wanted to leave."

Her eyes searched mine for something. Understanding, maybe? The judgement she just spoke of? Who the fuck knew? This was as unusual for me as it was for her.

"I thought he would have figured out I'd applied and wavered my application before it had arrived in Duke's mailbox. I didn't expect to receive a confirmation of my place. I definitely didn't expect him to give in and let me go. But I also didn't expect this," she said, untangling her hands and waving a finger between us. "The night I told him... I assumed he was calling them to toss my application. I didn't think he'd organise something this crazy."

"Well, you succeeded in pissing him off, and you're still here. What would you have done if he hadn't?" I asked.

"Hadn't pissed him off?"

"Hadn't let you go," I clarified, trying to read into her.

She turned back to the window, pressing her fingers against the glass. "I can't answer that," she said after a beat. "But I know he'll soon realise that I'll be just fine without someone holding my hand."

"Maybe, kid." My line of sight fell to her hands as she

dropped her fingers from the window and clung on to the material of her dress for dear life. "Then again, maybe not."

She whipped her head back in my direction, her gaze following mine as I took note of her confused expression before I dropped it back to her stiff fingers.

She was giving away more than she realised.

"Would it make it better if we pretended I wasn't holding your hand and you were holding mine?"

I smirked in spite of myself.

I never regarded myself as the type of man to use sarcasm to mask my problems–and to a kid, no less. But as it went, there was a first for fucking everything.

Blue

MY BROWS PINCHED TIGHT. Despite the sarcasm I detected in his tone, I couldn't help but feel as if there was some sincerity in his words. It was hard to believe the asshole sitting beside me would ever need someone to hold his hand. Regardless of the little sympathy I felt for him, I threw it to the wind when I found myself growing defensive. If he was going to continue to be a dick, then he didn't deserve my kindness.

I licked my lips and gave him a hard stare. "Somehow, that sounds even more tragic, don't you think?"

A frown replaced his smirk as he hit the light off in the car. I got the impression I may have offended him—my comeback not entertaining him as it had me. Though it hadn't really entertained me as much as I'd hoped. I didn't like being mean. I didn't like having to put up a front. But as it went, it was easier than confessing the truth. Nobody cared to understand the broken girl. The silence resumed then, weighing heavily on my bones. I suppose it was expected with what we didn't have in common and how little we knew of each other. I'd been in some strange situations before. And being my father's daughter, I'd walked into them blindly. But this was up there with being one of the most abnormal situations I'd ever experienced in my life so far. I'm not sure I'd have been here if I had known the plan he'd made behind my back.

It felt like a long drive, but the time on the car's centre console said it had been less than thirty minutes since we'd left Heathrow Airport. Still, I was itching to exit the vehicle.

Noticing me staring through the windshield, Walker's driver's eyes briefly met mine through the mirror before finally slowing the car to a halt.

I turned away, looking out my window to see a large white building lit up like a palace with wraparound glass windows. Walker's arm reached over my lap, opening the car door from inside. Startled, I'd reached out to grab it.

"We're here," he said, looking down at my fingers tightly grasping the sleeve of his jumper.

I caught the faint whiff of his breath before he'd moved away, my grip on him loosening. And then I stepped out of the vehicle, looking between him and the building in front of me.

I was about to go into this man's home. And based on the scent I just inhaled, he was intoxicated. I failed to understand my father's logic. Why he thought Walker housing me was the better option. Why he believed I was safer with a practical stranger than with people my age? It's not like I was a complete hermit, despite his efforts to keep me locked away or within a reasonable distance of what he perceived as anything danger-ous. He'd never admit it, but I believed his issues were worse than my own.

Of course, he'd never known the extent of my experiences. He'd assumed the parties I attended over the summer were the slumber kind. Sexual encounters–non-existent. And as for drugs–prescription only. I was an angel in his eyes. The truth of my experiences may have just pushed him over the edge. His little princess was not entirely as sheltered as he'd hoped for.

If he'd had known what happened on the days when he let me out past my curfew, he'd have had a lock on my door. When you combined rich kids, alcohol, and narcotics, it made for one big happy family. And my father was no clean-cut man. He attracted women like flies to shit. He owned controversial businesses that had more write-ups than Disney had Dalmatians. He fucked twenty-year-olds in our backyard without regard for those watching.

And if that was grief, I didn't want it.

It was probably why he didn't like Ebony. She did what she wanted, just like he did. Not that we were related, but if I took after my father like she did her mother when her father died, I'd probably be more like her and less like *me*.

Walker chose not to be conscious of me as we made our way through the attended lobby. I'm not sure if he'd intended it for the presence of the pretty young woman on the night shift, sitting behind the tall desk, but he nodded at her as we passed by. She returned his nod with a dimpled smile, tucking a strand of brown hair behind her ear. She didn't look too much older than me–and she was unquestionably flustered as he walked past her. I briefly wondered if there was something between them or whether they were sleeping together. No strings attached. Walker struck me as the type of man with a revolving door of attractive women to fulfil his male fantasies. The chances are he did, considering he was close with my father. I just hoped I didn't have to bear witness to the sounds of slapping bodies and porn star moans as I did at home.

We walked the length of the room and into the elevator, where I hiked the strap of my bag over my shoulder and stared up at Walker like, dare I say, a lost puppy dog.

He stared ahead, swiping his elevator key across the keypad without looking. Before I knew it, we were heading up, and as quick as the doors had closed moments ago, they were now gliding open with a smooth transition. We stepped out and straight into his apartment, the doors closing automatically behind us. Walker touched a button on the wall, and a few lights came to life, illuminating the expansive place.

"You can take the master suite for now," he said, sliding his elevator key into his pocket.

His words didn't register. I was too busy taking in everything. Inside was more than just your typical London apartment. It shouldn't have surprised me since he worked for my father and had a personal driver, but he lived in a penthouse boasting panoramic views of the famous Hyde Park. Though unlike the outside–bright white and vibrant–inside was moody and black.

I walked over to the floor-to-ceiling windows, taking in the views of the city before twirling around and decidedly falling onto the couch that stood facing the view. "Do you own all this?"

"The view?" He smirked. "No."

I turned to give him a condescending smile.

He sighed. "It's leased. Ellis and Frey real estate own the building."

As he left the room and wheeled my suitcases down the hallway, I allowed my eyes to survey the layout. A large TV was attached snuggly to a wall between two of the windows, and a small rounded table stood off to the side of the couch beside an armchair. There were no walls between the kitchen and the living area. The space was large enough to remain completely open. Barely any boundaries, except for the hallway leading to other rooms.

He came back into view a few minutes later, arriving at the charcoaled granite of the kitchen island. He watched me as I relaxed back into the couch, letting out an instinctive moan when the cushions moulded to my back like a hug. The tension from my body seemed to ease, and I found my eyes begging to close. It didn't seem to matter how much sleep I'd had already. Perhaps the exhaustion stemmed from so much happening in my life at once. Things I didn't think possible.

It was crazy to think the impossible was... possible–sort of.

"Take the master suite," he instructed, ruining my Zen.

I glared. "Isn't this my home now too? Can't I enjoy a few minutes on the couch without you telling me what to do? Do you think my dad would be comfortable with the way you're speaking to me?"

My words lacked the conviction I'd hoped for, but I was trying to make a point. I didn't care how much my father was paying him. The man really had no power over me.

"You ever tire of being privileged?" he bit out, stepping away from the kitchen. He raised a thick eyebrow but tore his eyes away from my face, staring through the window at the city below us instead. But it didn't matter where he looked. Not when he'd made it obvious he was still waiting for my response.

In all honesty, I didn't have one.

I guess I hadn't truly known anything but privilege. But being privileged wasn't me. It was the second reason I wanted to leave Miami if anybody would bother to listen before making their assumptions. But why waste my breath?

The drop lights above Walker illuminated half his face, so I could only see some of him, including the lustre of his green eye. I wondered if he knew just how handsome he was, if he knew the effect he had on the girl downstairs, or whether he was oblivious to both. Though how could he be when he looked the way he did? He was undeniably good looking. And not like the most popular boy in school kind of way. But in a grown-up, *I bet I can show you all kinds of things*, kind of way. Like a teenager with a crush, I couldn't stop checking him out every chance I got. And how was it my brain wavered back to how handsome he was instead of how much of a dick he was acting?

His eyes sought me out, pulling at something inside me and making me retreat into myself. I hated when people tried to read me so obviously. Out of habit, I reached onto my head for my sunglasses but came up empty-handed.

"Shit."

"They're in your bag."

When I stared at him, dumbfounded, he finally turned back to look at me head-on, sliding his hands into the front pockets of his sweats. "Your sunglasses? You fell asleep with them on your lap. I asked the air hostess to put them in your bag on the plane."

My head dropped to the side. "Why would you do that?"

"I told your father I'd take care of you. So that's what I'm going to do." He took a breath, removing a hand from his pocket to swipe over his jaw. "Go to bed."

"I didn't ask for this," I said, growing just as agitated as he looked. "Any part of it."

"I know." He nodded. "But this is the way it is. And while you're here with me, it'll make it easier for both of us if you just fucking listen."

I debated telling him I'd done most of what I was told my whole life, but he clearly preferred dictating over listening. And just as I'd felt with my father back in his office, I knew it wasn't worth the fight, especially when I'd only just got here.

Instead of arguing, I climbed to my feet and snatched my bag from beside me, fleeing to find the room he'd assigned me to. He said something behind me, but I chose to let it go through one ear and out the other, making a show of tossing my hair over my shoulder.

Screw him.

Screw my father.

And screw whatever arrangement they'd assembled without me.

CHAPTER FIVE

Blue

AFTER TWO NIGHTS of rough sleep, I spent my Monday morning in bed, watching the city of London slowly come to life below me. Early morning joggers, pedestrians hailing cabs, and the unmistakable sound of emergency sirens (which had been a constant since arriving) played a small part in my new morning routine.

When I grew bored, I pulled back the covers and grabbed myself a shower in the en-suite attached to my room.

Walker had been absent yesterday, leaving me alone to acquaint myself with his home. There wasn't much to find in the penthouse. Besides the office and the few empty rooms I'd stumbled across my first night here, I'd discovered a set of stairs that led to a luxurious bathroom, a home gym, and an outdoor balcony. There was nothing to indicate who Nate Walker was as a person unless the colour black was anything to go by. And after a quick Google search on my phone, because the dick had no social media that I could find under the name Nate Walker, the only thing I learned was that the colour black was associated with a list of things. The first on that list was 'mystery,' and given that I didn't know much of him at all, I guess it seemed to fit him quite well. There wasn't a better word to describe him unless I went by looks alone. And although I was just seventeen, I was yet to meet a man who was as handsome on the inside as he was on the out.

After my shower, I fixed my hair into loose waves and painted my face with make-up, all with forty minutes to spare before my first day at Duke. Boots on and fully dressed, I lazed casually on the king-sized bed for the second time that morning, composing a text to Ebony that consisted of a complete rundown of my last few days. I hit send, and then I began writing a less kind text to my father. I'd been avoiding his calls between yesterday and today. I couldn't decide if I was more upset that he'd changed my plans or that he'd changed them without discussing them with me first. But that was my father, always treating me like an act, despite my trauma being my circus.

Midway through texting, I heard Walker's raised voice carrying through the penthouse. After finishing the text and hitting send, I pushed my phone into my skirt pocket and tip-toed to the bedroom door, pressing my cheek to the hardwood as I attempted to hear what was being said on the other side.

It was a bad habit–something I'd picked up through the years. I hated being a child walking into a room full of adults, only for them to stop talking mid-sentence. Everyone seemed to be afraid of damaging the damaged girl further. Worried their words would cause more trauma to my already traumatised life. Well, what they knew of it. The worst was when our maids would speak about my father, as if I were oblivious to how many of them had been in his bed or how many of them quit because they'd felt disgusted knowing his daughter hid behind a door further down the hallway.

I'd googled that in the past too. My internet search history would show me questioning why my father was so keen to sleep around instead of replacing my mother. But I always came up empty. Which, as always, brought me back to the only thing that made sense.

My father liked control.

It was... psychological.

And it's all I'd known for a long time.

Though Walker's conversation seemed one-sided, I could only assume he was on the phone. He wasn't arguing with a maid or a one-night stand or about to fire someone for accidentally falling in love with him like my father had done plenty of times. And though I considered he was talking to my father and regretting taking me into his home, it wasn't that either.

"I told you, I'm not coming back. I don't know what you expected–" he said before pausing. "Am I *happy?*" He scoffed. "Are you?"

And then...

Nothing.

Not long after, I heard the opening of a cupboard, followed by the faint sound of a blender. I assumed either he or whoever was on the other end of the line had hung up the phone. Given his parting words, I believed it was him.

How much had I missed?

Why did I even care?

Slowly, I opened the bedroom door and softly stepped into the hallway that led into the open layout of the penthouse, pausing at my view. Walker was shirtless. His ass perched against the kitchen island, a protein shake to his lips.

"Trouble in paradise?" I asked, my hand pulling the bedroom door closed behind me with a click.

My voice carried the length of the hall, and Walker's upper body shifted to face mine. His eyes narrowed, his gaze lowering down my legs in my school skirt before coming back up to meet my eyes.

"No paradise, no trouble," he replied dryly.

I ignored his blatant perusal of my bare legs and held his stare. "Attachment issues," I murmured to myself, feeling the material of my school skirt bouncing over my thighs as I walked towards him. Maybe he liked control as much as my father did.

He pulled his eyes away from mine, darting between his protein shake and my legs, but I was no better, my own eyes absorbing every exquisite inch of him as I broke the distance between us. A sheen of sweat covered his abs, down to the muscles that formed a V into his black workout shorts. There was no denying it; Nate Walker oozed sex appeal with little effort. It was a shame he ruined that with his personality.

Without answering, he swallowed back the last of his shake and walked to throw the plastic container in the sink.

"It's cold out," he expressed. "Do you have to wear that?"

I rolled my eyes. The answer was no, but the school trousers were disgusting, and I didn't like the constraint of too many clothes against my skin, knowing my anxiety could cause a hot flush at any time. It was so much better to be prepared than it was to be overcompensated. It was a pity I didn't think the same way about my father's little setup.

"I like the cold," I said instead. "What does it matter?"

He shook his head as I circled the kitchen island, perhaps thinking of me as a nuisance.

"Do you have flavoured water?" I asked, hoping I'd missed it yesterday in my search.

He shook his head again and murmured, "Just tap." So I made my way over to the kitchen sink.

My stomach clenched with uncertainty when I realised how close we stood. The heat from his torso radiated onto my pebbled skin, coating me in a warmth far from the anxious kind. The scowl on his face didn't help. To top it off, I wasn't sure if it was me or his phone call that put it there.

"Early workout, huh?" I found myself asking. I opened the cupboard above me for a glass, only for my fingers to graze a half-empty bottle of Bourbon that I was almost certain wasn't there the day before.

"Wrong cupboard."

My fingers lingered on the bottle while my eyebrows dipped into a frown. Then he reached up and closed the cupboard for me, forcing my arm to drop.

"Sets me up for the day."

My frown didn't waver. "What?"

"A workout," he said slowly. "What about you?"

"What about me?"

He sighed. "What sets you up for the day?"

"No one has ever asked me that before." I looked down at myself. "Guess I can't answer that."

Silence settled between us as he boxed me against the counter and reached into the cupboard on the opposite side to retrieve a glass. I swallowed hard at our close proximity, and then, chancing a look at him over my shoulder, I asked, "Where... were you yesterday?" It was none of my business, but I couldn't deny my curiosity.

He was frowning deeply, or maybe that was just his face.

"At the club. I tried to tell you the night you got here, but you were too busy being a brat." Then, without giving me a chance to reply, he placed the glass into my waiting hand and changed the subject. "Have you got everything you need for your first day at Duke?" He turned on the water flow over my shoulder and directed my hand under the tap when I didn't move to do it myself.

What the hell?

I inhaled a subtle breath when I felt his weight against my back. Was he serious? The dude was giving me whiplash with the swift change in his personality.

What was it he said? Something about the club...

"Blue Lagoon?"

"If there's anything you need, I can have Finley take you to the store on the way."

I tried desperately to keep up. "Finley's your driver?"

With him nestled behind me, I felt the warmth of his skin through my school shirt. And then I felt him nod against my temple.

"And you work at my father's club?"

He sighed. "It's not just your father's club. I own a share."

Once he'd helped fill my glass, he turned the tap off, and I turned to look at him again. I took a sip of my water as our eyes met and attempted to have their own conversation.

One of us had to speak, so I broke the tension, dropping my glass onto the counter and saying the first tangible thought that came to mind. "Still, having your boss's daughter living in your home must feel weird, right?"

That frown hadn't left his face. "It's not a situation I believed I'd ever find myself in," he agreed. And because he was still hovering over me, his warm chest against my back, I felt the need to keep talking. "So why did you agree to house me? It's hardly practical for a newly single man like you to be putting someone like me up in your home. What if you want to bring women back here? Do you expect me to stay out of sight?"

His jaw ticked, though it was subtle. "Newly single?"

I raised a brow, mimicking, "No paradise, no trouble."

He was silent for a beat, so I turned my whole body to face him. I expected him to move his arms from beside me and back away, but he didn't. He kept me boxed in, his fists clenched against the edge of the kitchen counter, as he angled his hips away from me. "Let me get one thing straight," he began. "I might value your father's work ethics, consider him a great mentor even, but further than that, me and your father are nothing alike–that goes for the way he treats women like they're no more than accessories."

I felt an inkling of jealousy before it disappeared in exchange for my sass.

"Really?" I questioned, dropping my head to the side like it would make me hear him better. I plastered on a fake smile. "Sorry, but it'll take more than pretty words to convince me."

The tick in his jaw seemed to intensify, but he didn't retaliate. After a moment, he stepped back and sank his hands inside the pockets of his shorts. I didn't miss the movement of his hands through the material as he re-arranged himself. As if to take my attention away from what he was doing, he grit, "He wouldn't have asked me to care for you if he didn't trust me, kid."

Kid.

"I'm not a kid," I snapped. And by the way his body had responded from being so close to mine, I think he knew as much.

My cheeks heated, but my eyebrows drew into a frown that matched his. I took my phone from my pocket, ignoring his lingering stare and feeling the need to retreat. "It's eight-thirty. Registration's at nine."

"And?"

This guy. I fought to not roll my eyes. "How far away is Duke from here?"

I peered up to see him looking down at the time on my phone screen. I had less than thirty minutes, and I had no idea how far away it was, only that I had to collect my schedule from the office administrator and find my way around. It didn't feel like much time at all, yet I'd been awake for hours.

"Finley's been waiting on you for over an hour," he spoke matter-of-factly.

I dared another glance at him, hoping the blush on my cheeks wasn't as noticeable as it felt. "He has?" Why didn't he tell me this already?

He nodded, pulling one hand from his pocket to palm his jaw.

"Um, will you take me instead? And can I sit with you.. in the front?" I asked, clearing my throat.

He studied me closely and then huffed an almost silent "Jesus" under his breath. I didn't have enough time to read into what it might mean before he walked from the kitchen and towards one of the empty bedrooms. "Grab what you need while I throw on a T-shirt. I'll meet you out front. I'll take you this once, but I really, really don't have time for this shit."

Walker

I RODE the elevator down to the underground parking lot and hopped into my G-Wagon, resigned to the fact I wouldn't have time to shower before work. Then I drove around the front of the complex to collect Blue, who stood shivering outside the lobby doors. Her school skirt was too fucking short. Her white shirt too fucking thin. Yet, for someone who said she liked the cold, she clutched a large Prada tote bag against her chest like a hot water bottle.

I lowered the passenger window, knowing I wasn't visible through the black tint. She spotted me and then began walking towards my vehicle. Like a pervert, I watched her hips sway from left to right through the open window as she all but strutted her way across the pavement. When she reached me, she opened the door and slid into the passenger seat, placing her tote bag at her feet with an exasperated roll of her eyes. As if it was *my* fault she was running late when she was the one batting her eyelashes in the kitchen.

"Do you know where you're going?" she asked at the same time the built-in sat-nav said, "Make a U-turn."

I muted the robotic voice, closed her window with a button on my steering wheel, and then manoeuvred the car with a three-point turn.

The sat-nav answered for me, but I still tipped my chin in a subtle nod and mumbled a "Yeah" to clarify it for her.

Once we were en route and the engine had warmed up, I cranked up the heat in the car, though not by much. I knew if I made it too warm, she'd feel the cold further when she stepped out. This wasn't Florida. The weather was at least ten degrees below what she was used to. Her "liking the cold" was bullshit. No doubt, "cold" was a metaphor for attention. And I'm sure she got enough of that without using miniskirts as an excuse.

After another five minutes of travelling in quiet, this time, it was me who broke our silence. "Why didn't you say something at the airport?"

She crossed one leg over the other, and I couldn't help but notice how her skirt hiked further up her thighs with the movement.

"What do you mean?"

I glanced at her face before shifting gears, and then my eyes were back on the road. "You were tense as fuck in the car ride from the airport. You asked to sit in the front today. It's obvious you–"

"I get carsick," she mumbled before I could finish my sentence.

But she wasn't fooling me.

I'd observed her same body language in the car two nights ago, her hands virtually turning blue as she wrung them together on her lap. She'd given me enough pieces to puzzle her together.

"Does your father know you don't like riding in the backseat?"

"Of course he does," she was quick to reply. "He just doesn't understand it. Me. He doesn't understand me," she clarified. "He's always trying to fix me."

"Has he used those specific words–has he told you he wants to *fix* you–because that doesn't sound like something your father would say."

"No, but..." She inhaled a deep breath. "I'm broken. And if he hasn't told you that, then let me tell you myself... I have issues, okay?"

My stomach dipped, and I caught myself glancing at her again before switching lanes. I'd figured it out already, but hearing it was different. It was on the tip of my tongue to tell her she wasn't broken. That calling herself broken was not only an insult to her but to anyone else with the same disorder. But that's not what came out.

"The car accident," I muttered. She didn't need to tell me why when I already knew the cause. I'd spent the last two nights thinking about it myself. I didn't understand why James hadn't mentioned his daughter's PTSD, given the circumstances and our new living arrangement. However major or minor it was.

I sometimes swore that when I was between dreaming and reality, I still felt her tiny fists beating against my chest. Her broken voice screaming for her mummy. And fuck, if that was my trauma, I couldn't begin to imagine how it would feel to re-live hers.

"Do you remember it?"

She turned to look at me, and my paranoia made me feel like she was trying to place me to memory. I frowned, growing impatient when she didn't answer me as quickly as expected.

"Sometimes," she murmured. "In bits."

In bits?

I don't know what my face conveyed, but she felt the need to explain. "I take medication and stay away from potential triggers if I can help it. Like sitting in the backseat of a moving vehicle. Hanging upside down." And then she went on to mumble, "Thunder. Fire."

My shoulders tensed at her words, but as I settled onto the new road and switched into a higher gear, something possessed me to reach out and take her hand, the same way I had on the plane. I didn't have words, and she didn't say anything else. But this time, she hadn't fought me. She linked her fingers through mine and held on. Surprisingly, her skin was soft to touch and not as cold as I expected. I wondered if she was heating up because we were talking about it and that just talking about it was a trigger too.

Still, by the way she squeezed my hand back, I was under the impression she'd never received a response like it before.

We stayed like that until I was forced to use my hand again to change gears, and after that, I resumed their rightful position on the steering wheel. My fingers tightened around the rich leather with the urge to reach out to her again as I drove her the remainder of the way to the university. I'd never wondered until now why it was that James never told her who'd saved her. Was it because she'd never asked? Or was he waiting until she was old enough to understand it better? Though now, just being with her, I realised it was probably in her best interest that she never knew. Maybe *this* was why.

We reached the gates of the university at ten to nine. I parked in the parking bay beside an empty Bentley and stifled the engine's growl, but Blue made no attempt to open her door. On almost every occasion, I'd been a cunt one way or another. So when she remained seated, I was half expecting her to lash out at me like Sophia would. Only she didn't.

"You good?"

She gnawed on her bottom lip, her features showing more of her nerves than they did her excitement.

"Do you want the truth or a lie?"

"Either works."

"I'm good."

I relaxed back in my seat, contemplating if that was her truth. She didn't look like she wanted to be here any more than I did.

And that there was my lie, which was why I found myself second-guessing her answer.

A small part of me enjoyed her company, even if it wasn't my usual kind. Even though it somehow felt wrong.

Still, I held out my palm. "Give me your phone."

Her forehead creased, and instead of reaching into her pocket to get her phone like before in the kitchen, she leant down to the footwell to fetch her bag. She took her phone out, typed in the four-digit passcode, then handed it over.

I looked from her phone to the Victorian building in front of us. "You know where you're going?" I asked while inputting my number into her contacts and texting myself so I had her number too.

"I'll figure it out."

"Look at me," I said, handing back her phone and not letting go when she tried to take it from my hands.

Slowly, she raised her head to meet mine; her eyes–more green than blue in the morning's dim sunlight–looked into my own in question. I didn't know what the right thing to say was or if I were on track with the things she'd just told me, but I said, "There's nowt wrong with you."

"There's a lot wrong with me."

"Says who?"

Her expression was unamused. She couldn't answer me because the only person to think of her as broken was herself.

I sighed.

The more time I spent talking with her, the reality of everything she'd been through began to hit me. Slowly, but brick by fucking brick. The night James's wife died had somehow shaped this girl's entire life. And it wasn't fair or kind. It was fucking tragic. I couldn't help but feel responsible for the part I had to play in it.

The look in her gaze wavered, and for a brief second, she allowed herself to drop her guard. In a split second of vulnerability, I saw the frightened little girl who heard her mother's cries grow distant as I ran us away from the heat of the flames. And she didn't even know that I knew.

Fuck, *I knew.*

Perhaps I was the closest person who could understand just a semblance of what it was she felt.

I cleared away the lump of emotion that had lodged itself into my throat and shook my head of the memory. "I'll text you to check in. But if at any point you need me, text me first."

Did I mean that? I wasn't sure. But she nodded anyway.

I could just make out her blush under her make-up as she took her phone from me and placed it securely back into her bag. It was the second smile she'd graced me with today. And it made me feel all torn up, dislodging things from inside me I hadn't known were even there.

"Shit, one more thing," I said as I watched her place her hand on the door handle. I reached into the car's backseat and pulled out a hoodie from my gym bag. I probably needed it, considering it was baltic outside. But she needed it more. "It's cold out." I repeated what I'd told her earlier.

She held back another smile by pulling her bottom lip between her teeth. I could tell she didn't want to take my hoodie from me, but she shoved it into her bag anyway.

"Finley will pick you up," I said, as she climbed from the car. "This was a one time thing," I reiterated. "I work late."

When she got to her feet, she settled her bag on her inner elbow. Then, lifting her chin with false confidence, she said, "And it's fine to sit with him in the front?"

Involuntarily, the one corner of my mouth tipped up. "If that's what you want."

"Maybe you're not as bad as I first thought, Nate Walker. As obvious as you make it that you don't want me around." She looked at the ground and then back to me with a raised eyebrow.

And then the door slammed closed.

I refrained from opening the window and correcting her. My name. And what she thought she knew.

My eyes lingered on her as she raised her shoulders and chin, taking a few deep breaths. And then she stepped awkwardly over the dewy morning grass, steadying herself onto the pavement that led to the large Victorian building in front of us. She stopped mid-stride, and just when I thought she might look back, she raised her arms and brushed her fingers through her long hair. Only then did she carry on walking towards the building. The further she moved away from me, the harder I mulled. I wondered if she knew anyone here or if she was about to be on her own. It wasn't in my interest to care for trivial things such as who'd she eat lunch with or sit beside in her lectures.

But I couldn't deny the feeling that took root in my chest. I felt an urge—a desirous need—to learn everything there was to know about Blue Sterling while she was in my life.

Before I could digest any further what that might mean, my phone rang through the car's Bluetooth. Sophia's name lit up the screen. I sighed audibly and ran a hand back through my already dishevelled hair. After already speaking with her on the phone this morning, I wasn't ready for another round. She had the nerve to ask me to make more of an effort in our marriage. To go back so we could work on it as if we hadn't already tried to fucking love each other like a normal couple.

We tried.

We failed.

How could we repair something that had never been whole?

And what was there to repair? Almost everything in our life had been built on false ground. If we didn't fall for each other in the years we'd already been together; chances were it would take another lifetime to discover anything real.

Despite Blue not being able to contact me, I decided to turn off my phone so that Sophia would take a hint on the basis that the next time she called, she'd reach my voicemail. Then, shutting down every thought but work, I threw the car in reverse and began my drive to The Lagoon. I had too much to do before considering adding more shit to my plate.

I ARRIVED at The Lagoon to find Noah in my office, overlooking the nightclub below through the one-way windows. I wasn't surprised, considering I was late. He often wanted to discuss business first thing before something else demanded his attention. Besides Sophia and James, he was the only one I trusted with a keycard and access to my office. Though I'd have to get Sophia's back. Fuck, the last thing I wanted was her cornering me at the club.

Noah turned away from the window and glared at me as I stepped further into the room. "You're lookin' grumpy as shit and unapologetically casual today," he remarked. His jade green eyes glinted with mischief as they ran down the length of me in my lack of business attire.

"Fuck me for breaking the rules. Unlike you, I didn't have time to curl my hair."

If you asked me, the boy cared too much for his appearance. But it made sense. When some people grew up with nothing, they tended to appreciate the things money could buy.

He winced. "I got some bad news. You ready for it?"

"No."

"Tough shit. I'm just gonna lay it all out."

I rounded my desk and sat myself down on my office chair. Then I kicked my feet onto the desktop, giving him the go-ahead. Not that I wanted to hear it, but when it came to my job, I didn't pussyfoot around.

He took a breath and slid his hands into his pockets. The move was something I did myself when I was on edge, which immediately had me glowering.

"Hudson has an MCL grade two injury. There's a possibility he'll have to drop out of his title fight."

I blew out a heavy breath and allowed my mind to process this information, ticking off a mental checklist of what I knew versus what could change. There wasn't a ton of time to handle this, but there was still a chance it could be worse.

"He's torn his ligament?"

Hudson Barnes was our number one ranked middleweight fighter of The Lagoon, which meant the situation would only put us in a predicament if he couldn't fight. He'd worked hard for this, and we'd spent the best part of two months organising the next big event. Every spare moment we had was spent conversing with inspectors, having our licences regulated, getting bouts approved, and ensuring all the paperwork was correct and up to date for every regulation. It was one big fucking ball ache.

"Well, it's too late to cancel the main event. If that happens, the gym and the organisation will lose a shit ton of money."

In a perfect world, money wouldn't have been my first concern. But the world I lived in, the world our fighters fought for and into, was cutthroat. It went without saying that James and The Lagoon's organisation had such an important role in the industry, and a lot of it was held together by bank. Our bank.

"What about Wez? Where is that blonde-haired tattooed fuck?" I asked.

Wezley Bright was our standby fighter, but the last time I'd had a conversation with his coach, he'd mentioned how he seemed distracted. His head wasn't in it. When he stepped into the Octagon, he was throwing sloppy punches and not moving his feet. A sitting duck, which for a twenty-four-year-old on a six-fight win streak and one of the promotion's hottest prospects, was baffling. There was the possibility he would do more harm to himself than he would to his opponent. It would be the wrong call, perhaps one we'd have no choice but to make.

"Wez isn't up to par either, so it's not looking good."

"Wez hasn't been 'up to par' for at least twelve fucking months now. There'll be repercussions if we have both fighters withdraw. Hudson needs to get a feel, see what he can do with his injury." I looked off to the side. "This couldn't have come at a worse time. Make sure the press doesn't get wind of it. We've only just recovered from their last story."

"It's cool," he said. "I'll speak to him. We'll figure it out."

I dropped my legs from the desk and rolled my chair forward.

Resting my elbow on the hardwood, I dragged my hand back and forth over my forehead. "Shit."

With my inner turmoil not only etched into the planes on my face but out in the open, Noah took a few steps towards me. "If you need to take a step back, I can handle it."

He was too fucking good to me.

"I can manage."

Besides, both he and the club were the only things in my life worth a shit.

He seemed to accept it. "How is Sophia handling having James's daughter living with the two of you? Is she her usual bitch self?"

Although I could hide my emotions from most people, I couldn't hide them entirely from Noah. When I'd married Sophia and was finally granted custody of him, he'd not long turned fourteen. It was inevitable that he'd come to learn Sophia was the bigger picture behind my irrational mood swings through the years. He knew of my failing marriage. He just didn't realise that it was essential for me to marry her to save him from another two years in foster care. I'd have gotten him out sooner if I could, but the courts wouldn't allow it no matter what I offered. We didn't have the same father, yet I was his brother, and that complicated things. I didn't have the kind of money then that I had now, so bribing the courts wasn't an option. If it were, I'd have done it.

Besides asking him to handle the club while I flew to Miami, I hadn't found time to fill him in on everything prior.

"She's not. Me and Sophia are through." I dared a look at him and cleared my throat, embarrassed at having to explain myself to my kid brother. "I've leased a penthouse in Kensington while I figure things out."

"Divorce?"

I nodded. "I couldn't have predicted this shit when I married her."

"Does anyone?" He cocked his head and studied me. "Did you ever love her?"

I looked up at him. "That obvious, huh?"

He clucked his tongue. "Anytime she asked for more–for kids–you shut her down."

"I had you to think about. I had this place."

He sighed, removing a hand from his pocket to scratch his jaw. "Come on, bro. I'm not stupid."

No, but maybe I was stupid to think he hadn't cottoned on to the reasons behind my marriage to a woman I despised more than I relished the company of. But if he were to ask outright, I'd never admit it.

Maybe it was one lie I'd grow comfortable taking to my grave. He didn't need to carry the guilt of my choices. When it came to my marriage, I'd chosen his life over my happiness. It really was that simple.

And I'd do it again if I had to.

I'd do it twenty times over.

He looked through me then as if he'd had some kind of brotherly intuition. "You can run from the truth, but you can't hide from a lie, brother."

His words made me think back to Blue, who offered me her own truth or a lie less than an hour ago. It made me think of how I hadn't told James the entire truth and led him to believe Blue was staying with both me and my bitch of a wife.

"You should have left her the night she admitted she fucked around on you," he said, still on the subject of Sophia. Because why wouldn't he be? It was my mind that was wandering into blu*er* territory.

Still, his words filled my lungs with relief, thankful we weren't about to dive further into the past than I first thought.

The past was already set in stone. While a lot happened between now and then, there wasn't much I would change.

"Hindsight is fifty-fifty," I muttered.

"Twenty-twenty."

"Whatever you say," I responded, pretending to be interested in something on my computer screen.

With that, he didn't seem to be focused on our earnest conversation any longer. His hand dived back into his pocket to pull out his phone, and then his fingers were brushing over the screen. "I best crack on then. Sort out the lads before fight night becomes a shitshow."

I wasn't in the right mindset to figure it out, so I was glad he was already on the case. The two of us could put all our personal shit to the back of our minds, away from any more torment.

This time, when I re-focused on my computer screen, I got to work, loading up my emails and last week's financial report. "Keep me updated. Oh, and tell whoever's on duty downstairs that we have some new bar stools being delivered before we open. They'll need to let them in through the warehouse and help reload the ones they sent last week."

"What was the matter with them?"

"Wrong shade of blue." And just like that, at the mention of her name, my mind wavered. *Again.*

And then, an email from James drew my attention. "They were the wrong colour," I clarified.

"Alright..." he said slowly.

For some reason, I'd replied "Yeah," as if it were a question.

His back was to me as he made his way to the door. The moment he opened it, he stopped. "Nate?"

I looked up, feeling the torment come back to the forefront of my mind at the way his eyebrows drew together.

"What?"

He debated his next words. "I was a shit in the past. A real shit–sneakin' out late and disappearing without a word. I'm sorry if the arguments between you and Sophia back then were my fault. Maybe if I wasn't so difficult, if I tried to get on with her better, if I was a better kid, you mighta wanted one of your own–"

"I knew where you were," I interrupted. "You think I didn't?"

"You never said anything."

"Because I knew you were safe."

"How?"

"Does it matter?"

"Guess not."

"Well, then." I nodded, returning my eyes to the email in front of me. He didn't move from his spot. Assuming he was still expecting me to answer him, I chose my following words carefully. "Nothing me and Sophia argued about had anything to do with you. It's just the way we are. *Were.*"

He waited a beat, then ran a hand back through his short curly hair. "You deserve to be happy, man."

He coughed as I looked up. But before I could tell him to piss off, he'd already let himself out and was in the process of closing the door behind him.

CHAPTER SIX

Blue

WALKER GLANCED at me from over the head of the couch as I walked into the room. "Do you always wear so little clothes?"

I looked down at my lace trim pyjama shorts before looking back at him. "Are you rude to everyone, or just me?"

It was the first time I'd seen him since he'd dropped me outside of Duke this morning. I'd been hauled up in my temporary bedroom since Finley drove me back to the penthouse, and I was beginning to get—what do adults call it—*cabin fever*. Except back home, my version of cabin fever often began at ten p.m. and ended at seven a.m. the following morning. It would be easy to blame my new living arrangement, but truthfully, it was just the old habit of having a curfew.

I rounded the couch, noticing the bottle of Bourbon from this morning on the table beside him, only now it contained much less than earlier. Maybe his mood depended on how much or how little he had to drink. It would at least explain his attitude on the plane. Unless he was just a dickhead period.

He balanced his half-empty glass of brown liquid on his thigh. "Who knows?"

It was out of character for me, but still I questioned, "Do you always drink so much?"

"What's it matter to you how much I drink?"

"What's it matter to you why I wear so little clothes?" I shot back. "It's not like I'm walking around in my underwear."

"It matters," he said dryly before his attention shifted away from me and towards the television. He was lazed on the couch in fresh workout gear, legs spread apart, watching a sports channel—well, some interview with a news reporter and a guy called Hudson Barnes. The news reporter seemed to be grilling him outside The Lagoon for information about his upcoming title fight and whether it was hearsay that he might not be fighting in the coming weeks due to a rumoured injury.

"Fuck." He grabbed the controller and muted the television before I could hear Hudson's response. And a mumbled "News travels fucking fast" left his mouth before he downed his drink, lurched forward, and slammed his glass onto the table.

Hesitantly, I walked over and sat beside him. I hadn't intended to sit so close, but the angle had my knee colliding with his thigh. It brought to life a new sensation under my skin. I wasn't sure, but something told me he was trying to ignore it with the way his jaw ticked and the way his eyes shifted to the place our skin brushed before they refocused on the screen.

"What's the problem?"

He side-eyed me and pointed to the television. "Hudson. He's our number one ranked middle fighter of The Lagoon, and if he can't fight, we may as well hand the title and a hefty cheque over to the opposing team on a silver fucking platter."

"So they aren't just rumours, then? Has someone leaked this information to the press? And your backup fighter is... what? Not... good enough?" I didn't know a lot about the industry my father and Walker worked in, but I'd overheard enough phone conversations to understand when my father was pissed off with other agents, and I'd always been intrigued. I did know a lot of fighters in the industry got used for their bodies the same way a prostitute would. Of course, it was a personal choice, and the fighters didn't just love what they did; they lived for it. It was just the culture of the sport. It still came with the hypocrisy that the organisation made more money than the fighters did though, especially if their own fighters came out on top. The only difference was, the organisation got rich without bleeding all over the Octagon.

To summarise, it meant trouble was looming over Blue Lagoon, the same way our view through the windows suggested rain was threatening to fall from the clouds. And, based on what little I did know, it was terrible for business.

"Our backup fighter has some mental health issues, but I shouldn't be telling you this, so don't think about repeating it."

"Who am I going to tell? Why would I jeopardise your livelihood like that?"

"Why would anyone?"

"Well, I guess you've already made up your mind about me."

His voice was much lower than a moment ago when he mumbled something like, "I... shit."

After what felt like an awkward stare-off, he shifted his line of sight. I shot my tongue into my cheek. And like our previous conversation had never happened, he threw me the most mundane question.

"How was your first day?"

I didn't answer.

"Blue," he encouraged, nudging his knee against mine as if to break the tension he'd created.

"Come on," I sighed. "You don't have to force small talk. We both know I'm here because I have to be. And you're clearly getting something worthwhile out of this, or you'd never have agreed to let me stay here with you."

He pinned me with an amused glare. Thirty seconds later, he spoke again, refusing to acknowledge anything I had just said.

"So, it was alright, I take it? After this morning?"

I nodded subtly, resigned that he wasn't giving up. But how resigned was I, really? I'd wanted his company, else I'd have stayed in my room.

"It was fine."

Liar.

It was awful.

All three of my tutors took an apparent distaste for me from the get-go. It only made me not want to be there. I couldn't concentrate on anything they had to say in their lectures and wished I could be somewhere else. My anxiety sat like a parrot on my shoulder. And I was so far out of my comfort zone, I couldn't help but wonder if I'd made a mistake moving here. Still, *fine* was the most straightforward answer.

Unaware, he seemed to have angled himself towards me. "Fine?"

I sucked in a lungful of air, breathing it back out with a prolonged, "Yep."

"And you're studying...?"

"Media and Journalism."

His jaw ticked. I knew what he was thinking. He didn't have to voice it. After what he just told me about The Lagoon–about his fighters–he'd assumed because I was studying Media and Journalism, I was chasing gossip and crossing my fingers for something juicy to fall into my lap.

"What will you do with your degree?"

That was one question I didn't mind answering. And maybe, after hearing my answer, he'd realise just how wrong he was about me. Even if my first day at Duke wasn't anything like I'd imagined it to be.

"I'd always dreamed of becoming a social media specialist for a successful establishment. But it had never been a possible reality before now. I guess it's still sinking in that one day I'll have the opportunity."

"So you've accomplished pissing off daddy and establishing the start of a dream in just a few weeks, huh?" he said it like a joke, but I detected a sense of gravity in his tone.

That's what he took from that?

I threw one hand across my waist. "I guess?"

"And then what?"

"Then what?" I frowned.

"What comes after that? When you've got the job you've always dreamed of?"

"I haven't considered that far ahead." I scrambled for a thought. "I don't know... maybe happiness or something."

"Happiness?" he scoffed, his chest rising in silent laughter while a grin grew on his annoyingly handsome face. "Fuck."

"Why are you laughing at me?"

His eyes darted between me and his surroundings, and then he smirked, his tongue coming out to suck his bottom lip. "It's cute that you think happiness plays out like that. It's a rarity in life that anyone is truly happy. It takes more than achieving your aspirations to get to the point of happiness you're probably referring to." He held up his ringless finger. "All those fairy tales are full of shit."

"Clearly," I muttered. He probably couldn't hold down a relationship because he had a problem with his attitude and was fond of a drink. Ugh, he infuriated me so much that he made me do the one thing I hated. He made me judge him.

With a roll of my eyes and a confidence I didn't feel, I leant over his lap to grab the controller to the television and began browsing through the channels, unprepared to get into something so trivial. So what if I wanted to be happy? What did he want to be? Did he want to remain miserable as fuck forever? Would he have preferred me to be grumpy and rude, just like him?

I sighed with no other angle than to ease my own stress. To keep the rest of my judgement to myself.

Eventually, I paused on a documentary called *The Blue Planet*. For a few minutes, we watched penguins get hurled about by heavy waves as they tried to get back to shore.

I struggled to concentrate.

With my leg touching his and his body somewhat angled towards mine, it seemed I was aware of his every breath, and those few minutes seemed to feel like hours.

It wasn't until I was about to turn over again that he finally spoke.

"Why were you named Blue?"

"My mum." I cleared my throat. "Apparently, she thought I was a boy."

He was silent for a moment, and then, "What's your middle name?"

"Really? Do you care?"

He straightened as he made a show of rubbing at his eyes, leaning back into the couch while a mumbled "I don't" left his lips.

Ignoring his bluntness, I wavered between looking at him and scrolling through more television shows I'd never heard of. For some reason, he was making me nervous. Every time we locked eyes, my stomach twisted, and I couldn't decide if it was because I was frustrated with him or *into* him. He really was something to look at, and it wouldn't be the first time I'd been attracted to a guy's arrogance. I'd just never been on the opposite end of it. I could only blame the attraction on a surge in my hormones.

"If we're talking names, then why does everyone call you by your surname and not by your first name? Why not Nate?"

"Less personal," he muttered.

"Less personal?"

He hadn't mentioned that I'd called him by his first name earlier, but the way he tipped his chin and the corners of his eyes crinkled made me feel like he wanted to. For some reason, maybe one I'd never learn, he preferred Walker. I couldn't help but wonder at what point in his life did people stop calling him by his first name and begin replacing it with his surname? What was wrong with everyone calling him Nate? Why did he choose to hide it from the world? More pointless questions that would take up residency in my head to go with the other senseless questions I'd often find myself thinking. Maybe one day I'd learn that every question I had couldn't always be rationalised. Or perhaps I'd forever try to find an answer in everything and get over my brain being wired somewhat differently from most.

"My father–Nathaniel. Growing up, everyone said I took after him. I was Nate, Nathaniel's boy," he scoffed. "My father was a good man until my mother got pregnant by another bloke. Then he turned to drink, and when Noah was born, so did she. I guess *Nate* reminds me of what could have been. Of who my father was before."

I frowned. "Where's Noah now?"

"He lives ten minutes away–in Chelsea."

"I don't understand why he can call you Nate, but nobody else can."

"He always has. He's the exception."

"You're close?" I wondered. My father had slept with enough women to make it possible to give me a sibling if he'd wanted, but he hadn't. "I'd always wondered what it would be like to have a brother."

"As close as we can be, given our differences," he said matter-of-factly. "There're things we have in common, and things we don't."

We were silent for a moment, and then I asked something I probably had no business in asking. "What about your parents? Where are they?"

He shuffled in his seat, and though he hadn't moved much, I immediately noticed the loss of his body from beside mine. "Likely in the same sorry place they were when we left."

I realised he had a shitty childhood, and I wasn't sure how to respond. Convinced he was about to ask me to go back to the bedroom, I dropped the controller on my lap. I wasn't ready to call it a night. "Can we... watch a movie?"

His gaze darted to his watch as he debated it.

While I waited, I threw my head back onto the couch. I didn't know where my courage came from, but I rolled my head in his direction and began fluttering my eyelashes. Maybe it was a good enough distraction from where his head was at. And perhaps I could sway him. Though it may have been my eyes that won him over with the way he was looking into them so intently.

When the corner of my mouth rose in a smile, his eyes narrowed. Besides his obvious life experience, the thin lines surrounding them were the only thing I noticed of his appearance to highlight our age difference.

I took a breath. "So, how old did you say you were?"

"I didn't." And then, with nonchalance, he said, "I'm thirty-four."

I did the maths in my head, quickly working out our age

difference. There were at least sixteen-seventeen years between us, depending on his birthday, but it didn't feel that way. Sitting beside him and conversing like we were—it didn't feel like I was talking to someone who'd been born over a decade before me.

"Noah's closer to your age than I am," he admitted.

Two fingers brushed across his bottom lip. Then those same fingers were on my naked thigh before he stole the controller from my lap. As quickly as he'd turned away, he loaded up a movie. I couldn't comprehend anything he'd said as something low in my stomach prickled with awareness.

Nope.

No way.

He couldn't and definitely shouldn't have had this effect on me.

"Have you seen *The Sixth Sense*?" he asked.

I tried to relax, pulling my knees up on the couch. "Nope. Kinda embarrassing to admit, but my movie knowledge is pretty poor." Unless I counted every Disney movie ever made, but I refused to tell him that, worried it would only highlight my age.

"Then prepare to be spooked, kid. It's a favourite."

"Not a kid," I mumbled, grabbing the massive cushion from behind my back and throwing it in his direction.

He plastered a cocky smirk on his face, anticipating the move and seizing the cushion before it caught him on the chin. Then he brought it down against his chest in a death grip, show-casing the veins in his arms as he tucked it between his elbow and the couch's armrest. The move only brought us back together.

I felt the burn of his eyes on me as I leant back into the couch right beside his shoulder. Weirdly at ease and comfort-able in his presence, regardless of knowing him only a few days, and not forgetting the small tidbit that he may or may not suffer from alcoholism. Was it genetic? Many signs were there, but what did I know about something I had no experience with?

Still, there was something about him. Something I felt when I was around him that wasn't the typical feeling of anyone else I'd met in my entire life.

As the movie started, he hit another button on the controller that turned off the lights above us, playing into the whole movie night ambience. It was something I'd craved, yet never had. And I wouldn't admit it to anyone, but it beat *slumber parties* and being felt up by shitfaced jocks who claimed I was the most beautiful girl they'd ever seen.

I eyed the Bourbon on the table. I probably shouldn't have pushed it, but if he could, why couldn't I?

"How about a drink?"

It was dark, but I was sure I saw his lips twitch. "Watch yourself, brat."

Walker

WE WEREN'T HALFWAY through the film before Blue leaned into my body like I could comfort her from what was happening on the screen. I had no fucking business liking it, but I did. I couldn't remember a time me and Sophia ever sat down and spent time together like this. She'd choose an expensive dinner date over a night in; somewhere she could show off the latest addition to her wardrobe. Somewhere she could brag to whoever gave her just an inch of attention and be sure to tell them how incredibly wealthy she was. The richest thing in our marriage was my bank account. Still, I only had myself to blame.

I'd encouraged it. While she played doting wife, I'd played the part of *hubby*. Fuck, I'm surprised the word alone didn't make my balls shrivel up, and I, myself, grow a vagina. The same could be said for how I opened up to Blue, giving her parts of me I'd never shared with anyone.

There was something wrong with me, and I don't think it was just the booze talking.

My gaze drifted to her arm. She had it aligned across her chest, her fingers holding her neck. From my position, I noticed goosebumps on her skin.

"It's not real," I said, referring to the movie.

"I know that, but it doesn't make it any less uncomfortable. You're enjoying this?"

"What?" I grunted. "You're not?"

My issue was, I was enjoying her company more than I was enjoying the movie.

I felt the shrug of her shoulder, but her eyes stayed wholly engrossed on the TV. I knew because I couldn't stop looking at her. Regardless of her words, she was watching the movie with such a high level of concentration that, as uncomfortable as she was, the film still had her undivided attention. And why wouldn't it? It was a great film. A story of a troubled young boy who was able to communicate with the dead, partnered with an equally troubled child psychologist who attempted to help him.

I'd watched this film so many times I could watch it with my eyes closed and not miss a thing. Perhaps it was the sole reason I'd chosen it. Because despite me obliging her, I didn't truly want to watch some boy being haunted by ghosts. Which was ironic because it would only suggest I wanted to watch her before I even began to. Ironic because, in some weird way, I was being haunted by her.

I hadn't considered in too much detail about just how close we were seated, suspicious of the way it made me feel. At least not until she moulded her body into mine, and that suspicion felt like something welcoming. Her being so close almost felt as good as a drink. Almost.

Without thinking, I raised my arm so it laid above her head on the back of the sofa. Untouching, but near enough for me to feel the pull of her below me. She fell with me when I shuffled down into a slouch, which meant her head was now resting against my chest.

Comfort, I told myself. Shit, it seemed I'd grown fond of lying lately.

Blue tilted her head back to speak, her voice barely a whisper. "Am I–do you–do you want me to move?"

"No," I murmured. "You're safe where you are."

Safe.

The word, like my arm, surrounded her like a fucking shield. Safe was the sole reason she was here. A delicate little flower, though much too soft for anything more I had to offer than a roof and security for the next however many months. And then, she'd be gone.

I swallowed a sigh, focusing my attention on the screen instead of her. I had no idea what was wrong with me, but whatever it was had to be shut away in whatever box it sprouted from. And the wires crossing in my head had to be fucking straightened out before they completely malfunctioned and fucked up everything I'd worked for.

The club.

A life of forced solitude.

Blue remained flat against me for the rest of the movie. When the end credits finally rolled around, I expected her to move; only she didn't. And because I'd always loved to torment myself, I didn't force her to either.

Eventually, my eyes grew tired enough to close them, but I couldn't sleep. Somehow, the warmth of her body nestled against me loosened the stiffness that had been nailed to my chest for so long. I'd never been a religious man, but I imagined Jesus probably felt the same way when he was brought back from the dead.

Only when she began to tremble against me, I opened my eyes and realised she must have fallen asleep herself. She was breathing harder, her lips turning down at the corners, while her long lashes fluttered against her cheeks.

I frowned, unsure of how to soothe her in what could–from the outside–only be described as a bad dream. In the end, I settled for dropping my arm from the back of the sofa and holding her wherever most convenient. And given our position, it was easiest for my fingers to spiral over the skin at her waist. She was warm to the touch, despite the little clothes she had on.

"You're safe with me," I murmured, extending my other arm around her and lifting my fingers to move her hair away from her face.

A few seconds into assuring her, she began to wake. The intrusion had her eyelashes fluttering open, and realising where she was, she quickly sat forward, breaking my loose hold of her. The dim light of the television highlighted her clammy skin. She looked flushed for all the wrong reasons, but there was no denying it did something to me.

"Sorry," she whispered. "Sorry—I didn't mean to fall asleep."

Her tone was velvety, and I found myself craving to stroke it with my tongue. It was the first fucked up thought I'd had.

A thought I had no right indulging.

A thought that had me hardening like a steel door.

No fucking entry.

Turn the fuck around.

"Best idea you've had all night, kid," I said, making sure I punctuated every word to sound like the truth. "James never said I had to entertain you."

She breathed a heavy breath in, her chest rising before she slowly let the same breath out between her lips. Slipping from the sofa, she shot me a look that I was familiar with. It only told me that I'd subconsciously taken more notice of her than I realised. Somehow, I knew what her words would be before she even spoke them.

"I'm *not* a kid. And *fuck* my dad."

And with that, she twisted on her heel and began her exit from the room.

In the midst of the quiet, when I assumed she was out of earshot, I mumbled a very grave, "I know."

As soon as the words had left my mouth, I clamped my lips closed.

The way her feet faltered on the floor between the kitchen and the hallway told me she may have heard me. I could only blame the Bourbon for making me more susceptible to getting to know her. For getting so close to her. And obviously, making me so fucking negligent. It wasn't an excuse. Anyone who was anyone could see she was far from a kid–to look at. Her attitude may have said otherwise, but I was still undecided. And it was best to keep it that way.

As I stood from the sofa, I pressed a button on the TV controller to turn on the drop lights in the kitchen behind me. Then I grabbed my empty glass and near-empty bottle from the table.

Did I forget that Blue Sterling was nothing more than a means to an end? The juvenile daughter of my boss? And did I forget that, by law, I was still a married man, regardless of what little it meant?

My feet drove me to the kitchen island, where I poured myself my final drink of the night. I tore my eyes away from my full glass of amber liquid and to the shadow of Blue's retreating back as she made her way to my bedroom. And it was *my* bedroom, though I was yet to spend a night in my bed.

I had the means and the money to furnish the entire building–buy the whole building–and yet, for some reason, I chose to sleep on the sofa. In an apartment—a penthouse that wasn't mine. But fuck, what was less sleep when you weren't sleeping well, regardless? And what was a roof over your head when it wasn't really your home? I wasn't sure I'd ever known what 'home' was supposed to feel like. Who knew... maybe I was lying to myself, or I'd forgotten how it felt.

Blue reached the bedroom door as my hand wrapped around my glass. I brought it to my lips while she lingered with her hand on the doorknob. I pondered the possibility that she might look back for the second time today–that there was something else she wanted to voice–but that never happened. She pushed down the handle and stepped into the room, the door closing behind her with a gentle click.

My head shook as I took a breath and brought my Bourbon to my lips. But at least, finally, I could fucking breathe without the smell of her perfume making me delirious. It was like black coffee and sensual vanilla.

Daring.

Sweet.

And too fucking much.

The heat of the bronzed liquid lined the back of my throat, then my chest, until somehow, gravity pushed it into the pit of my stomach. I stood in my kitchen alone, and now, with nothing left to focus on now that Blue was out of sight, I realised I hadn't had a phone call from Sophia all day.

I breathed with ease, relief flooding through me for less than a second before my mind began to protest the reason why. Stroking the pocket of my shorts with my free hand, my other threw my glass to the counter.

"Shit."

A glacier may as well have replaced the warmth in my chest. My heart, the fucking titanic.

I walked from the kitchen, down the length of the hallway, then rounded the corner and all but jumped up the stairs and into the bathroom. Both the fan and light turned on as I entered. It was the darkest room in the penthouse. All black tiles and no windows. An open shower and a granite bath that doubled as a whirlpool I was yet to utilise. If ever.

Hidden inside an aperture of the wall was the washing basket. I retrieved my dirty gym shorts from earlier today and took my phone from their pocket. Every muscle in my body grew tense as I turned it on, and messages and missed calls pinged one after the other like a spitting cobra.

Sophia.

Sophia.

Sophia.

They just kept coming.

Something close to disappointment poked at me when I realised there wasn't one text from Blue. Though why did I expect one? I never texted her today to check in as I promised, and she'd said herself everything had been "fine" for her first day. She hadn't needed me. Perhaps that should have been my first clue to stop convincing myself she had the attitude of a kid and just accept she was a young adult.

My phone continued to buzz in my hand with text after text from my wife, and all I could think was what sane woman believed this was fucking normal? What healthy, wholesome, ordinary relationship experienced this?

Are you with her now? Read one of her messages. For reasons unknown to me, my fingers flew over the screen, texting back. **With who?** I responded. There was no way she was talking about the teenage girl in my home. She couldn't have known the reverie plaguing me.

Her reply was instant. **Whatever slut you keep on the side.**

A scoff forced its way up my throat at the hypocrisy.

I've told you time and time again, Soph, there's only ever been you.

Her call came through within seconds, but I didn't answer. I glanced at myself in the bathroom mirror. My eyes were glazed—alcohol and lack of sleep playing their part. My phone rang out, but before she could call again, I switched off my phone. She was the one regret I'd have to live with. Just another hurdle I'd cross tomorrow.

And the day after.

And then maybe even the day after that.

Definitely the fucking day after that.

CHAPTER SEVEN

Walker

PISSED OFF that The Lagoon had made this morning's headlines for all the wrong reasons, I stood with my arms folded beside Noah, watching as Hudson went through the motions on the canvas mats alongside his trainers.

"You think he'll be good for fight night?" I asked, my eyes glued to the swelling on Hudson's knee as he pushed his injury to his limits.

"So far, he seems to be working through the pain. There's no telling that his training won't do further damage. He needs rest, but ultimately, the ball's in his court."

"What about today's image in The Liberty? Have you asked him about that? It's not like the boy to be caught off guard."

"I asked. He said it's nothing to be concerned about."

I sucked my teeth and scoped out the remainder of the gym. "Where the fuck is Wez?"

Noah ground his jaw. "You're asking the wrong guy. His phone's off. Nobody but coach has heard from him for a couple of weeks."

"If Hudson's injury worsens, we need Wez to take his place. Get his address off the system, have someone scope out his apartment and someone who isn't coach find out what the fuck he's playing at. I want him in this fucking gym, working out his issues on the floor."

He took his phone from his pocket and nodded, sending a text to whichever staff member he'd assigned the shitty job to. Hopefully, someone with a good enough persuasion technique to have him back where he should be. If he didn't have to work hard before, he would have to go at it harder now that Hudson was toeing the line between stepping foot in the Octagon and watching from the sidelines.

"Sophia called me late last night," Noah said suddenly, his eyes still on his phone.

"She was asking where you were, whether you were with James's daughter or if you'd abandoned your work as you had her for your mistress."

"My mistress?" I scoffed. "Jesus. What did you tell her?"

"I didn't." He tipped his head to meet my glare. "I didn't know what the fuck to say. I had someone over, so I hung up."

I fought the urge to grind my teeth, tightening my already crossed arms. It hardly felt appropriate to file an injunction against my wife, though the idea crossed my mind momentarily. It seemed she'd try anything to get under my skin. She knew she held cards I'd never planned to reveal to my little brother. And I had no doubt she was ringing him to try to spite me. It didn't matter that I'd stood by her, even after she'd openly admitted to fucking around on me with whatever sorry fuck wanted her at the time.

"You shouldn't have answered," I said. "Next time, don't."

He frowned, the lines on his forehead making him look older than his twenty-five years, making him look more like me. "No need to be a prick. I didn't know why she was ringing me. Besides, your phone had been off all evening. For all I knew, it could have been an emergency. Hard time or not, don't take your shit out on me."

"She's not listed as my next of kin," I muttered. "That's you. So now you know, for future reference, her calling you warrants no kind of emergency. Fucking none." Then, I added for good measure, "*If* there's ever an emergency, you'll be the first person to be notified."

"Noted."

As he pocketed his phone, an agonising groan sounded from Hudson in front of us. And then, in a span of seconds, my day worsened. We both turned to see Hudson hit the floor, shielding his knee between his hands. His ocean eyes met ours, signifying that this wouldn't be an easy feat. The chances of him stepping into the Octagon without rest were slim. And I didn't want to think of him not stepping into the Octagon at all. At the moment, the latter seemed to be likely.

"Fuck," Noah said.

Fuck was right. I needed a fucking drink. "Someone better find Wez. Today. We have less than two weeks, and time is not our ally. If Hudson can't fight, Wez needs to be prepared. I swear that lad's head has turned to fucking jelly since his last fight."

I couldn't begin to think how I'd repair further damage to The Lagoon's reputation if both our fighters were to withdraw from our event. And as it stood, the media shat on James, on us, any chance they got. For whatever reason they could come up with.

When the main event took place, I needed Hudson to win the title and The Lagoon to come out on top. Because ultimately, when it came to business, I couldn't afford to do if, buts, and fucking maybes. I could only do absolutes.

———

I WAS SITTING behind my office desk with a glass of Bourbon to my lips, my gaze on my staff through the window as they worked their jobs beneath me. I was beginning to resent the taste, yet it still served its most important purpose. And it did its job much better than most.

Finishing a gruesome phone call with my solicitor was all it took to start the process of divorcing my wife and for me to pick up the bottle. Typically, this was the easy part. The rest would be a headache. I was setting myself up for a game I didn't want to participate in, a game where I didn't hold all the cards. But my hand was forced anyway.

Interrupting me from my thoughts, my phone vibrated on my desk with a text.

Blue's name stared back at me.

Holding my phone in one hand, I begrudgingly slid my finger across the screen and opened her message.

Beatrix–my middle name. In case you still don't care.

I couldn't help myself. I sat back in my chair with a smirk pulling at my lips, thoroughly amused at her ability to be sassy and endearing even through a text message.

"Beatrix," I mused. It was delicate, rich, and soft on the tongue.

A text back acknowledging its delicacy could be construed as wanting to get to know her. Which ultimately was the plan. But did I want her to know just how much? A battle with my sanity had me putting down my glass and texting back; only I disregarded her message.

Why aren't you in class? I replied.

Three dots appeared on the screen before disappearing. Some part of me felt disappointed and regretful that I had been so cold in my response that it had scared her away. But then an image came through, the edges of her school skirt curtained across the top of her sun-kissed thighs with the message: **I am.**

I stared at the image a little too long before my fingers flew over the screen. **Should I be concerned that you're not paying attention to whatever it is you're supposed to be doing?**

I waited a minute until that minute turned into four, into nine, and then into double figures. And still, she hadn't replied. I felt like a man possessed. Was this how Sophia felt when I avoided her texts? Pocketing my phone, I stood from my chair with force, allowing it to roll back towards the wall. As it bounced off the black metalled wall, I paced over to the window, staring down at what was in a matter of months, soon to be solely mine.

No one would ruin this for me, and no one could take it away.

Not Sophia.

Not Hudson.

Not that blonde-haired tattooed fuck by the name of Wez.

Definitely not Blue Sterling.

"MISS STERLING."

My name being called from the front of the old auditorium had me sliding my phone into my skirt pocket and my eyes widening. I looked up at Mr Smith, my Journalism tutor, staring at me with blatant authority. He looked the opposite of kind-faced, his glasses perched on the end of his nose, making his nose look a few inches smaller than it was. We were almost two hours into his lecture on what it meant to be a journalist. It was my last lecture of the day, and a lot like on my first day, I was struggling to pay attention, wondering if it was too soon to regret choosing Media and Journalism as my degree.

I hadn't realised how many connecting factors there'd be. All I wanted was to learn how to create compelling social media strategies and excel in my creativity. I didn't want to gather fake news and disseminate it to the public. Only, when there was a curriculum to follow, what I wanted was a lot different from what I got.

"Do you want to be here, Miss Sterling? Or is there somewhere more important you need to be?" He spoke loudly, encouraging almost every student to stare in my direction. All of them seemed to stop what they were doing–either easing down their pens or closing down the heads of their laptops to get a better view of me.

How the hell Mr Smith knew my name out of the other thirty students here wasn't just embarrassing, but beyond me. Unless he had an excellent recollection of his students' first introductions, he'd gone out of his way to single me out and embarrass me in front of the others.

I cleared my throat, faking a confidence I didn't feel as I sat straighter in my seat and attempted a smile. "I have nowhere more important to be."

He raised a curious eyebrow and pushed his glasses up his nose. It must not have been the answer he was looking for because the next thing out of his mouth was, "Stay for a chat after my lecture."

"Sure," I mumbled, looking down at my lap, where I was holding too tightly onto the pleats of my skirt.

I spent the remainder of the lecture with my head down, half-heartedly taking notes where I could. But mostly, I spent my time where it wasn't warranted. I may have–okay, I did–Snapchat Ebony with ridiculous filters on my tutor's face to cheer myself up. And although I refused to text Walker back–he was a little too close to the truth, and I wasn't entirely sure how I felt about that–I still considered it.

I googled everything there was to know about The Lagoon, surprised to find it lacked almost any kind of social media presence, which was crazy to me, especially when The Lagoon had made such a big name for itself. Despite it being my father's business, there was so much–away from what the media wrote about it–that I didn't know. And now that I was in London, I found myself wanting to learn more about the business my father chose to leave behind and put into the hands of someone else.

When Mr Smith turned off the projector that was on view to the students, ending his discussion and signifying the end of the day, I packed my belongings into my tote bag and remained seated in my chair until the rest of the students had cleared out from the room.

As the last student stepped through the doorway, Mr Smith walked over to the door and closed it behind them. From a distance, he met my eyes. Then he walked over to his old wooden desk, took out a rolled-up newspaper from his drawer, and proceeded to walk up the stairs towards me. I seemed to shrink into myself as he towered over me. Up close, I could make out an indent in the middle of his chin and his beady eyes staring at me through the frame of his glasses.

"Yesterday," he said with disdain in his tone, "despite efforts to put it down to first day nerves, I couldn't help but notice how you looked like you didn't want to be here." He threw the rolled newspaper down on the chair beside me. "I've been given the same impression today, Miss Sterling. I hope you realise that places at Duke and for this particular degree are limited. Given that it is day two and you've paid more attention smiling into your phone than you have your textbooks and our discussions, I'm forced to warn you of that. There is a list of waiting students, ones I feel would be more respectful of your place. Students that would appreciate my time and efforts."

When I made no move to open the newspaper, he leant to unroll it for me. Then, he proceeded to flatten it down with his palm. I didn't understand what he was trying to show me until he moved his hand away and the back page came into view. My father, or more precisely, The Lagoon, had made today's sporting headline. This, of course, was no surprise to me. They may have had a lack of social media presence, but there were enough journalists and sporting forums to make up for what The Lagoon didn't share. Even if half of what they wrote were lies.

Mr Smith pointed to the image of Hudson "Bully Boy" Barnes. He'd been caught vulnerable outside The Lagoon, and although he had his cap pulled down over his face, tears were noticeable on his cheeks. Alongside the image, the headline read, "*No Bully left in Barnes.*"

My brows pinched together as I studied the paper and scanned the article. Like the television interview, the article stated how Hudson had acquired an injury and then went on to talk about the club's previous drug raid.

None of the article explained why he was *crying,* which was exactly where my mind lingered.

Walker said the Lagoon's backup fighter had mental health

problems, so why was Hudson the one to be crying in broad daylight? This image was probably porn to his component.

Mr Smith sighed, air blowing down on me through his nose.

"Why are you showing me this?" I asked, looking up at him with narrowed eyes. He must have had an ulterior motive.

He looked me hard in the eye and placed a hand on the back of the chair beside me. The faint stench of his dried sweat assaulted my senses, and I struggled not to let it show.

"Miss Sterling. *Blue*. Do you want to make headlines, or do you want to write them?"

The only thing I heard from his mouth was judgement.

"I... what? I wouldn't be making headlines. I'm... nobody, really."

He sighed again, his tone sounding both resigned and annoyed. "We check the history of every student that attends Duke. We know who you are, and we know who your father is. This article here is considerably tame compared to the others I've read. If you want to be here, Miss Sterling, we need to see it. We hold a high standard, and we don't take kindly to uninter-ested students when there's another hundred that would be more respectful of your place."

"Isn't it a little unfair to judge me based on my father's repu-tation? On his business's reputation?"

"I'm not judging you, Miss Sterling. Quite simply, I'm just telling you how it is."

I wasn't sure how to respond to that, so I didn't respond at all.

"Perhaps you need to rethink your degree of choice," he said, stepping back from me. "Maybe something less strenuous would suit you."

He made his way down the stairs and towards the door, where he waited for me to follow. For some reason, I was still sitting in my seat. I collected my tote bag from beside me, bypassed the newspaper, and headed towards the exit.

"If you want to keep your place here, you need to do better. By that, I mean focus. Despite the money I'm sure you'll inherit, that air in your head won't get you very far."

With that, he opened the door for me to exit through, and as quick as I stepped through it, he closed it again behind me.

Finley didn't say anything when I slid into the passenger seat of his BMW ten minutes later and threw my bag to the floor. With shaking hands, I fastened my belt and waited for him to start the car.

Noticing he was a little sluggish starting the engine, I glanced at him to find him staring at me, the wrinkles on his forehead showing concern.

"Everything okay?" he asked.

This was the fourth time I'd been in the car with him, but it was also the first time he'd spoken more than his usual hello to me.

I was too embarrassed to tell him what had just happened. So I said, "I think perhaps I'm just a little jet-lagged."

It was some of the truth, at least. Really, my anxiety was making itself known by weakening my muscles. And my conversation with Mr Smith was likely at the root of that, but now, sitting in a car on an already bad day, was not the time to confess. Since being on medication for my anxiety, it wasn't often I was triggered unless a night terror got too much, and because I understood enough about the disorder itself, I knew that identifying how I felt often helped limit the occurrence of a panic attack. I wouldn't allow Mr Smith that privilege over me.

Finley stared at me a beat longer before reaching over to open the glove compartment and signalling inside to a packet of Kleenex and an unopened bottle of flavoured water.

I was relieved he didn't ask any more questions. And although my throat was drying by the second, and I wanted to take the water, I couldn't help but feel guilty for accepting something that wasn't mine. "I can wait till we get back to the penthouse."

"No, it's yours. Walker said it's what you like. He ordered for the penthouse to be stocked this morning and told me to keep a bottle in my car at *all* times."

"He did?"

He nodded.

"Well, um, thank you." I uncapped the water bottle, not wanting to read too much into the gesture. First my sunglasses, and now this? I knew it was because he'd told my father he would take care of me–he said as much himself–but I wasn't used to being catered to so... thoughtfully.

I almost felt... cared about, which was ridiculous because these two things were hardly anything at all. I definitely shouldn't have been reading into them like I was.

"If it's not an inconvenience, can we make a stop on the way back to the penthouse, please? I noticed we passed a home and furniture boutique this morning that I'd like to check out."

Without another word, Finley side-eyed me and gave one gentler nod of his head.

Grateful that the man barely spoke, I sipped my water. Only the calm that settled over me didn't stay long, and my mind began to drag me to a discomfort I only wished I could escape from.

I tried to convince myself I was strong, but it wasn't always as easy as telling myself so in my head. And it seemed even far from home, with the path paved towards the future I thought I wanted, nothing in my life would quite ever be that simple.

CHAPTER EIGHT

Walker

IT WAS after eleven when I found myself stepping from the elevator and into the darkness of my penthouse. It was quiet–too quiet. Finley had driven Blue over to Duke this morning and was told to fetch her back at the end of the day, just as he had yesterday. I hadn't heard from him, which wasn't out of the ordinary. Finley didn't often speak unless he needed to be heard.

I removed my suit jacket and placed it over the back of the sofa as I walked through the room, taking in my surroundings for any signs of life as I neared the kitchen. My feet came to a halt as I reached the entryway that separated the kitchen from the hallway. My fingers dug into my palms as I stared at the floor, itching to step back and pour myself a drink before taking a late shower. But before I could succumb to the craving, my attention was stolen. It was minimal, but the faint sound of someone crying echoed down the hall. I frowned, my chin raising and my line of sight falling on Blue's bedroom door. *My* bedroom door.

The crying, I realised, was coming from Blue. Hesitantly, I strode quietly across the floor until I reached the door that separated us. I wrapped my fist around the handle, seconds away from letting myself in before thinking better of it. Loosening my grip, I slid my knuckles against the hardwood and instead, very gently, double-tapped.

"Blue?"

The crying lessened, and a muffled "What?" came from the other side.

I scrubbed my free hand over my forehead. "Can I come in?"

"It's your room," she said. "You can do whatever you want."

Not the entire truth, but I bit my tongue, knowing she was upset, and whatever I was about to step into could only be made worse by saying the wrong thing.

I opened the door and stepped into the bedroom, barely closing it behind me. The first thing I noticed was the white glow illuminating her, courtesy of the tall pink lamp nestled in the corner of the room. My eyes lingered, knowing it wasn't there before. But then I turned to Blue, and suddenly, the lamp became irrelevant. Freshly showered and sitting up in bed, she wiped at her cheeks. In an otherwise black room, the white quilt pooled over her thighs, leaving her visible in a satin cami from the waist up. Tears were falling from under her dark lashes, creating wet lines down her makeup-less face.

My hands slid into the pockets of my slacks. "Why are you crying?"

"I'm not," she said, avoiding eye contact with me whilst continuously wiping at her face.

I stared at her with a mixture of amusement and concern. "You're crying."

"I'm not crying anymore," she clarified, finally meeting my eyes.

A smirk threatened the corners of my mouth, but I turned my attention away from her and took a few steps towards the window. It was dark out–late–yet London traffic was still relatively busy below us. I remained quiet. If I didn't push, maybe by her terms, she'd let me in.

"What's the latest on Hudson?"

Puzzlement covered my face as I turned to look at her over my shoulder. "Hudson?"

She pursed her lips. "He made headlines today. Did you know that?"

"I know that, but how do you know that?" I turned to face her, studying her for answers. She wasn't the type of girl to purchase a newspaper. *Vogue* or *Harper's Bazaar* was likely more her style.

She looked down at her hands, clutching the blanket over her legs and then back to me. "My tutor, Mr Smith."

"Mr Smith," I repeated. "He's a fan, huh? Have you been using that name of yours in vain? Letting people know who your daddy is to climb Duke's social ladder and get the status of teacher's pet?"

She rolled her eyes, which had me walking closer to the bed in annoyance. One minute she was crying, and the next, getting under my skin. In the moment, I didn't care that James founded The Lagoon and was the majority owner. It was me who had managed it for the last however many fucking years. It was me who got it to where it was today. And it was me who had to deal with both Hudson and the aftermath of the press. I didn't need her stirring the pot and creating more gossip for sources to sell to third parties.

I quickly realised it was a mistake letting her in on Wez's mental health problems yesterday. It was the same thing Sophia used to do. I'd tell her something in confidence, and the next thing I knew, I'd be receiving texts from news outlets because a "source" had shared something they shouldn't have. Sophia had always denied selling the information, but she had enough fame-hungry friends to do the honours on her behalf. You'd think I'd have learnt my lesson, spouting my mouth to untrusting women. Apparently not.

That's not to say it was true every time. There were plenty of people in the world wanting to see something fall in hopes they could resurrect something better.

"What?" I questioned. "Am I wrong?"

I wanted to be. I wanted to be so fucking wrong.

"You are," she said, looking up at me from under her eyelashes. Though her eyes were still wet and glossy, there was a determination that wanted to be seen. "Quite the opposite, actually."

And fuck, maybe to be known.

Maybe it was worth reminding myself she wasn't typically anything like Sophia. I had no reason not to trust her to fuck me over. Still, I wasn't sure. And I didn't care how pretty she was. Or that we shared something minuscule I couldn't comprehend yet.

I studied her for a moment, and uncertain, I tipped my chin to the bed. "May I sit?"

There was a brief quiet moment, her lips threatening a small smile. Something so simple, so natural, had me questioning what it could mean. I couldn't read her, and it seemed I kept getting her wrong, no matter how right I thought I was.

I didn't like it. Not one bit.

"Be my guest."

The irony wasn't lost on me.

My hands slid from my pockets as I took another step closer and sat myself down beside her. I kicked off my shoes, allowing them to fall to the floor with a soft thud. Then I shuffled myself up the bed, my back angled against the headboard. Raising my arms, I positioned my hands to double as a pillow behind my head. Three nights on the sofa, and the comfort of Blue's bed, *my* bed, felt like pure fucking bliss. I needed to get her set up in her own room, pronto.

"Comfy?" she asked, amusement in her tone. Her features had softened, and now a smile really was gracing her face.

I frowned, but there was likely a sparkle of something in my eye because my gaze was drawn to her mouth. Rolling my lips, I wondered what they'd feel like on hers. Pouty and pink, and oh so soft. Her tongue peeked out, and then she pulled her bottom lip into her mouth. My eyes raised, catching hers, as we sat there in a silence that began to feel so incredibly suffocating. I thought, for one second, I might have stopped breathing. And if I didn't know better, I'd think she was looking back at me the same way I was her, with nothing but pure unfiltered lust and a promise of a good time.

My head spun, yet my cock perked up with interest. *Seventeen,* my mind protested. Yet legal in more ways than one.

What was wrong with me? How had I allowed this girl into my penthouse and my head so freely? And what the fuck did it mean? This was a business deal, yet the things I was thinking would have James burying me in a shallow grave and Sophia standing over it screaming, "I fucking knew it!"

"No," I said.

Her smile fell. "No... you're *not* comfy?"

I cleared my throat, somehow hoping that it could clear the weird tension brewing between us. Or in me.

"Where'd you get the lamp?" I asked, changing the direction of our conversation while staring at it over her shoulder. Anything to will away the sudden urge to touch her. That wasn't me. And for fuck's sake, I was still married. Even if that marriage never really meant shit.

"I noticed a furniture boutique on the way home from Duke and asked Finley if we could stop for a little retail therapy."

My eyes found hers again, and that sadness that was there when I first stepped into the room was brewing in them once again. "Retail therapy?"

She nodded.

"What happened today that had you crying and seeking retail therapy?"

"Do you remember what we spoke about in the car when we first landed? About people having a perception of me before getting to know me?"

"Vaguely," I muttered. And also, *yes*, because I was incredibly guilty of it. But she didn't need to know that.

"Well," she said. "Mr Smith did exactly that–"

I smothered a chuckle with my palm over my jaw before she'd even finished her sentence. She clamped her mouth closed and then threw her arm over her face with a groan. It amused me–her thinking she was an exception to others' judgements. I'd put money on her being guilty of judging others herself.

Removing a hand from behind my head with quick reflexes, I caught her wrist in my grip to pull her arm back down. "Less of that," I mumbled. She didn't try to remove it. In fact, she raised an eyebrow at me while staring at me through those glossy eyes. They were so full of depth, I imagined it would be effortless for the right person to drown in them.

"Are you upset that he judged you?" I asked. "Or was it because he misjudged you?"

Her eyebrows sank together. "Is there a difference?"

I loosened my grip on her wrist and allowed myself to sink back to my side of the bed.

"You have a lot to learn if you want to make something of yourself, kid. The world is full of bastard opinions and people who think they have everything figured out. Judging is our own bullshit personal hierarchy." I tucked my elbow behind my head and nestled back into a slouch. "What was it he said?"

She huffed out a heavy breath and slumped back against the headboard beside me. I tried not to notice that her head was almost resting on my shoulder, but I couldn't deny how connected I felt when I was near her for reasons I couldn't explain.

"He didn't like how uninterested I was in his lecture. He said Duke does a background check on every student. He brought up my father. He showed me today's paper—the image of Hudson—and then he had the nerve to ask me if I wanted to make headlines or if I wanted to write them! He said there'd be more students respectful of my place. That I should consider changing my degree to something less strenuous. He basically called me an airhead."

My eyes closed with a sigh, and I wondered if I looked as tired as I felt. I wouldn't allow this minor inconvenience to stand in the way of me and my end goal. I felt for Blue, how perhaps she was being judged by her father's reputation in society. But fuck that, it was merely the club at the top of mine. Which was why I said, "Don't worry about it. I'll sort it."

Although my eyes were closed, I could feel her looking at me when she asked her next question. "You'll sort it? How?"

"With money," I answered dryly. "How the fuck else?"

Almost everyone, and everything, could be brought for the right price. Her father taught me that.

MY EYES FOUGHT TO OPEN, constricting with a stream of light forcing its way through the luxury curtained voiles. It took a minute to comprehend, but no longer than two, to realise I'd fallen asleep beside Blue.

With my arm under her neck, I'd threaded my fingers through her hair and, at some point, pulled her head to lay in the crevice of my neck.

I lifted my chin from the bed and towards the lamp in the corner of the room, careful not to wake her. The light had been switched off, which only confirmed she hadn't tried to wake me and that I must have been out for the whole night and not for a few hours, as I'd initially hoped.

The last thing I remembered was telling her I'd sort out the situation with her tutor–the next... nowt.

The predicament I was in was made worse when I realised that Blue had forgone her blanket during the night and had one leg hooked over my own. I held back a curse as she shuffled sleepily against me. Any closer, her bare thigh would be nestled over my cock. Which seemed to be hard and excited at the probability of being so close to a nice warm cunt. The first in a long fucking time.

Wanting to untangle my fingers from her hair, I eased back my hand and stretched my arm above her head, slowly manoeuvring my way out from under her. Despite my body aching to stay, I felt a sense of clarity as I left the bed. She stirred but, to my delight, didn't wake. Absently, I reached down to collect my shoes from the floor, like some backward walk of shame. Even then, I admired the dusting of freckles on her cheeks and her dark feathered lashes. I found myself wishing I could run a finger down the length of her nose, grip her jaw between my fingers and stroke my thumb over her luscious lips without it being...wrong. They were so damn kissable, I wondered if anyone had ever had the privilege. Whether she'd ever had a kiss to light her up inside–if she'd had a good enough kiss to make her pussy wet and eager for cock.

Jesus.

I shook my head at my absurdity. Now wasn't the right time to be thinking those things. Never was the time to be admiring the sleeping brat.

Her lips.

Or her pussy.

Without waking her, I made my way from the room. And then, on route to my morning shower, I decided I'd leave the penthouse without acknowledging how I'd fallen asleep beside her or how fucking good it felt to wake well rested with her body nestled against mine.

However, by the tightness in my trousers, I imagined my cock wouldn't be able to forget it as easily.

FORTY-FIVE MINUTES LATER, I'd completely skipped on my morning workout and instead was pulling to a stop outside Duke.

Without Blue.

She could hitch her usual ride with Finley. And given that there was still at least an hour to go until her classes started, I had plenty of time to find this Mr Smith and demand he treat her with a little more respect than he had the past two days.

I'd say I was minding my own business when a trio of attractive blonde females strolled past me with hearts in their eyes, but I couldn't help but notice them. I merely returned the hearts with a smirk as I refastened the cuff links on my suit, and just as quickly as they checked me out, they were scattering towards the building to get in from the threatened rain.

Making my way through the tall doors of the old building, I immediately noticed a pointed arrow with the word 'office' and headed straight to it. I didn't bother knocking, immediately trying the handle. However, it was locked. Sighing, I pulled up the sleeve of my jacket and checked the time on my watch.

"The office doesn't open for another twenty minutes," a female voice spoke from behind me. "Mrs Berry needs at least three cups of coffee before she decides to start her day like the rest of us mere mortals."

"I don't have twenty minutes," I said as I turned to face the voice in question.

It was one of the females from outside, all big brassy blonde hair and blue eyes. Who, not so many moments ago, had given me heart eyes. Pretty would be a word used to describe her. She looked at me from top to toe with interest. "Can I help you with anything?"

"Are you a student?" She looked young-ish. Younger than me. Maybe five years older than Blue. Though she wasn't wearing a school skirt like the one Blue had, but dark fitted trousers with kitten heels.

"No." She laughed. "I'm the librarian."

I studied her for a moment. What were the chances she could point me in the direction of Mr Smith?

"I'm here to talk to Mr Smith."

"There are a few Mr Smi—"

"Media and Journalism."

"Ah." Her eyes breezed down the length of my Armani suit for the second time. "Are you here to discuss a conference?"

What's another lie? "I am."

"Well, my name is Kirsty–"

I interrupted her. "I'm not here for introductions. I'm just here to speak with Mr Smith. Can you point me in the right direction or not?" I glanced another look at my watch, realising I'd wasted another two minutes of valuable time. Time that could be spent at the club, organising the final preparation for fight night. Not cleaning up silly little situations so Blue would feel more comfortable here.

She pursed her lips, then nodded. "Follow me."

I matched her slow strides down the corridor and through two sets of automatic doors before we took a sharp left.

"I've just realised who you are," she expressed. "You're the face of that club, right? Blue... something."

"Lagoon."

"Yes! That's the one. It's not really my scene."

"No?" I tried to sound surprised, but she was a *librarian*. Of course, it wasn't her scene. Only certain types of people entered The Lagoon, and she didn't strike me as any of them.

"Mm." She glanced a condescending look at me. "I mean to say that I heard it can get pretty wild there at times. What with the fighters and the club being so close together. All that confined energy. The paper said you'd been raided not so long ago for drugs? Actually, just yesterday in the canteen, I read that one of your top fighters sustained an injury, which could be extremely damaging for his career and your business. The paper made it seem like that was drug-related too."

I'd never known someone to go from heart eyes, to not interested, to nosey as fuck so quickly. Not that I cared for the attention of a woman who had no idea what she was talking about. It wasn't often someone recognised me. My face hadn't been in the paper since our last event. But that's not what bothered me. I was hoping the old news of our drug raid was just that. Old. And clearly, this Mr Smith hadn't just shown Blue the article about Hudson but assumedly had been passing it around to his colleagues. It was expected–people purchasing newspapers and magazines. But I'm sure, by what Blue had told me of this man, he only had unkind things to say. As did many people who didn't understand the sport or the scene. But given that Blue was his student, it was unprofessional. And to be frank, it pissed me right the fuck off.

Many small-minded people assumed the club was a story away from being finished. And there was always someone trying to sell fake news.

Our fighters may have come from tough backgrounds, with enough baggage to fill every bin in a ten-mile radius, but that meant nothing. Not in the grand scheme of things. The Lagoon's nightclub wasn't just any club. It was high end. Luxurious yet daring. And of fucking course, drugs slipped through my doors undetected, but what establishment could ever say they were one hundred percent drug-free? As long as my name wasn't associated with the hobby and that Blue Lagoon's fighters were keeping clean, I didn't give a fuck who snorted coke off whoever's fucking cock.

Or tits.

Or took a bump in whichever fucking toilet.

There was a reason I paid my staff so well and a reason my cleaners got a tidy bonus every year.

"Perhaps you shouldn't believe everything you read. Or share gossip without knowing the facts."

Embarrassed she'd offended me, she placed a hand on my arm as we walked. "Oh no, that's not what I meant."

"Please be quiet," I said, removing her arm.

The rest of the walk I spent composing an email to James while brassy big hair led us through the maze of Victorian walls. A few lies scattered here and there in my reply to drive home the fact his daughter had settled in *so well*. That *she and Sophia* had bonded over a movie night. Lies, lies and shit, more lies.

I didn't have it in me to tell the truth to James or feign politeness to the woman beside me, when the sole reason I was here was to put an end to Mr Smith's judgement of Blue. Perhaps the next email I sent would tell more of the truth. Or not. I hadn't given it much consideration at this point.

Brassy big hair slowed her steps, and I slid my phone into my trouser pocket when we finally stopped walking.

"His office is through there," she said, signalling towards a door a mere few feet away from us.

"Thanks." I tipped my chin. "I'll find my own way out."

She bit back a tight smile, understanding that I wasn't interested in idle chit chat. Or anything else she had to say. Or offer.

I entered the room to find Mr Smith sitting at his mid-century desk. I didn't expect him to look like a cartoon character with his butt-chin and glasses bunched on the end of his nose, so it was only natural I was holding back a chuckle when he turned his head towards my intrusion.

"I was unaware I had any meetings this morning," he grunted.

"You don't. I'm not staying long. I'm here on behalf of Blue Sterling."

His eyes narrowed as he stood from his chair. "And you are?"

"A man willing to write you a decent-sized cheque if you get off her back and not single her out in a class full of students because her last name happens to be one you dislike," I said without a breath. "Her association with The Lagoon is second-hand and has fuck all to do with her degree." I tried not to raise my voice, but just knowing I was a few feet away from the prick who made her cry was invoking something territorial in me.

"She's been here two days, and I'm yet to see her show any interest in anything I have to say, Mr...?"

"Walker." I ground my teeth together as I did a quick scope of the room.

Recognition seemed to flicker over his face. He knew who I was, just like the librarian had. He was someone who didn't like what The Lagoon represented. He probably considered himself above it like half of London.

"She's just not an intellectual girl. If she put effort into raising her hand and answering questions like the other students here, I may think differently. She spends most of her time on her phone or staring off into the void. Now, this would be something I'd perhaps expect further through the term, but on day two?" He shook his head. "I won't tolerate it. She should have never been accepted into my class."

"How much?" I asked. "Name your price."

"Excuse me?"

I unfastened my suit jacket and took a thick wad of cash from my inner pocket, watching as his gaze fell to the fastened paper bills in my hand. "How much is it going to cost me for you to treat her as I hope you respectfully treat all your other students?"

Four thousand pounds sat in my palm, and yet he waved his hand in the air as if to shoo it away.

"I don't want your money, Mr Walker."

Lying greedy cunt. He wanted more of my money.

"Everyone wants my money. There's a lot more of this." I expressed by flicking through the cash in my hand. "Consider this a down payment. I can write you a cheque through a third party if you'd prefer. Nobody would know."

"No, thank you. Now, if you'll see yourself out. I have students' work to review. Students who want to be here," he went on to say.

I was half tempted to pocket my cash and punch the smug look clean off his face, but with what I had at stake, I chose not to be such an irrational fucking bastard. Instead, I lifted my chin, more than adamant about getting my point across to the receding bald prick. "Blue wants to be here."

He scowled, placing a finger on the centre of his glasses as he pushed them up his long nose. "She'll have to convince me."

Frowning, I ground out, "How. Much?"

The tone of his skin was already pinker than most, but it was apparent he was becoming flustered. "I—I—this is absurd." He shook his head from side to side, that smugness he wore like a second skin seeming to disappear by the second. "I could lose my job."

"I'm not asking you to fake her grades, Mr Smith. I'm offering you money, and in return, all I'm asking is that you show her some respect. Unless...?"

"Unless?"

"I pay you enough to retire, and someone else takes your place." Looked like I was willing to do whatever it took. It was like my mind had been replaced by another. As if I was living outside my body, and my mouth was moving without being granted permission to fucking speak.

He continued to shake his head. "Mr Walker. You may consider yourself better than me because I am a teacher, and you are an entrepreneur, but I will not be bribed. With the utmost respect, if you offer me payment again, I will contact both the school board and the local authority and have them investigate."

My jaw ticked, but I gave no fuck for threats. Striding forward, I made my way to Mr Smith's desk and placed the wad of cash over yesterday's paper. Hudson's sad face looked back at me. Whatever he was hurt about, I felt for the poor lad.

Leaving my money on the desk, I took time to refasten my jacket before I turned and breezed back to Mr Smith. With a foot between us and his self-assured attitude that wreaked of stale sweat, I couldn't help but disclose my examination of him.

"Perhaps you're above accepting bribes, but I've seen more bully in you in the last five minutes than I've seen in Barnes since he stepped through my doors and asked if someone could teach him how to fight."

With that, I left him with his mouth agape and steam shooting from his ears.

Okay, no steam.

Still, I'd never seen such a cartoon character of a man. I was disappointed when the steam *didn't* happen.

When I slid into my G-Wagon another ten minutes later, I threw my head back against the leather of my seat with a heavy exhale. I couldn't help but crave a drink, but still, I fought against it.

CHAPTER NINE

Blue

FIN WAS DRIVING me to Duke, when my phone vibrated with a call in my pocket. I was expecting it to be my father as I was still dodging his, but when I retrieved my phone, I was surprised to see an English number I didn't recognise.

"Hello?" I answered.

"Good morning, Miss Sterling. Is now a good time to talk?"

"Um, that depends. Who is this?"

"This is Mrs Berry, the office clerk from the University. I apologise that I have to do this via the phone, but policy states that you are to be contacted as soon as the decision has been made."

My brows pinched. "The decision?"

"Unfortunately, a staff member has made an accusation this

morning, and until a thorough investigation can take place, you have been issued an immediate suspension."

"An accusation?" I questioned, confused. "What am I being accused of? What do you mean, I've been issued a suspension?"

Finley's concerned gaze switched from the road to me.

"A suspension, Miss Sterling. As of this morning, you have been excluded from Duke. Should you wish to appeal this decision, an email will be sent to the address on file with information on how to do this. The faculty appeals committee will consider your application, and once a decision has been made, we will notify you."

Adrenaline hit my chest.

"I'm sorry, what? What the hell is happening?"

"I apologise, Miss Sterling. It's completely out of my hands."

"Are you going to tell me what I've been accused of?"

I heard the clicking of a keyboard, and then she said, "Failure for academic dishonesty."

"But I didn't do anything," I argued.

"You'll find all the information to appeal the decision in the email. Again, I apologise for doing this over the phone. I hope the rest of your day is better."

I lowered my phone to my lap and opened my emails after the call, and precisely as Mrs Berry had said, an email was sitting at the top of my mailbox with the subject line: **Immediate Suspension.**

"Fin," I said with a heavy breath. "Please take me to The Lagoon."

He exhaled a breath through his nose and tapped a wrinkled thumb against the steering wheel, doing a double-take of me in my school uniform as I relaxed further into the leather. Though his eyes weren't eating me up the way Walker's often did. No, if anything, Finley was staring at me like I was a porcelain doll. It was the same way my father looked at me. Like I was between two states and on the cusp of emotional despair. Perhaps I just had that *look* about me. A look that screamed, *"Fragile, don't touch."*

"Do you need to change? I can turn the car around."

"No," I mumbled, reading over the email. The words *failure of academic dishonesty* and *grounds of expulsion* made my stomach turn.

I'd been at Duke *two days*.

Two fucking days.

What Walker said the night before flew to the forefront of my mind. His side of the bed was still warm when I woke up this morning. How the hell had he worked so fast, and what the fuck did he *do?*

I lifted my chin. "I'm going to kill him."

I noticed Finley shaking his head in my peripheral vision. "Walker?"

"Yes. Do you think I won't? I will," I said, turning my head to face him. "He told me he's nothing like my father, but he is. He's so much like him, he may as well be a clone."

Finley chuckled at my enthusiasm, though it seemed forced. "It's probably some kind of misunderstanding. I'm sure it can all be worked out."

"Finley, you do realise what a suspension means, don't you? And I don't know what exactly he's done, but what I do know is it's all his fault."

He signalled onto a slower road, but this time, chose to keep quiet. I sighed with the lack of conversation, locked my phone, and fiddled with it on my lap.

A misunderstanding?

Unlikely.

How the hell would this be worked out? How could I be suspended for something someone else did? Did Walker understand what the hell he'd done?

We reached a T junction, and where we usually took a left towards Duke, this time we took a right. And as the first of the day's rain hit the window, my head fell to the glass. Outside, traffic drove in either direction and pedestrians waltzed in and out of shops lining either side of the street. Though only temporary, the distraction of other people's lives helped me mask my anger.

"How long have you been a chauffeur?" I asked absently.

"A long time."

"Vague." I raised my head from the cool glass and positioned my head back against my headrest.

"I'm an old man. When I say a long time, I mean it. Now, if you asked me how long I'd worked for Walker, I'd have another answer for you."

I frowned at that. "What do you make of him?"

The tap of his thumb sounded against the wheel. "He's a good man. Always grafting."

"A good man," I murmured. "I want to believe it. Maybe a part of me does."

"Hmm, give him time."

"He confuses me. I never know what version of him I'm about to get. He's hot one minute, cold the next. A little bad." I side-eyed him. "A little good. And yet... I have the strangest feeling when I'm around him."

His brows pinched in concentration as we waited in traffic, and then he steered into another lane and headed towards a large roundabout. "Go on."

"I don't know how to explain it. I feel safe with him. He makes me want to drop my guard. It's silly, right? The feeling holds no ground. And now look where it's got me," I scoffed. "Suspended."

"Hmm."

"Seriously, Fin? Just *hmm*? Why don't you have more to say?"

"Perhaps the quieter I am, the more I can hear."

"Right. So you can report back to Walker. Got it."

He opened his mouth as if he wanted to say something, but closed it again quickly.

"Just because I said I feel safe with him doesn't mean I'm not angry. I am angry," I punctuated. It seemed he didn't want to reply to that either. This time, I didn't even get another "hmm."

He drove us in silence, and after taking the second exit at the roundabout, and another five minutes of driving through the city, eventually we entered a large parking lot. A large, almost stadium-like building grew closer as we neared, the words "Blue Lagoon" attached to its front.

"You'd think I'd remember it, but I don't. I'm not sure if my father ever brought me here."

"If he did, things have probably changed some since then. Walker ordered the place to be re-gut with your father's approval back in February."

I pursed my lips, staring ahead. I was excited to see the inside, but I couldn't forget the real reason I was here, even if Finley chose to ignore it.

"Arena entrance," Finley expressed, aiming a finger over the head of the steering wheel. "You'll notice some cars, but not many. Those who use the gym tend to park here, as it's cheaper than a roadside permit in the city. It looks quiet now, but this whole lot will be full for fight night." He drove us over an electric barricade, bypassing the front doors and into an underground parking lot. "The nightclub is open to the public from seven p.m., though their entry points are on the opposite side of the building, closer to the city's hustle. Staff parking is this way, as is access that grants the staff entry to each sector of the building." He rolled the car into a space near a steel door and produced a black metallic ID from his pocket–like the one Walker showed me on the plane. "My keycard is programmed to all three sections. This door right here gains you access to the staff elevator." He pointed behind me, and I shifted in my seat to follow his line of sight. "The nightclub is on the third floor. That's likely where you'll find Walker. If not, someone should be about to point you in the right direction."

I took the keycard from him and slipped it into the pocket of my tote bag. "Thanks, Fin."

He grunted. "Whenever you're ready to leave, I'll be here."

Feeling my eyes well with unshed tears, I blinked hard before refocusing on my surroundings. I knew his words weren't meant the way I took them, but I chose to reply like they were.

"That's okay, old man. I don't think I ever really arrived." And then I removed myself from the vehicle before he could say anything else.

I STEPPED out of the lift and into a box room with glass windows. And before the elevator could close behind me, I was already walking through an open door and down a clear staircase lit with blue LEDS. My boots hit each step, vocalising my presence to whoever could hear my arrival in what was otherwise a quiet atmosphere. When I reached the edge of the nightclub floor, I realised the room was empty, which was obvious for a nightclub early in the morning, I guess. But Walker was there somewhere, meddling in business that was actually his to intervene in.

I inspected the area for any sign of him, but found myself distracted by my surroundings. I didn't think I'd ever been somewhere quite like it before.

A bright blue painted the walls, and darker stalls stood against a black metal top bar in the shape of an octagon. It wasn't how I pictured it to be by any means.

I began walking further into the large room, observing every detail my eyes could touch. It had Walker written all over it. The place was hard around the edges, yet soft with delicate fittings and fixtures–bright blue and white lights illuminating where it fell dark.

Unlike the clear staircase, black metal booths separated the seating area from the white dance floor. I quickly realised that the nightclub represented who Walker was more than his penthouse did. And it held more of him than he'd ever care to show first-hand.

"Hey," a male voice spoke from behind me, and I spun on my heels, startled at the sudden interaction.

Hands shot out to grip my arms when I almost crashed into the stranger's chest. "Easy." He chuckled. "Fin may have let Nate know you were on your way up."

Nate?

"Noah?"

"The one and only." The grin he shot me was devilish, and I could see how he used it in his favour. His gaze brushed over me like a wave from head to foot. I stared at him. He was more of a pretty boy than he was a grown man, and though his skin was a shade darker than Walker's, I could still see the resemblance to him in his features. I wasn't angry at Noah, but I couldn't help but swallow down the angry bile that stung my throat. Or want to shake away the discomfort that settled over my skin.

"Noah." Another voice came from nearby, and that's when I lifted my head and found Walker watching our encounter from the bottom of the steps I'd just come from, mere metres away.

"How long has he been standing there?"

Noah narrowed his eyes at me while Walker's eyes focused on where Noah was holding my arms. All at once, my body was heating up, except I couldn't quite pinpoint the significance.

Not wanting to embarrass myself, I didn't say anything in

front of Noah. Though I didn't have to worry because Walker ignored my presence as if he no longer cared I was there, speaking only to his brother. "Wez is waiting for you downstairs."

"I'm going, I'm going." Noah loosened his grip on me and gave me another cheeky smile. "Nice to see you, Blue," he said, tapping two fingers to his temple in a salute, "but duty calls."

Walker watched Noah retreat in the opposite direction before finally refocusing his attention on me. Apparently, I was worthy of his time now. He didn't say anything if he noticed my fists clenched at my sides.

Maybe he didn't care.

He still hadn't moved from the end of the staircase, and I hadn't made any move towards him.

I had every right to be angry at him, didn't I?

I'm not sure why I was even questioning myself.

"Kid."

To no surprise, he sported his usual look of disdain. He gave nothing away to signify what he'd done. Perhaps he didn't know himself.

He turned around and began walking up the stairs, only he seemed to stop mid-step when he didn't hear the sound of my footsteps following. Perhaps this wasn't the right environment to discuss what he'd done, but I wasn't his bitch. He swung his head, not enough to face me, but enough to steal my attention. And then he spoke loud enough for me to hear his next words from where I still stood rooted to the spot. "Are you coming?"

I scowled, called him a dick under my breath, then meandered after him, planning all the ways I could hurt him with every step like he'd hurt me.

His trousers tightened against his body as he slid his hands into his pockets and walked ahead of me. He glanced at me over his shoulder, his brows pinched as he went. I had no doubt he wanted to know what I was doing here, unless Finley had told him already. Though I assumed he hadn't with how little he spoke and from the confusion etched into Walker's features. Besides, this was my business. Not his.

When we reached the top of the stairs and entered the box room, Walker slid his keycard against the elevator's control panel. And once we were inside, he opened an encasing on the wall and did the same again. The panel beeped, the red-light flashing green, and then the opposite side of the elevator split into two and opened like a door.

"After you," he instructed, allowing me to step past him and into the room.

I quickly came to the realisation the room was his office, and it covered the whole expansion of the nightclub below us.

A caged black metal wall decorated one side of the room–like the walls of the octagon, while one-way glass windows lined the other. A black desk was situated in front of us, and off to the left was a discrete wall of filing cabinets and a door that I presumed led to his private bathroom. There were no papers sprawled across his desk as there would be in my father's office, but the latest iMac. Beside it, his office phone. There were also no family photographs to show off anyone in his life except for a single picture of him and Noah. However, there was more personality here than at the penthouse. Framed black and white artistic images of martial arts fighters were fitted to the wall, and spotlights in the ceiling brightened the otherwise dark room. The very last thing I noticed was a lounge set-up at the far end of the room with a private bar. Because duh, Walker liked a drink and easy access. It made perfect sense, despite there being a bar no more than fifteen metres beneath us.

Both frustration and anger lingered in my mannerisms, but I was distracted enough not to jump down his throat straightaway. "Did this used to be my father's office?"

He made his way behind the desk. "Years ago. Now it's mine."

He was as vague as Fin seemed to be back in the car.

He sat down in the chair at his desk, widening his knees as he leant back, though his gaze didn't waver from my face. "Let's not bother with the little talk. Why are you here and not on your way to Duke?"

It felt natural to walk towards him. I only halted when I was between his thighs, vaguely aware of how close I'd gravitated. It was like he had me on a string. Pulling, pulling, and pulling.

Gritting my teeth, I muttered, "You know why."

His eyes dropped to my legs before he caught himself. When he looked up, he must have noticed my sullen expression.

"What's going on?"

I sighed, but it was a failed attempt at keeping myself composed. "What's going on is whatever you did backfired. I've been suspended, and the only way I'm allowed back is if they accept my appeal. My appeal, Walker. Maybe I should be the one asking you what's going on? What the fuck did you do?"

He rolled his neck, seemingly agitated. "That cocky cartoon-looking motherfucker."

"*What?*"

"I'll sort it."

"You'll sort it? Just like you said you would last night," I argued. "Whatever you did, you made things worse. Just wait until my dad hears about this."

"Fuck, Blue." With no warning, he shot forward out of his chair and pushed me back against the desk, his knuckles gripping the woodwork on either side of me. "I said I'd sort it. You're really going to run and tell him about this? A minor mistake?"

I pushed back but was barely able to move, too distracted by his scent. The freshly showered fragrance of him tickled my senses instead of the usual lingering liquor. "No, I'm not going to 'run and tell him.' But he will find out, and that's only if Duke hasn't contacted him already. I'm not sure if you remember this, but I told you I wanted to make my own mistakes. Not have someone make them for me."

Glancing down in the little space between us, I watched his hands as they inched closer to my waist before he balled them into fists. Was it silly to think that perhaps we had each other on a string? That I could pull him into me, the way he pulled me into him?

"Let me worry about that." He dropped his eyes to his watch, and the tick of his jaw drew my attention to the sharp lines of his face. "I have vendors coming now. This couldn't have waited until later?"

My eyes widened in disbelief. "Waited?"

"Yes, waited. Evading me at work isn't part of the deal."

"The deal? I'm unaware of any deal. Are you insinuating that I'm part of some lousy business goings between you and my father, is that it?"

"That's it," he said, all matter-of-fact. "I was hired to accommodate you in my penthouse and help you settle into your new life, nothing more. There's no fucking reason for you to be in my club. Suspended or not, we could have spoken about this tonight."

"Sorry–what? Help me settle? It's your fault I've been suspended! And, uh, isn't it more my father's club than it is yours?" I replied innocently. "Oh, and I'd call it an arrangement–one between you and him. I had no say in it, remember? If I did, I probably wouldn't have been in the same position as I am now. I wouldn't be suspended," I squealed. "On day fucking two! I feel like I'm in an alternate universe. God, Walker... These things... these things don't happen in real life."

His gaze fell to my mouth, perhaps disgusted with my words, or my tone, but he didn't argue with me, knowing I only spoke the truth. His shoulder barely rose in a shrug, and still, he didn't move from where he had me trapped against his desk. Despite the two of us feeling frustrated, for the first time since being in his presence, I noticed how well rested he looked.

"Why did you sleep beside me last night? Was that a part of the arrangement? Or did you think by disappearing before I woke up you could pretend it hadn't happened, only to then go and screw up my future?"

I didn't care who he thought he was; there was no way he'd get away with having my place at Duke revoked. I wanted to push him. I wanted to push him until he told me how he was going to fucking fix this.

"No." He wet his bottom lip. "But trust me, it won't happen again."

I swallowed, needing clarification. What did that say about what I wanted? "Which part? Because I doubt you're able to do any more damage than you already have in the four days I've been here. I don't get why *he* chose *you*."

"You know, it would help if you kept your lips sealed. Fuck, I really can't think clearly when your pretty mouth is moving so fast."

Pretty mouth?

What?

My stomach somersaulted, and still, I continued to push. "Would it make it better if we pretended you weren't sleeping in my bed and I was sleeping in yours?" I mocked, just as he did in the car from the airport. "I wonder what my dad would think about how well you're taking care of me."

He gripped my chin hard between his fingers in a move I didn't anticipate, but all it did was increase the fire in my belly. His following words lacked less conviction than his touch. "Are you threatening me?" His tone was husky, his mouth a fraction from my own. If I was a braver girl, I could've swiped my 'pretty

143

mouth' across his and tasted him on my tongue. How clearly would he think then?

I didn't move my mouth any closer to his, but I licked my lips, showcasing what he deemed pretty while inclining my body back into the desk. Then I allowed my legs to slip between his as he towered over me.

I wasn't going to... but maybe I could.

Seeming to read my mind, he narrowed his eyes. "You better not be threatening me, Blue."

"What if I am?" How far could I push? "And what if you like it?" I murmured.

Utilising my body wasn't something I'd done before, but that didn't mean I didn't know how to use it. I'd been to enough parties, and I'd witnessed enough women try to seduce my father. Maybe the one thing I detested of my father was the one thing I could use against Walker.

He shook his head, but he didn't make any move to stop me when I lifted my knee and hooked my leg around his waist.

"Blue," he said, agitated, though his voice was breathy. His grip on my chin wavered as he looked down at our new position. My school skirt had risen up my thigh, showcasing some of my underwear, which was a movement away from being pressed against his obvious erection. He was attracted to me, and he couldn't admit it. He couldn't admit it because it was obscene; a thirty-four-year-old man being sexually attracted to a seventeen-year-old girl.

I'd be the first to say so.

I was the one that didn't like others' judgement, yet he was the one trying to stay within the lines of social perception, fighting with himself over the way he felt. But as much as he couldn't admit it, he couldn't deny it either.

And ultimately, I was only fooling myself.

I wasn't any more of a threat to him than he was to me.

"You can deny it if you want," I said quietly. "But I feel how hard you are for me."

Guilt marred his features. The heat in his eyes was as undeniable as the flames in my stomach, but so was the newfound worry.

I angled my hips forward, feeling the outline of his cock through the lace of my underwear.

His grip on my chin grew slacker, and then he dropped it, hissing between his lips. "Fuck, brat. What are you doing?"

Even though he asked the question, he didn't move away. Our eyes danced with each other, our pupils portraying more honesty than our mouths as I rolled myself against him. Slow and subtle.

Our frustration became intimacy. And really, what good was a threat when it meant so little and felt so good?

Ever so slowly, his gaze ran from the marks he'd left on my chin to my collarbone, lingering over the material of my school shirt where my scar hid beneath it. I wondered what it was he saw when he looked at my imperfections. Did he think back to our conversation in the car, when I referred to myself as broken? Did he think I was fragile? Did he wish me to be a little more pristine? My self-consciousness tried to eat at me, but I refused to let it take this from me too.

I rolled my hips again, embarrassingly desperate for a little more friction.

"Blue," he warned. His hands moved to hold my hips, and before I could ease more of the growing ache, his grip tightened, stopping me from going any further.

My lips parted, inhaling what little air I could, and regardless of our arousal, regardless of him stopping something that had barely begun, I couldn't help but tell him what'd been plaguing my mind.

It felt bigger than my threat.

Bigger than the both of us.

Bigger than the moment I could've easily lost myself in.

"I can't help but feel as though there's more between us than what my father has asked of you."

"Maybe."

"Maybe?" I repeated.

And as if he was backtracking, all he said next was, "Maybe the only thing between us are my secrets."

I was annoyed that he refused to admit to more. Still, I murmured, "What secrets?"

His demeanour shifted as he put up a front. It seemed our roles of who controlled who in our situation had reversed. "Why?" he remarked. "Are you afraid?"

Was he mocking me? Did he see through me that well?

"Afraid?" I feigned indifference. "Is there something to be afraid of? Should I be afraid of you?" I rolled my eyes with sass. "Of your secrets?"

Not for the first time, his gaze dropped to my lips as he murmured, "Maybe you should be afraid of both." And then his fingers squeezed my hips, almost bruising, as if to drive home his point.

Regardless, I didn't flinch.

If he thought he could scare me away with his bullshit, if he believed he could hide from our chemistry, he had both all wrong.

"Don't you remember what I said on the plane?" I whispered. "Or did that slip your mind too?"

I couldn't focus my attention as his mismatched orbs came back to mine and held me hostage with a strength I wasn't sure it was possible to break from.

"I remember," he replied hoarsely, but the corner of his mouth lifted in a smirk. "You're not afraid of anything."

How big were his secrets in comparison to this? In comparison to our undeniable attraction? What could he possibly be hiding that would make this feeling any less than what it was?

My heart thundered in quick succession as he leant further into me and wrapped his hand around my neck. The anger was long gone, our strings were free, and in their place, something else entirely.

The pads of his fingers laid firm against my pulse, his hardness creating the smallest amount of friction between my legs. Only this time, he had control. And I was grateful, for once, that someone wasn't treating me like glass.

Fuck, he was choking me, but not with his fingers.

With his secrecy.

With his masculinity.

With his heat on my heat.

First, I hesitated, but then I reached up and wrapped my fingers around his wrist, wanting to touch his pulse and feel if it was beating as hard as mine. He went to pull away, perhaps startled he'd got it all wrong, but I held him there. His eyes searched mine, and time seemed to stand still. It seemed my threat had backfired, because there was nothing in this moment or the moments before that I didn't want myself. There was nothing I'd want to take back. There was only me wanting to take more.

He spoke his next question quietly, almost as if he were unsure of it himself. "Surely you're afraid of whatever this is?"

Maybe he was.

Maybe the question was meant for himself, because admitting this was something would only make it real.

But this time, I didn't hesitate. "Can I be afraid of how safe I feel when I'm around you? Can I be afraid of not understanding what it might mean?"

The need to blanket myself behind some kind of armour was strong once the words left my mouth, so I closed my eyes, concentrating on the feel of his fingers absently caressing my neck. I wondered if he was conscious of the action. I wondered if we would both live to regret this.

I couldn't see him, but I felt his breath across my lips. "Shit, Blue, I–"

My eyes blinked open, and he halted whatever else laid on the tip of his tongue. And then the sudden ringing of his office phone disrupted our moment, dousing us in icy water. I should have been glad for the interruption, but all I felt was disappointment.

My lips turned down at the corners, but I didn't sink from my position as he pulled away from me.

I flattened down my skirt, hiding my underwear. They were damp, and he knew it. His jaw clenched like it irritated him to give in to our chemistry–as if already regretting what just happened. Like the phone ringing hadn't just saved him from making a big mistake.

He didn't hide as he re-adjusted himself inside his slacks. But it wasn't until he picked up the phone and the shrill of the calling stopped that his eyes returned to mine. Though unlike before, I couldn't read much into them.

"Walker," he said, announcing his name to the caller. "What do you want?" he argued more than asked. I wasn't sure if he meant his tone for them, or if he was angry because of me. "I'm obviously at work. You called me."

I searched his eyes as I seated myself on his desk, eager to know who it was that had the power to aggravate him so easily if it wasn't my doing. The same caller from three mornings ago, or someone else entirely?

He swore under his breath and pinched the bridge of his nose. "Yeah, and there's a reason why I've been avoiding your calls," he said, slamming the phone down only for it to bounce from the hook. He didn't bother putting it back on; instead, he dropped down, lowering a hand under his desk to pull out the wire. And though he tried to hide it, I didn't miss his hard swallow as he tore his gaze away from the space between my legs.

The atmosphere took another turn after that, and he didn't meet my eyes again as he stood. He didn't look at me at all. He walked over to the edge of his office to distance us, focusing his attention through the window.

A few minutes passed, then breathing out a heavy breath, he said, "Shit."

With the space between us, I worked to ignore the feeling between my legs and how my heart palpitated at the thoughts of what it all meant. Of everything that happened and how it couldn't be taken back.

I swung my legs back and forth, deliberating.

"Blue," he muttered.

"No. Don't say anything."

I didn't want to hear how he regretted what almost happened.

Remembering why I came here, I crossed my arms over my chest as I stared at his back, and then my eyes fell to the floor as I stopped swinging my legs, and instead, frantically shook my head. So much was at stake here. Too much more that could go wrong. I had to wise up. Reassert myself into my big girl shoes and own who I wanted to be. I couldn't let these complicated feelings or this infatuation for a man I barely knew mess everything up.

It was a complete three sixty but–

"Please, Walker. I don't want to go back to Miami. I've barely landed on my feet, and already the rug is being taken out from under me."

In my peripheral vision, I noticed him turn around, standing stoic in his suit and listening intently.

I looked up at him, a little nervous. "Whatever deal you've

agreed to with my father must be worth substantial money. Is that one of your secrets? Why else would you go through all that trouble to help me? Because that's what you attempted, right? You said something or did something, thinking you could fix Mr Smith's issue with me?"

It was the only thing that made the most logical sense, given the timing.

He worked his teeth against his jaw, clenching his fists before sliding his hands into his pockets. "I may have offered him some money in exchange for his respect," he said, somewhat flustered. Then he laughed humourlessly. "Fuck, that daft wanker has some balls. I'll go to the education board if that's what you want me to do. I'll pay off the appeal and force them to take my fucking money. Or I can get rid of Mr Smith. None of this needs to be an issue."

"No."

He took one hand from his pocket and dragged it through his hair. "What do you mean, no?" His words seemed forced.

I contemplated the jumbled thoughts I couldn't string into sentences as he took steps towards me. We weren't in as close proximity as before, but we were still close enough that I could feel the pull towards him.

"I just mean no." I frowned.

He seemed exasperated, but that made two of us. I didn't have any idea what I was doing, and it seemed neither did he.

"Who are you, Blue Sterling? And what is it you want? Because fuck, I didn't expect you. And now I'm here, questioning my morals and doing things I'd never usually do." He slid the hand from his head to grip the back of his neck. "It seems every time I think I've figured you out, you go and prove me wrong."

"You're not the only one confused, Walker."

"No?"

Now it was him with those two letters, though I knew he meant it as a question.

"We've known each other for four days. It's... I don't..." I shook my head, reminding myself again that whatever this familiarity between us was, wasn't the reason I was here. That just because he made me feel things–sexual or not–didn't mean we were destined for something more.

"That's not why I'm here. It's not... you can't just..."

"For fuck's sake, kid. Spit it out."

I snapped. "Fuck my life. You can't throw money at people and expect them to take it! Mr Smith might have bullied me into thinking I wasn't smart enough for his class, but what you did was just as wrong."

Quickly, I planned the threat I was about to put between us. One that had potential. The one I considered before it became... something else.

It was easy to twist it–simple enough to turn it into something it wasn't.

He came on to me, dad. He wanted me.

Would it make me a hypocrite?

Probably.

I could've appealed Duke's decision, but who was to say they'd rule in my favour?

"Blue."

My head continued to shake.

What evidence did they have against me?

"Whatever you're thinking, stop. I said I'd sort it. Your father doesn't need to know shit."

It seemed like I'd gotten under his skin. But he'd put me in this predicament, and it was his fault we were in this mess, wasn't it? I didn't have many options. Desperate people sometimes had to do desperate things.

I looked at him. "What choice do I have?"

"I really don't give a fuck for threats," he said. "It wouldn't hurt to remember that."

Who was he trying to convince? I could make this so bad for him. Was that what I wanted?

"You've taken away something important to me. The only way you'll make this right is if you give me something better."

He frowned deeply, but I was certain I saw a glimmer of remorse shining through his eyes.

"I don't have all the answers, but I know what I want." My lips moved before my mind could comprehend it any further, the words tumbling from my mouth before I realised what I was saying. "And you're going to be the one to give it to me."

CHAPTER TEN

Walker

A JOB.

A fucking job.

Blue had asked for the one thing I was easily capable of giving, and yet, I didn't want to give it.

I slid my glass across the metal bar from one hand to the other, listening to the ice hit the circumference. Until now, I hadn't had a drink all day, so it was only fitting I'd drank my Bourbon before the frozen rocks could serve their pursuit. Before they served a chance to alter the flavour.

Much to my dismay, Blue was mingling with Noah in one of the booths behind me. Seventeen years of age, yet acting like she had every right to be exactly where she was, in the midst of my fucking club during happy hour. My best efforts to send her back to the penthouse had been futile since she'd spent the whole day learning every square inch of my building. It was the same way my soon-to-be ex-wife thought it was okay to ring my office, warranting my attention when we were no longer together. Except Blue was different. As much as I tried to convince myself I didn't like having her around, I knew I was lying to myself. Fuck, she probably knew it too after what happened in my office.

I scoffed at how easily she had me eating out the palm of her hand. Clearly, my brain was too slow to play catch up with my cock.

"A third, boss?" my barman, Louis, asked me. However, he was subtly checking out Blue over my shoulder while he spoke. I made it a habit to know the names of all my staff. Even those dressed like they were part of a prestigious boy band and didn't know their arse from their elbow. Blue Sterling wasn't a name I wanted on that list or Louis's bedpost. I chose to ignore how his eyes lingered on her legs, knowing I had my erection pressed against her underwear not so many hours ago. And how my mind conjured up dirty thoughts just this morning. Thoughts that I could have easily indulged in across my office desk.

Blue had killer legs.

Legs I'd want wrapped around me as I fucked her religiously, if she was only a little older. A little fucking wiser. A little less of a Sterling.

How far was I prepared to go if the phone hadn't rung? How far was she?

She was pushing me, and she knew it. In fact, I had every belief she liked it.

Guilt ate at me.

"Have you ever been blackmailed, Louis?" I asked, my eyes shifting from Blue to him. Because that was essentially what was happening. It was a poor attempt at best. It may have started out as a petty threat, but then it became something for her to hide behind. Blue Sterling was attempting–very terribly–to blackmail me into giving her a job in the pretence of telling her father I'd slept in her bed. Amongst other things too little to count. In my gut, I knew she wouldn't go through with it. Something inside of me was realising I could trust her, despite what she said.

More fool me if I was wrong.

The issue was, she was just a naive fucking girl with her head to the clouds, wanting to live in a big man's world. But maybe, on the other hand, she was someone who knew what she wanted.

She walked into my office, stood her ground, and handled me like a fucking puppet. And I wasn't used to that.

I'd never experienced that.

I'd never been at a woman's mercy.

I'd never found myself wanting to see how far a woman could push me the way she did until I snapped and pushed back.

Thank fuck that phone did ring.

With a chuckle, Louis shook his head. "I have not."

He took a fresh glass from beneath the bar and poured me another of The Lagoon's top-shelf Bourbon. Before he could throw his frozen rocks in my glass, I put my hand out, halting him. "No ice."

He nodded and then placed my drink in front of me. "Dare I ask who's blackmailing you?"

I snickered. "Not if you want to keep your job."

He held up his palms, eager to back off. He knew I'd sack him on the spot, given any wrongdoing. Then he left me alone to wallow in my mood and instead found his way to the commotion awaiting him at the far end of the bar. It was relatively busy for midweek and would likely get busier within the hour. Everyone who was anyone wanted to be in my club, eyes open and ears alert to get their heavy bets in for fight night.

I looked over my shoulder at my brother and Blue conversing in whatever idle chit chat they'd been at for the last however many hours before diverting my attention to my drink. It concerned me some, and I didn't want to see her smiling at my brother, who happened to be much closer in age to her than I was.

Worse yet, I didn't want him to slip up.

What did that say about the way I was feeling?

My hand wrapped around my glass, then I brought it to my mouth and threw the warm liquid to the back of my throat. A bittersweet sigh left me, only partially appeased, while I placed my glass back on the bar.

Another, and maybe then I'd taste comfort.

Another two, and maybe only then I'd taste relief.

I STUMBLED through the elevator with bodies on either side of me, hands and arms holding me up. I couldn't have said how many, my eyesight too foggy, and my mind too fucking slow.

"Blue," I muttered, raising my head in search of her. "Where is she?"

A scoff sounded from behind me. I wasn't confident it was from her mouth, but part of me knew it was. She'd been in my life less than a week, and I'd memorised more of her than I cared to confess.

"Don't worry; we got her. You should get into bed."

"We?"

"Me and Fin, big bro."

I rumbled in response, then murmured something meant to be "Bed," but it didn't come out quite as I hoped. It was on the tip of my tongue to tell them Blue had been sleeping in my bed.

That I'd taken the sofa. That I couldn't just go and... "Shit, why'd you let me drink?"

My body and head felt ready to drop as Noah's and Fin's arms grew slack. Then it was Noah I heard scoff. "That's all on you, man."

Fin didn't need to say anything for me to know what he thought. It wouldn't have been the first time he'd questioned my alcohol intake. And if he chose to tonight, I imagined it wouldn't have been the last.

Forcing my legs to hold my weight, I stumbled away from them and through the penthouse. Muffled voices spoke from behind me, only growing distant when I reached the door of the master suite. Blue's perfume invaded my senses as soon as I entered, inciting a groan from me as I slammed the door closed.

I told myself just a laydown, and later I'd drag my ass back to the sofa.

I sat on the bed, my fingers moving to my collar, where I began loosening my tie. Then with my tie all but hanging around my neck, I fiddled with the buttons of my shirt. Before I knew it, drowsiness had me lying on my side and my eyes growing heavy.

Ten minutes.

I'd give myself ten minutes.

It didn't feel any longer than five when I heard the faint sound of the door opening, but I was too out of it with the room spinning around me to give a shit who entered.

Nah, I wasn't getting up.

The sofa could go fuck itself.

Blue

WITH THE CURTAINED voiles wide open, the city illuminated the room enough for me to see Walker in a state of undress. He still had his trousers on, but his shirt was hanging open, his toned chest on display. I walked over to the bed, placed a glass of water down on the bedside table, and then slipped two aspirin from my pocket that I'd raided from the kitchen drawer before placing them beside it.

When I turned to face the bed, I found Walker's eyes on me. He didn't need to say anything. There was something in his gaze that told me he was thankful, maybe even surprised, for the small gesture.

"I'm still angry at you," I explained. I couldn't forget what had happened–what he did–or how much my life had changed. That he was the culprit at the cause of it.

"Be angry at me, then," he mumbled. "Trust me, I deserve much worse."

I paused. "If we're going to talk about it again, I'd rather do it when you're sober."

He didn't respond, his eyes having closed again. I couldn't explain it, but I felt the need to care for him like he'd been taking care of me. And because of that, I stepped further down the edge of the bed and removed his shoes before placing them on the floor. Then, I pushed his legs up onto the bed so at least he'd be somewhat comfortable.

I couldn't do much else, so that's how I left him while I took myself to the en-suite with a clean pair of pyjamas. Once I'd redressed, cleaned my face of the day's make-up, and brushed my teeth, I took my medication from the bathroom drawer and popped one pill from the foiled packet.

I wished that taking them at night meant they'd keep my nightmares at a distance, but there were often times that one slipped through the net. I told myself a vivid dream was still just a dream, but I'd dreamt of my mother and the night she died so much in recent years, I knew my dream held more of my memories than it did my imagination. Though it was never the accurate recognition of the night–a child as young as I was wouldn't have remembered the event that decidedly mapped out their future. At least, that's what I tried to convince myself when I suffered the horrific flashbacks.

They were purely something my overactive brain had conjured up over the years as I tried to place together the night which changed me. The night that altered both my father's and my life. It was how my mind tried to understand my father better. His need for control. His reasoning for being so protective. It was how I pieced together the jigsaw puzzle that made up the traits of my character. Heightened by the fear of dying before I'd ever lived, contradicted by the fear of being afraid to.

Afraid to live.

Scared to die.

I'm certain it made little sense to anyone who wasn't me. Which was a reason I kept it locked away. All padlock, no key.

I swallowed my medication before making my way back to the bedroom. Walker laid on his side, his eyes still closed. I didn't mind that he'd slept beside me last night, which was why I climbed onto the bed beside him. Only I got under the covers while he remained on top. Though I'd attempted to blackmail him, I had no interest in telling my father what'd happened. In my frustration, I'd said some things I didn't mean. But making Walker's life miserable because he made a mindless mistake wasn't me. A life back in Miami wasn't *me* either. I'd appeal my suspension as a backup. But a job at The Lagoon–working as a social media specialist for an already established business–my father's business–was essentially a step up. I had no idea why I hadn't considered it sooner.

Rolling onto my side, I stared at Walker's back. I never believed I'd find myself in a situation like ours. Let alone with an almost stranger. It was odd how I'd never slept beside the opposite sex until the night before and how it felt so incredibly *ordinary*. I'd expected the first time to be much different from how it played out, which was why, despite a barrier between us, I found myself snuggling against him for the second time. If he was awake, he didn't say anything. And amidst the quiet, and the tug of our unseeable strings, I didn't either.

CHAPTER ELEVEN

Blue

FOR FORTY MINUTES, I'd been standing at the bathroom counter in my en-suite, with the contents of my make-up bag spilt over the granite as I applied the finishing touches to my face in between replays of what happened in Walker's office.

It had been four days.

Four days since I pathetically blackmailed him with a threat I had no intention of following through with.

My phone rang against the counter, disrupting me from my trance, and seeing Ebony's name on the screen, I lowered my make-up and hit answer.

"Blue!" Her drunk voice sounded down the line before I could address her.

"Hey." I frowned at myself in the mirror, holding my phone with one hand as I brought my make-up brush up to my cheek.

She couldn't see me, but if she could, she'd know something was up. Something close to guilt was written all over my face.

Walker had to know I never meant to threaten him, right?

Swiping the fluffy end of the brush over my cheekbones, I listened down the line as Ebony rattled off her address to whoever gave her a ride.

"Were you at a party? How drunk are you?" I asked, keeping my tone even.

"Pretty steaming," she said. "I need pizza."

"Who's giving you a ride?"

"I don't remember his name," she whispered.

I stopped mid-brush. "Eb, you're not in a random's car, are you? Tell me you didn't just meet him, at least."

Her conversation with the stranger was no more than muffled sentences, and then she gave me back her attention. "He's not random. We've hooked up a few times in the last five hours."

"You've hooked up, but you don't know his name? What happened with *banks262?*"

"He wasn't who I thought he was," she admitted. "That day we were meant to Skype at the beginning of summer? It never happened."

"What? Why didn't you tell me this before?"

"It doesn't matter. Hey, this Walker guy you're staying with, is he hot?"

Thoughts of his breath against my lips, the lingering glances, the subtle touches, and the way he'd continued to sleep beside me every night without a word only made me realise how deep things had gotten between us so quickly.

And there Ebony was... putting things into perspective for me by asking one simple question.

Is he hot?

He was everything if not completely unexpected.

I looked over my shoulder and then turned to close the door. Walker had already worked out and left for work, but he'd organised a team of interior designers to turn an empty room into a bedroom after spending the last five nights beside me. As if he suddenly decided he no longer could. I didn't understand it, but how was I suppose to?

Ebony wasn't on loudspeaker, and I was keeping my anxious self away from the strange men in the house, but I still didn't want them to overhear anything from my mouth that wasn't for their ears. And I definitely didn't want them to see the disappointment on my face, even if they had no clue why it was there.

Ebony remained on the line, waiting on me, while I took time to answer her question. "Yeah, I guess."

"I guess," she mocked.

"Okay," I groaned, feeling a pang of sorts in my gut. "He's a real ten out of ten. Happy?"

"Very. Hold a sec."

"Okay."

"Hey, no name, pit stop at Pizzahole, please and thank you."

"Ugh, Pizzahole, I'm wounded."

"I know. I wish you were with me. Nothing is the same without you. How have you only been gone a week? It already feels like forever. Is Duke everything you expected? Remind me why I didn't apply for college again?"

Now would have been the perfect time to tell her what happened on Wednesday, but I was still waiting to hear back after submitting an appeal. Walker was yet to give me an official job. And everything was...what it was.

"Yeah," I said with little enthusiasm. "And because you said college was for people who knew what they wanted to do with their life. And you didn't."

I rolled my eyes, but even with my tone, she didn't notice my lack of enthusiasm, and instead cursed through the line as a beep sounded. "Shit. My battery is about to die. Love you. We'll catch up soon, 'kay?"

"Love you. Charge your phone when you get home so I know you're sa-" Before I could finish my sentence, the call was cut. I stared at my phone screen before lowering it to the counter alongside my make-up brush. And then my phone rang again before I had time to consider what I was doing next.

This time, I didn't bother looking at the screen.

Relief settled through me. "It didn't die?"

"What didn't die?" my father's voice spoke down the line.

"Dad," I muttered, confusion etched between my brows. "Sorry, I thought you were Ebony. I'd barely been on the phone to her before her battery died."

"Why is Ebony ringing you at gone four in the morning?"

"Dad," I said again. "You're ringing me at gone four in the morning. Ebony just missed me, that's all. I don't understand why you have such a problem with her."

"I know her type; she's tried to lead you astray plenty of times. Do her parents have any idea of the type of daughter they're raising?"

"Do you?" I shot back.

"What is that supposed to mean?"

"I don't know, dad. What do you think it means?"

"Where has this attitude come from?"

"Perhaps I'm still waiting for an apology."

"If you had bothered to answer any of my calls or respond to my recent messages, you may have gotten one. The only thing I am now is disappointed."

"That makes two of us," I muttered, staring at my reflection. If I was honest, being disappointed came part and parcel to being the daughter of James Sterling. It seemed I couldn't escape him, and I couldn't escape his name. No matter where in the world I was. No matter who in the world I was with.

He sighed. "Where is Walker?"

"He's at work." I frowned. He always seemed to be at work. "Why?"

"No particular reason," he said, his tone softening. "I just haven't heard from you, princess, and Walker's emails have been few and far between. I expected to hear how you're getting on at Duke."

More focused on how Walker had been emailing him updates on me, I ignored the latter, partly relieved to know Duke hadn't gotten in touch with him regarding my suspension. "You emailed Walker to check up on me?" I tucked a loose strand of hair behind my ear. "I can't believe you at times. I'm days away from turning eighteen, and you still treat me like I'm eight."

"That's not true."

"Isn't it?" I scoffed. "If you're just ringing to see how I am, to spy on me, I'm fine. Everything's fine."

"Just fine? I expect Walker's taking care of you. I trust that man with your life."

My eyebrows lowered. "With my life?"

That was a big statement to make. So big he probably wouldn't have believed me if I did spin a web of lies and tell him Walker had come on to me.

"That's what I said. Look"—he breathed a weighty sigh—"I have to go. I have a business meeting in a few hours. But next time I call, you best pick up. Or I'll fly my plane over myself and see that you're safe."

"Sure, dad," I mumbled bitterly. "Or you could just ask Walker for an update, as you seem so certain you can trust *him* with *my* life."

But he didn't let me have the last say.

"Don't be petty, princess. It's not pretty," he said, and then he followed it with, "One day you'll understand."

Walker

IT WAS after ten when I stepped out of The Lagoon. Hudson's injury was improving, and he'd dismissed his setback Tuesday. According to him, it felt a lot like a grade one injury and less like a two. I wasn't going to argue. If that's what he said it felt like I couldn't tell him otherwise. As far as things went, fight night was still going ahead, and it would be one less weight off my back once it was all over and dealt with.

I greeted Finley as I slid into the backseat of his BMW. "Finley, four days in a row. It's like I've won the lottery," I said dryly.

There was a slight resemblance of a smile on his face, but I'm sure he was just as pissed off with my sarcasm as I'd intended him to be. I'd given Blue access to him since she'd arrived, which meant I was driving myself around up until my overindulgence of alcohol in front of my audience on Wednesday. Because good ol' Finley had taken it upon himself to go back to being my personal chauffeur. Granted, he didn't need to take Blue anywhere since I'd got her suspended. That was something I was fixing behind the scenes. Mr Smith had a distaste for my money, but there were members on the committee that accepted it without question. All I was waiting on was the cheques to clear. And with any luck, Blue would be off my back and back in Duke by tomorrow morning.

Finley nodded at me in the rearview mirror. "Nowhere else to be, boss."

It was without question that he'd rather pick me up every night and not risk me being behind the wheel when I was under the influence, but he couldn't be held accountable for my actions. In truth, he was my most loyal employee. And although he tried not to make it too obvious, he was evidently worried about me. About my drinking habits. And he was perhaps concerned with how I was treating Blue. I was confident he'd come to the rescue of any damsel in distress. Especially if he happened to have a soft spot for the same one I did.

"To Kensington?" he asked.

"Later. First, can you drive..." Home was on the tip of my tongue, though I'd already established that it had never been my home. "To the townhouse," I said, running a hand through my hair. It was the last place I wanted to go, but, "Needs must."

I palmed the breast pocket of my beige coat, feeling for the envelope I'd placed inside it not so long ago. All I needed was Sophia's signature, and our divorce would be well underway. Although some part of me didn't want to go ahead with my choice because of the aggravation it would cause. Still, I knew it was the right call to make. And at the end of the day, what was a marriage without love? The answer spoke for itself. It was inevitable both me and Sophia wouldn't last. Our marriage was both materialistic and convenient. We weren't a wilting house plant needing water. We weren't the roots of a tree or branches that blossomed flowers. We were merely weeds, growing where we weren't sown.

Finley drove down the dark streets of London while I closed my eyes and relaxed my chin on my fist. It was nearing eleven by the time he parked on the curb outside the stone townhouse, and I was tired. Tired of pretending. Tired of every encounter. Tired of wanting it to be over and done with.

He gave me his usual nod of acknowledgement through the rearview mirror and switched off the engine.

An orange glow came from the downstairs oval windows of the grey brick property, which told me Sophia was home. However, I couldn't seem to get myself out of the vehicle. It was as if I was back in primary school and my feet were stuck in mud.

I took a deep breath before exhaling. "Just a moment, Fin."

Finley's kind eyes watched me through the mirror, a silent show of support. And then I placed my hand on the car door and swung it open before forcing myself to my feet.

"I won't be long," I spoke through the open door. Then I closed it before making my way towards the property.

I probably should've just posted the letter, but the masochist in me wanted to see the look on her face when she realised I'd no longer be funding her lifestyle. The paper in my hands was clear evidence of my final straw.

Before I could climb the steps to the front door, someone swung it open. The person I saw staring back at me was the last person I expected to see walk out.

I did a double-take.

"Wez?" I said, a questionable edge to my voice as I stared at his unruly blonde hair and the tattoos peeking out from the edges of his creased t-shirt.

"Uh, Walker." His brows rose while he closed the door to the property behind him and meandered down the steps.

"Care to explain?" I asked, signalling to my–*to Sophia's*–home.

"I just dropped by to see you."

I frowned. "For what reason? I'm not your coach. Since when do The Lagoon's fighters just drop by unannounced and out of business hours? There's no reason for you to be here."

"I... came to apologise."

"At this time of night?" My head tilted to the side as I observed him. If he were a dog, I imagined his tail would've been between his legs. His eyes were wide, alert, and slippery as fuck.

When I heard the distinctive sound of the door reopening

behind him, I looked up. Sophia's head inched through a small space, keeping the door enclosed on her body. Wez cleared his throat uncomfortably, and like a shot, Sophia's startled hazel irises zoned in on the situation in front of her. Her eyes drew me to her first, but as soon as I dropped my own to her flushed red cheeks, everything else snapped into place.

It had been a while, but... "The only time my wife looks like that is when she's been thoroughly fucked."

Sophia spoke with no delay, which told me more than she probably ever would. "I can explain."

Typically, her words couldn't have felt any more scripted. Wez looked between us in annoyance, his knee bent as his feet lingered between two steps. His hands were fidgeting at his sides, like he often did in the cage before a fight. Eager for that first throw.

A humourless laugh hurled from me. "Him?" I said while tipping my chin to the boy in question. "Was it him the first time too, or some other poor fucker?" I looked to the ground, clenching my jaw and scrubbing my forehead free of tension before focusing my attention back on Wez. "This is the reason you've been absent from the gym? Because you've been fucking my wife behind my back? Jesus."

I rose to him with a snigger as he settled his feet on the bottom step closest to me. "Everything The Lagoon has done for you. The best coaches, the best prep, one of the top organisations in the fucking country, and you've given it all up. And for what?" I pointed harshly at Sophia. "That crazy fucking bitch?"

His fist collided with my chest in a half-hearted jab, the step giving him higher ground over me as his nose looked down onto mine. "Don't fucking talk about her like that."

"Are you serious...?" Another humourless laugh made its way from my throat when he didn't answer. "Jesus fuck, you are."

Seething, he got in my face, forcing his head against mine.

Pushing him back a few steps, I practically spat my next words. "All this time, you've been fucking my *wife*. All that wasted potential because your mind's been on pussy, fuck."

"It was him, wasn't it, Soph?" I asked, turning to her again as Wez retreated with a bounce in his step. "It was Wez the first time?"

Wez scoffed and ground his jaw, seeming to be disgusted I'd even questioned it. Sophia looked guilty, but somehow innocent all at once. That was her, an award-winning actress when the mood struck. All she needed was a red carpet, and she'd be in her element.

"You know, there were times when I looked at you and I thought how fortunate I was to have something so beautiful. Now I'm standing here wondering how I'd ever been so deluded. How did I ever find beauty in something so damn fucking ugly? In something so damn fucking fake?"

The door closed suddenly with a slam, and she ran down the steps, her silk camisole barely covering her breasts as she tied her silk robe around her waist. Disgust filled me as tears she brought on herself fell from her smudged eyes and sexed-up her make-up further.

"Head down, was it? Did you think of me when he fucked you? Did you moan my fucking name?"

"Walker, stop."

She forced her way to me on the pavement, driving Wez off to the side as she passed him on the steps.

"I'm sorry," she said. "I'm so, so sorry."

"Stop?" I scoffed. "I didn't realise it was possible to make yourself look any more desperate. What was it you said not so long ago, that you fucking *loved* me?"

Wez shifted down the steps and to the pavement, his shoulder level with mine as he stared at Sophia, confusion etched between his brows. "What the fuck, Sophia?"

"My thoughts exactly."

"You told me you didn't love him."

Sophia reached out to grab my coat, her eyes pleading with her apology.

It was a mess of all fucking proportions. My mind spun, wondering if she'd told Wez about our sham of a marriage. Though I stood stoic, waiting on a verbal response to both him and me.

Her fingers clutched at the midst of my coat, completely ignoring Wez as he began pacing beside us. Not being able to watch on while she fought for someone that wasn't him.

"Walker, please. I promise. I promise now that you're home, this will never happen again."

"This isn't my home." I pointed over her shoulder. Frantic, she continuously clenched and unclenched my coat as she tried to force another reaction from me.

I looked over my shoulder to Wez, who seemed to be wearing a hole in the tarmac, clenching his best hand. If he knew what was good for him–for his fucking career–he'd leave.

After sliding my hand into the breast pocket of my coat, I pulled out the envelope that had been safely tucked away in there. Sophia's gaze followed the paper as I pushed it into her chest.

"This was never my home, Soph. You were never my home." Even through my revulsion, my heart still plummeted. "I came to give you this." I held the envelope against her chest until her hand reached to take it from me.

My eyes focused on the rock on her finger, shining under the streetlights. The psychopathic bitch still had the nerve to wear a ring like it meant something.

"What is it?" she asked, her voice shaking as she held the envelope in front of her.

I made space between us, glancing another look behind me.

This time, I noticed Finley stepping out of the car, watching the three of us with some kind of authority, though he held none.

Sophia tore open the envelope with her finger and pulled out our divorce papers.

"Why? How?" she questioned, her gaze darting over every word.

"I had them fast-tracked," I admitted. "A lot like our marriage, huh? But to question why is ridiculous. This was a long time coming."

Her eyes returned to mine; only instead of tears, they shone with violence. She wore a look I knew just as well as the last. The same regard she always gave me when she accused me of doing something I hadn't done.

"I knew there was someone else," she said, dropping the letter to the floor as her eyes began inspecting any visible skin I had on display for something that wasn't there. A sign that another woman had her lips or claws on me.

"Seriously, what the fuck, Sophia? What the actual fuck?" Wez cursed, stepping between us.

He gripped her arm, and my eyes followed the movement, my jaw clenching. The kid was going to fuck his whole career because he couldn't keep his dick in check or his hands to himself.

I took a step back and spoke to Sophia over his shoulder. "I couldn't give a fuck anymore what you've done, Soph. What were you thinking fucking someone associated with my club? Did you think it would hurt me? The lad's got nothing but trouble attached to his name and less than an average salary. Fuck. You'll be disappointed to hear he won't be able to take care of you the way I fucking did."

Maybe my ego was a little wounded, given our eleven-year relationship.

I saw it coming–Wez pivoting on the spot and lunging into

me. But with alcohol in my system, my reactions were slow. I stumbled to the ground when his fist caught me in the jaw. Sophia squealed, and then I felt Finley's arm pulling up my own. I didn't know how drunk he believed me to be, but I was already up from the pavement before he could assist me any further.

Blood filled my mouth and seeped between my teeth, yet I stood taller. "Fuck you both," I said, hurling bloody spit to the concrete. "You deluded fucks continue your affair. Please"—I placed my palms together, lowering them as I bent at the knee— "don't stop on my account."

Sophia turned on the waterworks as she turned to Wez and pulled him back up the steps with shaky hands. At this point, she'd pass as a fucking panda. And Wez... fuck him. After everything The Lagoon did for him, it was karma's turn now.

"Pick up the papers, Sophia," I growled, walking back towards the car with Finley at my side. "You better sign them, or so help me fucking God, I'll take everything and leave you with nothing but what you had when we met. Do you think I give a shit where you end up? You think I'll give a shit when you've got no place to go? If you think for one second I'll be there to pick up the pieces when I've offered you an easy way out, you're more desperate than I ever gave you credit for."

Her lip wobbled, but she didn't dare speak. And neither did Wez.

By the time I was seated back in the BMW, false composure kept me eerily still. Finley drove us through the dark streets of London, only speaking when we finally arrived outside the doors of my complex.

"Don't take it out on the girl."

I snickered.

Don't take it out on the girl?

He meant no harm. I knew that. But what the fuck did he take me for?

"You know me better than that." I looked at his reflection in the mirror. He wasn't looking at me, which was a first. Except I wondered if I'd look at me too, given who I'd become.

Maybe my father had shaped me more than I was willing to accept.

Maybe Finley saw something in me I didn't.

I placed my hand on the car door and swung it open, but he spoke again as I was about to slip out.

"Walker."

With one foot on the pavement, I turned to face him grimly. "You got something to say, Finley, you fucking say it. By all means, don't let your salary hold you back."

"I mean no harm. You're a good man. But do me a solid and lay off the booze. That girl upstairs, she's a pearl. Break her, and there's no way to repair the damage."

Disregarding Blue, I replied only to the latter. "I'm still functioning. Big difference." And with that, I climbed from the car and slammed the door closed behind me.

CHAPTER TWELVE

Blue

MY CHEEKS BURNED *as daddy opened the door of his club, and mummy led us outside and into the dark. The wind was crazy, and my nose scrunched as droplets of rain landed on my cheeks and danced down my clothes. I'd only just got dry. I looked up at both of them, but as I did, the raindrops started to fall in their thousands. It made sense to close my eyes so they wouldn't get wet too, so that's what I did.*

"Not again."

Clutching my bunny to my chest, I peered open my eyes to find daddy bent down beside me, pulling my hood onto my head and tightening its strings. It was so windy, I thought I might get blown over, but then he picked me up and placed me into mummy's arms.

"I'll be home late," I heard him say as he kissed mummy over my

shoulder. "Don't wait up. And drive slow, okay? Never mind this wind; the roads will be terrible."

My eyes grew tired, so I snuggled into mummy's shoulder. Late? I thought. Mummy said it was already past my bedtime.

"I'll wait up," mummy said.

I felt her smile against the side of my head.

"Love you, princess," daddy said to me, kissing me too.

"Love you, daddy. Bye."

He closed the door, and then mummy and me made our way to the car. Her warmth enveloped me as she secured her arms around me nice and tight, perfectly content until I realised I could only see one of bunny's big floppy ears.

"Bunny!" I wailed, wriggling and trying to pull him free. "He's stuck, mummy!"

As she walked, she glanced down into the small space between us. The rain hit my face again as she moved one hand from my leg to cradle the back of my head, allowing me to lean back and tug bunny from between us.

"Don't drop him," she warned.

I would never!

Silly, silly, mummy. I cuddled him nice and tight between my face and her neck while she skipped us over puddles. Droplets of water splashed our clothes with each step, getting us wet. When the sky broke out in a loud rumble, I whimpered and pinched my eyes closed tight.

"It's okay, baby, it's just thunder."

"And wind," I said.

"You're right. Thunder, wind, and rain."

It felt like a long time until we reached the car. Mummy leant me against it, balancing me on her knee while she one-handedly opened the door to the backseat.

"No," I cried when she placed me in my car seat and took my bunny from me.

"Ssh, hold on. Let's get you out of this wet coat, and then you can have him back." She began pulling my arms free from my coat, but I continued to fret. I wanted my bunny, and I wanted him now.

She manoeuvred me around, taking my coat from me, and then she threw it onto the seat beside me. Water dripped from her brown hair and onto my face when she pulled each of my arms through the straps of my seat and leant forward to fasten me in while I continued to cry.

My wiggling hands reached out for bunny, Mummy's brow pinching as she placed him back in my waiting hands. I pulled him to my face as I cried.

As I did, the sky rumbled, only it sounded much louder this time and made me cry harder.

"Ssh, baby. Sleep," she cooed, her gentle fingers stroking my hair away from my damp forehead. "You're overtired, huh? I'm sorry. We'll be home soon."

Her lips touched my cheek, and then the door closed with a thud.

THE SOUND of thunder startled me awake, my eyes blinking open in the darkness of the room. I realised then that I'd fallen asleep on Walker's couch. With the recognition of a dream in the midst of my mind, I figured the thunder was a figment of my imagination. But then I heard the rhythmic pitter-patter of rain against the windows and another bout of thunder in the distance.

Regardless of what I'd woke from, it felt like I'd lived it.

Rolling onto my side, I noticed Walker slouched, legs spread, on the armchair beside me. His eyes floated over me, from my head to the tips of my toes. Despite feeling exposed under the gravity of his stare, I didn't shy away. There was no reason to. Not when we'd slept in the same bed for the past five nights. No less dressed now in my pyjamas than I'd been beside him.

The moon's light illuminated everything from his naked chest to the glass of amber liquid in his hand, which settled on the skin just below his shorts. Though my own eyes focused on the tortured look in his.

"Bad dream?" His voice was hoarser than usual, almost a rasp, as if he'd drank so much liquor he'd burnt his throat. As if he'd worked out so hard, he hadn't much air in his lungs.

"How did you know?" I slowly crawled back on my palms until I was seated, only blanching again at the sound of thunder. It was going to be one of those nights, it seemed.

Walker frowned, studying a path down my neck until he paused on the scar nestled above my collarbone. It wasn't the first time I'd noticed his eyes drift to the mark engraved in my skin, but for the first time since we'd met, I felt like he saw under the armour I often buried myself in.

By instinct, I raised my hand to trace its length with my fingers, watching him as his eyes followed my slow caress.

"You were restless," he murmured. "You said thunder was a trigger. The night it happened–"

"Yeah," I said, interrupting him. My brows drew together. He may have had an insight, but that didn't mean I wanted to talk about it. I only hoped he could understand why and not pressure me to talk it over like my father often did.

His eyes came back to mine with a look of understanding beneath their depths. Only when he licked his lips, I realised I was staring at him too fixedly. I dragged my eyes away, to the glass in his hand, and hoping to steer the conversation away from my nightmares, I asked, "Bad day?"

"Not the finest," was his response. There was no uncertainty in his tone–just honesty. With that, he brought his glass to his lips and swallowed the remainder. Something about the action made my stomach dip.

"My dad called me today," I said casually.

"He did? Why?" He refused to meet my eyes, and upon emptying his glass, he kept the rim against his lips.

"He said he was worried about me."

"That's it?"

I frowned. "Mostly."

"What else?"

"You don't have to worry. I know I said those things in your office, but I haven't told him anything."

His only response was to smirk.

"You haven't been around much. It's like you're ignoring me," I stated. "The new bedroom is all set up. I wasn't sure if it was for you or for me. The decorators locked the door behind them. I couldn't find the key."

"It's for you," he murmured. "You're a temptation I can't afford."

My heart rate kicked up a notch, and my words came out in a whisper. "What does that mean?"

He glared at me, gnawing his cheeks before he spoke again. "I think you know exactly what it means."

Maybe that was true, but still, I asked the question anyway. I was becoming borderline obsessed with him. Too conscious of our chemistry. We'd known each other only a brief amount of time, and it didn't matter how hard we tried to convince ourselves nothing was there; the truth still lingered between us like something foreign. Which was precisely why I slid off the couch and strode over to where he was seated with the urge to be near him.

He dropped his empty glass to the arm of the chair as I approached, his chin held high as if it could discourage me from advancing any closer. He wanted the space between us, but he couldn't deny that he liked being as close to me as I did him. It was why he'd chosen to sleep beside me in bed in replace of the couch. It was why the two of us never acknowledged it in words and instead let it play out.

I stepped forward and climbed onto his lap. He grunted at the intrusion, though he seemed neither satisfied nor displeased when I placed my knees on either side of his legs.

He kept his lazy, reclined position, but his hands moved to my waist. It was to either hold me still or push me away, but I wasn't confident which until his thumbs protruded into the waistband of my pyjama shorts, and he secured me down onto his lap.

Relief settled in my chest and joined the warmth in my belly.

"What is this, Walker?" My voice was breathy, if not hopeful. I was sure he understood what I was asking. No way was it just me searching for answers. Not when he all but asked the same question in his office. Maybe differently; but nothing could convince me it didn't mean the same.

His hands wrapped around my hips. And as if it stung him to say it, he replied, "I don't know."

I wished for an explanation that didn't feel like a riddle. But riddles seemed to be all we had.

ALL MY MORALS had evaporated along with my sanity as my fingers dug into her waist, itching for more.

Another touch.

A little taste.

Temptation.

The word was like glue.

The air was potent with unspeakable chemistry as I followed her every move. From the rise and fall of her chest to the way her fingertips made their journey into her hair, where she brushed through the tendrils with her fingers and pulled it over one shoulder. My cock twitched at the sight of her above me. And my mouth salivated to kiss the skin of her exposed neck.

Desperate to have her taste in my mouth, I worked hard to suppress a groan. But even so, I hardened beneath her.

"It's almost my birthday," she said, swallowing a breath. "I'm turning eighteen."

She didn't need to fucking tell me. I was completely aware of how old she was. It was one of the reasons she was here. And it didn't matter if she was seventeen or eighteen because this wasn't Florida, and she was a British Citizen. With her permission, if I wanted to fuck her, I could. Legally. Her age wasn't what held me back. At least, not completely. There were many factors.

There was James.

There was the past.

There was the future.

And regardless of them, it wasn't right.

I shuffled in my seat, which was a bad move because my cock created friction against her pussy, and her lips parted on a soundless gasp.

Swallowing, I told her what I was thinking. "I know how old you are."

"I was just reminding you."

I didn't need reminding, but I was sure she knew that.

Positioning my body upwards, so I was no longer slumped in the armchair, I moved so her chest was pressed against mine. And then, with my fingertips on her waist and her head in line with my own, I shuffled forward in my seat. It felt good being so close to her. Probably too good for me to keep my intentions pure if I relished in the position too long. Which was exactly why I couldn't.

"Wrap your legs around me," I murmured.

The corner of her mouth tipped up. It wasn't much, but being so close to her, it would have been impossible to miss it. And then her legs were wrapping around my waist and locking behind my back.

With my cock hard against her stomach, I was sure she was thinking the most carnal thoughts. If my night weren't such a clusterfuck of emotion, if I wasn't so fucking intoxicated, no doubt I'd be thinking more of them too. But maybe that was my issue, because I was thinking of them. So maybe this was me fighting it. Maybe this was me trying to convince myself I didn't want her, even though I did.

Despite the fantasy, I said, "I'm not going to fuck you, Blue." God knows she deserved more than a drunken fucking lay.

She stiffened in my arms and bit her bottom lip, giving off the impression she was disappointed in my honesty. I shouldn't have been, but fuck, I felt a little disappointed too. And jealous. Jealous that some other fucker would get to sink his cock into her one day. And jealous of all the other cunts before who had.

In spite of my better judgement, I found myself saying, "Not yet anyway."

It was impulsive.

Stupid.

So fucking moronic.

But then her arms encased around my neck like it was music to her ears. Like she was the damsel, and I was some kind of forbidden prince. And by their own accord, my hands gripped under her thighs as I raised us from the armchair and began walking us to the master bedroom.

But then, given our position, I thought, how much could I

take? And how much would she give? And how would I feel when it was all said and done, knowing that I'd handed my wife our divorce papers only a few hours ago, no matter how little our marriage ever meant?

I wasn't a prince.

This wasn't a love story.

Not even close, because fairy tales didn't exist.

The proof was in my shorts as I carried her through the room and down the hall towards the master bedroom. In the way my teeth fought not to bite into her sunshine skin. In the way I squeezed the skin of her thighs between my fingers, with the urge to creep closer to the place between her legs.

"Am I heavy?" she asked as I stepped through the bedroom door with her in my arms. She'd left the lamp on in the bedroom, and as my eyes adjusted to the light, I gently shook my head with a silent chuckle.

"You're a lot of things," I rumbled. "But heavy isn't one of them."

The smell of her perfume lingered through the penthouse since she'd moved in, but in this particular room, it assaulted me from every direction that I couldn't stop myself from wondering how I'd ever forget it when she was gone.

I walked us to the bed and placed her back onto the mattress, but she didn't choose to let me go straightaway, keeping her legs locked behind my back and her arms around my neck.

"Blue." I moved my hands from her thighs to either side of her shoulders and pulled back, forcing some distance between our upper bodies, not trusting myself while I was intoxicated. "Unlatch your legs."

"I thought you wanted me to stay in the new room."

A frown pulled at my forehead. "I do."

"Then why am I in your bed?"

I felt the urge to drop my head to the bed with a groan, but I didn't. Why was she in my bed? Why didn't I just take her to the new room that I'd had all set up for her? The fuck was wrong with me?

"Consider it your room until tomorrow. You're already here."

She darted her eyes from the window to me as rain hit and thunder sounded in the distance.

"Are you?" she asked.

"Am I what?"

"In here with me tonight?"

Her hands slid into my hair, gripping the strands between her delicate fingers as she attempted to pull my head closer to hers. I pulled back to look at her, and with one hand still in my hair, she moved the other to my face, smoothing out the lines on my forehead.

"Well?"

"I don't think it's appropriate," I said honestly. These deep-rooted feelings–these deep-rooted memories–and the urge to sink my cock into her warm cunt were too tempting. I'd already spent the last five nights beside her. I'd felt her snuggling against my back like I was a comfort. And every morning, I'd wake before she did with her head cradled in my neck and my fingers tangled in her hair.

It appeared even in my sleep, I was drawn to her.

Though right now, I was too wired and too infatuated with her body, with what this was, to keep myself under control. Staying beside her tonight would only end one way. There'd be no cuddling or sneaking out from on top of the sheets. Instead, I'd be balls deep, and with every thrust, she'd be screaming my name.

Her eyelashes fluttered as her fingers followed a path down the bridge of my nose, to my lips, and then along the length of my stubbled jaw. It threw me for a moment, my chest aching with something I'd never felt with a woman. Neither sober nor fucked up. Why the hell was she looking at me like that? Touching me like that?

She tore her hand away when I flinched, as if I'd scolded her. The ache of Wez's hit lingered, but there was no swelling, so she hadn't known her touch had hurt. And not only in the literal sense, because this... this.. longing I felt was a different kind of pain. The truth was, I didn't have it in me to explain or worry that I'd hurt her feelings. And clearly, I hadn't hurt them that much. Because although she was mimicking my frown, her eyes–her beautiful come-fuck-me eyes–were now glued to my mouth. She couldn't make it any more obvious how much she wanted to kiss me.

"No," I said, reading into the dumb idea. Absolutely no way would I let her close the space between us; the complication could ruin me. Shit, how did I go from one extreme to the other with her? Why the fuck did she continuously push me?

Annoyed, I took her wrist in one hand and pinned it above her head. "Whatever you're thinking, you better stop."

Her breath hitched, and her hips lifted, moving against my straining cock in one gentle movement. It took all my goddamn willpower to keep myself from grinding back. From stripping those goddamn skimpy pyjamas from her perfect skin, fucking her raw, and showing her who possessed the control here. It had been too long since my cock had been inside another woman, and it was begging to be hugged by her warm wet centre.

We were a long way from my office. She was no longer hiding behind a shitty threat.

With no words, solely touches, she suddenly inclined forward so our lips were grazing. I gripped her wrist tighter, but my eyes closed as I bathed in the feel of her mouth against mine. I'd fucked up by all accounts. And still, when her tongue came out and dampened my bottom lip, I let it happen. I didn't make one single attempt to stop her. I did the opposite. I drew her bottom lip between my teeth and nibbled in a way that was anything but romantic.

It was mean, and punishing and fuck–

"Nate."

Just *fuck!*

My first name on her lips sounded like a prayer, and the little moan that followed only made me want to do dirty, dirty things to her. I drew my lips away from hers, down her chin, and across her pulse before dipping into the hollow of her neck. She shivered when my breath hit the damp skin, and when my lips pressed against her throat and my teeth pinched, she raised her hips and ground herself against me, loosening the lock she had around my waist.

With a pained curse, I inhaled her scent. I knew if I were to do anything when she was gone, it would be to use my money for the greater good and pull this scent from every store in the whole of England and any country I ever planned to visit.

"What perfume do you wear?"

Knowing the name of it would be a good start.

Distracted by my vicious lips, she could barely get her words out. "Do you like it?"

Do I like it?

Do I fucking *like* it?

"No. I fucking loathe it."

I didn't give her a chance to think about what I said before I was nibbling and sucking at her skin again, marking her like it was my very right. She continued grinding herself against my cock, eager to chase the high I shouldn't have been assisting her with. It was PG compared to some of the things I'd done with women before Sophia and with Sophia, but still, I let her take what she needed. I convinced myself I was being a good guy. A real fucking gent.

I groaned, low in my throat. "Does that feel good, baby?"

She responded by moaning timidly in my ear, rubbing and grinding and grinding and rubbing. It threw me for a loop. But it wasn't enough, because the next thing I knew, I was letting go of her wrist, pulling away from her, and staring down at her covered pussy. A damp patch covered the satin of her pyjama shorts. And before I could question it, my thumb was there, softly rubbing her clit through the material.

"Oh."

Fucking *oh?*

I couldn't look at her.

If I looked at her–if I saw her face, all blushed and sexy as sin–there was no saying I wouldn't lose it. I was close. Close to dipping my hand into her shorts and feeling that wetness between my fingers. Close to feeling that wetness on my cock. My cock that was currently leaking pre-cum because I was being deprived of one of my favourite fucking activities. One I hadn't participated in in too long.

She crept forward, moving her hands to my bareback. "I think–I think–"

"You think what?" I said, looking up. "Do you want me to stop?"

Shit.

Why, just why, did I look at her?

Her face was glowing, her cheeks the colour of cherry blossom, her lips parting as she mewed like a fucking kitten. Her nipples hard and pointed through her top. Jesus, this girl.

"No. No, please don't stop," she breathed.

Thank fuck.

She inclined her hips into my touch, and then I was cupping her, my fingers sprawled over the material between her ass cheeks as my thumb continued its spiralling assault on her clit.

"Nate, *oh.*"

I grunted. "Fuck, you're wet. I can feel you through your shorts. Don't be shy, baby. Take what you want."

What I really wanted to say was, take it all. Take *me*. Take my cock. But then–then it happened. Her legs shook as she clenched her thighs around my hand, and her lips parted with a final moan as her release finally broke. It seemed to last a few moments, and then she was closing her eyes, spent and completely satiated.

Despite wanting to bathe in her presence a moment longer, I removed my hand, swallowed a breath, and took myself to the en-suite before things could get any more heated.

My fists clenched the sink as I spoke to my dishevelled and equally flushed reflection. "Shit. That wasn't supposed to happen."

That wasn't supposed to fucking happen.

With the hope she fell asleep before I returned, I sponta-neously stripped from my shorts, took a few steps back, and reached behind me to turn on the shower. A second later, I stood under the flow of the scorching water. The wet heat wrapped around me, temporarily abolishing the mess I'd got myself into as it beat down on my skin and relaxed the knots in my back. But with my cock still hard and standing to attention, I couldn't do anything but take it in my fist.

And then, my eyes closed, and all I could picture was Blue's face.

Her lips.

Her sexy as fuck legs in her next to nothing pyjamas.

The way they moulded to the perfect globes of her ass.

The way she purposely strutted her hips whenever she walked, as if she knew the power she held over the entire male species. Over me.

With one hand holding my weight on the wall of the shower, the other squeezed the head of my cock before beginning slow, torturous tugs up and down. It was all so fucking wrong, but it felt so good. So goddamn good.

I forced myself to think of something else. Relay an old memory of me and Sophia, or fuck, some recent porn. But it was no use. All I saw was Blue's eyes looking into mine. All I felt was the wetness between her legs. Her legs shaking against my thighs as she came. It was her sassy mouth as my imagination stirred up a new scenario—her down on her knees, parting her full pink lips, ready to take me between them. A naughty glint in her eyes that told me she could take it.

She could.

And I knew what I'd do.

I'd let her deep throat my cock until I forced tears from her eyes. She'd like it. No, she'd fucking love it. Then I'd strip her bare. Lift her up. And once her legs were around my waist, I'd bury my cock deep in her pussy, and fuck her hard against the wall of this shower. Nothing but skin between us. My cum filling her up.

And up.

And up, and up.

"*Fuck*, Blue."

My movements became faster, and then my head dropped down to see my release coating my fist, low groans leaving my mouth before my breathing could even out.

As soon as it was over, the guilt began to rot, leaving me feeling no more than a filthy fucking deranged pervert.

Shit, what was wrong with me?

I was *sick*.

Stepping out of the shower, I reached for Blue's towel from the heated rail. No doubt another thing that was covered in her scent. I wasn't sure how to feel that I'd still smell her all over me, even after getting clean. I wrapped the towel around my waist and picked up my gym shorts from the floor, popping them into the washing basket. By the time I returned to the bedroom, Blue was sleeping silently. And that's where I left her as I made my way back to the kitchen, where I opened a fresh bottle of my favourite beverage.

Before I even had the chance to pour myself a glass, my phone lit up with a text from Noah. It was almost one in the morning, which only told me he was still at work.

Just a heads up, The Liberty Daily got wind of yours and Wez's fight. Were you planning on telling me wtf happened, or was I gonna have to read about it in the paper tomorrow?

"Shit." I threw my phone to the counter, poured myself a glass, and sank another three. Before I could even attempt to get a night's sleep, I had to figure out what the fuck I was going to do about all the bad press we kept receiving. There was only so much bullshit a business could take before people believed it.

Fight? I texted back. **It was nowt but child's play.**

CHAPTER THIRTEEN

Blue

I WOKE to the sound of the bedroom door opening and the feel of someone watching me from its threshold. My eyes opened but immediately closed again, sensitive to the light coming through the bedroom windows.

"Who opened the curtains?"

"I did–forty minutes ago. Now get up." Walker's voice tore through the subtle calmness of my morning. Not just his words, but his tone demanding my attention.

I groaned. "What?"

"I said get up."

My fingers wiped the sleep from my eyes as I sat up. "I heard you," I mumbled, dropping my hands to clutch my blanket as it pooled at my waist. I checked him out as he leaned against the doorframe, already dressed in his business attire. I doubt I'd ever tire of seeing him in a suit. "But why? I assumed after last night, you were going to go back to trying to pretend I didn't exist."

"Your existence isn't one I'd forget." He cocked an eyebrow at me, and though he was trying hard not to stare at what I presumed to be the mess he'd left on my neck, he'd have to try harder for me not to notice. "Now, would you get the fuck out of bed and get dressed?" He was silent for a beat before adding, "Please?"

"Are we going to talk about last night?"

"No."

"Then what's going on?"

I'd fallen asleep after... what'd happened between us. He didn't want to speak of it, but I wish he'd still have stayed the night beside me. I'd be in the new room tonight, and he'd be in here. Alone.

Agitated, he said, "You want a job or not, kid?"

"What I really want is for you to stop calling me *kid* when it suits you," I complained, raising my elbows and fluffing up my bed hair before giving him a pointed stare. "You're serious?"

"As a heart attack," he replied dryly. His jaw ticked when I didn't make a move to get out of bed, but he just lifted his chin towards the en-suite. "You've got twenty minutes. Fucking chop-chop."

Despite the sleep in my eyes, unlike last night, I noticed what appeared to be the shading of a bruise along the edges of his jaw. "Has someone hit you?"

I didn't want to pry, so I didn't chase after him demanding answers when he left the room without a reply and nothing but a scowl. Being shut down once was enough for one day. And ignorance wasn't new to me, being my father's daughter. Instead, I fumbled out of bed and into the bathroom, stripping from my sex infused clothes as I moved and leaving them in a scramble on the floor.

My nose scrunched at the state of my hair in the bathroom mirror. I brushed my fingers through my untamed mane, my brown and blonde balayage looking worse for wear. I needed to find a hairdresser, pronto. And then my eyes turned wide at the red and purple bites on my neck. It would take me at least fifteen minutes to cover them up.

After loading my toothbrush, I stepped into the shower and brushed my teeth. I bathed myself in hot water, clearing away the events of last night's rough sleep from both my skin and my mind. Initially, I got a good few hours, but the thunder throughout the night had only made me restless. And without Walker to snuggle into, I couldn't seem to relax.

Spitting the minted foam down the drain, I stepped out of the shower, opened the bathroom drawer, and reached for my medication. Droplets of water ran from my skin and spilt over the floor while my fingers probed a pill from the foiled packet. I placed it on my tongue, then stepped back into the water and aimed my head upwards into the steady stream. Opening my mouth, I let the hot water veil my tongue as I swallowed back the one thing that kept my anxiety at bay.

Maybe this was what Walker meant when he asked what set me up for the day. This was my equivalent to him working out every morning.

Twenty minutes later, I walked from my en-suite with my towel wrapped around me, feeling a fraction lighter than when I stepped into my shower. I found Walker sitting on my unmade bed with his head in his hands, his suit pulling tight against his muscular back.

He looked up at me when he heard me approach. "I said you had twenty minutes, not twenty minutes to shower."

"Sorry, I guess."

I walked in the direction of the closet, and once I stepped inside, I began fingering through my clothes hanging on the rail, unsure what to settle on for my first day of... work. The task of having to move all my clothes down the hall later and into my new room, I couldn't bear thinking about.

Popping my head out of the walk-in closet, I gave Walker a timid smile. "So do you know something I don't?"

He looked at me, dumbfounded.

"Has my appeal been declined?" I clarified. It had to be the reason he was giving me a job now and not days ago.

"No, the opposite. If you want to go back to Duke, you can. Do you"—he paused, searching for something in my eyes as I stepped back out of the closet and into the bedroom—"want to go back to Duke?"

"Not if I can do what I want to do working at The Lagoon. Can you guarantee me a permanent position? Can you guarantee that you're not going to take it away from me? Could we have some paperwork drawn up or... I don't know... have you spoken to my father? I have a feeling he's not going to like this. At all."

Tension was visible in his shoulders. "Slow down, and I'll explain," he said, clicking his neck from side to side. "I've filled out the application to enrol you into Duke's Apprenticeship Programme. Instead of what you'd previously signed up for, once a month, if you want to do this"—he raised a brow—"then you'll attend Duke for a face-to-face with a tutor, but you'll complete the rest of your degree online while working for-"

"How?" I interrupted. "I mean, when did you arrange all of this?"

"This morning," he grunted. "Before and after I worked out."

Figured.

"Are you going to tell me why?"

Did last night change things? I wondered. Though I was too

nervous to ask him that out loud. What could change when neither of us knew what this even was?

He ground his teeth against his jaw, and then, as if he was mentally ticking things off in his head, he said, "The media hate us. No matter what we do or what The Lagoon does, they always have something bad to report. If you can get even a handful of media outlets to alter their views on us by creating a positive media campaign, it's worth a shot. Second, your name is already associated with the club. And third, if you're there, I can keep my eye on you. I employ the best staff, so I know they won't bother you. And if by any means you happen to piss someone off, I can see to it that you're reprimanded."

"Reprimanded?"

"That's right." He licked his full bottom lip. His eyes dropped to the bottom of my towel, and his head tilted as if he wanted to look at what was underneath as I pulled on a strand of my wet hair.

I was too busy considering what he'd offered to say anything. Why did it seem too good to be true?

"My name is on the building. I guess it makes sense to associate myself, right?"

His eyebrows raised like it was the most obvious choice as he nodded and quipped a dry "Yes," but wanted to say duh.

"And what about my dad? You know we don't have much of a relationship. He won't agree to this."

"I'll handle that." He looked to the floor, then back to me, not meeting my eyes. "Considering it's been five days since your little stunt in my office, I think we've already established your threat holds no intent. You said as much last night."

I leant the side of my head against the door jamb of the closet. "You seem to have it all worked out. So why do I feel like there's something you're not telling me?"

"There's a lot you don't know. A lot of things that don't

concern you," he replied. His tone was complex and cold while he fiddled with the clasp of his watch.

"So you admit it, then. There's something you're not telling me?"

"There is something I haven't told you yet that I suppose is deemed important."

My lips pursed, and I watched as he clicked his fingers one by one. When he got to his ring finger, he stopped and moved his attention back to his watch. My line of sight moved back to his face when I felt his gaze on me.

"I've hired someone to mentor you. Someone with experience. You'll meet her later, and then the two of you can do whatever you need to do to paint The Lagoon in a better light." He shook his head, more to himself than me, then released an exasperated sigh.

"That's it?"

"Get dressed. And cover your neck."

I didn't move. I stayed exactly where I was. I didn't mind a mentor. I knew I couldn't learn everything I needed to learn without one. It was another reason Duke appealed to me–the tutors there had first-hand experience in the industry I wanted to be involved in. It's the way he'd handled it that upset me. The way both my father and Walker figured they could dictate my life. If they told me to jump, I was expected to jump. If they told me to sit, I was expected to sit.

Well, I expected him to say more, but he remained quiet. Meanwhile, resentment coated my tongue like tar.

"What will you tell my dad?"

"Technically, even with the Apprenticeship Programme, you're still enrolled at Duke, so we don't necessarily have to tell him anything."

My eyes narrowed. "You want to lie?"

"Lying is a stretch. I'm merely withholding information." He smirked. "Besides, I'm sure you've lied to him yourself about worse things, considering how under wraps he keeps you."

I ignored the latter. "When I spoke to him yesterday, he said your emails were few and far between."

His eye twitched as he focused back on his watch. "There's been nothing to tell him. You've settled in, minus the hiccups. What more can I say?"

"Maybe the truth."

He hesitated, then stood to his feet. "The truth, huh?" he asked, taking steps towards me.

I lifted my head from the wooden frame of the doorjamb as he approached.

"The truth would be telling him how I made his little princess come with my thumb on her clit."

His response was unexpected, and he chuckled low in his throat as I inhaled a lengthy breath through my nose.

I could feel the heat of a blush as it appeared on my cheeks.

"I don't mean that truth," I said on an exhale. "Why don't you just tell him that instead of studying at Duke five days a week, I'm working at The Lagoon... for him? For you? And attending Duke once a month? If anyone can make him believe that I can handle myself in his world and not the one he created around me, it's probably you. Given that it's coming more from a business standpoint and not a personal one."

"He doesn't want you of all people involved in his affairs. Especially The Lagoon."

"Why? I'm already here. And I'm eighteen in a few days, so he can't exactly drag me back home unless I go kicking and screaming. If you just spoke to him, then maybe...." I tipped my shoulder. "Maybe he'd be more inclined to listen."

"Blue," he said, pocketing his hands as he stood before me. "Your father is a businessman. Has been all his life. Sometimes it can be hard to step away from business when you invest all you are into your work. But he did. He stepped away from the mess of The Lagoon and into safer territory because a good portion of the public perceived The Lagoon to be this big criminal organisation, what with the nightclub and the gym combined. Some people hear the words 'martial arts' and think of it as a violent sport. Some of those people don't understand that the sport is competitive. Our fighters aren't outside kicking each other to death on the street. Still, there are people out to get us. To shut us down. To shut the whole building down because our USP is out of society's norms. It's not the life your father wanted for you."

"My father doesn't want any life for me."

"That's a little far-fetched. He doesn't want any harm to come to you. He loves you."

"I never said he didn't." My brows pinched as an awkward silence fell over us like an old stiff blanket. "Is this the reason you're so cold? Because you invest all you are into your work?"

"I am what I am," he said quietly.

I dwelled on that for a moment, watching his every action as he arranged himself to stand less than a fraction away from me. I felt the heat from him on my exposed skin. I smelt the freshness of his shirt and the subtle touch of his cologne. My heart seemed to stop when he raised a hand from his pocket and tucked a strand of my wet hair behind my ear.

His usual frown told me he was brooding over something.

"That's what you think of me?" he asked, eyes mapping out my face before pinning his gaze on mine. "You think I'm cold?"

"Truth or a lie?"

He moved his hand from my ear, placing his knuckles on the door jamb beside my head.

"Truth."

"Yes," I said, my voice breathy. "I think you're cold." Even as I admitted the words, I couldn't seem to break from his glacial stare. So, to distract myself from the gravity of the moment, I weaved my hands under the lapels of his suit jacket and pressed my palms against his hard chest. He didn't detest. We stood fixed like stone; his head tilted down so our only line of sight was each other.

How was it the man kept his cool when from the outside it felt like his heart was going to burst?

I felt him pulling away as he worked his jaw. And then he admitted, "You're right. I am cold." He drew back from me then. All I could do was pull my bottom lip into my mouth and chew on it in an effort to keep my lips sealed.

He might not have realised it, but I liked who he was. Because despite the coldness in him, I'd witnessed his warmth. He first gave it to me when he held my hand on the plane and again when he gave me his room. When he let me snuggle against him on the couch. When he carried me to bed, gave me pleasure, yet didn't fuck me.

The feel of my teeth against the cushioned skin of my lips made me think of our kiss, reminiscing about the way I'd pressed my lips to his and the way he'd pulled my bottom lip into his mouth. It had my heart in overdrive. I wondered if we'd do it again. I wondered when.

"What, now you disagree?" he questioned.

"What makes you think that?"

He didn't falter. "The hearts in your eyes." He leant into me, forcing me into the closet until I took steps back, hitting its mirrored wall. He placed his knuckles on either side of my head, and they cracked as he pushed his fists tight to the reflective glass. He scrutinised me and then allowed his gaze to peruse the length of my body. "If I asked you to drop your towel, you would."

I swallowed, feeling his words in my core. "Yes."

"It wasn't a question." He closed his eyes. "The line between us is blurry." When he opened his eyes again, they shone with lust. "I want to do things to you I shouldn't."

"And? What if I want you to do them?"

"No."

"You don't make any sense," I said, placing my hands back onto his chest and digging my nails into his shirt. His eyes followed, seeing the soft creases of petite half-moons I'd created.

"None of this fucking does," he replied, dropping his fists from the mirror and stepping back. He avoided my eyes as he turned to leave through the closet door. "Get dressed."

I stopped him before he was gone entirely from sight. "Nate."

"What?" he grumbled.

"What should I wear?"

He brushed a hand back through his hair as he glanced an annoyed look at me over his shoulder. His gaze fell to my legs. It sounded like it pained him to say it, but he mumbled something I could just make out.

"Clothes."

Walker

"WHAT IF I *want you to do them?*"

Blue's words were all I'd thought about on the drive over to the club. She didn't understand what she was saying.

Finley's eyes had darted from me in the backseat to Blue in the front as he looked between us–the two of us staring out through our windows, utterly ignorant of each other. I'm sure our body language conveyed that we'd fought to anyone who didn't know what was going on between us. Not that I truly understood it myself. But maybe I was done questioning what was happening, and perhaps I was done feeling the way I did over something that happened years ago.

Since we arrived at the club over two hours ago, I'd hidden upstairs in my office, finalising everything for Friday's fight night. I'd told Blue to "get acquainted" with the staff. Olivia–the social media expert I'd hired to work alongside her, was due to arrive later today. Together, I'd leave them to do whatever they could to bring the media and public back on our side.

I knew Blue wanted to impress me, and I wanted to see how she'd go about it. What was the worst that could happen?

For the past fifteen minutes, I'd been watching her from my office window, speaking with Louis, my barman, while helping him shine the bottles behind the bar. I twisted a rogue pen between two fingers, trying not to snap the plastic in half every time I saw Louis check her out when he believed she wasn't paying him any attention.

I'd told her to wear clothes, and given that her choice of attire was usually minuscule, I shouldn't have been as surprised as I was to see her in a pair of daisy dukes. There was no point reminding her that this was England and not the magic city. After all, the comment she made in the kitchen on her first day here–when I pointed out her little school skirt–had come back to me in full force when she'd referred to me the same way this morning.

"I like the cold."

Only now, I wanted to inject those words into my veins like a junkie would crack. No doubt they'd feel good at first, but like the drug, probably wouldn't bode well.

Addiction wasn't the correct term for whatever this was. I wasn't addicted to Blue Sterling or her idea of me.

Although my office windows were tinted to those outside my office, Blue kept looking up. There was no way she could have known I'd been watching her. In fact, it was something I found myself doing more often than not in the time she'd been living with me. It was all in an effort to figure her out, though I still wasn't much wiser to her as a person. But what I did know of her, I liked. And that alone somehow felt like a lie. Just like addiction, *like* also wasn't the right way to describe whatever this was. What we were. I still had no fucking idea what word I'd use to describe the way I felt and if there was more to it than the typical lust. Lusting after a seventeen–almost eighteen-year-old–didn't feel right. Still, it seemed to be more than the need to get myself off, but less than the need to do more about it. Seventeen-year-old girls were rarely written into the lives of thirty-four-year-old men. And when they were, I imagined they weren't written into them the same way I was.

The noise of the elevator pulled my attention away from Blue, and I spun around to catch Noah stepping into my office, watching how his gaze was drawn to the bruising on my jaw.

"You don't look as bad as I imagined," he said. "The Liberty made out it like it was a KO."

"No images, and still, you believed the media's bullshit?"

He sucked his teeth. "Of course not. I know it's rare that they ever print the real version of any story. So, you gonna tell me what the fuck's going on?"

Dropping my head back, I closed my eyes to the ceiling and rolled out my shoulders. "Short version?"

"I'll take anything."

"I showed up at the townhouse last night to hand Sophia our divorce papers. Only I ran into Wez leaving the property. It turns out, it was him who Sophia had been shagging behind my back for the last twelve months."

"Wez? But–"

"But what? His mental health issues?" I sniggered, opening my eyes and giving Noah a pointed stare. "They likely stemmed from his guilt or her crazy. Maybe both. Either way, he got a little heated when he realised Sophia wasn't fully invested in him as he was her. He caught me in the jaw with his left hook." I tipped my head to the side so he could get a better look at my face.

"Is it broken?"

"Does it look broken, you dopey cunt?"

He held his hands up. "Fuck, forgive me for being worried about you, man. You've been all over the shop recently."

Shaking my head, I muttered, "I'm good."

His eyes moved from me to the window, where he lengthened his neck to get a better look at Blue below us. "And the girl? Is something going on?"

My shoulders hiked up as I cleared my suddenly dry throat. He couldn't know. She'd covered her neck with enough make-up to hide every bite I'd inflicted on her skin. "What?"

"Why is she here again?"

"Apprenticeship." My body seemed to relax, knowing he hadn't caught on to whatever the fuck was developing between me and 'the girl,' but something else was brewing in my gut. A new surge of protectiveness that wasn't quite there before. And this was Noah I was talking to. My brother. A man who wouldn't wound me on my worst day. Perhaps it stemmed from last night. Sophia. Wez. Or maybe I was just fucked in the head, feeling things that didn't make any sense for me to feel. Things that validated and unvalidated everything I now felt for the girl who was no more than three years old when I was just nineteen.

"Nate."

"What?" I swallowed.

"You look ill. What the fuck is wrong with you, man? Are you pissed?"

"Am I pissed?" I repeated with somewhat of a laugh. "I'm living in a permanent state of stress, little brother. Unless you have any good news to sprout, go make yourself useful down-stairs where you're sought after."

He scowled and brushed a hand back through his curls. "If you want to take a few days off, I can handle this place. I can have everything ready for fight night by Wednesday."

"I don't doubt it." I walked around my desk and sank into my office chair, placing down the pen I held onto my desk before I snapped it. "But I'll have it ready by tomorrow." Lifting my chin, I hesitated before I said, "Terminate Wezley's contract and have someone else take his place. I don't want him anywhere near my club."

He rubbed his palms down his face. "If that's what you want."

"It is. Oh and before I forget, we have a new employee starting later today, so make the introductions. Olivia Blake. She's going to handle all our social media. Blue is going to be working alongside her. I'm hoping it'll aid in tidying up our reputation."

"Anything is worth a shot at this point," he agreed.

I woke up my computer and clicked on my emails. No doubt there was a new email waiting for me from James, especially with it being his daughter's birthday tomorrow. And I was right. His name sat at the top of my mailbox.

"Is there anything else you need me to do for you?"

Looking up at Noah, I shook my head. Not to be a dick, but I'd almost forgotten he was there. "Nope."

He tapped my desk twice and then left me alone to wallow in whatever awaited me in James's email today. But before I did that, I chose to open and respond to any emails related to Friday's event.

Weigh day was Thursday, which meant vendors were prep-ping the events arena and everything surrounding fight night over the course of the next few days. And, of course, the stage was due to be set up for the ceremonial weigh-in. A lot of people failed to recognise that UFC fighters weighed in twice. Once in the morning, the day before the fight–which was when their official weight was announced. And once in the evening–the ceremonial weigh-in. Which, in short term, was a little show for the press, staff, and the fans. In truth, I found it a total ball-ache, and I probably wouldn't bother hanging around for the both of them. It was the official weigh-in that was deemed the most important. And the last thing I wanted was a microphone in my face and questions about my not-fight with Wez. When they realised he was no longer listed as our backup fighter, the chances were they'd only get more ruthless.

Closing an email from a vendor, the following email I opened was from Olivia with written acceptance of the job I'd proposed just hours ago. I'd never hired someone so quickly. Between the early hours of this morning and now, the paperwork was settled, and she was due to arrive in just a few hours. I found myself wondering why I hadn't hired a social media manager sooner. Because after finding her on LinkedIn, I was sure her skills would only benefit the club.

It was only when I was done responding to work-related emails that I opened the email from James, completely surprised to find documents attached to his email, including a valuation and buyout agreement for The Lagoon.

My attention piqued. "Well, shit."

I hadn't expected it so soon. But then, that was James. When he wanted to do something, he did it. There was no second-guessing. No going back on his word. There'd never once been any qualm between us when it came to business. Unless we factored Blue into it, and in this case, I supposed she was the main factor in our business dealings, if not the only factor. And James was still under the impression that both me and Sophia were taking care of her. I wondered how long I could keep up the false pretence. I wondered if it was possible to tell him part of the truth, like Blue had suggested. Perhaps I should have never kept news of mine and Sophia's failing marriage from him. I couldn't even recall my reasoning except for embarrassment. And then there was the incident where I accidentally got Blue suspended.

Not my finest moment.

And since then, I'd only fallen further down the rabbit hole.

I'd touched her.

James trusted me to take care of his daughter, and as her guardian, I'd gone and broken that trust. I was building lies on top of fucking lies. And at the risk of losing everything I worked for in my life, telling him the truth seemed like the most brainless idea. I only hoped he wouldn't lose every inch of respect for me once he found out the whole of it. Better yet, perhaps there was a way to keep it from him. All of it.

Clicking off the documents, I read over his email. He'd planned to fly to London today and had arranged a dinner date for the four of us tomorrow. A celebration for Blue's birthday.

The *four* of us.

But as I dragged my trackpad through the rest of his email, that moment of panic shifted to relief when I read he could no longer make it. Still, the reservation stood, and he insisted the three of us would still attend without him.

My hands flew to the back of my head, where I locked my fingers together and attempted to stretch my tense muscles. Sophia was no longer in the picture, so dinner for three was absolutely out of the question.

It seemed I had two choices.

Come clean, or take Blue out for a birthday dinner.

Just the two of us.

It shouldn't have felt like a dilemma, but that's precisely what it was.

If I fucked up–if James's didn't like how I'd lied to him–he could withdraw the buyout agreement before we finalised the contract. And on the other hand, when it came to Blue Sterling, I felt nothing but a weak man.

What was *one* more lie?

I'd already told enough of them.

I dropped my hands from my head and emailed him back.

It'll be our pleasure.

CHAPTER FOURTEEN

Blue

OLIVIA WAS PROBABLY the most gorgeous girl I'd ever seen. She wasn't what I pictured when Walker said he'd hired someone to mentor me. Her perfectly styled brown waves fell on either side of her centre parting and hung over the swell of her breasts. Her lips were bow-shaped, yet bottom heavy. And her eyes were such a unique shade of blue that they almost looked silver. And I was envious. Envious that someone could be born with genes like that and look like a supermodel. And it wasn't just me who thought she was gorgeous.

We were seated in the lobby, a square room that stood in the second section of the building, just off to the side of the gym. It was a place for both the fighters and the staff to interact. To socialise so everyone could feel like they were one big family.

And Hudson, well, he couldn't stop looking over at Olivia. His eyes were practically glued to her face.

"Do you have any previous experience in social media management?" she asked me.

"No, this will be the first time. Unless you include the time I spend browsing socials on my phone, but I'm guessing that's not what you mean."

She smiled, and woah, I couldn't fault Hudson for staring. It seemed I had a total girl crush.

"No, that's what I would call experience. It helps to know your way around socials. I think it's best to focus our attention on Facebook and Instagram for the time being, and we can work The Lagoon up to a social media presence on other apps once we've built that initial following."

"Seems easy," I hummed.

"This part is easy. But technically, we're jumping ahead of what you should be focusing on purely because it seems too good of an opportunity to miss with the event happening Friday. But it's cool; we'll have plenty of time to get you where you need to be for every assessment Duke will carry out."

I was about to respond but became distracted when Noah stepped into the room, his eyes going to Hudson, then to us, then back to Hudson. "Hudson, a word."

Olivia lowered her eyes when she caught Hudson's smirk, then a moment later, he was following Noah out of the room.

"Do you two know each other?" I asked. "You and Hudson?"

"Um." With both hands, she tucked her hair behind her ears.

"We did once." Then she lowered her hands and drummed her fingers rhythmically on the table, going straight back into work mode. "Walker said that you won't be here tomorrow, so if we set up the basics now and create a little hype surrounding Friday's event, you can help me continue the campaign on Thursday, which according to my calendar"—she opened up her spiral diary—"is weigh day. Perfect. We'll be able to create momentum around the fighters and snap some images for the gram."

Although I was excited about everything we'd planned, I stopped to ask, "Why aren't I here tomorrow?" It was the first I'd heard of it.

"When I got all the information I needed from Walker, he also mentioned tomorrow was your birthday. That the two of you have plans?"

"We do?" I said out loud, seeming to stare at her a moment before shaking myself out of a stupor. "Right. We do," I agreed falsely.

I slid my phone from my pocket, opened my texts, and sent Walker a message. **Since when do we have plans for my birthday?**

He replied in an instant. **Did I forget to mention it?**

Though I was grateful I'd be celebrating my birthday, I rolled my eyes at his lack of communication. **I wish you'd have told me. It would have been nice to get my hair done. Maybe buy a nice outfit. Get my nails did. You know, a lil birthday girl prep.**

Ten minutes later, I received a hair and nail appointment confirmation. Noon tomorrow at Herschel Boutique with one of London's top stylists.

Five minutes passed, and then my phone was alerting me to another message.

Aren't you going to thank me, brat?

With warmth in my belly and a smile on my face, I texted back a heart emoji and pocketed my phone.

It wasn't until later on that I realised he'd responded with a kiss.

Walker

AFTER HANDING over the remainder of my to-do list to Noah and sacking off work, it was still early evening when Finley dropped both Blue and me back at the penthouse. I was lazed on the sofa, still in my shirt and trousers, while waiting for a phone call from downstairs to let me know our takeout had arrived. Chinese. Because Blue had never had the pleasure of tasting Chinese cuisine in her life, and I wanted to show her exactly what she'd been missing. I may have gone a little overboard, ordering too much off the menu, hoping we'd find something she'd enjoy. It seemed the brat was pulling strings without any inkling of the things I would do for her if she just asked. Though while I lazed, she was following my orders. I'd asked her to move her belongings from the master suite–my bedroom– into the bedroom I had made up for her. She hadn't even seen it yet, and already she was sassing me. I'd probably have found it cute if I wasn't itching for a drink.

"You know, a gentleman would help me move everything from one room to the other."

"You had two suitcases when you arrived. I'm sure you can manage." I looked at the time on my watch. Takeout would probably be another fifteen minutes at least. It would take her no more than ten. "What ever happened to you 'wanting to do things on your own?'"

She made a noise in her throat that sounded like a *hmph*. "That wasn't entirely what I meant, but whatever."

It wasn't whatever. But it wouldn't hurt her to do it on her own. She was more than capable. And until she outright asked for my help, I wasn't going to assume she needed it. Maybe I still needed her to convince me that she wasn't a complete brat.

She disappeared down the hallway but came back into view not long after. Only this time both her hands were busy with clothes hangers pinched over her fingers. "Please, can you unlock the bedroom door?"

My lips twitched. She looked one second away from being swallowed by all the material gathered around her, her fingers losing their blood supply as she held tightly on to the metal of each hanger.

"I unlocked it before I sat down," I replied. But because I didn't enjoy watching her suffer, I rose from the sofa and headed towards where she stood to help her with her things. Before I reached her, she tipped one hip out to the side and pouted.

"Brat," I murmured half-heartedly, grabbing some hangers from her before making my way down the hall and to the bedroom door. *Her* bedroom door.

I'd finally be getting the master suite back for myself. I should've felt excited about it, but a small part of me felt deflated. It was the right thing to do. And yet, I'd no longer be waking up with a mane of hair between my fingers. Or a naked leg wrapped around my thigh. Or the scent of her perfume gassing me out in the best fucking way. I was selfish. A selfish cunt who wanted to take more pleasure from something that wasn't his to take.

I stood off to the side as I pushed open the bedroom door and allowed her to enter the room before me. Following her in, I clicked on the light switch off to the side of the door. Although there was one large glass windowpane opposite us that would let in a considerable amount of light during the day, it was currently dark out, and this side of the building overlooked another, so there wasn't as much light outside as there happened to be in the master bedroom or the living area during the evening. The only light came from apartments lower down. And I suppose, the walls too, given that I'd asked them to be painted in a greyish blue.

The thing about stepping in after her was I couldn't see her face. I internally cursed myself because I had no way of knowing if she liked the room and everything inside it. It wasn't what I imagined it to be myself. But it was evidently... all her.

"Do you like it?"

I looked over her head and around the room full of all the things I'd had shipped from Miami. And then I watched as she walked over to the double bed beside the window, lined with fresh white linen and full of different coloured scatter cushions.

Once she emptied her hands of the hangers, she turned to face me. I was taken back because... she was fucking frowning. Not one sign of a smile on her face.

Immediately, I mimicked her expression.

"This is my stuff," she stated.

I nodded.

"Like, my actual stuff."

I nodded again. "Except for the bed–that's new."

She walked to the end of the bed and stroked the tips of her fingers over the hood of her yellow ottoman. While she glanced between me and the rest of her belongings, I made my way to the walk-in closet and put the clothes I was holding inside with the rest of them I had shipped from Miami. And while I was there, I took and deep breath and gathered my thoughts. She hadn't known, but I'd agreed to it with her father and arranged a courier mid-week after I suffered sleeping beside her every night. It was a bit of a fuckery having to change the delivery address to the penthouse once the items were shipped, but money–it talks. I wasn't sure what I was expecting, but she had fewer items than I imagined she would. That went for clothes, accessories, shoes, furniture. Books and wall art. It seemed Blue

Sterling was a minimalist. But of the items of furniture she did own, they all happened to be colourful and buoyant.

"Perhaps you could put that ugly pink lamp somewhere in the corner," I suggested when I walked out of the closet.

She followed my line of sight to the almost empty corner, where a green chair sat beside a white desk. "The bulletin board was my idea. I figured it may come in handy for study purposes." I tipped my chin at the thick linen square above her desk.

"Walker."

"Our food will be here soon, so you better get the rest of your stuff in here quick, huh?"

She smiled.

Finally.

"Nate."

There was something about the way she said my name that made my chest yearn.

I drew my finger to the collar of my shirt and edged it away from my skin. "What?"

"Thank you. This is... was, completely unexpected."

Before I could reply, she'd taken three steps towards me and was rising on her tiptoes, her arms encasing around my neck in an embrace. For a moment, I stood stoic, but then her fingers threaded through the hair at my nape, and I found myself wrapping my arms around her waist.

We were hugging.

Fucking hugging.

And it would have been normal if just last night she wasn't riding my hand to the point of orgasm. If I hadn't touched myself to my dirty pipedream of her in the shower. If her lips weren't currently creeping closer and closer to my own.

When she brazenly kissed my mouth, and her soft, plump lips nestled against my own, I didn't protest. Her lips lingered, and her nose brushed mine, slow and tormenting. Our heated breath spanned between us, and I knew, I just knew, she wanted me to take from her like she just took from me. To give back some of what she was giving.

So I did.

I kissed her.

She kissed me.

And we stood there, embracing as we kissed. And I couldn't get enough. I couldn't get enough of *her,* and that was a big fucking problem.

When her lips grew more fierce, a low growl slipped from between my lips, and in one quick, measured movement, I gripped her hips almost too tightly and forced my tongue into her mouth. She didn't pull away to acknowledge me with words. She responded by tangling her fingers in my hair and pushing my head lower while lifting hers higher. And with each swipe of my tongue, she drew her body to mine. We were close. Close enough I felt her nipples pert against my chest. Close enough that I had no doubt she could feel my erection grow against her stomach. Yet somehow, I wanted to be closer. I wanted inside her. I wanted inside her more than I could remember ever wanting anything else—more than I wanted a life without solitude.

My hands trailed from her hips to her denim-clad ass, where I took two needy handfuls and squeezed. A moan left her mouth, one which I swallowed as she leapt up and wrapped her legs around my waist.

It was a lot.

Too much.

Absolutely not enough.

I spun us around, planting her down on her desk before easing away. As much as I wanted her, I was getting carried away. My hands gripped the back edge of the white wood as I compelled myself not to touch her. "Fuck, why are you so hard to resist?"

She smiled again, bigger, and gripped the desk by my waist as she leant forward to chase my lips.

I pulled back. "Blue. I want you. Fuck, do I want you. But this isn't right." I hated what I was saying. I hated how I felt utterly sane one moment, and then the next, I felt insane. And given the email I received from James today, with him handing over The Lagoon like a father would a son, it felt like the worst kind of betrayal.

"It feels right."

It did. In the same way it was wrong, it felt right. Despite thinking it, I couldn't seem to deny that.

Removing one hand from the desk, I ran it up the length of her back and wove it into her hair. "We need some distance. This—last night, your father, your age." I shook my head as the list grew, inclining her head back with the little grip I had on her hair. I wasn't able to articulate everything I wanted to say, nor the realness of how I felt. I'd never been one to speak so freely when it came to my feelings, but on the other hand, I'd not once in my whole fucking life been stumped for words.

She pouted, but in the same second, the light in her eyes dimmed, and she dropped her chin. "I get it."

"You do?"

I didn't get it. I didn't get why I was lusting over her or why things felt different with her than with my wife of eleven years. A kiss was a kiss. A fuck was a fuck. I didn't care for women above that. I didn't care because I'd witnessed how love ruined people and how easy love could be taken away.

Still, when she nodded and looked up at me with those blue-green eyes that could easily break hearts and said, "Yep," I didn't question it.

It was me who put a stop to it. And for once, she didn't sass me. She just accepted it, dropping her chin as I loosened my grip on her hair. And then, with no time to think about how I'd ease us back into who we were before the kiss, my phone rang from the pocket of my trousers.

"Chinese."

Maybe it was perfect timing.

The distraction we both needed.

An out of an awkward conversation.

I remained standing between her legs, my stomach in knots and my cock the only thing hungry, but slipped my phone from my pocket and hit the answer button. "Send it up."

When I hung up, Blue had a timid smile on her face. It made me want to kiss her again. But I wouldn't. I tore my eyes away from her mouth and stepped back, rearranging myself from the outside of my slacks. And when I heard the distant sound of the elevator opening, I made my way out of the room, promising myself I would never touch her again. Yet wishing–shit–*wishing* like fuck that I could.

CHAPTER FIFTEEN

Blue

I SAT in the salon's chair with my phone in hand, reading through the numerous happy birthday messages my friends had sent the night before, while the stylist finished straightening my freshly coloured hair. I ignored the incoming call from my father as I browsed, and my lips turned down when I realised I still had nothing from Walker. Not that he had any reason to text when in just a matter of hours I'd see him again. But after last night, when we ate our Chinese with nothing but a "Do you like it?" and a "Yeah" passed between us, I guess I was left with a sour taste in my mouth.

The night ended abruptly once we'd finished our takeout, and when he went to his room, I went to mine. As suspected, when I woke up this morning, his empty protein shake was in the sink, and he'd already worked out and left for work. It was

Finley who came up to the penthouse with a bouquet of white roses, wishing me a happy birthday. And it was Finley who ushered me downstairs and into his BMW.

With instructions from Walker, he drove me to Mayfair, where I shopped religiously in Balmain. It was fun, yet lonely. Freeing, yet repressive.

Actually, I wasn't entirely sure how I felt. I'd always imagined that turning eighteen would make me feel more of an adult, when up until now, almost every day of my life had reminded me of my childhood. And those thoughts festered as I purchased two dresses for tonight's dinner and the event Friday.

The festering only leered me to want to make a statement. Something that said I was all woman. Grown. An adult. That the past was the past, and today was another core memory towards my future. Because of that, I settled on a metallic green mini dress with a plunging neckline for dinner, and for fight night, I purchased a short black leather dress which left little to the imagination.

I had to ask myself if I was doing this for Walker's attention. But regardless of me falsely agreeing with his admission yesterday–that he wanted me, but it wasn't right–I wasn't going to dwell. It was one thing attempting to persuade my father into doing what I wanted; it was another when it came to a man I'd barely known for a week and a half. As crazy as it seemed, our brief time together felt like nothing, when in his presence, I felt the strange familiarity of knowing him my entire life. Perhaps that was the hopeless romantic in me. Or an illusion of the broken shards of my memory that I'd never entirely pieced together.

Half the day later, dressed in my metallic green minidress, my hair pin-straight, and my make-up simple yet sexy, Finley pulled the car up outside a luxury restaurant not so far from the penthouse. With my feet inside my Loubigirl heels, he took my hand and helped me from the front seat.

"You look magnificent," he told me as I righted myself on the pavement with a thank you and a smile.

"I don't think anyone has ever called me magnificent before."

He gave me a friendly wink, wished me a lovely time, and then I was on my way up a set of marble steps, either side of me encased by tall green vines. Once I reached the door, I gripped my clutch bag and made my way inside. My eyes scanned just how busy the restaurant was, a flutter of nerves filling my stomach.

Standing at the entrance of the restaurant, I waited to be acknowledged. Or at least spotted by Walker. But looking around the tables in view, full of people dressed exceptionally well, I didn't spot him anywhere.

My attention was stolen when the maître d' greeted me, her hazel eyes and brown hair darkened further by the ambient lighting and greenery surrounding us. "Welcome to The Grant. Do you have a reservation?" Her smile seemed genuine. Kind, even. And she didn't attempt to rush me when I found myself lost for words. Assuming Walker was there somewhere, I swallowed back my nerves and nodded.

She clicked something on the tablet in her hand and then blinked at me, expectant yet completely at ease.

"Name, please?"

Shit. Did I give her my name or Walker's?

Before I could answer, I felt a presence behind me and the warmth of a palm on my lower back. Even through the material of my dress, I could feel the heat of Walker's skin. Butterflies took off through my body from his touch alone, replacing the nerves in my stomach with something more giddy. Subtly, I took a breath between my parted lips, and then his lips were against my ear.

"Happy birthday, brat. Sorry, I'm late."

As hot as he'd made me only a moment ago, a chill now floated down my spine. He couldn't have known, but I'd grown fond of the nickname. Whether he meant it as an endearment or not was still to be decided, but it beat *kid*.

"Mr Walker." She smiled up at the man behind me as if he wasn't a stranger. "It's been a while, Mr Walker. Are you here with–"

"Blue Sterling," he said with a tone I couldn't decipher.

I hadn't looked at him yet, and as eager as I was, I wanted to wait until we were seated, hoping I'd have calmed my racing heart and pulled myself together. Why was it that a public dinner with him felt so... so... intimate? We hadn't even sat down yet. And it's not like it was a date. He was being kind, taking me out for a birthday dinner, knowing I had no one else in London besides him to spend it with. There were no friends or family to celebrate, what with my father in Miami, distant relatives abandoned, and my mother... dead. If she were here... If she were alive and my parents were still married... I wondered how we'd celebrate my eighteenth. I wondered if I'd have grown up in London. I wondered if I'd have been the same Blue I was today. Would I have been a little less broken and a lot more whole? Would me and Walker have met in different circumstances? Would we have met at all?

My hand crept to my neck and clawed at the ghostly restraint around my throat. All the what ifs seemed to restrict air from flowing into my lungs. The atmosphere around me was so dry and irritable, I was surprised I hadn't choked on it.

Walker's hand on my lower back, rubbing circles with his thumb, helped me regain some sort of composure. Did he know? Did he understand? Did he read into my thoughts as if I'd spoken them aloud?

I blinked out of my stupor, noticing the maître d' opening

and closing her mouth, looking over my shoulder to Walker and then down at the computer tablet in her hand. Then, nodding to no one in particular, she swiped a pen over its screen. Time felt slow, but I was aware it had barely been minutes. That was the thing about anxiety. Though life seemed to continue on around me, it often felt like I was stuck in a box. A box I was unable to completely crawl out from.

"You happen to have the best seats in the house tonight," she told us.

She led us to a table in the far corner of the restaurant, a more secluded spot beside a bifold door that looked out into the darkening sky. Walker pulled out my chair for me, and I obliged him by sitting down.

Still a little on edge, I told him, "Thank you." Yet, I wasn't ready to look at him. Too apprehensive about what I might find in his gaze. And perhaps a little nervous that whatever was going on between us was, in fact, really gone.

I heard him sit down in his seat opposite, but instead of looking up at him, I turned in my chair, glancing outside the window. It was beautiful–a path of white marble which led to a fountain. Except, at a closer glance, I realised the fountain wasn't a fountain at all.

It was a fire.

I spun around so fast in my seat, my knee bumped the table and the cutlery rattled against the cloth.

"Breathe easy, Blue."

I didn't have to look at him to know he was concerned.

"I'm breathing."

"Not easy."

Blinking slowly, I took a deep breath and found something to focus on that didn't remind me of my mother. That didn't make me wonder the what ifs. That didn't make me wonder more of why or have me seeking solutions to questions without answers and answers without questions, like that dredged night when I was three.

Dryness lined my throat as I stared at the table and asked, "Why is the table set for three?"

And then, I was three again, and all I heard was the faint sound of Walker rising from his chair before everything went dark.

I woke to the sound of a horn—my body stiffening when a hard thud hit our car. My lips parted in a scream, and as we skidded across the road, I felt something wet against the side of my face. Thunder sounded, and I was hanging upside down from my car seat. With bunny's ear still clutched in my little hand, his legs touching the roof, I screamed for my mummy, who sat silently in the front seat. When I looked back down at my bunny, he wasn't pink anymore—he was red. I turned my head to the side, and all I saw was the upside-down face of a boy, punching his bloody fist through the broken glass of my window.

My body trembled, but only when I felt fingers under my chin and light returning inside my wet eyes did I finally allow myself to look at Walker, who was no longer seated in front of me but crouched at my side.

"Hey." He swallowed noticeably. "Where did you go just now?"

From the shadow of facial hair against his perfect jaw to his lazy styled chocolate hair, I forced myself to forget about the flames burning not so far behind me, about the memory that probably wasn't an accurate recollection. About the innocent child I used to be or the woman I could have been if only things had panned out differently.

Instead, I focused my attention on him. I allowed his eyes to take me someplace else. The green and brown were so prominent, so alluring, that I barely noticed the crinkles lining either edge or the usual frown glued to his forehead.

"They're staring at you," he murmured. "You look... exceptional."

I looked back up at him with a smirk of my own. "Exceptional? Finley said I looked magnificent. Is the word beautiful no longer in a gentleman's vocabulary?"

He bit back his full bottom lip, his thumb pausing and pressing into my skin as his eyes darted from my cleavage to my mouth. His eyes lingered there for a moment before he met my gaze again. "You wouldn't consider me a gentleman if I told you what I really thought, and considering you lost yourself just then, it's better that I keep it to myself."

As he stood and rounded the table back to his seat, a waiter appeared and popped the cork on a bottle of champagne. Walker kept his eyes on me while my own followed the waiter. He filled my glass with champagne, and only when he went to fill Walker's glass did Walker shake his head. "No thanks. I'm good with water." And then he gestured to the third table placement. "We won't be needing these."

My heart jerked, dropping into my stomach, although my lips twitched simultaneously. I was a ball of emotions. On edge, yet delighted. And then, I felt confused as the waiter set the champagne bottle down on the table and took away the third cutlery set. Because... "Wait. You're not drinking?"

"Nope. It's your birthday. You get to have all the fun tonight."

"Are you babying me, *Mr Walker?*"

He dropped his head to the side and studied me, his finger running down the handle of his knife. "I'm just taking care of my asset," he said with a smirk, and then, in a second breath, "There's one guess how the night would end if the two of us were intoxicated."

"With me under you?" I took a sip of my champagne, staring at him over the edge of my glass.

His jaw ticked. "When it comes to restraint, you make me lose it."

Of course, he hadn't denied it. How could he? Our sexual chemistry was unquestionable.

I finished off the rest of my glass, only to fill it again.

"Steady. You haven't eaten anything yet."

"Two glasses of champagne are hardly going to do any damage now, are they?"

He'd know.

We were in a silent stare off when the waiter appeared back at our table, placing my meal in front of me. Pulling my eyes away from Walker, I looked down at the food in front of me in question.

"We're not having a starter?"

He hiked an eyebrow. "Did you want a starter? I didn't think you'd be too hungry with how much food you ate last night."

"The chow mein was delicious," I agreed.

He moved his gaze from me to his plate as the waiter set it down in front of him. "Tonight's a set menu. Lamb loin with caramelised onions and rhubarb compote." Holding out a finger to the waiter, they both waited patiently for the answer I was yet to give.

"Are we having dessert?"

"It's your birthday. If you want dessert, baby, you can have dessert."

Realising his accidental endearment, he cleared his throat and tipped his chin at the waiter beside him, taking my question for what it was and giving the man permission to leave us to dine in peace.

He didn't mention the endearment once we were alone. And he didn't apologise or proclaim he'd never meant to say it. He simply picked up his cutlery and dug into his meal, watching me under his eyelashes as I did the same to him.

"Baby?" I spoke under my breath.

Little did he know, I'd be his baby. I was beginning to believe I'd be his anything if he'd let me. Though perhaps that's where it was all going wrong, because given our situation, I didn't think he wanted me to be his.

CHAPTER SIXTEEN

Walker

IT WAS an accidental slip of the tongue. Still, I'd said it. My only saving grace was it wasn't the first time I'd called her that, so instead of correcting myself, I only smirked.

"I wouldn't have chosen to dine here," I told her as I sliced into my lamb loin.

"What?"

"Your father had already made this reservation. He was supposed to be here tonight. Have you heard from him today?"

"The third placement?"

As I chewed my food, I studied her face. She seemed somewhat disappointed. Had he not called her and wished her a happy birthday? I looked to where the placement was and then to the opposite side, where a fourth was supposed to be. James must have called ahead to eradicate his place before he emailed me yesterday. Why hadn't I considered that when it came to Sophia's? Not thinking forward only pushed me to lie. And for reasons unbeknownst to me, I didn't particularly enjoy lying to the girl sitting in front of me. Admittedly, I was a wanker, asking for her truth when I couldn't give her mine.

"Yes."

She rolled her eyes, cutting into her lamb loin with force much more potent than I had. "God, I'm so stupid."

My frown deepened. "What makes you say that?"

"I knew this was a kind gesture. But I thought it was your kind gesture. Not my father's."

"I never said I wouldn't have celebrated your birthday with you. I said that I wouldn't have chosen to dine here." I looked over my shoulder, recognising some of the guests. "At this particular restaurant."

The disappointment in her eyes wavered. There was a possibility it was there because her father hadn't called her or taken a flight over for her birthday. Perhaps she'd felt neglected somehow. But then I realised it was there because of me. For some reason, like when I lied, the idea of disappointing her only made me disappointed in myself. It was a new feeling. Something I hadn't felt in a long time. And weirdly, although perhaps a little fucked up, it was something I wanted to feel more of. An ache that felt better than the usual resentment or nothing at all.

"Where would you have taken me?" she asked.

"Where would you have wanted to go?"

She looked around us, raising a neatly shaded brow. "Is this not your scene? I was under the impression you came here a lot. The maître d' remembered your name."

I placed down my knife and fork. Talk of being here, of the memories with Sophia, had me quickly losing my appetite. "I've spent a lot of money here, yeah. But my scene... nah." I picked up my napkin and dabbed my mouth before refocusing on her.

"This isn't about me. I'm asking you, birthday girl. Where would you have wanted to go?"

"I'm not sure. I don't know London the way you do."

"What if you weren't in London? If you were back home, how would you be celebrating?"

"Well," she said slowly. "Usually, my dad would take me out for a birthday dinner. A lot like this one." She tucked her hair behind her ear. "Just us."

I encouraged her to go on, sitting back in my chair as she spoke.

"He'd try to make it special, but given that, he'd always try so hard to bring up my... my... *mother*. How proud she'd be of me. Of how alike we were in our mannerisms. How every year, and the older I got, I became more and more like her." She frowned. "It's not that I didn't care. I just..."

"Didn't–don't–want to remember," I finished.

She nodded, her eyes glossing over. "My last memory of her haunts me. I can't speak to him because he makes me feel like something is wrong with me, and I don't want to feel like something is wrong with me. I don't want to feel the way I do. I've opened up in the past, and look how that played out. He gave me a curfew and attempted to control my entire life."

Between guilt and wanting to reach out and comfort her, I didn't know what to do with my hands. So, even while sitting, I slid them into the pockets of my slacks.

"Anyway," she went on, a small smile framing her mouth. "I'd spend the following evening with Ebony–"

"Ebony?"

"My best friend. And we'd go to Pizzahole, where usually we'd try our hands at bribing Donny into buying us a bottle of wine from the nearest off-licence. My father assumed I was having a sleepover, or maybe he allowed me to break the rules after he experienced some guilt for making me sad on my birthday. But it was probably the only occasion he didn't question my whereabouts. The only time he let me out past my curfew."

I heard everything, but the only question to leave my lips was, "Who's Donny?"

"Donny's the guy who owns Pizzahole. It's this tiny outdoor restaurant. He has this little brick building with a hole in the wall. I swear, he cooks the *best* pizzas."

Her smile was contagious, but I didn't like the idea of some guy called fucking *Donny* buying her alcohol when she was underage. I was a teenager once. I knew the excitement that came with underage drinking. The rush of the occasional pill before I was forced to grow up. But getting pissed at some lousy fucking hole in the wall in the middle of Miami? Doing fuck knows what? When she looked like that, and everything about her screamed wealth? And James, one night of the year, allowed it?

I shook my head.

"So what you're telling me is that, even though you're here, in one of London's finest restaurants with me, you're wishing for pizza from some manky hole in the wall with fucking *Donny?*"

The sweetest laugh escaped her for the first time since she'd been here. I wanted more of it. In fact, as quick as it came and left, I craved to rewind the moment and hear it again despite what I said being completely unfunny.

"No, not at all. That's me telling you what I did. Given the choice, I have no idea what I'd want to do."

"I'm giving you the choice, Blue," I said, remaining nonchalant. I took my hands from my slacks and leant forward, placing my elbows on the table as I stared down at her full plate. "I don't know a Donny, but if you want pizza, we can go and get pizza."

I'm sure she presumed I was joking, as she tilted her head to the side and looked at me inquisitively.

"I don't want pizza. I'm enjoying this."

"You haven't taken one bite of your food."

She poked her fork into a cut of her lamb and brought it to her mouth. "Happy now?"

"If you are."

With that, we continued to eat, and the two of us finished off our meal within five minutes. That was the thing about fine dining. The portion sizes were child-like. Maybe I should have pre-ordered a starter after all. But the truth was, I didn't want to be in this restaurant longer than necessary. Not with it being a regular spot between Sophia and me. And with Blue filling her glass with her third champagne, I was beginning to grow antsy. I wasn't sure if it was because I was dying for a drink or because I didn't want her to get drunk. But I did want her to enjoy her birthday, which was why I didn't stop her. Which was why I didn't drink.

Either way, she was much safer drunk in my presence than at some outdoor pizza restaurant with fucking *Donny*.

"How old is this guy?" I asked after the waiter collected our empty plates. I tried not to sound jealous or angry over a guy I knew nothing of, but I'm not entirely sure I convinced her.

"Donny?" Her eyes shot up to her forehead. "He's... He has grandchildren. Why do you keep saying his name like that?"

That should have settled me, but it didn't.

I ignored her question. "Back home, he's brought you alcohol when you've asked him?"

"God, no." She grinned. "No matter how hard we batted our lashes or pleaded, he would always refuse. It usually resulted in Ebony doing something... stupid." Her grin became something curious. "The thing is, me and Ebony are total opposites. She likes to break the rules, whereas I tend to follow them. Unless..." She dipped her head, hiding her growing blush.

"Unless what?"

"Unless I don't care about the consequences." When she

lifted her chin, my eyes absorbed that cherry blossom blush that ran down her neck and into her cleavage. That's where I had to drag my eyes away from when our waiter appeared beside her once again and set down our trio of desserts. Lucky for me, she was too intrigued by her food to notice.

"Chocolate torte, pavlova, and a lemon cheesecake," he said before leaving us.

Blue licked her lips and picked up her spoon, diving straight for the lemon cheesecake. When she placed it in her mouth, the quietest moan spilt between her lips. I wanted to taste that lemon on her tongue, but I promised myself I'd never devour her kisses again. They were bad for me, and like hot water on an ice cube, they melted away my purpose.

"So, so good."

I swallowed, doing the same, and then I agreed with a hum of my own. Though if she were to look at me too intently, I'd be worried that it'd be obvious that my enjoyment wasn't for the dessert at all, but for her.

Jealousy, anger, disappointment, lust, empathy, and optimism–every emotional neuro in my brain, seemed to be fighting all for her.

I HELD my palm over Blue's lower back as we stepped out of the restaurant, and using my free hand, stole her phone from her grip as she took a selfie for "the gram."

"I left my phone at the office rushing to get here," I explained. "I'm letting Finley know his services aren't required this evening." And then, texting one-handed, I sent Finley a message to say I'd be driving us back to the penthouse.

I had every suspicion that he'd be trailing behind my car to make sure I didn't swerve into the wrong lane, worried for Blue's safety. But that wasn't going to happen, considering I hadn't touched a drop of alcohol in over forty-eight hours. I fucking felt the withdrawal of it too. Irritability seemed to be infusing my body like the onset of a virus, and my body temperature only seemed to increase by the hour. If Blue noticed my distress, she didn't mention it. My suit was making me claustrophobic, and I couldn't wait to get the thing off. Formal wear wasn't much my style, but as it went, it attained me a lot more respect than my sweats.

Handing back Blue her phone, we waited for all of sixty seconds before the valet drove my G-wagon out front. I gave him a tip in return for my keys, and then we were on our way.

As I drove through the streets of London, I noticed Blue seemed to lose some of the spark she had throughout dinner, and for some fucking reason, it had me scowling. She'd barely spoken, but I could feel her mind moving a mile a minute. I could hear her even when she wasn't speaking. Because though I had no idea of her thoughts, they were making noise. And like hearing static through an old radio, it only irked me further.

"What's wrong?" I asked, glancing between her and the road.

Other than the lights on the dashboard, the car was dark, but that didn't disguise how her freshly coloured hair shone like the fucking moon. Which, as it turned out, was full tonight. A clear sky–rare as fuck when you lived inside the polluted city of London.

"Nothing's wrong," she mused. "I was just thinking."

"About…"

"What you said at dinner. When you asked me what I would have done for my birthday if I had the choice."

"You said you enjoyed dinner."

"I did," she sassed. "Obviously."

"But?" I encouraged, extending my question.

She tipped her head so she could face me better. As much as

I wanted to give her my full attention, I knew I had to be mindful of the road, so I returned my line of sight to the windshield before she spoke, conscious of the traffic lights.

"It's not really me, I guess. I like dressing up to go places. I like buying clothes and getting my hair done, and I like everything a girl like me should like. But dinner in a lavish restaurant, that's not really who I am underneath all that, is it?"

I noticed her poking at her fancy white manicure in my peripheral, and upon taking a heavy breath, I asked, "Are you asking me that, or yourself?"

As I indicated towards The Lagoon, she lifted her shoulder and then dropped her chin onto it, smiling gently. "Did you mean it?" she asked. "When you said you were giving me the choice to go somewhere else. To get pizza."

"If I didn't mean it, I wouldn't have said it."

She returned to face the windshield, her smile still intact, and still a little tipsy from her three glasses of champagne, I realised. The moment she discovered we weren't heading back to the penthouse, her smile only grew.

Though as soon as I rolled up at The Lagoon, parked in the staff parking lot, and told her to wait inside the car while I grabbed my phone, her cheeks hollowed and she formed a pout.

"Can't I come with you?"

I unfastened my seat belt and shook my head as I told her, "No." Only as I climbed out of the car and walked ahead, so did she. Exasperated, I turned to her and said, "Get back in the car, Blue."

She strode up beside me, but as I pushed a hand into my pocket, she went and took me completely off guard by linking her arm through mine. I looked down at our new position with confusion as she said, "No can do. I'm choosing to come with you."

My jaw ticked, but I couldn't argue with her when she was

using my own words against me. "In and out," I said. "Then we're going home." I realised it was the first time I'd called the penthouse "home," but whether it was home or not was still to be decided.

Once I'd locked my car, I withdrew my metallic keycard from my wallet and we both waltzed inside the elevator before travelling up to the floor of my office. Unfortunately for me, Blue didn't seem to take my "In and out" too literally, because by the time I'd grabbed my phone and we'd made our way back into the lift, she was pressing the small black button labelled 'R' and asking, "Where does this go?"

I rubbed my cheek on a sigh and then looked to the ceiling. "To the roof."

The elevator carried us up, and within seconds, the doors were opening on top of the building. As well as the elevator, a metal door separated the roof from us, but it was noticeably open, which implied Noah had been up here recently and hadn't locked it behind him.

I'd never understand it, but my little brother had a thing for heights.

Blue's heels tapped against the metal path of the roof as she walked ahead of me. It wasn't the full expansion of the roof, so to speak, but a pathway that wrapped around the perimeter of the building. The only barrier between the path and thin air was a one metre metal fence, but it was safe enough, providing we kept enough distance between us and the edge. Not so much if you were drunk–which was why I was mentally cursing Noah in my head. If we weren't careful, anyone from the building could get up here and fall to their fucking death. And the last thing we needed was an inquiry.

Stuck in my head, I stood watching Blue as she swung her head around to mine with a smile, and the wind softly blew the skirt of her dress higher up her thighs. My feet only moved from their position when I noticed her moving further and further to the edge of the roof. No, she wasn't drunk-drunk, but she had had three glasses of champagne tonight. I convinced myself everything I was about to do next was for her safety, and not because I wanted to be near her.

As she leant over the fence to get a look at the world around us, I gripped both her hips and saddled up behind her, and then, without any deliberation, wrapped my arms around her waist to hold her still. I was aware the gesture could be considered intimate, that I was giving her mixed messages, but she didn't even attempt to withdraw.

"The view is amazing," she said. "Better than your penthouse."

For the first time, I took my eyes away from her and looked up. First, at the moon, and then to the city of London and the bright lights which surrounded us. It was the first time I'd really taken it in, because I hadn't been on the roof in, well... maybe years.

"Yeah," I said, lowering my cheek against her temple. "I guess it is."

"The world is so busy, isn't it?" she murmured. "But up here, it kind of feels like there's no one else in the world but us."

I wasn't sure how to respond.

Talking so openly didn't come as naturally to me as it did her.

Her head fell against my shoulder as she breathed in a lungful of air and raised her chin to meet my stare. "You have a faraway look in that gaze of yours," she murmured.

My lips twitched. "I do, huh?"

I dropped my eyes to her lips as the corner of her mouth rose in a smile. And suddenly, I was reminded of how just yesterday, I'd felt those luscious lips against mine. If there was no one else in the world but us, I knew without a doubt I wouldn't be holding myself back as hard as I was.

Her lashes fluttered with some sass. "Yeah, you do."

"And you'd know something about that? That faraway look?"

Now she was looking at my mouth, and it seemed we were moving closer and closer to a line I forbid myself to cross again. I swallowed, hard. And then, forcing clarity, I pulled back and squeezed her hip in warning.

"Blue," I sighed softly.

"I know, I know. This isn't right." She repeated my words from yesterday with a roll of her eyes. And then, moving away from me, she wrapped her hands against the top of the metal fence and squeezed. "What did you do on your eighteenth birthday?"

I'd moved my line of sight to the floor, but looked up to answer her question. "Pretty sure I got so fucked up I had a three-day hangover."

I cringed at the memory, but that three-day hangover wasn't shit when I compared it to the way I lived nowadays.

"Do you have those now?" she asked, and I raised an eyebrow in confusion.

"Hangovers," she clarified.

I palmed my jaw, refusing to answer the question. Every day felt like a fucking hangover, but she was too innocent for me to unleash the weight of that, so I told her, "No."

She looked at me then, in a way like she knew more of me than I let on, but I didn't want things to get any deeper. It was her fucking birthday–we happened to be on the roof of The Lagoon–and since dinner, she only seemed to be shrinking more and more into herself. Into her head.

Wanting to bring back the Blue I knew was in there, I took my phone from my pocket and pulled up the only playlist I had on there. It was my gym playlist, but what the fuck, who cared. I hit shuffle, and placed my phone down at our feet, letting chance lead the way. Just because I didn't believe in fate didn't mean I couldn't pretend for the three minutes it would take for the song to finish. Just because I didn't believe in happy ever afters, didn't mean I couldn't relish in the vision of there being nobody in the world but us.

"It's your birthday," I said as the opening verse of *Chainsmoking* by Jacob Banks began to play. "Don't girls like you like to dance on their birthdays?"

One hand unclenched from the fence as she turned her body to mine, her blue eyes alight with something that reached into my stomach and twisted my gut. I held out my hand for her to take, and ever so gently, she linked her fingers through mine. Despite the late-night chill in the air, her skin was warm against my own. And as much as I wanted to stay in the position we were in–face to face, and almost chest to fucking chest–it felt too personal. We couldn't risk another accidental touch of our lips. We just couldn't.

So, with that, I spun her around and held her. With my arm around her waist, one palm flat against her stomach, and the other to her hip, I nestled behind her.

Within seconds, we were moving, our bodies in sync.

I never fucking danced, but insanely, this girl had me honing against her like it was something I'd done countless times before.

She moved her body with mine, lowering the hand I held in hers to the skin of her thigh and hiking up the material of her dress as the words of the song rose from the ground and vibrated through every part of our being.

Something about chain-smoking–something about love.

The meaning was easy to digest, but it wrestled with my core just the same.

When she pushed her ass back against my growing cock and

the vocalist said something about it getting harder to breathe, I felt the sincerity of the lyrics squeeze all the air from my lungs.

She knew I was hard for her.

There was no way she couldn't.

She continued to trail my hand up her thigh, under her dress, and to the edge of what felt like laced underwear. My palm floated across her skin like butter, which only made the battle to pull away that much harder. I was internally kicking myself when I squeezed her hip with my free hand in warning. I got the reaction I hoped for, because she did the right thing and eased off.

There was only so much restraint a man like me could hold on to, so when the song finished, I loosened my hold on her and picked up my phone, exiting the playlist before another song could start.

Focusing on my phone, I said, "What else do girls like you like to do on their birthdays?"

When she didn't respond, I gave in to the temptation and slowly lifted my head. I don't know what I expected, but as I met her gaze, the twinkle in her irises was most definitely not it.

"I think girls like me like watching movies," she answered with a newfound confidence.

I took a deep breath to slow my heart rate as I straightened, reminded of the night she fell asleep against me on the sofa. But nonchalant with my words, my only response was, "I'm good with that."

She looked at me then, like she knew what I was thinking because she was thinking it too. But she didn't say anything, and a second later, she took off in the direction of the door, her words moving with her. "I'm choosing this time."

I followed after her. "That right?" And I tried my absolute best, but apparently it wasn't good enough, because I still couldn't pull my gaze from her legs as she strutted ahead of me.

Not until she looked at me over her shoulder, and that smile of hers directed my attention to her face.

"Yep," she quipped.

That smile of hers turned knowing.

"No more ghost shit."

WE ARRIVED AT THE PENTHOUSE, and I led Blue from the garage and into the elevator with a hand on her back. With it being her birthday, I didn't have it in me to decline her decision to watch a film. I was beginning to think that this girl could ask me for anything, and the only way I'd feel content was if I obliged.

"I'm going to take a quick shower and change into something comfy," I said, ecstatic to be removing my suit.

"Sure. I'll find something for us to watch."

And with that, I left her alone in the dimmed room, forcing myself to stay clear of the kitchen cupboard and away from my favourite bottle of booze.

It didn't take me long to scrub myself free of my withdrawal–I'd done well forcing myself to not think about it. But by the time I'd showered, towel-dried my hair, and changed into a casual T-shirt and grey sweats, I came back into the living room to the sounds of a movie already playing.

"Didn't want to wait for me, huh?"

The volume was so low I was taken aback when she didn't turn around at the sound of my voice or my footsteps moving across the floor and towards her.

Observing her from the head of the sofa, I realised her eyes were closed and she was fast asleep. And as I watched the slow rise and fall of her chest, I couldn't help but notice for the first time tonight that when putting her dress on, she'd forgone her fucking bra. I couldn't help but notice how her perky tits were almost falling out of her birthday dress. All sinfully angelic and tempting as fuck. So fucking captivating it made it hard not to stop and stare.

I visualised the last time she'd fallen asleep on my sofa–on my chest–where she'd woken up abruptly from a bad dream. A small part of me was expecting the same thing now, especially where her head took her at the restaurant. The way she spoke on the roof about the world being busy.

But there was no thunder tonight.

Nothing here to remind her of the accident.

Not unless she suddenly remembered me.

My feet took backwards steps towards the kitchen, and while my eyes flicked between her and the kitchen cupboard, I absently felt around for my favourite bottle before pulling it towards me and uncapping its lid. A voice in my head told me I had to stop this. I had to stop reaching for the bottle any time I felt a strain. But another voice said it wasn't hurting me. That the throbbing behind my eyes would disappear with every drop.

I knew if I drank enough of it, I'd feel the relief I craved.

And that was why the second voice always won out.

The first voice needn't bother to convince me at all.

I took a small swig as I made my way back towards the sofa with the rim against my mouth, feeling a small amount of comfort as it sank into my stomach. And again, I helped myself to another taste of the sweet liquid before lowering the bottle to my side. My head dropped to the left as I stood at the end of the cushions, studying Blue sleep while my cock twitched beneath my sweats, begging for the attention of my hand.

She rolled onto her back, and my gaze was drawn to her lips as they parted in a dreamy sigh. A few seconds later, her arms stretched above her head. I watched, transfixed on her, as her back arched with the movement, which made the material across her chest part, giving me the near-perfect view of her tits. They were creamier than her tanned neck, her tanned legs, and I found myself wondering what other parts of her body hadn't been touched by the sun. Shit, maybe hadn't been touched by anyone.

I muttered a quiet "Fuck" and palmed my cock with my free hand over the material of my sweats. My feet were rooted to the spot, unable to drag myself away even though it was the most rational thing to do. And as one of her arms came down from above her head, her hand trailing the length of her dress, my whole body only grew tenser.

Her lips parted, her hips raised, and then her hand sank ever so gracefully underneath the hem of her dress and into her panties.

What I now knew to be black laced panties.

It was like she'd known I was there, battling with my feet to move and my cock to relax as I regretfully soaked in everything that was her.

My jaw ticked.

Was she aware of how badly I wanted her? Was this another attempt at threatening me? Seemed I did well to encourage her the last time. Hadn't I played into what she wanted? Did she think because it was her birthday, I'd give in?

"Blue, if you're fucking–" My sentence came to a pause when I noticed movement inside her underwear. I groaned. She was touching herself. Rubbing her little pink pussy in her sleep while I lurked over her.

What the fuck was I doing still standing here?

I'd told myself we couldn't do this.

My fingers itched around the neck of my Bourbon. This time I wasn't sure if it was because I wanted another taste or because I wanted to round the sofa, push my hand into her panties and thrust my fingers into her pretty pussy. And I bet it was pretty. So fucking pretty and wet for my cock.

Fuck. Fuck. Fuck.

Equal parts guilt and pleasure travelled through my nerves and doused my skin with heat. I should've stepped away, forced my eyes closed and pretended this hadn't happened–that I wasn't a witness to this. This... torture.

But instead, I took one last hefty swig from my bottle before lowering it down onto the table, focusing my eyes on Blue's movements and the material of her underwear being disrupted by the motion of her hand. Completely entranced by the way she was pleasuring herself. Replacing one weakness for another.

An almost silent mewl travelled up her throat and between her lips. Suddenly, I found myself gripping the thickness of my cock through my sweats as I imagined her fingers strumming against her clit, remembering her face when I brought her to orgasm not so long ago.

It was fucking painful. My dick fucking hurt. I wanted to touch her. Take my cock out, bathe in her pleasure, spill my cum all over her body and mark my fucking territory like it was my right. But I couldn't. There was an inner turmoil I was in constant back and forth with. She was a stupid fucking teenage girl. Sort of. But still, too damn young for me, the daughter of my boss. The end to my abstract beginning. It was the same shit I was bored convincing myself of since she sat beside me on the plane.

Couldn't.

Wouldn't.

Definitely shouldn't.

But fuck, I'd never felt so weak.

"You're making me lose my mind, baby. And not in the way I'm used to."

I didn't think I was loud with my words, but her eyes blinked open and caught my own, right as I pushed my hand into my sweats and took my cock in my fist. The scent of her arousal filled the air, and I swear if the walls could speak, they'd ask me why the fuck I hadn't accommodated myself with her pussy yet. Why wasn't I pleasuring her and filling her with my cum?

"Nate," she murmured, grazing her teeth over her pink cushioned lips.

"You're awake." I cocked a brow, relaxing my shoulders as I held a stance that I hoped conveyed indifference, unconcerned that my cock was, in fact, in my fist.

Her hand didn't let up. If anything, the movement of her fingers grew quicker as a blush crept over her cheeks. My eyes told her I wanted to see that blush all over her naked body. But I held my cock in a chokehold as a means to keep myself grounded. This was wrong. So fucking wrong. Yet the cracks in my armour began to form with every little thing she did. Every move she made.

"Come here," she whispered. "I want you to touch me."

My voice was nothing more than a pained groan. "I can't."

"You can. I know you want to. I feel the way you look at me." As if to prove her point, she bucked her hips up and began riding her hand. "Right here. I feel it right here."

I felt a bead of pre-cum tickle the end of my cock while visions of me up close and personal with her pussy penetrated my mind. Licking my lips, I couldn't help but wonder what she tasted like. Sweet? The kind of taste a man like me couldn't get enough of?

"Fuck," I hissed, squeezing my cock again but refusing to give myself anything more. I couldn't enjoy this. Not in front of her.

Her eyes fell closed, and a soft moan poured from between her lips like hot air.

"Nate," she whimpered amongst these quiet little mewls of pleasure that I wanted against my ear. "I'm close."

My gaze hopped from her face to where her hand continued to bounce beneath the material of her shorts. "Yeah?"

"Yeah."

Her eyes were still pinched closed as she indulged in her pleasure. Her legs began to shake, her cheeks turning a brighter shade of pink. That's when I knew she was tethering on the edge, moments from slipping over.

My cock was so big and hard for her; I really believed I could come in my pants like a young boy watching the show of his teenage dreams. But then her eyes finally opened, settling on me.

"Are you hard for me, Nate? Will you show me?"

Fuck, this girl had some power over me. She was making me snap, minute by minute. It was rare anyone could tell me what to do, and she seemed to do it with ease. My cock throbbed, but her words sedated me. I was at the temple of Blue Sterling, moments from resisting the temptation and giving in to her glory.

Before I gave my guilt a chance to carry me away, I stepped towards her and took myself out of my sweats. Her thick black eyelashes fluttered over her cheeks, and then those blue-green orbs that I often found myself lost in dropped down to where my cock was wrapped in my fist as I began stroking myself with almost vicious strokes.

My blood ran hot, and I watched as a timid smile pulled on the corner of her mouth.

"Is this what you wanted?" I rasped, running my thumb over the head of my cock.

She licked her lips, and a glint shone in her eyes that told me *yeah*, it was exactly what she wanted. Except, as she watched me, she slowed on pleasuring herself, and the relief was bittersweet.

"Don't fall shy on me now," I warned her. "Put your fingers inside that pretty pussy. Imagine it's me."

Her lips parted on a soundless gasp, and I could hear her wetness from where I stood.

"Good girl," I murmured. "Such a good fucking girl."

Another moan travelled from her throat and trickled from her kissable lips at the compliment. Her hand moved again, and I imagined she was playing with her clit, unable to hold back any longer.

I smirked. "Yeah, that feels good, doesn't it baby?" As I said the words, she came, right then and there, looking like an angel but sinning like the fucking devil.

But I wasn't finished.

Because right then and there, I decided I wanted to sin too.

As if warning me to stop, I could hear the melodic tune of my phone ringing in the distance. But I was past the point of return, and this time, no chance was a fucking phone call going to stop me.

Looking at the cleavage spilling from her dress, I said, "Part your dress. It's my turn to see you."

She gnawed on her bottom lip as I continued stroking my cock. Only now, I was holding myself with a softness I'd never got off on before. As I looked down at her before me, the slow removal of her hand leaving her underwear and the glistening of arousal on her delicate fingers, I wanted to remember every detail. I wanted to remember every moment so I could replay it again when the mood struck. So when she was gone, I could get myself off to the image of her, the thoughts of her, the fucking feel of her.

With unsteady fingers, she parted the material of green that barely covered her and revealed her breasts. My brows pinched, and before I knew what I was doing, I was leaning over her, holding myself up with one hand while I pumped my cock with the other.

"Your tits." I gave her a sideways glance, groaning at the sight. Her nipples were the perfect shade of pink.

I wanted to take one in my mouth.

Shit, I wanted more of this.

More of her.

She was still gnawing on her lip so hard I expected her to split it. But her gaze... her lustful gaze, was on my cock.

What was she thinking? Did she want it in her mouth?

Fuck. I wanted it in her mouth.

"Blue." I slapped my cock against her breast and watched as it bounced. "I'm about to come all over your tits. If you don't want that, then tell me to stop right fucking now."

She popped her bottom lip free, and then, like she knew exactly what would push me over the edge, brought a palm down to her chest and rolled a pert nipple between her fingers. "I want it, Nate."

Biting back a smirk, I felt my balls draw up, and then I squeezed the end of my cock. With two more tugs, I came all over her. Strokes of my cum covered her from her breasts to her chest, surrounded by skin that looked hot to touch with the faintest shine of perspiration. I think I may have even stained her pretty dress.

Jesus, I hadn't even fucked her, yet her body responded like I had.

She licked her lips, surprising me further by rubbing my cum into her skin. Turning my head back to hers, my semi-erect cock still held firmly in my hand, we locked eyes. I couldn't explain it, but it was at that precise moment I realised the multitude of my actions. As if I suddenly had some colossal epiphany. However, it seemed that the epiphany was still to be deciphered.

A hard lump formed in my throat as I tried to swallow, and my skin crawled with a combination that felt a lot like guilt seeping into undeniable pleasure. If I knew anything, it was a sure fact that the two didn't belong together. They felt immiscible, like oil and water.

"Shit," I cursed. "What the *fuck* is wrong with me?"

I FROWNED, watching his face wash with regret. He straightened, refusing to look at me as he tucked himself back into his sweats.

"Nate."

"No."

Flinching, I smoothed my dress over my breasts and pulled the hem down to cover my damp underwear.

He tossed his head back to the ceiling, the veins in his neck bulging with the movement. I found myself hyper-focused on them, wondering why he was fighting this so hard? Why couldn't he just accept that there was something between us?

"Nate. Please look at me."

He swallowed. "Don't call me that."

"Why?"

"Because you don't get to call me that," he bit out. "Because you don't get to come into my life and make me feel things I've never felt. Or care about things besides the things I already care about."

I sat up, swinging myself around to plant my feet on the floor as I looked up at him. "I think we have something worth exploring."

He snickered. "You have no idea what you're talking about."

"Don't belittle me."

He closed his eyes and ran a hand back through his dishevelled hair. "We can't happen. We're never going to be something that grows roots and flourishes."

I rolled my eyes. "Because you work for my father? Because of my age? Of our differences?"

"That and because I'm not who you think I am."

"Oh, please. Cry me a fucking river."

Tipping his chin down to maintain eye contact with me, he smirked, half-assed. "Does your daddy know his little princess has such a dirty mouth?"

"He isn't here. You are."

His jaw ticked, and then, with the same hand he'd brushed through his hair only moments ago, he held it out for me to take.

With my palm in his, he led me through the penthouse and then upstairs and into the large bathroom. The lights came to life as we entered, and then he let go of my hand to reach inside the shower. With a twist of the lever, water cascaded from the shower head. He turned back to me, eyes on my own. A silent question, one he needn't ask. The only sound to be heard was our controlled breaths and water hitting the tiled floor.

I bent down, slipping off my heels, and then stepped into him. Affliction could be read from his stare, but he held my eyes as his fingers trailed my collarbone, my shoulders, until he pulled down the metallic material of my dress and removed it from my skin. His eyes didn't waver from my face as I edged my underwear from my hips and arched to remove the flimsy lace once it dropped to my ankles. His want for me was evident as I climbed back onto the soles of my feet, his erection noticeable through the material of his sweats, ready to go again.

Unembarrassed, he held my gaze and then turned me around, encouraging me into the flow of the water.

I looked at him over my shoulder, his eyes not once falling to my body. He had more constraint than he realised.

"Are you joining me?"

He swallowed, then pulled the neck of his T-shirt over his head. I turned away, facing the shower to give him the privacy of undressing as the water cloaked me, washing away the evidence of his arousal from my breasts.

Moments later, he pressed his body against my back. His hard length nestled between us, my arousal reverberating through me once again. But as his head lowered and his lips pressed against my temple, and as his hands pulled tight around my waist, it felt like an intimate moment between lovers.

A moment, so he believed, never meant for the likes of us.

"The fuck are you doing to me, brat?"

My words were a whisper when I replied, "No more than you're doing to me."

CHAPTER SEVENTEEN

Blue

WITH LAST NIGHT pushed to the back of my mind and my day focused on work-based learning, the evening came fast. I stood with Olivia in front of the makeshift stage. It was weigh day, and although we'd captured images of The Lagoon's fighters' official weigh-in this morning, Olivia said this set-up was what made the difference between an average image and an Instagram-able post.

Music played through the room, which in turn, blurred the noise of the lively audience behind us. All the while, high-tech cameras broadcast the stage for their live streams.

The Lagoon was one night away from its prestigious fight night. Walker had been in full work mode. And Noah, every time I'd seen him, was either dabbling in business or pleasure. Though he was mostly flirting with the octagon girls in between running every errand imaginable for his brother. It seemed he did everything outside of the legalities, and he often did it all while attesting for The Lagoon's fighters the same way a coach would. Currently, he stood on the edge of the sponsorship stage, handing out bottles of blue liquid to every fighter which passed him.

"I thought you were going to stay put in your office for this one," I said to Walker as he came to stand at my side, primed in one of his many designer suits. I wasn't sure what version of him I enjoyed best.

This one.

The man flushed from a workout.

Or the man I had last night, in his white T-shirt and grey sweats.

"Things change."

"They do." I frowned. They had last night when something transpired between us during our shower. It never led to another sexual encounter, despite our bodies desperate for a second release. And we didn't need to speak about what transpired exactly to know something had. I was sure we both felt it more than we each let on, and I knew Walker wouldn't voice it, regardless. He'd probably fight it until he couldn't anymore. Until he was forced to tell me how he truly felt without using my age or father as an excuse.

We both watched the stage as the announcer, once again, through his microphone, called out the names of each under-card fighter and their opposition.

"Hudson's up soon," Walker told me as a fighter from the opposing team walked across the stage and stepped onto the scales. I knew this already, but I was under the impression he just wanted to speak to me.

From beside me, Olivia moved her camera away from her face to glance at us. Intrigue shone in her eyes, likely wondering why I'd stopped working, but without questioning me, she continued snapping photographs with her camera pointed towards the stage.

I smiled up at Walker and nodded encouragingly. "Hudson looks good, considering his injury. Noah said he's worked hard."

We already knew he'd made weight after his official weigh-in this morning, and he was back fighting fit, ready for fight night. The ceremonial weigh-in was more for the media and the fans than anybody else.

Walker slid his hands into his pockets, though he stood close enough for our arms to be touching. Something like jealousy stirred in my gut when I noticed his eyes were on the array of beautiful octagon girls dressed in tight black and white shorts and push-up bras.

"And you say I wear little clothes," I attempted to joke, speaking quietly up at him over my shoulder. I regretted it as soon as I'd said it. But maybe he'd missed it with the noise of the crowd howling around us.

He turned his head back to me, his eyes piercing into my own. "What are you on about?"

Okay, so he heard me. I had no choice but to follow through.

"The girls," I said, a little embarrassed. "Until last night, they wore fewer clothes than I ever had in your presence."

A smirk pulled on the corner of his lips, and then his head was swivelling back to the stage. I don't know what it was–perhaps the uncertainty of what was happening between us–but I seemed to crave his attention, his acknowledgement, now more than I ever had since I'd been here.

I was itching to discuss things with him and talk through what happened. I was itching to talk about how things were changing between us. But with company around us, and the media at every angle, it wasn't the time or the place. It was an itch I couldn't scratch, not while surrounded.

"How much did Hudson have to lose to make weight?" I found myself asking when Olivia glanced another look at the two of us.

"He had five days to shed twenty pounds."

"No way."

My brows creased as I studied his face for any sign of a lie. But all I could take note of was the heaviness under his eyes and the contradictory excitement in his irises.

"I can feel you looking at me, Blue," he said dryly. "What's on your mind?"

It's you, I wanted to say. But... "I'm just thinking, how is that even possible? There were girls in my school who would kill for that kind of weight loss in that little time."

He flared his nostrils and turned to look at me, dropping his line of sight to my figure. My sleeveless crop top was tight against my chest, and my leather pants were taut against my waist, showing just a hint of tanned skin above them.

I'd showered with him last night. I'd felt his naked skin against my own. But he hadn't once looked at me in the way he was now–like he'd stop at nothing to protect me.

Not even my father had looked at me that way. No matter how many times he believed I was at breaking point.

It was different.

A look that said he wanted to take care of me, not that he *should.*

"Were you one of those girls?"

"No," I murmured. "Ebony, though..." I let my sentence trail off. Ebony was a fool for the latest fad diets or living off chewing gum and cola to shed pounds she didn't need to shed.

He lowered his lips to my ear. "Your body is unreal," he rasped. "It took everything in me last night to not take further advantage of it."

Time passed by before he lifted his head and turned back to

the stage and then back to me in quick succession. My heart was wild, my cheeks flushing pink as I clenched my thighs together.

He cleared his throat knowingly. "The fighters dehydrate themselves to lose most of their weight. It's about manipulating water and sodium levels. Putting your body in overdrive to flush the weight off."

Tucking my hair behind my ear and re-focusing on the importance of the conversation, I eyed a bottle of blue liquid that a fighter took from Noah. Walker followed my line of sight, and I wondered how the hell he managed to keep so composed after the things he had just said to me. Was he not hard from thinking of all the ways he could take advantage of me? Thinking of all the ways I'd let him?

"Liquid electrolytes."

"Those help put it back on after making weight?" I tried to take a leaf out of his book, feigning his careless stature, though the images in my mind were so far from careless.

He nodded. "One litre an hour until bedtime, plus a good portion of protein will give them a competitive advantage." Turning again to the stage, he murmured, "Hudson's up."

I'd been so invested in Walker, I'd barely taken any notice of the undercards or the replacement backup fighter I overheard Noah mention this morning. I mumbled a "Sorry" to Olivia, who still stood a small distance away. She smiled, shaking her head. I'm sure she was confused why the boss was giving me his attention when sports reporters were behind us desperate for it.

I turned around to look at them, noticing some eyes on us and some on the stage. Then, all at once, the announcer's voice robbed my attention, and the audience's noise fell behind me as I resumed my previous position.

"The main event takes place in the welterweight division. Ladies and gentlemen, let's introduce the challenger to the stage... Hudson "Bully Boy" Barnes!"

Walker tipped his chin at me. "You good?"

I rolled my eyes mockingly and told him, "Yep."

And as I did, his gaze fell to my mouth before he caught himself and looked back to the stage.

My heart hammered.

I wondered if he wanted to kiss me again. I wondered if he thought about the kiss in my room as much as I had. Or.... was he thinking about the roof... about last night?

I forced my head free of those images and tried to concentrate on the stage. *Tried* being the key word. It was incredibly hard when the man standing beside me brought something out in me which nobody else had ever come close to unravelling. Which I'd never allowed someone to come close enough to me to unravel.

Noah caught my gaze with an amused glare, but I looked away, worried I was wearing my feelings on my face. I had no guise here. Nothing and no one to hide behind that, as if he wasn't doing maddening things to both my head and my heart.

Rolling my shoulders, I settled my line of sight on Hudson, dressed in an all-black shorts and T-shirt combo. He appeared effortlessly handsome. Clean but rugged. His short brown hair was freshly tapered, and his deep blue eyes seemed to lock onto Olivia's silver.

Hudson's posture showed confidence as he stepped onto the scales, but his facial expression gave nothing away. He was the epitome of poised. I wondered if he'd practised that look for times like these or if it came naturally to him. Like a frown came naturally to the gorgeous man beside me.

With one hand, Hudson grabbed the chest of his T-shirt and pulled it up and over his head, messing up his hair and showcasing every defined muscle in his upper body when the material was stripped bare from his skin. For the first time, I realised he had a tattoo–script inked across his right peck. Though there was too much distance between us for me to read it. The crowd quietened down when he stepped onto the scales, and the announcer's voice boomed through the surround sound, "Official weight one-seventy!"

Hudson's, Noah's, and Walker's faces remained passive, even as the crowd erupted throughout the room.

I didn't get a chance to speak to Walker again before the announcer introduced Hudson's opponent, who happened to be a big deal in the world of martial arts. I still had so much to learn, but it seemed Killian "the Mercenary" Mahoney was the one to beat. Supposedly, he was motivated by money. And big money came by winning.

"Next up, introducing the reigning, defending welterweight champion of the world... Killian "the Mercenary" Mahoney!"

More noise flared from the crowd as Killian stepped onto the stage and headed towards the centre. He'd draped a Welsh flag over his shoulders like a cape and moved with a bounce in his step. He was as handsome as Hudson. His buzzed dark hair showed off his killer cheekbones, and a thin layer of sweat made his skin glow. But it was his grave, honey-coloured eyes and the brazen wink in my direction that warmed my already flushed cheeks. He had a persona about him–the kind that could probably charm his way out of trouble.

Walker noticed Killian's attention on me, and from my peripheral, I watched him tense.

He removed a hand from his pocket before subtly wrapping his fingers around the back of my neck and under my hair, not caring that we were in a room full of people. People that may or may not come to inaccurate conceptions and judge it for something more, or something less, than what it was. But what was *it*? What were we? And were we anything? And why did I care less about their judgement of us than I did being a rich man's daughter?

My chest constricted as he squeezed and leant down to my ear. Hot breath fanned my face, but before any words left his mouth and I could challenge the unexpected marking of what perhaps felt like his territory, he dropped his hand and abruptly stepped away from me, diverting his attention elsewhere.

I followed his line of sight, looking over my shoulder, half expecting to find a camera in our face. Only to the side of the sports reporters, I spotted a stunning brunette who hadn't been there before. She looked just how I imagined his usual type to look. Beautiful in the sense of Disney's Belle being a porn star. A red bodycon dress that matched the shade of her lips. The perfect complexion and just enough botox to be considered natural. She was definitely more his age than I'd ever be. And probably something more than I'd ever amount to.

It wasn't my business to feel defensive over where he placed his attention. Or on who he gave his attention, no matter how innocent it might've been. But I couldn't help the fact that I did. That I wanted more than he ever gave or had given me. That I wished to explore every piece that made up the jigsaw of who he was. I wanted him all for myself.

Was it too much to ask for him to want me back?

He walked towards her, and the woman smiled at something he said while glaring at me over his shoulder.

"Who's that?" I found myself asking as Olivia stepped up beside me. Probably as curious as me.

"She looks familiar." She tilted her head to the side. "But I'm not sure. I can't place her. Could she be his girlfriend?"

The two words made my stomach drop.

"He doesn't have a girlfriend."

Does he?

He wouldn't have done what he did with me last night if he had a girlfriend.

Still, something about the brunette made me feel uneasy,

and I wanted to follow Walker over there and introduce myself as if I was more than just the daughter of the less than iconic James Sterling. Though embarrassing myself wasn't an option. Especially when I had absolutely no claim to him whatsoever. So what we'd made each other come? So what I shared parts of myself with him I'd never disclosed to anyone?

If I were jealous over the way he looked at the octagon girls, this was something else entirely. And I just couldn't help myself seeking answers to the questions firing off in my head.

Who was she?

Had she been the one on the other end of the phone calls I'd bore witness to?

Maybe she was his paradise.

Maybe I'd got this all wrong.

I didn't understand how he could be intimate with me if he had someone in his life that meant something to him. Because that's exactly how it looked–they had a familiarity that looked like they meant something to each other.

Did they mean something to each other?

To calm my annoyance, and to ease my racing heart, I looked back to the stage to refocus my attention as Killian's weight was disclosed.

"It's a match. Official weight one-seventy!"

The crowd cheered, their chants and screams filling the room, stealing every spare molecule of silence as they stomped their feet and raised their voices. The sound made it almost impossible to focus.

Walker couldn't have a girlfriend.

He just couldn't.

"Are you okay?" Olivia asked.

"Fine."

Though it seemed, without Walker by my side and with him by the brunette, an ache settled over me. I pulled my lips into my mouth to gnaw on them–an attempt to distract myself as the pace of my heart continued to increase. It seemed my anxiety was threatening to take me away just because my emotions were disorientated. Just because my mind was in turmoil.

Amplified by the noise of the crowd.

Amplified by the heat in the room.

Amplified by the eyes burning into my back.

I tried not to draw attention to my jealousy as I breathed through my body's fighting urge to be near Walker. To have him take care of me the way he had in the restaurant last night. To find answers to my questions and understand what they meant. To find out if that woman was, in fact, his girlfriend.

He'd given me so many mixed messages. He was so against feeling anything for me, of admitting he had something with me. Was I naive to think it was just because of my age? Just because of my father?

Forcing my thoughts away from Walker and my attention to the stage, I flitted my eyes between Hudson and Killian. I watched as the two fighters moved centre stage and faced each other before Killian began shouting incendiary remarks, all in a bid to get under Hudson's skin. And as he did, I felt Olivia tense beside me, not liking how Killian seemed to speak so derogatory of Hudson. Of his upbringing–of his past.

I crossed my arms over my chest, feeling the power in Killian's remarks as they burst between his lips like shot fire flying towards Hudson.

But Hudson wasn't weak like me, and he didn't tense like Olivia when Killian spoke shit about him. He didn't crumble when others judged him. He didn't seem to care for the way Killian was staring him down. No, Hudson deflected every word from Killian's mouth with silent strength.

Though I did wonder one thing. I couldn't understand why Hudson was nicknamed "Bully Boy" when he seemed less like a bully than Killian. Either way, Hudson took it, nestling every word into his skin like it built resilience. He stood tall, unbothered, his lips in a thin line, his eyes speaking what his mouth didn't.

Tomorrow we'd watch as he threw those exact words back at Killian's body, using nothing but his strength.

Eventually, my heart rate began to settle, and with that, I uncrossed my arms and dropped them to my sides. And then, because I was unable to keep away, I took a deep breath and chanced another look back at Walker. Only this time, I caught eyes with the woman beside him.

A slow, almost chilling smile broke across her face. And as if Walker felt my attention on her as hers was mine, he looked over his shoulder and stole it back for himself.

Walker

SHIT.

I turned back to Sophia, feigning indifference towards Blue, who had captured my soon-to-be ex-wife's attention. "Any particular reason why you're in my club today, of all days?"

She stepped into me, handing me an envelope, forcing more decorum than necessary as she placed a kiss on my cheek. "Is that any way to greet your wife?"

It was an act.

I knew it; she knew it.

But those around us wouldn't have known our marriage was in ruin without looking between the lines. We'd held it together for so long that they probably wouldn't have known our marriage was a sham unless it was spelt out to them. And still, even if it were printed in big, bold letters, perhaps they still wouldn't have believed it.

"The divorce papers." I realised. "You've signed them?"

My brows pinched as I studied the envelope in my hands. I hoped she didn't notice the slight tremor in my fingers. With the small amount of alcohol I consumed in the last few days, it would be embarrassing to admit that I was experiencing withdrawal.

When I looked up at her made-up face, set like stone and not giving too much of anything away, I realised I needn't have been concerned. Or at least concerned over that. I had an entirely different reason to be uneasy, because she was still too busy looking over my shoulder.

At Blue.

"Who's that?" Her red lips parted, and her tongue slowly crossed over her top teeth, lingering on a pointed canine. A sinister smile continued to play at her mouth as she turned back to scrutinise me.

"Who's who?"

I kept my nonchalance, except I'm not sure my tone convinced her. She'd ambushed me, and I was sure she knew more than her stony face let on. Though maybe I was overthinking. Overanalysing every day I'd spent with Blue. Overanalysing what I'd done. Why I'd done it. What it meant.

In the eyes of the law, I'd committed adultery, and if Sophia were to ask if there had been someone else, the truth would be much different than the last time she'd asked me.

I could lie, of course. I'd done so much of that recently that I was surprised I could differentiate between the truth and a lie anymore.

But what did it matter? The last eleven years with the

woman in front of me happened to be the biggest lie I'd ever told.

She glimpsed another look at Blue. The move only had me clenching my jaw and my eyes peering into the envelope's seal as I pried it open. I realised I'd do almost anything to deflect her attention from Blue with what I had at stake.

Though what I had at stake was a conflict with how I felt.

"I've signed them," she mused, refocusing her eyes on the envelope in my hands.

I couldn't see her signature on the document, but I could make out a "fuck you" scrawled across the first page in cursive red lipstick instead.

She laughed. "How's my handwriting?"

I clenched the envelope in my fist, which crinkled the paper. What good was it now?

"Why bother making this difficult for yourself, Sophia?"

"Because I haven't decided what I want yet."

I allowed her words to sink in before responding.

Had I heard her right?

"What you want? What more could you possibly want?" I'd raised my voice, but it didn't warrant any extra attention and instead merged with the noise of the audience around us. "I think I've been more than fucking generous."

"The townhouse is barely a scratch of your worth. Don't embarrass yourself by fighting me on this. I'm entitled to a fair financial settlement."

I scoffed. "Of course, you wouldn't make this easy. Nothing with you ever is. I should have known I married a fucking narcissist."

"Now, now." She reached out, stroking her palms down the lapels of my jacket. Her nails looked like talons, likely to claw at me any second. I tried not to feel repulsed, but my face must have conveyed otherwise. "I've no idea why you're looking at me like that. You know, these same nails used to draw blood from your back as you'd fuck me."

"Emphasis on used to."

I had the intrusive urge to break her fingers. The vision of her hands on my bare skin after I'd slept with Blue in my arms, after I'd felt her naked skin against my own last night when we showered, made me want to douse myself in bleach. I should've known she was never going to relent.

One-night stands were once my MO, but Sophia being Sophia, she kept coming back. She hadn't relented then. It took longer than it should have, but eventually, she made me feel how I imagined a guy in love was supposed to feel. And she gave me dirty, mind-blowing sex which served as an escape from my responsibilities.

Lost in my head and desperate to get Noah out of foster care, I was turned away by the family court time and time again. A twenty-three-year-old working a full-time job in an industry that promoted alcohol and aggression wasn't the face you ever saw on a child adoption brochure.

It was James who told me money could buy me anything. So when I had nowhere else to turn, and with desperation paving my way, I married Sophia and painted the picture of a perfect family.

I knew we were never meant for the long haul. And I was right because with each day that passed, and each year went by, she only grew harder to tolerate. She only grew harder to like.

But I wouldn't cause a scene.

Not with the press here.

Not with roaming eyes.

Not with Blue standing not so far behind me.

It would warrant too many questions. It could jeopardise everything I'd built.

Regardless of the hardships, I'd re-live every fucking lousy day for my kid brother and me if it still got me to where I was.

"There must have been something more you saw in me; else you'd have left me much sooner," she murmured, looking up at me from under her eyelashes. "I think we could fix us if you gave it a chance."

I sensed sincerity there, but not enough for me to care. I couldn't begin to understand why I had stuck around so long. It was like asking someone why they smoked when it caused cancer.

"There's nothing for us to fix. You made your bed. I made mine. If you're upset that your sheets itch, that's a you problem."

She drummed a patronising palm on my cheek. "Then I suppose you've given me no choice. You'll be hearing from my lawyer. You know how the saying goes, don't you, Walker? The one about a woman being rejected in love?"

I didn't.

She took another lasting look at Blue, who I prayed to fuck was no longer paying us any mind, before turning back to me. By the look on her face, I could have sworn that she knew something I didn't. Or maybe I did know and hadn't enough time to analyse just what it was before she spun on her heels, delivering one final blow that carried with her as she strutted towards the exit.

"Hell hath no fury like a woman scorned."

Hell hath no fury like a woman scorned? Yeah, she'd always been a psychotic bitch.

CHAPTER EIGHTEEN

Blue

WALKER DIDN'T ACCOMPANY me back to the penthouse, and I didn't get a chance to speak with him about the brunette for lack of privacy. I rode with Finley, and although I was tempted to ask him if he knew who she was, I convinced myself it would be better hearing it from Walker. He didn't owe me anything, but maybe he'd be honest after everything that had already developed between us.

It was two in the morning when I woke in a hot flush to the sound of breaking glass. At first, I regarded it as a remnant of a dream. Of the boy pulling me from my mother's car and through my window, tearing my skin in the process. I couldn't make sense of how I was able to put more of a face to the stranger all these years after the accident. But as I sat up, pulling my covers tight to my chest, I heard Walker's distinct accent cursing from down the hallway.

I abandoned the warmth of my bed and made my way to my bedroom door. Goosebumps coated my skin with the early morning chill, and although it didn't warm me, I still pulled up the straps of my pyjama top as they'd dropped from my shoulders with my movements.

The white glow from the kitchen drop lights illuminated my path as I tentatively made my way from my room and down the hall. When I reached the edge of the kitchen, I spotted Walker perched against the side of the couch, one hand in his pocket, the other on the top of his shoulder, his jacket hanging haphazardly over it. Dropping my head to the side, I studied him from a distance. He didn't have to look at me to know I was only feet away.

"Careful," he said, pitching his chin to the floor. "Glass. At your feet."

I inclined my head down to the floor where a broken glass lay not so far from my skin, a brown puddle of liquid surrounding the debris.

Sidestepping the glass, I made a safe way over to where he was before placing myself between his legs. He watched me curiously, his drunken eyes holding interest as I looked up at him.

I had no discipline.

"Who was that woman today?"

His body remained stoic, but his lips twitched. "I don't know how I feel about you getting all territorial on me, baby."

I frowned. "I don't know how you feel about me at all."

He let go of his jacket, and I watched it fall onto the couch as he manoeuvred his arms to wrap around me. His warmth embodied me, and his lips came down to my temple. "Truth or a lie?" he asked, using my phrase against me.

I didn't need to think about it. "I never want your lies."

He waited a moment, as if he were gathering the words up before deciding whether to speak them. And then he took a breath before letting them out. "I think I'm in over my head when it comes to you," he murmured. "Because since you sat beside me on that plane, I haven't stopped thinking about you."

My breath hitched at his revelation. This was new, but he was drunk... so how was I meant to know if he really meant it?

"You haven't?"

"How can I? You're everywhere."

My voice was muffled when I leant into his chest and asked, "Why?"

He dropped his head, and I felt him smirk against the sensitive field of skin beneath my ear. His touch remained tender, but his breath against my neck had my blood pumping faster. "Why?" he repeated, somewhat amused. "The way you look." He pressed a kiss to my neck. "Who you are." I tilted my head, giving him more access. "Your scent." He nibbled the skin he just kissed, then groaned into my neck as though I was torturing him. "And your taste, I can't forget it. Fuck, the way I feel about you is chaotic. You make me feel like I'm going fucking crazy. Do you know what crazy feels like to a reasonable man, Blue?"

I breathed hard, feeling the steady thump of his own heart under my ear as I curled my body around his. "Explain it to me," I whispered.

He shook his head. "There's no way easy way to explain crazy. You know we're doomed to fail, you and me."

"You and me? I think we're all doomed, aren't we? Nothing's forever."

"Maybe," he murmured. And then, in one second to another, he went from soft to hard. He swallowed a growl and in a fluid movement, picked me up. My legs wrapped around his waist, locking behind his back, and his hands held steady beneath my thighs as he walked us forward.

"This doesn't feel like crazy," I whispered.

"No?" He frowned. "So what does it feel like?"

"It feels like you were meant to hold me like this."

"It seems a given for us," he mumbled, his tone thick.

Something pulled at my heart, but I couldn't comprehend my next thought before he'd dropped me onto the kitchen counter, and his needy lips were on my own.

My lips parted for him as his tongue sought entry. And when my tongue found his, the kiss we shared was unlike anything I'd ever experienced before. He didn't hold back. Everything he gave, I returned. He pushed and I pulled, until all I could taste was the distilled honey on his tongue. I was desperate for every drop. He swallowed my every moan, and I drank his every kiss.

I was intoxicated.

Completely drunk on everything that was him.

Squeezing the backs of my thighs, he thrust me to the edge of the counter, tearing his mouth away from mine and nipping my bottom lip in the process.

"Do you like kissing me?" I spoke against his lips.

"I shouldn't like it as much as I do," he grunted.

It wasn't a yes, but I wasn't ignorant. Just because we'd grown closer didn't mean his opinion over how wrong we were for each other would change overnight. He confirmed that when he looked down between us, when he noticed the wetness visible through my pyjama shorts and ambled back. My eyebrows dipped, frustrated he was pulling away, but then he slid his fingers into the edge of my shorts, pulled them from my hips, and followed them with his touch down the length of my legs.

My breathing grew heavier as he dropped the flimsy material to the floor, leaving me sprawled out in front of him in nothing but my pyjama top and underwear.

"Lean back," he ordered, his eyes glued to the thin scrap of material between my legs.

I dropped to my elbows, my blonde hair falling over my shoulders as I watched him lower his mouth to my left thigh.

A shiver ran through me when his hot, damp breath climbed my skin. But when his lips met the restraint of my underwear, my body tensed. He must have felt it because he paused, and the next words from his mouth were, "Has anyone ever ate this pretty pussy?" His fingers pulled the laced material to the side as he wet his lips. "Or am I going to be the first?"

My skin warmed as he looked up and scrutinised my face. And by the smirk lining his mouth, I knew a blush was visible on my cheeks. Lost for words, I shook my head. He dipped his chin, teasing my clit before he licked a path down my folds and dipped his tongue inside my centre.

"Oh, fuck," I moaned, sloping my head back and raising my hips, begging for him to push inside me further.

He held me down with his grip on my thighs to keep me from squirming on his face, knowing the only thing between me and an orgasm was a little more friction. He was teasing me—teaching me—showing me it was him who had full control of my body. That he could prolong my pleasure, and we didn't have to rush.

The pads of his fingers dug into my skin, forcing my thighs open wider, and when he dragged his mouth back to my clit and began teasing me with his skilled tongue, the weight of my elbows gave out and I collapsed against the kitchen counter.

He lifted his head, just barely. "You like my tongue in your pussy, huh?"

"Yes," I whispered. I was almost afraid to speak in case he decided this wasn't the right thing to do. In case I gave him any doubt. I needn't have worried because I felt his cheeks expand against me in a grin.

His hold on me loosened, and then I felt his fingers trace the length of my slit. "What about my fingers?" he murmured before edging inside of me.

Oh God.

I breathed hard. "Nate."

"Baby, you're tight. Relax."

My hips bucked up and into his hand as his two fingers pushed into me and continued their incline.

This time, when he lifted his head, it was high enough for him to stare down at me. Though his eyes were dark with desire, that frown of his I grew to enjoy so much seemed to replace the smirk on his lips.

There was an edge to his voice when he said, "Blue." And then, with nowhere for his fingers to go, he curled them against my wet pillowed walls. "You didn't think to tell me you're a virgin? Shit." But even through his words, he didn't cease touching me.

"There wasn't a right time to bring it up," I whimpered as he pumped his fingers in and out of me in long, drawn out strokes; not once going past his knuckle. His fingers curled every time he met the resistance, eliciting needy moans from my lips.

"Fuck," he groaned. "So pretty and tight, I can only imagine what you'd feel like encased around my cock."

I raised my head to look at him, and the primal way he was looking at me and his explicit words only drove me closer to release.

"Don't imagine," I mouthed. "I want you. I want it all with you."

I meant it.

I'd give it all to him if he wanted it.

I'd be his, completely.

He cursed as my eyes became heavy, but he spoke again before they could close. "No, baby. Eyes on me." And as I obliged, he followed with a, "That's it."

He dropped his head and tongued my clit as he continued to finger fuck me nice and slow. And then, as though he knew when I was about to come undone, he gently seized my clit between his lips and sucked until my orgasm exploded on his tongue.

My thighs trembled around his head as I moved back up onto my elbows, flushed and breathing heavy. With a smirk, he peered up at me from under his eyelashes and pressed a kiss against my pubic bone before springing my underwear back into place.

He straightened, and not caring that I was a damp, quivering mess, he wrapped his arms around my waist and pulled me towards him in an embrace. He was hard as hell between my legs, which dangled from the counter on either side of his hips. But he didn't push for anything more as he kissed me.

This time, our kiss was gentle, but as I tasted myself on his lips, my nose scrunched.

"Fuck, you're cute." He smiled drunkenly. "Even when you're not trying to be."

"You just made me come and you're calling me cute?" I rolled my eyes playfully.

The low chuckle that crept up his throat had me sobering, and then he was forcing my legs to wrap around him.

I expected him to deposit me back into my bed, but instead he carried me past my room, down the hall, and all the way to his en-suite, where, like last time we were intimate, he turned on the shower. Only this time, he didn't join me.

I think my face conveyed something like hurt, because he said, "I need to clean up the glass. I don't want you accidentally cutting yourself in the morning."

He waited for me to say something, but all I could manage was a nod of my head. His chest expanded, and he leant into me, pressing a kiss to my forehead. "Shower," he murmured. "I'll be five minutes, tops."

With that, he left, and I undressed.

I wasn't entirely sure why he'd brought me to shower in his room when he'd made it obvious he didn't want me there by giving me my own space just last week. But did I care if it meant I was on his mind? Did I care when he considered me 'cute?' Did I really care when he was giving me the attention I wanted? If anything, it only made me feel closer to him. It felt like another way he'd cemented me into his life, into his routine, like I belonged.

Even if I didn't.

Even if he already said I couldn't.

He may have said he'd be five minutes, but he hadn't come back by the time I'd finished showering, and for a moment I wondered what I was supposed to do and how I was supposed to act.

Our relationship was still unknown. We weren't really anything, but at the same time, we were something. I guess the two of us were in reckless territory with no map to navigate.

But when he found me stepping from his en-suite and into his room, wrapped in nothing but a towel, he didn't say anything. And when I walked into his closet and replaced that same towel with one of his shirts, he remained unreadable.

I climbed onto his bed, kneeling on top of the sheets. "Can I stay in here with you tonight?"

He unfastened his belt as he looked at me and then re-focused on undressing. I could tell by his movements he was still slightly intoxicated. It was probable he'd had another bottle of something alcoholic in the kitchen cupboard. Perhaps with the time it took, had another glass or more while I showered. But he murmured, "If you want," coherently.

He pulled his belt from his slacks and then disappeared into his closet. When he came out, he was wearing nothing but his boxer shorts. With the voiles still open against the floor to ceiling windows, the city still full of light below us seemed to bring light into our darkness, illuminating him like a work of art.

He loosened his watch as he neared me, and then placed it on the bedside table. And then, once he'd pulled back the quilt, he sat on the edge of the bed.

He looked at me over his shoulder, the angle of his jaw so sharp I was desperate to line it with kisses. Tonight, he felt like mine. And in some strange way, I was already his. And maybe he didn't know it, and perhaps I wasn't entirely sure, but what we had felt like something real.

So what I was eighteen? So what I'd never had a boyfriend or been in love? He was thirty-four, and his experience probably outdid mine. But if this was what love could feel like–if this was what it took to get there–I wanted it forever. I wanted to be his, in whatever way he'd have me. And it didn't have to make sense, as long as it was ours.

"Stop thinking so loud," he said roughly.

I inhaled sharply, pulling back the remainder of the quilt as I climbed underneath. "Sorry, I... do that sometimes."

"A lot," he murmured, doing the same. And unlike all the other times we shared a bed, this time was different. He didn't face the opposite direction but instead laid on his back, wrapping one arm under my neck to nestle me against his chest. His other hand hiked my thigh up and over his. Even now, he was still hard–I felt him under my leg. But when I reached out to touch him, he gripped my wrist and pulled my hand up to his stomach before linking our fingers together.

I wanted to please him as he pleased me, but I was tired, so I didn't argue. I had a feeling we would have plenty more intimate moments together. Somehow, tonight felt like the beginning.

"Promise me something," I murmured.

He stroked a finger across my cheekbone with the arm he had wrapped around me. "What is it?"

"When you crave a drink... think twice."

He inhaled deeply. "You care about me, huh?"

"Mmhmm, and I think you care about me too."

Time passed as he continued to stroke my face.

"You didn't answer my question," I said sleepily.

"What question?"

"The brunette. Who is she? Is she the reason you drink?"

He squeezed my hand but didn't reply. I knew he was keeping her from me, but sleep took me before I could question why.

CHAPTER NINETEEN

Blue

I WOKE up alone the following day, but I could hear the faint sound of the shower running from where I lay in Walker's bed. With the sunshine attempting to break through the grey clouds and drops of rain silently trailing the window, I briefly wondered if I'd overslept. Sitting up on my elbows, I noticed an unopened bottle of flavoured water on my bedside table. I reached over, uncapping the top and smiling to myself before taking a sip. Immediately, the citrus water coated my taste buds and soothed my dry throat.

The shower stopped running, and I resumed my position on my elbows as I waited for Walker to re-enter the room from the en-suite. A click sounded, and then he stepped through the door.

And I saw all of him.

Every solid, naked inch of him.

He smirked in my direction, peering down at me from under his lashes as he towel-dried his hair.

"What?"

Sure I was blushing, I murmured, "You're hard."

He dropped his towel in front of his dick, partially covering it, and without a fraction of embarrassment, he said, "I was thinking of you. Of last night."

"In the shower?"

He nodded.

Feeling bold, I pushed the quilt away from me and sat up on my knees, like I had when I crawled into his bed last night. His shirt dropped off my tanned shoulder, and its bottom fanned along my thighs.

He tracked my movements, and in a moment of honesty, he admitted, "I'm afraid of how easily I could fall for this view."

My head dropped to the side in a smile as I studied him, and I watched as he sucked his full bottom lip into his mouth. His cheeks hollowed as his brows dipped and, if he hadn't spoken, I don't think I'd be able to tell if he was tormented or turned on.

"Ever had a cock in your mouth?"

Sex oozed from his tone, but I temporarily lost my ability to speak. I just watched him as he dropped his towel to the floor and took his hard cock in his fist.

"A game of spin the bottle and four strawberry daiquiris would say I have."

Shyly, I placed the tip of my thumb between my lips. His eyes followed the movement, his nostrils flaring as I pushed my thumb fully into my mouth and sucked.

"That so?" He tugged on his cock, his eyes not wavering from my mouth. And then, because it all felt so natural, I dropped my hand and began undoing the buttons of my shirt, giving in to my urges.

He raised his chin, his confidence such a turn on I already felt myself growing wet. "Move to the edge of the bed."

I was still undoing the buttons on the shirt, but as he walked towards the bed, I stopped to do what he asked until we were just inches from each other. With the shirt parted but a few buttons remaining, he released his cock to separate them for me, allowing his fingers to purposely graze my pussy with his movements.

"I have no idea what you're doing to me," he murmured, watching me as I whimpered. I had no time to speak before two of his fingers entered me. And as he drew them back out, I found myself chasing the loss. He smirked, teasing me as his thumb drove to my clit and his fingers pumped in and out of me nice and slow.

With each stroke, quiet moans spilt between my lips, and his eyes darted between my face to what he was doing to my body. He was just as turned on from watching what he was doing to me as the way I felt with him doing it.

"You're perfect," he remarked in a tone infused with awe, using his free hand to part my shirt. He clutched one of my breasts in his palm, feeling its weight before he squeezed.

My knees grew weak, and I reached out, gripping his shoulder and digging my nails into his skin for balance as I felt my release draw closer.

He hissed, continuing his assault on me, drawing his fingers in and out of my pussy as he added more pressure to my little nub. And with his other hand, he alternated between rolling my nipple and pinching my breast.

I was so turned on I didn't want it to end. But he knew exactly what to do, and it felt so, so good.

"Oh, God, I'm going to come."

"Then come," he grunted. "Come now so that your mouth can fuck my cock."

With his dirty words and a last pinch of my nipple, my nails drilled into his shoulders as wave after wave rippled through me, and I burst around his fingers.

When he didn't retract straightaway, I had to force myself back, too sensitive to his touch.

"Your turn."

"My turn?" He chuckled. "You sure you're good?"

His fist wrapped around his cock, and I watched him stroke himself; my eyes transfixed on a bead of pre-cum that escaped from his tip.

"Yeah, I want to taste you."

He groaned. "Drop onto your elbows. Ass in the air."

I followed his instructions, and he pushed forward, directing the head of his cock onto my lips. It was soft, like velvet. My tongue darted out to lick the pre-cum declining down his head, and although the position I was in wasn't the comfiest, I wanted to please him. Which was why when he told me to "Open up," I parted my lips.

He pushed his cock between them, and as he did, I looked up at him from under my eyelashes, tasting the saltiness of his cum. His gaze was on me. His brows lowered like he was trying to control himself, but his eyes had become dark. I took him deeper into my mouth to show him I was willing to do anything he asked. I wanted him to lose control with me. I wanted his raw, primal honesty, even if it came like this.

Either he understood or he gave in, because he let go of his cock, giving me complete access. His hand came to the back of my head, his fingers weaving into my hair, securing a tight grip as he pushed me further down his length, praising me with words like "Good girl" and "That's it."

I moaned around his cock, and he used his hold on my hair to pull me back up. He looked down at me, eyes smouldering with want.

"Do that again, and I'll be tempted to lay you down and fuck you." His words were thick as he thrust into my mouth. "Right here." Then he pulled himself back out. "Right now."

I hollowed my cheeks, unsure I was doing it right. I'd only ever done this once, and it lasted all of thirty seconds before the guy pulled out and came all over himself. But Walker wasn't just a guy. He was a man. A man that knew what he wanted and how to get it. So when he tightened the grip he had on my hair and fucked my mouth, pulling me back and forth along his cock and groaning every time he hit the back of my throat, I did my best to oblige, allowing him to use me for his pleasure.

"You look so fucking pretty with me in your mouth." He pulled my hair back so just the head of his cock was between my lips, as if wanting to savour the moment. I was so turned on I swear I was dripping all down my thighs and over his sheets.

After a beat, he thrust to the back of my throat, and I couldn't help myself. His words–the way he was using my body–only turned me on further. My eyes watered as he continued to thrust, and though he'd warned me, I moaned around his cock for the second time.

With his free hand, he held his palm against my cheek, effectively halting me. I leaned into his touch, noticing his jaw tick as he looked down at me, my mouth still full of his cock. "What did I say? Do you want me to fuck you?"

I was so needy for every inch of him that I whimpered an incoherent yes around his length. I wanted it all. I'd take anything he'd give me.

"You don't mean that."

But I did mean that.

I pulled back from his cock, and his hold on my hair loosened. He watched me as I sat back up on my knees, shirt parted, my body entirely on display.

He looked from my glossy eyes, eager and hungry for more of him, to my bare pussy, wet and willing. "Blue..."

His brow pinched when I bent my legs and laid back on the bed, bracing myself on my elbows. "Nate. I want this."

"You're serious?" He clutched his cock in his fist and began pumping himself, torn between waiting for my response and getting himself off.

"Do you have a condom?"

"I can't have kids," he said, observing my expression. "I had a vasectomy."

"Okay," I spoke slowly. Though he was looking at me like he expected me to ask why, I didn't. Instead, I stored that information away for a future conversation and said, "I trust you. I want this, and I wouldn't say that if I didn't mean it."

His nostrils flared, but he climbed on the bed and held his weight above me. I felt his cock against my pussy, but that was it. He didn't force his way in. He didn't make a move except to drop his head into my neck and speak against my throat. "If we do this, it's done. You can't take it back."

"I know," I murmured. "I won't want to."

He lifted his head from my neck to peer down between us, watching as he slid his cock back and forth against my folds. Getting himself nice and prepped.

"Final warning," he said, needing me to be sure.

"Take it," I told him with a shy smile. "My virginity's yours, Nate Walker."

His eyes danced with my own, searching for any sign of uncertainty. But he wouldn't find any. I'd never been so sure of anything in my life.

I held on tightly to his shoulders as he angled himself at my entrance, and as he slowly edged inside of me, I lifted my hips to encourage him. His jaw ticked as he kept moving, and I whimpered as he met the resistance.

He paused. "Do you want me to stop?"

"No," I breathed. Sweat coated my skin as I clenched around the pinch of intrusion.

"Blue, baby." He dropped his forehead to mine, rubbing it from side to side. "Don't do that." I could hear the restraint in his voice when he said, "If you don't want me to stop, then you need to relax. I don't want to hurt you."

"You're not." My voice shook. "Keep going."

He wasn't fully sheathed inside of me yet, and it seemed my nerves were getting the best of me. He withdrew and then pushed himself back in again slowly, taking my lips in a kiss and tangling his fingers in my hair as my pussy opened for him and my walls embraced his cock. His tongue fought with mine, and then he began to pump in and out in shallow thrusts, allowing me to get used to his girth.

Gradually, and with each thrust, I felt his resolve slip until he forced his way through the barrier and completely sheathed his cock inside of me, stretching me wide open.

I sucked in a breath at the uncomfortable pinch, but he didn't stop, continuing to kiss me through my pain.

"Nate," I breathed. "I'm so full. You're so big." I dug my nails into his back so hard I was sure I'd broken his skin.

He pulled out slowly, then pushed back in a little faster, a little further.

"I know, baby. You feel so fucking good." He kissed me back greedily, angling my head to meet his and burying his cock inside of me before retreating and doing it again. "You're taking my cock like such a good fucking girl."

The discomfort lessened as he moved in and out of me, and I wrapped my legs around him, needing to feel him closer, needing to feel every inch of him as he entered me.

He pulled away from my mouth, untangled his hands from my hair, and raised on his arms. His gaze watched my tits as they bounced and then moved to his cock, where he made a show of thrusting in and out, painting himself with my arousal. It was sinful. Dirty. And I was utterly enamoured, because I never expected my first time to be with a man like Walker. A man who knew how to work my body into answering the way it did for him.

I whimpered, unsure if it was in pain or pleasure. His eyes darted back to my face, but he didn't slow his thrusts. "*Relax*, baby. Lift your hips. Take my cock."

I moaned his name between breaths until he leant back down, pressing his lips to mine in another tantalising kiss. Our chests touched, and the heat from our skin moulded as if we were one, the perspiration of our bodies glowing as I raised my hips and began meeting him thrust for thrust.

"Yeah, just like that," he murmured over my lips as we found a steady rhythm. Again and again, he eased in and out of me until all I felt was him. Until all I breathed was the scent of our arousal. Until my toes were curling, my walls were squeezing, and he was forcing pleasure from somewhere no one else had ever been.

"Oh God, Nate."

"Jesus, the feel of you..." he groaned.

My clit rubbed against him as he propelled his hips into me, and I found myself arching off the bed as he picked up the pace and plunged deeper inside my pussy. Only then did I convulse, clenching down around his cock while my whole body vibrated with release.

He dropped his head into my neck whispering a "fuck," and I moaned as he continued to milk my orgasm out of me. In his next thrust, I felt his cock pulsate as he filled me with his cum.

Less than a minute passed before he rolled from me, pulling me with him to lay across his chest as our breathing levelled out.

"Are you sore?" he rasped, trailing his hand across my thigh and then to my centre.

"A little."

My pussy tingled as he soothed his fingers through my folds. His cum dripped out from me, mixed with my blood, and in the next second, I felt his finger push it back inside.

"Nate," I gasped, embarrassed at the quantity of blood running from me. At the way he was watching where he touched me. At the mess we made over his sheets.

"Don't do that," he whispered. "You're mine, Blue. You hear me? Mine. No one else gets this."

His finger dipped in for the second time, and I clenched my thighs, trapping his hand between my legs and bathing in the burn of our repercussion.

"Yours?"

With his free hand, he brushed away some damp tendrils of hair stuck to my forehead and then pressed a gentle kiss against my temple.

"Mine."

"Is it always like this?" I asked breathily, fixing my eyes on his.

Our eyes danced, but instead of an honest answer, all he said was, "We should shower."

I wished we could stay like this all day, but I knew it was impossible with the day ahead of him. It's why I didn't protest. It's why I didn't repeat my question. And it's why, after a few more quiet moments, I let him carry me from the bed and into his en-suite the same way he had the night before.

Walker

ME AND BLUE showered together and then went our separate ways to get ready for our workday. Last night wasn't planned, but I wasn't sure how to respond with alcohol in my system and her questions over Sophia. Even for me, deflecting her questions using physical advances was a low blow. I shouldn't have gone there, but I had. And then this morning happened. Was there any point resisting when we kept moving further and further away from a line we'd already crossed? Just remembering how she felt wrapped around my cock made me hard again. I couldn't seem to get enough of the girl, and I couldn't decide if taking her virginity was righteous or foolish. Whether I'd made a mistake when I told her she was mine, knowing there was so much against us.

The events of last night and this morning had to be put on hold though, because tonight was fight night. I still had shit to do. I couldn't be thinking of Blue with so much on my mind. Not when I was already running behind schedule. I only hoped she understood how important the event was to me and the club. It contained not just mine but the whole of The Lagoon's blood, sweat, and tears. It was a big fucking deal, one that I knew had the potential to get us back on the straight and narrow as long as nothing went tits up. Which reminded me that I still had the situation with Sophia to contend with. *Hell hath no fury like a woman scorned.* She was up to something, and if there was one thing I was sure of, it was that I didn't have time for her ridiculous games. I needed to contact my solicitor again and have him tell me what the fuck I was meant to do. Perhaps offer me a solution on how to solve this.

Why couldn't she just sign the divorce papers or attempt to be amicable? Why couldn't she take what I'd offered and disappear from my life the same way she entered?

Me and Blue met Finley outside the penthouse, and I opened her door for her to climb in before I got situated in the back, careful to stand behind her, so no bystanders saw up her skirt. If she wanted to wear clothes that showed more skin than I thought necessary, that was her prerogative. But I wouldn't allow perverts to upskirt her or take a mental image so they could jack off to it later.

I sat in the middle of the backseat, legs spread, and as she fastened her seat belt, she looked over her shoulder at me, holding back a smile. I was mid-way taking my phone from the pocket of my beige coat when I caught it. My mouth pulled into a smirk, and I couldn't seem to tear my eyes away from her glossy lips. Fuck, I wanted to kiss her again. I wanted to do a lot more than kiss her. Again and again. Over and over.

Finley cleared his throat, and Blue swung around to face the front.

I met his eyes in the mirror before refocusing on my phone. "To the club, please, Finley."

Of course, he already knew that, but he also knew better than just to assume.

Before I opened my emails, I found myself texting Blue. I didn't want Finley to know, and the two of us were yet to discuss this morning, but I knew I couldn't have anyone looking at us and thinking something was going on. Not when her father was so close to handing me The Lagoon. And not with Sophia showing up at the club unannounced. How the fuck was I to know that she wouldn't weave Blue into her twisted discord with me? How do I know that she wouldn't take away the first bit of uncharacteristic happiness I'd experienced in a long time? Because that's what this feeling was, wasn't it?

Blue. She made me... feel some type of way. And not the way I ever felt when I was with Sophia. I was becoming attached, and I didn't want to think how that attachment would be fleeting. How if we did become something more, we wouldn't last because the stages in our lives were so vastly different. She had her whole life ahead of her. And I'd already experienced so much of mine–even if I had to grow up a lot sooner than most.

My fingers flew over the screen, and I hesitated only a second before hitting send.

Strictly business at the club, brat.

Her phone chimed, and I peeked up from my screen, watching as she slid her hand into the Prada bag at her feet.

She pulled out her phone and read my message, and as my eyes darted back to my own, I watched the three dots appear to indicate she was replying before disappearing again.

I frowned. She had to understand that me and her... were temporary. That she was mine *temporarily*, and I was... *fuck*. How could she know any of it when she didn't know why she was here? How could she understand it when I barely understood it myself? Whenever she neared anything resembling the truth, I diverted us in another direction. Anytime I felt like this was something–anytime we acted on impulse–I found myself unwilling to accept it. I was unwilling to be honest with myself because it was fucking ridiculous that I'd begun to feel things for her I definitely shouldn't have felt.

I quickly typed out another text before she responded with something less than sassy, deciding to be honest, not just with her but with myself. For once, I wasn't going to tell a fucking lie.

Whatever you're thinking, know that this morning meant something to me. You mean something to me.

The dots appeared again, and two seconds later, I received her reply.

Okay.

"*Okay,*" I read aloud.

Blue shifted in her seat, and Finley looked to me via the wing mirror, a touch of a frown on his ageing forehead. But he didn't say anything, because why would he? His words of wisdom and supposedly caring lectures only came about when I'd had a drink. Or two. Or nine.

But "*okay.*" So what the fuck did *okay* mean, exactly?

And what the fuck was I doing?

CHAPTER TWENTY

Walker

THE ELEVATOR OPENED, and both me and Blue stepped out, but not before I planted a kiss on her temple. As much as I wanted to kiss her thoroughly, with tongue, teeth, and my hands in her hair, I was afraid if I started, I wouldn't be able to stop. That I'd drag her to my office and have her writhing on my desk with my fingers in her pussy.

"What did you mean by okay?" I asked as we walked. I'd never had that response. Granted, I hadn't much of a relationship with a woman outside of the bedroom other than Sophia, so I couldn't help but feel like *okay* was a trick or some code I was supposed to decipher. This was all new to me. Like a toddler who'd gone from Velcro to laces. When in actuality, Blue was probably less experienced than I was when it came to whatever the fuck it was we were doing. I knew better than to believe in fate. In serendipity. In fairy tales. But Blue... she made me believe in something. Fuck, maybe she was the one to give me something to believe in. Even if I had no idea what the fuck that something was or what direction it could go in other than one which turned around to bite me on the ass.

"I just meant okay."

"Okay," I repeated.

"Yes," she replied slowly, her eyebrows pulling in a frown. "You're overthinking, Nate."

"Girls overthink. Not men."

"I understand that this is work. The club is important to you. And we... *me,* I'm something different," she explained. "It's separate."

"Separate." The word left a bad taste in my mouth. If only she knew just how close to work she was. If only she knew that she was with me out of not much more than a trade.

It seemed that ship was no longer smooth sailing because I'd hit rough and murky waters.

I breathed deeply, walking with her to the lobby to meet Olivia, leaving enough distance between us so we didn't attract any extra attention. Despite that, temptation made me want to reach out and devour her. Touch her. Just spend time with her. Just us, back at the penthouse, away from prying eyes. Back in my bed, where I had her body naked and content against mine.

When had I ever said that about anything, or anyone, ever before in my life?

Guess I was love drunk.

Not *love* drunk.

Lust drunk.

My cock was drunk on her pretty pussy and pert tits.

But it wasn't just that, was it? I'd gotten to know her. She'd gotten to know me. And not the me that everyone else knew. Not

Walker, but Nate. I was Nate with her. A little softer. A little more gentle.

I took a further step away from her when we neared the lobby. At this precise time in the morning, it was busier on this building level. And it was one thing if everyone believed me to be happily married, but it was another for them to look at me like I was having an affair with a girl almost half my age. Which... they weren't. But I couldn't be sure that the guilt for betraying James's trust like I had wasn't noticeable just by analysing me, which was why I needed to keep my distance and treat Blue like anyone else who worked for me and not look at her like I cared about her more than I did anyone else.

Separate.

I was fucked.

"Hudson," I addressed as we entered the lobby. He sat beside Olivia on the sofa, his hand on her thigh. I raised an eyebrow. "You shouldn't be here."

"Where should he be?" Blue asked from beside me. She was close. Close enough to get a whiff of her perfume. The one I loved to hate and hated to love. And it was very fucking distracting. The fantasy pulled me away, and I envisioned what it would be like to have her between my sheets every night, wearing nothing but that scent.

"Walker?" she said when I didn't offer a reply.

Walker.

Not Nate.

I didn't like it.

"On fight day, our fighters should be using that time to eat and relax," I stated. "Hudson?"

"I gave Olivia a ride." He looked from Olivia to me as he stood and then made his way towards me.

"I wasn't aware the two of you knew each other well enough to give rides." If I had known that, perhaps Olivia wouldn't have been my first choice when it came to picking a social media specialist and a mentor for Blue. I couldn't have my fighters fraternising with my staff or my team fraternising with my fighters. Shit, the hypocrisy. But it was my own irresponsible decision to hire Olivia before we had the opportunity to go through the whole employee handbook.

"We go way back," Hudson mumbled.

Good to know, but I wished I'd known sooner.

"You're blocking the door," he said when he reached me, his features not giving any more away. He was good at that, the whole closed off thing he did with his face. It's what worked so well for him in the cage. His moves were unpredictable–unlike Wez.

Fuck that kid.

Fuck. That. Kid.

"You good?" I asked him.

He nodded. "I'm good."

With that, I gripped his shoulder in silent support and stepped out of his way, allowing him to walk through the door without more of my scrutiny. He didn't need me winding him up before the biggest fight of his career. He knew what he was in for. And I had to trust he knew what he was doing. "See you later."

"Olivia," I tipped my chin in her direction, wondering if I could get a better read on her than I had Hudson. "And you, are you good? Our social media's looking spot on. I trust Noah's been on hand for anything you need, and Blue has been a good student in the little time you've had with her?"

Blue shuffled on her feet beside me. She liked it when I gave her praise, I realised. It turned her on. In fact, I bet she was wet just thinking about me calling her a good girl. My cock twitched just thinking about it. So much so that if it hadn't been such an important day, I'd say fuck what I said in my first text and drag her upstairs into my office.

"Yep," Olivia said with more enthusiasm than I cared for this early in the morning. "Thank you. Actually, Blue, Duke has been in touch and has passed on all the relevant material we need to prepare for your assessments."

"Cool."

I didn't need to look at Blue to hear the smile in her voice.

"Come on," Olivia encouraged, opening her MacBook. "I'll show you what you're in for."

Blue stepped past me, brushing her pinky against mine as she moved.

"Okay," I warned, subtly reminding her what we discussed. "If anyone needs me, I'll be in my office."

Blue sat down beside Olivia and mimed a thank you. I wasn't confident about what she was thanking me for, but I had a feeling it wasn't about this morning.

She finally could be who she wanted to be without her father holding her back. And that meant something. Maybe more than anything else I could ever give her. It didn't take me long to realise that if I could do anything for her while she was here, it would be to help her succeed. Especially when, for the last fifteen years, I'd lived with what I irresponsibly took away.

I entered my office to find Noah sitting behind my desk.

"We have company," he said, turning to face the couch and bar at the far end of the room. I followed his line of sight, only to find a man in a navy-blue suit striding towards me.

"James?"

"Good morning, Walker."

"What are you doing here?"

"I think the more important question is, what is my daughter doing here? When were you going to tell me?"

I looked to Noah, then back to James, my finger edging to the collar of my shirt to loosen the restriction around my airway. I knew Sophia was up to something, but she wasn't smart enough to figure out what was going on with Blue and me when I'd barely figured it out myself.

"Did Sophia call you?"

His brows pinched, but he didn't say anything, so I refrained from mentioning Sophia again and asked, "When was I going to tell you what?"

"Don't play stupid with me, son. I received a letter from Duke with confirmation of Blue being enrolled in their Apprenticeship Programme. You can imagine my confusion when I learned that Blue had an apprenticeship to begin with, never mind where that apprenticeship was taking place. So, I'll ask you again, when were you going to tell me that Blue was no longer studying at Duke, but here, working in a place like this?"

"A place like this?" I repeated, taken aback.

"It's not the life I want for her; you know that. She's not programmed to be a part of this world. Not the media and their savagery. She's too clean, too pure. This industry, this place–you know damn well she's above it."

I could have argued that she wasn't above it. That she was sassy, strong, and less fragile than he knew her to be. But fuck, it wasn't my place. He was her father, and what did my opinion matter when all of this could fuck up everything I'd worked towards? I couldn't protect Blue from everything, even if I wanted to.

Even if, up until a few weeks ago, I had never imagined standing in front of him, feeling the way I did about his daughter.

But why the fuck had James travelled across the world to tell me something he could have told me over an email or on the phone?

"I was going to tell you," I said, slipping my hands into my pockets. Why the fuck did I sound so meek? I wasn't afraid of James Sterling.

"When?" he interrupted. "Because in the last email you sent me, you failed to mention anything other than how nice a birthday dinner Blue had with you and Sophia on Wednesday."

Noah noticeably hissed from behind me, and my jaw ticked as I looked at him over my shoulder. He hadn't known I'd taken Blue to dinner, but he knew that there wasn't a chance Sophia would have been there, and he knew I'd rushed to leave work early. He'd have questions, and that was a problem because I wasn't ready to answer them. And I'm not sure if I ever could. It was bound to be temporary, what I and Blue had, wasn't it? Could it be more? Still, why complicate things by involving other people before we had the chance to figure it out between ourselves?

This was terrible timing.

Staring, I said, "You can leave, Noah. Louis should be arriving soon to prep the bar. Could you double-check everything is in order for tonight?"

I could tell he didn't want to leave me alone with James, that he would probably defend me no matter knowing my guilt or innocence, but he stood anyway and saluted the both of us with his phone as he exited the room.

"Well?" demanded James. "I want an explanation. I'm failing to understand why you kept this from me. I can understand why she would, but you—after everything. You owe me your loyalty."

I frowned. "Aren't we past that?"

"We are," he agreed. "I'd never use the past against you. It was a freak accident, I'm aware of that. You're not to blame."

"If I'm not to blame, why bring it up?"

"Because," he threatened. "You're supposed to be taking care of my daughter the way you did that night."

"I am taking care of her." Unfortunately, in more ways than he'd be comfortable with.

"So why, for the life of me, did you not consult me on this? Why did you believe it was acceptable to keep this from me? And whatever happened to her studying the degree she set out to study?"

My nostrils flared, and I took one hand from my pocket to palm my jaw before quickly returning it. He was here now, and with no time to prepare, it seemed in this instance, the truth was better than being caught in a lie.

"She had an altercation with one of her tutors."

"Details, Walker. I need details."

I took a deep breath, though as I was about to divulge the events that led us to the here and now, Noah stepped back into my office with Blue in tow. All I knew was that he must have fucking run to get her here so quick.

I pinched my nose. He believed he was helping, but he didn't realise that this might just make things worse.

I wasn't prepared.

I was a fucking fool. A mindless fool who hadn't thought any of this through.

This morning, I had my cock buried deep inside his daughter and was ninety-nine percent sure I had fucking *feelings* for her.

Idiot.

"Dad," Blue said warily.

"Princess." He stepped past me and walked towards her, holding his arms wide to greet her with an embrace. "You didn't answer the phone when I called you on your birthday. Neither did you, Walker." He side-eyed me.

Noah snickered. "That's because the silly cunt left his phone in the office."

How did he know that?

Jesus fuck.

He was implicating himself into shit he needn't get involved in. Yeah, I'd left my phone in the office, but I wondered what he'd think if he knew the real reason I hadn't answered James's call on Wednesday? That I'd come back for my phone, and the actual reason I hadn't answered was because I'd been too busy coming all over Blue's perfect tits?

Blue stepped into her father's arms, and they enclosed her. Staring at me over his shoulder, she looked as nervous as I'd felt. And fuck, did I feel it.

"He knows about Duke," I said aloud. There was no reason to hide it.

Understanding drew in her eyes, and I watched her face visibly relax. "I'm not sorry I didn't mention it," she told him.

I rounded my desk and sat back in my chair as they caught up, and Blue dug me out of that hole. As long as nobody mentioned Sophia, everything would be calm.

But shit, how had I managed to get myself into such a fucking mess? Of course, Noah's almost knowing stare and his eyes burning into the side of my head didn't help my frustration. He was still stuck on James's mention of Blue's birthday dinner, and though I was stuck on him knowing how he knew I'd left my phone in my office, I didn't need another revelation to come to light. Especially one which told James just how well I'd been taking care of his daughter. And how Sophia and Blue hadn't ever once met–unless I considered them catching one another's attention just yesterday as an introduction. Obviously, it was not.

Now that James was here, on my fucking territory, he threatened my whole charade. And all I could think was how the fuck could I tell the truth without losing The Lagoon, or Blue, in the process? Chances were, I wouldn't lose one without losing the other. And what a tragic story that would be if everything I worked for was for nothing.

Blue

MY DAD and I left Walker's office after I explained what had happened with Mr Smith. Except I purposely left out the part where Walker attempted to bribe him and accidentally got me suspended. I also left out the part where I tried to blackmail Walker in his office and softened the truth by telling him the apprenticeship was entirely my idea.

"I'm not happy about this," he said as we walked to the lobby.

"I didn't expect you to be. But, dad, I'm eighteen, and whether you like it or not, this is what I'm doing with my life."

"You've been in London almost two weeks, and already I see a change in you." He took me by my elbow and brought us to a halt outside the lobby door. "I'm not comfortable with it. And I don't appreciate how you and Walker lied to me."

I swallowed. "No one lied to you." I used Walker's words. "We just withheld the truth."

The way my father was acting was the exact reason I wanted to leave Miami. It may have only been two weeks, but it was the most freedom I'd ever had now that his noose wasn't around my neck. I was no longer living in retrograde but thriving and excited for my future.

My smile didn't reach my eyes. "I understand you're upset with me. But what I did wasn't worse than what you did when you asked Walker to baby me. I understand you didn't want this for me, but perhaps try to see the bigger picture?" I pushed open the lobby door with my shoulder and looked between Olivia and my father. "I want this, dad. It feels right. And if I show you what

I'm doing–if I show you what I can achieve–maybe you'll allow yourself to feel differently."

Olivia introduced herself to my father, and I was grateful he kept his line of sight on her face and didn't say anything that would be considered inappropriate, given his reputation.

The three of us moved to a table in the corner of the room, a quiet space away from the disruption of anyone who could have entered. And then Olivia opened her MacBook and, like she had with me, began a rundown on my apprenticeship with my father. She explained all the framework that Duke had emailed over that morning, and although my father seemed to agree and hang on to her every word, I wasn't entirely convinced he was supportive. Still, when he'd received all the information, and I showed him what we'd accomplished with The Lagoon's social media presence in the short time we'd spent on it, he perked up.

"Looks good." He nodded. "I'm impressed."

"Are you?" I asked, unsure if he was just saying it because we were in the presence of Olivia or if he meant it.

He looked at me again and then stood, checking the time on his Rolex. "I wouldn't say it unless it were true." Then he brought his attention back to me. "I have a business meeting I can't be late for. It was nice to meet you, Olivia."

"You too, Mr Sterling." Olivia smiled.

And while I refrained from rolling my eyes, he kissed me on the head.

"I'll see you tonight at the event." He raised a brow. "Though I rather I didn't. If you're going to work here, I'd prefer it to be between the hours of nine and five. This environment isn't for the vulnerable."

In my peripheral, I noticed Olivia looking up at us from her phone screen like she couldn't believe what he'd said. I could understand why. She didn't know my father. And she didn't understand the control he was giving up at that moment, not to say something worse or tell me I wasn't attending the event at all. Still, to her, it was as if everything we'd just been through with him went in one ear and out the other. But to me, it was progress. And although it wasn't much, slow progress was better than no progress, especially when I'd spent my teenage years struggling to make any.

OTHER THAN THE glitch with my father, Olivia was satisfied with the headway we made today. As well as making a start on my first module, which consisted of advertising and promotion, we also created a Twitter profile for The Lagoon and drew in some last-minute attention around tonight's event.

Which was why, when four o'clock came around, Walker was happy to let Finley take me back to the penthouse.

As soon as I stepped out of the elevator, I slipped off my Louboutins, grabbed a bottle of water from the kitchen fridge, and then made my way to Walker's bedroom.

I spotted his hoodie on the bed, and because I was feeling a little cold, I pulled it over my head before climbing into his bed without him–tired and in need of a power nap before I spent the rest of my evening back at the club, in the midst of what I predicted to be chaos.

I only hoped that my father was wrong. That when it came to this life, I wasn't as vulnerable as he thought.

It didn't take long for my body to become lax, but as my eyelids closed and my body moulded further into the mattress, I fell into a dream-like state. And it didn't matter how hard I tried to pull myself from it or how I subconsciously tried to force open my eyes, the dream took me hostage, and the memories I'd suppressed for so long waved a big white flag behind my eyes.

CHAPTER TWENTY-ONE

Walker

BACKSTAGE, The Lagoon was crawling with people. Those with media passes had set up their cameras in the Arena hours ago. The prelims were already through. And now we were further into the night, I had to strain to see an empty seat over the herd of the roaring audience.

As our youngest prospect, Teddy O'Sullivan, opener to the main card, bumped gloves with his opponent in the cage, I caught James through the fence, grinning beside a busty redhead. He'd disappeared after claiming he had a business meeting. Now I wasn't so sure if that was the case. With no sign of Blue at his side, I took my phone from my pocket to see if she'd texted me whilst I'd been otherwise occupied with a heated altercation between two undercards.

With a touch of the screen, the only notifications I had were ones I didn't give a shit for. I didn't have time to worry about Blue's whereabouts, yet I was. The Lagoon was heaving, she barely knew anyone, and the last I'd spoken to her was when I sent her back to the penthouse with Finley hours ago. She should've been back by now. On a whim, I decided to text her. **Where are you?**

I'd give her the benefit of the doubt before I chased up Finley. Today had been a long day, and it wasn't over yet. But if I had to, I'd send a fucking search party.

I turned my back on the crowd and strode down the halls of the Lagoon, making a pit stop at our next fighter's wardrobe with some words of encouragement, watching as his hands were wrapped, taped, gloved, then taped again over his wrists to keep them secure. Then, I returned on my way.

Entering the locker room we'd reserved for Hudson, I tipped my chin at my brother in acknowledgement, who sat not so far from his side. Noah wasn't just my mini-me around here. Everyone gave him their time of day. He walked into a room, and the people in that room would show him respect, and though he came across as my errand boy nine times out of ten, he did it because he was a genuine guy. A top friend. And the best fucking brother. It was precisely why he was sitting in support of our "Bully Boy," watching the event on the screen in front of him, instead of being in the arena, right beside the action.

Just as Hudson's opponent Killian had begun his pre-fight ritual in another room of the building, Hudson had done the same. I recognised the music playing through the speakers as DMA's *Silver*. Every fight since the song was released, he'd had it on repeat. Everyone else grew tired of hearing the same fucking lyrics time and time again, but Hudson seemed to come into his own when the song played enough times. He had a while to go until his turn in the cage. Members of our team were spread throughout the room, ready to give him whatever he asked for. But until then, it was pivotal that he kept his head straight.

"You seen Blue?" I asked Noah.

"Nah, is she with Olivia?"

At the mention of Olivia's name, Hudson side-eyed me from over his shoulder. With his back arched forward and his elbows resting on his knees, he spoke casually, "She's not with Olivia."

I frowned. I wanted to know how he knew that, but without wanting to disrupt his usual pre-fight routine, I dipped my head with thanks and slid my hands into the pockets of my slacks. "Alright. Noah, if you happen to see her before I do, tell her I'm looking for her."

"Is this about this morning?" he asked.

"How'd you mean?"

"Whatever went down with James. Blue's birthday dinner." His curls fell over his forehead as he mimicked Hudson's position and hiked an eyebrow in my direction. "Sophia. She didn't attend Blue's birthday dinner, did she?"

I sighed and scrubbed a hand across my jaw, glancing around the room. Six people too many occupied the four walls, making it easy for me not to divulge any details. "Not now. Later."

He pursed his lips and nodded slowly, his attention back on the television as Teddy passed his opponent's guard to full mount and started landing some vicious ground and pound.

The room erupted with hoots, and Noah blurted a "Get the fuck in there!" as Teddy's elbows rained down on his opponent's face, forcing the ref to jump in and stop the fight. With his opponent conscious but unable to fight back, it was declared a win by TKO.

The Lagoon was flying high. So far, every result was one I'd hoped for.

I smirked as I headed to the door, glancing at Hudson–the

only one to remain unbothered in his seat as his favourite fucking song ended and began again. Regardless of how well The Lagoon had done so far, it was his show. If he was nervous, the kid didn't show it.

My phone rang as I made my way from the room, back through the hall and towards the arena. *Finally,* I thought, as I slipped it from my pocket and answered without pause.

"Blue."

I heard a scoff and then, "Red is more my colour."

"Sophia?" I pulled my phone from my ear and took a glimpse at the number on the screen. "What the fuck are you doing in my office?" It didn't get past me that she mentioned red being her colour. And not because of the blood-red lipstick she often wore, but as if she was the champion and Blue was her challenger.

"I think we need to discuss a few things," she purred.

"We have nothing to discuss that can't be settled through our lawyers."

"That's where you're wrong."

I sighed and spoke dryly. "If you haven't noticed, it's fight night. I haven't got time for this."

"You'll want to make time, Walker."

I reached the door to the arena seconds after our next fighter stepped through. The audience's noise breathed into the hall before the door closed behind him, and then, glancing through the window, I drew my gaze to James. He hadn't moved, seemingly still content with the redhead at his side. It settled me, but only slightly. I took a deep breath, a little apprehensive that whatever move I made next could be damaging one way or another.

"What do you want from me, Sophia?"

Did I go into the arena and take my seat beside James, ignoring Sophia's idiocy?

Did I chase up Finley to figure out where the fuck Blue was?

What if Blue was with Sophia?

What if Sophia came down here and fucked everything up for me before I even had the chance to put things right?

"What do I want?" she hummed. "What. Do. I. Want?"

I heard the click of a mouse and then the sound of my printer. My brows bunched tighter. "The fuck are you doing? How did you get onto my computer?"

She laughed. "It took me a few attempts to guess your password, but I'm not completely dense. Noah's birthday. He always came before me. Before us. But then," she sighed, "so did work. I wish I could say I read your emails and found them... hmm, what's the word?" I heard the tap of her nails. "Lacklustre. But what you've told James–these lies you've fabricated–you've painted quite the picture. I'm touched, truly. It seems we've welcomed Blue into our home, and I've grown quite fond of her. *The Sixth Sense,* Walker, really? James believed me and his teenage daughter bonded over a psychological thriller? Give me credit. I have much more class."

My shoulders tightened, and when I didn't speak–because what the fuck was I supposed to say? she continued, "Come to your office. We need to discuss our future."

I ground my back teeth. "We don't have a fucking future. I've already wasted one too many years with you."

"That's where you're wrong. You need me. Maybe more than you did back then. Maybe now more than ever."

She hung up, and I pushed my phone back into my pocket, anger embodying me as I took off in the direction of the elevator. I hated to think it, let alone admit it, but if Sophia had read my emails, it meant she knew the extent I'd gone to. And it meant the bitch just might've been right. If I wanted The Lagoon, then perhaps I did need her. I required her to corroborate my story until the deal was done. At least where James was concerned.

The question was, how did I keep it from Blue? Was it even possible?

"Fuck!"

How had I been so fucking stupid?

There was no way I would crawl out of the mess I had made without losing something valuable to me in the process.

Blue

A FIST FLEW *through my window, and suddenly I was being pulled from my car seat and into the rain. Crying, I clung to the boy who held me, and as I looked up, he looked down, pulling something sharp from my jumper.*

Raindrops stuck to his hair, his brows pulled down in a frown.

"Shit," he said, looking between me and the car. "Fucking shit."

Warmth touched my back, but then it was gone as he spun us around and began jogging. Something crackled, and I wriggled, trying to see over his shoulder. But he didn't stop. We kept moving further and further away, and instead of letting me go, he only held me tighter.

"Mummy. I want my mummy."

"I know, kid. I'm so fucking sorry."

He lifted me higher, cradling my head, and that's when I saw it. Flames coming from the car. Someone was shouting for help, and my eyes followed the noise. There was another car, but it wasn't upside down like ours. A man had fallen from it and out onto the road. His face was covered in blood. But where was my mummy?

I whimpered, and the boy squashed my head into his neck. All I could hear was him cursing under his breath. Unable to move with his arms surrounding me, I cried into his neck, my tears falling against his skin.

A moment later, he opened the door of another car and spoke to someone over my head.

"Mummy," I sobbed. "I want my mummy."

"Did you call an ambulance?"

"Yeah."

"Good, take the kid. Keep her warm until the paramedics get here. She's bleeding a little bit. She had some glass near her shoulder. Will you remember to tell them that if I go and... If I go and... fuck! Just tell them. I have to go back."

He tried to hand me over to the person behind me, but I gripped onto the boy like I would my bunny.

Oh no, my bunny.

He swore as my hold on him tightened, and then, ever so gently, he angled my chin upwards. His fingers were damp and cold against my skin, but his mouth turned up at one corner, forcing a smile.

"Don't do that," he whispered. "Don't cry. Noah's going to look after you while I go and get your mummy, alright?"

My lip wobbled. "And bunny?"

"Bunny too."

His smile disappeared as he looked outside and off into the distance. He was frowning now. Frowning as he passed me to Noah, who sat me on his knee and secured his small arms around me.

"Nate, is her mummy okay?"

Nate swallowed.

He looked at me, then back to Noah. Then he shook his head, quickly pulling off his jumper.

"Wrap her in this," he said, right before closing the car door.

Through the rain covered windows, I watched him run back towards the direction we'd come from.

My body shook as I settled back against Noah's warmth. He settled the jumper over me like a blanket, and just as I closed my eyes—

my little body so tired–his whisper broke through the darkness. "My brother said if he had stopped at that red light, your mummy would have too."

STARING at my blank expression through the bathroom mirror, I robotically applied the finishing touches to my make-up. The girl in the mirror looked like she had her entire life together. An expensive dress–flawless skin. Nothing to suggest she continued to live through a tragedy unless someone were to ask, "How did you get that scar?" and she revealed her life story.

Wasn't it disappointing that I'd spent my whole life feeling threatened by others' judgement, when in reality, the judgement of others only hurt because it exposed precisely the image I portrayed? And wasn't it contradictory that I'd spent my whole life trying to outrun my childhood, only to find myself in the arms of a man who understood more of it than I could even comprehend?

I placed my lipstick on the counter and brushed my shaking fingers through my hair before settling my palms against the granite.

Unlike me, Walker probably remembered every recollection. The moment he ran a red light to the moment he left me in the arms of his little brother.

I leant over the sink, hurling, and though acid seemed to climb up my throat and my chest threatened a panic attack, I didn't succumb to the dread any further. But still, I felt it. I felt it from my head to my toes as it deflated me, second by second– moment by moment. And I wanted to be wrong. I wanted so hard for someone to tell me that I wasn't the little girl in my dream. That Walker wasn't the boy who pulled me from my mother's car while he left her to die.

How had I not known who he was when I sat beside him on the plane? Why had my father always referred to him as *the stranger who saved me*, as if he hadn't played a part in my mother's death and killed the woman my father claimed to be the love of his life? Perhaps my father was more messed up than I realised. Clearly, I was a lousy judge of character all around.

Walker... I didn't know him at all.

My phone vibrated against the bathroom counter, and I glanced at the screen, noticing a text from the man himself. The girl in the mirror would have laughed if she hadn't been me. The girl in the mirror would have run away if she wasn't finally ready to face her trauma. Both she and I deserved an explanation.

Had I been naive to think he began to feel for me what I had for him? That there was something between the two of us? That he actually cared about me? That this familiarity I felt towards him was more than the experience that outlined my entire life? That I wasn't just here out of his guilt? That I wasn't just here because my father didn't give him the fucking choice?

I felt dirty.

Every inch of me.

Inside and out.

My breath shook as I inhaled and exhaled again and again, until eventually, I picked up my phone and left the bathroom.

I ignored Walker's message and dialled my father, and on the fifth ring, he picked up.

"Dad." There was a ruffle, a giggle, the expansive noise of a crowd, and then the sound of the announcer opening the next fight. "Dad. I need to talk to you about something."

"Blue. I can barely hear you."

"I said I need to talk to you about something."

"Right now? I'm already seated; where are you?"

I paused in the kitchen, looking to the ceiling to hold back the angry and equally devastated moisture pooling inside my eyes. And I felt both. I felt both under my skin like burning shame. "I remember, dad. I remember what happened. You said a stranger saved me. But it was Walker. It was Walker that pulled me from the car."

He grunted. "Where are you?"

"I'm still at Walker's. Can you come here?"

"No. Stay there."

"What? No. Please. I need to talk to you."

"No, Blue. I said stay there. We can discuss this tomorrow. All these years refusing therapy, this can only be a good thing. Tomorrow," he repeated. "We can talk then."

"A good thing?" I scoffed, feeling frantic. "How is this considered a good thing? All this time, you've been lying to me. All this time, *he's* been lying to me. It's his fault, dad. Mum died because he–"

A beep sounded, and I realised my father had ended the call.

My phone fell to my side and hit my thigh as I blinked back my tears. There was no way I was waiting until tomorrow to speak with him. And if my father wasn't going to come here at a time when I needed him, then I had no choice but to go to him.

FINLEY PULLED up outside the doors of The Lagoon and stepped out of the car. He rounded the vehicle and opened my door. I hadn't spoken the entire drive over, so it didn't surprise me when he helped me from my seat and asked, "Is everything okay?"

It was funny how okay meant something entirely different just this morning.

So I didn't answer him.

I couldn't.

"Do you want me to call Walker and have him meet you?" He

looked around us. The noise of the crowd could be heard through the arena walls, and there were only a few people waiting to go inside.

"No," I said. "I need to find my father."

Finley nodded solemnly, then walked me over to a side door where he handed a security guard my pass. I walked through the door alone and followed the noise of the crowd to the arena. Despite wearing little clothes, my skin remained hot. And with every step, I grew more nervous.

My eyes immediately went to the Octagon as I stepped through the double doors and into the arena. The crowd felt overbearing; thousands of people cheering as they watched the fight before them. There was a large television screen against the room's back wall, giving those seated far from the octagon the perfect view. After all, it was the atmosphere as well as the enter-tainment that made the event what it was. I scoffed, somewhat ashamed to be a part of it now that I knew exactly the type of person Nate Walker was.

As the camera panned out, I spotted my father on the screen, sitting behind the cage. So that's where I went, bypassing rowdy crowd members as I made my way to him. I wished for my sunglasses to hide my eyes, though I held my head high and continued.

When he spotted me, he scowled. "I told you not to come," he said as he stood. Then, gripping my arm, he led me away from the cage and from the arena.

"I'm not waiting until tomorrow to talk about what happened. You've wanted me to face my trauma for years, so here I fucking am, dad. Right here, facing it."

"Don't you dare curse in front of me."

"Then don't treat me like a child!" I screamed. A lone tear escaped my eye, but I wiped it away before it could glide down my cheek.

He blanched back, dropping my arm, and those who stood near us all turned to look in our direction. A few camera phones pointed in our direction. Judging, I imagined. But for once, I tried to convince myself how little I cared. They could judge all they wanted. They could believe what they wanted, and I wouldn't let it bother me because they knew nothing of what I'd been through.

With a pinch of his nose, he said, "Walker hasn't sat down yet. Have you spoken to him? Do you know where he is?"

I shook my head to both, but a staff member must've been eavesdropping on our conversation because he darted his head up and said, "I saw him take off in the direction of the elevator."

"Then he must be in his office," my father stated. He didn't bother with a thank you, and maybe, for the first time in my life, I didn't either. My father waltzed off in the direction of the elevator, and I followed behind.

"How did you figure it out?" he murmured. "After all this time, what triggered the memory?"

I took a deep breath. The words were hard to get out, but I forced them through my lips anyway. "Subconsciously, Walker never felt like a stranger. And since being here, my dreams have only become clearer." I swallowed back the lump in my throat as I remembered how real my dream felt. How it felt like a moment I'd lived. "I don't understand, dad. It was his fault, wasn't it? She'd still be here if he didn't run that red light. I wouldn't have grown up without a mother. I wouldn't have grown up like *this*. How can you forgive him for taking her away? How can I forgive him for shaping who I am?"

"He made a bad judgement call, princess. As much as it kills me to admit it, your mother ran that red light all on her own. Walker cannot be liable for the mistake of another person. We weren't the only ones who lost something that day."

I shook my head, the new information only confusing me further. "I don't know what you mean—"

"Noah. He went into foster care. A police check revealed Walker had stolen his father's car. No tax, no insurance. When the police took the boys home, they realised their parents weren't fit to care for Noah. Walker had taken Noah from the family home. They'd run away. Only social services wouldn't allow Walker to take custody of him. By coincidence, Walker applied for a job at The Lagoon a few months later, and because he saved you, it only felt right I gave him something in return."

"I don't understand... Dad, he *took*. You didn't owe him anything."

"You're wrong, princess. I did. I owed him a chance."

I shook my head, unbelieving. "If you believed it wasn't his fault, why didn't you tell me any of this? Why didn't you tell me who he was before I came to London?"

"When you were younger, before you were old enough to refuse therapy, I was told by your therapist that it was best to let you explore your memories and your feelings without leading you in a particular direction. Nobody could tell me if you'd remember or whether your memories would remain repressed. You were already so fragile. I didn't want to push you over the ledge by filling in every blank."

What...?

"So the two of you lied to me?"

"I asked him to keep it from you, princess. And in the back of my mind, I hoped you'd figure it out on your own. Though I must say"—he pressed the button on the elevator, and we stepped inside—"you're making a complete show of it with your timing. You do realise how important tonight is for The Lagoon, don't you? How important tonight is for Walker."

I knew that, and maybe a small part of me—one I wished

wasn't there–felt guilty, but I wouldn't admit that to him. And this... wasn't this more important? Wasn't I?

"A show of it?" I wiped under my eyes, feeling my stomach sink as the elevator rose. Did I even want to speak to Walker now? How was I supposed to face him? I hadn't had any time to process everything my father just told me.

If he was telling the truth, it meant Walker wasn't to blame.

And why would my father fabricate a story when he lost my mother the way he did?

My mind swirled, my chest expanded, and I found myself growing dizzy with emotion.

"Yes, a show of it. You've gone this long. One more day wouldn't have gone amiss, princess. Just one more day while the dust settled in that head of yours."

"Is that what you think? You think this is dust, dad?" I held my palm against my heart, feeling it break. "Imagine being me– imagine having to relive it. Do you think I planned this? Do you think I wanted this?"

I felt sick with sadness, with anger, with confusion.

How was I to know that Walker wasn't who I thought he was?

I thought it was his fault, but it turned out his betrayal only stemmed from him hiding the truth.

I closed my eyes, counting the beat of my heart with each crack, unaware who, perhaps even what, was really breaking it. And how was I to stop it from breaking if I didn't understand? If I couldn't find the root of it?

Walker warned me he had secrets.

He tried to scare me off him.

So why didn't I listen?

CHAPTER TWENTY-TWO

Walker

I STEPPED into my office to find Sophia seated at my desk. With one leg crossed over the other, she sat back in my office chair like she owned it.

"No Wez today?" I remarked. "Did your little boyfriend come to his senses?"

She pursed her lips at me, mockingly. "He meant nothing."

"I don't actually give a fuck." I sneered, pulling at my sleeve. "Let's make this quick, Sophia. Whatever it is you're doing. Whatever it is you want to say. Whatever it is you want from me, speak it into existence, so we can get about our evening, yeah?"

She dropped her head to the side ever so slightly, staring at me with glee. And worse, she looked comfortable. Too comfortable.

I fucking hated it.

I hated how I'd spent the last eleven years of my life with this woman, and now I couldn't feel anything more than disgust. Disgust for myself–disgust for her.

But I didn't want to let it show, so I did what was deemed normal for *us*. I walked to the end of the room and took a glass from my office bar. Studying the bottles that lined the shelf, I picked up a bottle of Jack before thinking twice and placing it back down–remembering I made a promise to the girl that had somehow woven her way under my skin. I intended to try my damn hardest to keep it, even if it took every ounce of my strength.

Sophia was a fucking parasite, and alcohol had been my fucking antidote for so long. But who knew? Maybe Blue Sterling could be my remedy.

I didn't get a chance to ponder on that for long. At the sound of Sophia rising from the chair, I spun to face her, watching her from the short distance between us.

"You've got yourself in quite the pickle," she remarked, flattening down the faint creases of her dress.

She leant under my desk, taking the last printed email as it exited the printer. When she stood, she darted her gaze from me to the words on the page. I could've charged at her and ripped the paper from her hands. Though what was the point? The lies I'd told were bigger than the paper they'd been inked on.

"Sorry I missed your call. Happy to go ahead with the buyout. I've attached the required documents. Blue enjoyed her birthday dinner. Both her and Sophia enjoyed a few glasses of champagne, and then we called it a night," Sophia mimicked, reading the latest email I'd sent to James. *"She's a good girl."* She scoffed. "Yeah, that line doesn't surprise me. You've always been one for praise."

My fists clenched at my sides as she placed the email down on my desk on top of others. "I know what they say," I said dryly. "I wrote them."

My eyes followed her move for move, as she straightened out the paper.

"For theatrics," she said, looking at me across her shoulder with a smirk. "I've already forwarded myself copies."

I checked the time on my watch as she made her way towards me and mumbled, "Nothing you do no longer surprises me."

When she reached me, she placed her palm over my chest as she pushed up against my body. "The element of surprise is overrated," she cooed.

No doubt she felt every erratic beat of my heart, even if I refused to give her anything else she wanted.

I didn't move as she leant forward. She wasn't going to intimidate me. Not even when her lips were a breath away from mine or when her eyes darted between my own, searching for something I was yet to give.

"Tell me, does Blue know she's only here in return for something James offered? It's clear to me you've formed quite the relationship. What would James say if he knew me and his precious daughter had never met? That she's been staying with you and you alone after this image you've painted? How do you think that looks, hmm? How did you expect this to end?"

"I would've told him the truth."

Eventually.

"The same way I would have told you the truth if you hadn't shown up at our door and saw my affair for yourself? At the risk of losing something you love? Don't lie to yourself, Walker."

Fuck this. I stepped back, completely repulsed by her presence, recreating the distance between us. "I'd do whatever it took if it meant James would let me buy him out. In this instance, it was taking care of his daughter. So what? You already knew that. You heard him through the phone the night he asked. Don't pretend you didn't."

"Taking care of his daughter? No. I saw the way you were with her at the weigh-in. The way she looked at you when you were with me. It seems like you're taking care of his daughter all too well."

"It's none of your fucking business what I do. You think you have a leg to stand on?"

She stepped back into me, and though I felt disgusted with her body against mine, I held my ground. Even if just for the moment.

Without an ounce of shame, she placed her lips beside my ear. "Oh, but it is. Because like it or not, we're still married, and I'm an important piece in your very"—I felt the touch of her red lips against my neck—"*very* complex puzzle."

My hands went to her hips as I pushed her away, and a condescending laugh blurted from her mouth as she fell back a few steps.

I scoffed. "You're fucking crazy; you know that?"

"Crazy or not, you need me," she retaliated. "Or everything ends so badly for you. If I tell James I've never met his precious daughter, he's not going to give you the club. It's not hard to assume you took advantage of her, given your age difference."

My jaw ticked. "That's not what it is."

"No? So am I wrong? Do you believe James would welcome you into his family with open arms after you killed his wife? Are you that desperate for a father figure in your life?"

"I didn't kill anyone."

"That's right," she mused. "But it was your fault."

"It was a fucking accident, Sophia. You think you know, but you weren't there. You don't know shit."

"What about Blue? Do you think she'll still want you when she realises you've been lying to her? That you're the reason her mother is dead? You're not a stupid man, but it seems you've made some foolish mistakes."

"Mistakes escalate when you're too embarrassed to admit them. Marrying you was a mistake, if not the biggest regret of my fucking life." I crossed my arms over my chest, trying not to let her words infect me like the poison they were. "I'm done. Tell me what it is you want. Is it money? More property? Fucking spit it out so I can get back to a life without you."

"I want a baby."

"What?"

"I want your baby."

I shook my head, disbelief forcing me to laugh. "Funny."

"I'm not joking." She stepped back into me, her fingers moving to the belt of my slacks. I uncrossed my arms to grip her forearms, but I was too taken aback to stop her from unfastening my belt. "Let it be the last thing you do for me, and I'll leave you alone."

"Not this again, Sophia. We're getting a divorce. I don't want you. I don't want a family with you. Shit, there's no chance in hell I'd give you my child and be tied to you for the rest of my fucking life. You think I want to be a fucking father? *I don't.*"

She dropped to her knees, quickly fiddling with the buttons on my trousers. "I just want something to love. And someone to love me."

My jaw ticked. "Stop, Sophia. Jesus. Our marriage was a mockery. What makes you think I'd give you my child?"

The door to my office opened before I could stop her from going any further, and I turned my head, watching as James stepped into the room.

I was so swept up in what Sophia had said, I hadn't even heard the lift. My eyes dropped to his feet, embarrassed to be caught mid-argument–mid who the fuck knew what–with my soon-to-be ex-wife. It took me a moment to register, but I caught long sun-kissed legs behind him that led up to a little leather dress. And then my gaze was on Blue's face. And my multi-coloured orbs were locked on her sea glass domes.

And there I was.

Lipstick on my neck.

Sophia on her knees in front of me. My belt unfastened and her conniving hands inches from my fucking cock.

It didn't matter that I was as soft as a fucking sponge. It looked bad. It looked really fucking bad.

"Blue."

I moved back from Sophia and hastily buttoned up my trousers as Sophia climbed to her feet.

James laughed. "Are the two of you not getting much alone time now that my daughter is living with you?"

Blue's brows bunched into a frown, hurt and confusion both etched on her face that was noticeable even with space between us.

I did that to her.

I did that to her, and I didn't fucking like it. And worse, I couldn't go to her. I couldn't go to her because what the fuck was I meant to say? What the fuck was I meant to do when James was *right there*?

Sophia plastered on a fake smile. "Unfortunately not, James. I can't complain, though. After eleven years of marriage, the excitement of roleplay helps keep the flame alive. I'm sorry you caught us in such a predicament."

James licked his lips, looking up and down at Sophia as he nodded. Whether he believed her lie or not, I couldn't be sure.

All I could focus on was how green Blue's eyes looked as they began to gloss over. She directed her gaze to me, and then, like it was just us in the room, her lips parted, and all I could hear was disbelief in her voice when she asked, "You're married?"

A hard lump formed in my throat. Even if I could speak, I didn't have a chance to before James turned to his daughter and quipped, "Of course they're married." And then he turned back to Sophia and me. "Don't tell me the two of you have been avoiding complete PDA for the sake of my daughter? I assume this isn't the first time you've resorted to sneaking away?"

Swallowing roughly, I forced out, "It's not what it looks like." And of course, I was speaking to Blue, but James mistook my reply for himself.

"I'd fucking hope not. Blue's sheltered, but given who I am, she's grown comfortable with public displays of affection. No wonder she hadn't realised the two of you were married if you've been giving your wife a wide berth."

Jesus fuck. I sucked in a lungful of air through my nose and dropped my head as I began fastening my belt. Sophia didn't say anymore, but my chest tightened as I felt her presence surround me and dominate the room.

I didn't know what to do.

I didn't know how the fuck to navigate this.

My wife.

My business partner.

And an eighteen-year-old girl I'd slowly but surely been growing devoted to. All in one fucking room. And all too close for fucking comfort.

When I looked up, I studied Blue's face. She seemed to be looking between all three of us, from me, to Sophia, and then to her father. She was trying to figure everything out. In my mind, she assumed I'd taken advantage of her. That I'd used her to get myself off. That I'd manipulated her into being intimate with me and tricked her into a meaningless affair.

James's voice had my gaze snapping to his. "I have something to discuss with you before the main event, Walker. So if you don't mind, Sophia–"

"What is it? Can it wait?"

He pierced his gaze on me, hiking an eyebrow. The look told

me I could only assume he believed I wanted to wait because I was about to get my cock sucked.

"No. It can't. Sophia, would you mind escorting Blue downstairs while me and Walker have a conversation?"

"It'll be my pleasure," Sophia said much too willingly.

I clenched my jaw, feeling Blue's gaze cut to me like a knife. And then, without a word, I slid my hands into the pockets of my slacks because if I didn't, fuck knows what I'd do with them. And then Blue strode from the room, faster than I would have liked to see her go, and Sophia spun around, ready to take after her.

Before I realised it, I pulled one hand from my pocket and gripped her wrist, tugging her back with a look that conveyed not to fuck with me. James didn't seem to notice, but that's because his eyes were focused on the emails Sophia placed on my desk before he'd entered.

Sophia smirked knowingly, and reluctantly, I let her go. She left the room, and then it was just James and me.

He picked up the emails. "What are these?"

I cleared my throat, keeping the distance between us. But what I really wanted was to leave my office and go after Blue. "Our emails."

"I see that, but why are they sitting on your desk?"

I took a deep breath through my nose. "Sophia printed them."

His brows pinched. "For what reason?"

"Fuck." I palmed my face. "What a fucking mess."

"Walker." He placed the emails back down on my desk and turned to study me. "What on earth is going on?"

Looking between him and the door, I came to the conclusion I was short of options. Something had to give. Who the fuck knew what lies Sophia was feeding Blue? And now Blue knew I was married, that this whole charade wasn't going to fall apart

JESSICA GRACE

another way? In a way completely out of my control? In a way that was past repair?

"I left Sophia," I said begrudgingly. "The day after you called me and asked me to take in Blue, I left the townhouse."

"You did what?"

"I filed for divorce... and she's being a total fucking bitch. She's refusing to sign the papers. She's trying to blackmail me into giving her something she wants."

He held up a finger. "Wait a minute. Just wait a fucking minute. If you left her, where has Blue been this whole time?"

"With me." I sighed, palming my hand across my jaw. "But you have to understand, leaving Sophia was in the works before the night you called me. I leased a penthouse in Kensington, and it had been there, ready and waiting. Fuck, James. I'm sorry, but Blue didn't know Sophia existed until today."

"Which was why she was so shocked to discover you were married."

I nodded.

"So your emails..." he said, attempting to put two and two together.

"Are fabrications of the truth. Those things I said in my emails happened, but Sophia was never a part of the picture. It was just the two of us."

The baggage fell off my shoulders, but guilt sank to the bottom of my stomach like dead weight.

He crossed his arms over his chest. "I'm not sure I'm under-standing you, Walker. Fabrications of the truth? You mean to say you lied to me, son?"

I nodded again, ready to admit my wrongdoings.

This shitshow needed to be over with.

"Yeah," I confessed, my tone flat. "Yeah, I lied in my emails. I lied, and I can only apologise. You must think the worst of me. It was shitty of me, James. Fucking shitty."

Aware I was rambling, I sucked my teeth, all while he wagged his head from side to side. He hadn't moved his arms from where they were still clenched across his chest, his shoulders stiff. Confusion and discomfort surrounding us like black smoke.

Fuck, I was surprised to find I could still breathe.

That the revelation hadn't killed me already.

"I know it's a lot..."

"I'm just confused as to why you wouldn't have told me this before? Not only that, but you had the opportunity to come clean to me yesterday. Why didn't you mention it to me? Why was Sophia on her fucking knees just then if you two are in the process of separating? Are the two of you still–"

"No." Unable to explain everything, I scoffed in spite of myself. "I don't know why I hadn't mentioned it except for feeling so fucking embarrassed. I was taking it one day at a time. Plans to leave her were already in motion before you called me. Shit, I could barely see the light at the end of the tunnel, but I didn't want to let you down. When you mentioned buying you out, I didn't want to leave it up to chance." I slid my hands to my nape and locked them together, allowing myself a long exhale. "This place... the club. It's my fucking life. Sophia... she's just fucking deluded and doesn't want to let go."

He uncrossed his arms, not looking any less relaxed. How could I blame him? I'd fucked up, and worse, this was only the half of it.

"I'm sorry to hear that. Truly. I'm disappointed you kept it from me, but you should have known that wouldn't have changed anything." After giving me a moment of reflection, he continued. "That meeting I had yesterday? That was with my soliciting firm here in London. Blue Lagoon's yours once you transfer the funds over and the payment has been cleared. If this is all Sophia has over you, you needn't worry, Walker." He frowned. "What is it she wants from you anyway?"

"More than I'm capable of giving her." And then admittedly, I said, "More than I want to give her."

"Well, then." He strode towards me. "I'll never love again, that we know, but I loved once, and I of all people know that for someone you love, you'd do anything. Even if it meant breaking your own heart to see them happy." In what seemed like a rare moment of the old James, he smiled as if reminiscing a memory before shaking himself free of it. "So you must not love Sophia, and eh, that's okay. I realise this has been hard for you, but I'll have you know you needn't have worried. There's not another man I'd trust with my daughter. If there were to be a next time, one where you find yourself at a hard turn, perhaps put a little of that trust into my opinion of you."

His eyebrow rose as he held out his hand.

I was apprehensive to take it, wondering if he were to discover the things I'd done, would he still think so highly of me? And then there was the discomfort in my chest, a sad dwell when I thought of the night his wife died. He'd loved her beyond words, and I couldn't help but wonder what that felt like.

Maybe a part of me knew, but it hurt too much to think about.

Still, I decided to take his hand anyway.

It would be too obvious if I didn't.

"Congratulations. I'm disgustingly proud of you, Walker. You've come far, achieved a lot. There's never been a better fit for The Lagoon than you."

Though I was ecstatic to hear him speak the words–words I'd never experience from my own blood, the guilt still festered. Because despite *this* truth, there was so much more he didn't know. And I felt if he knew the extent of mine and his daughter's relationship, there wasn't a chance in hell he'd have held out his hand to me. Instead, he'd be throwing his fists into my face and wishing me fucking dead. Maybe there wasn't another man he'd trust with his daughter, but that wouldn't hold if he learnt what I'd done.

His words were a hard pill to swallow, and they seemed to get stuck in my throat.

"We do have other things to address."

I frowned, feeling anxiety creep up my spine.

"It's Blue."

Immediately, I was reminded of the hurt in her eyes when she stepped into my office. The hurt I caused her. He didn't know about us, and given that, I hadn't a chance to comprehend what there was left to discuss before he said, "She remembers."

My nails dug into the palms of my hand. I understood each word, but my mind didn't want to accept it. Hadn't I put her through enough? Still, I found myself asking, "Remembers what exactly?"

"She remembers the accident. She remembers you. She doesn't understand it–I mean, how could she?" He cleared his throat. "But, she blames you, Walker. She blames you for Lola's death. I explained everything, filled in what she didn't know, but..." He appeared to consider what he said next. "I believe it's for the best that I take her home with me."

"Home as in–"

"Miami, yes. I appreciate everything you've done for her these past two weeks. It can't have been easy, given your situation. There's no need to feel embarrassed. But it's clear that this life–life here in London and around you–isn't healthy for my daughter."

I didn't know how to respond, so with nothing to say except for "I should talk to her," I left the office with James in tow, and we took the elevator to the arena. It was hard not to show how antsy I was standing beside him. It was hard to keep my feet in place and my hands still in my pockets. Fuck knows how I managed it without him cottoning on to how desperate I was to find her and check she was okay.

Clearly, she wasn't.

I'd seen so myself.

"Alright," he said, looking down at his Rolex. "Don't take too long." And as the elevator doors opened, he followed with a "You're a good man." And gave me a double pat on the back.

He was taller than me, and the gesture felt like one I'd receive from a father if I had such a figure. A good man? I thought. Finley often said I was a good man. Occasionally, so did Noah. But I failed to see it. Especially now, when there was so much left unsaid. But with everything unfolding, perhaps it was best James never knew the truth of his daughter and me. That way, he'd still believe I was a good man, and fuck, maybe I could convince myself I was too.

With his approval, not that I needed it, I went in search of Blue in the hopes she would let me sit down with her and explain everything from my point of view. Given the situation, what else could I have done? Though I was eager to argue with James and demand Blue stay with me in London, I knew I needed to speak with her first. If she'd even give me that. Still, I wanted to make sure she understood. James said she'd remembered and that he'd filled in the blanks, but other than that, I didn't know much else. And fuck knows what shit Sophia had filled her head with since leaving my office, and with me not there to defend myself; I only imagined the worst.

I pulled at the neck of my shirt. Just the image of Sophia being close to her fucked me off.

I probably deserved it.

I probably deserved the hate Blue no doubt wanted to spit at me.

I knew I didn't deserve her.

I never had, and I knew without a doubt I should've never crossed that line with her when I had the answers she didn't.

Once I pulled my phone from my pocket, I dialled her number, only to meet her voicemail a second later. And then I did the same with Finley, only to meet his. As I bypassed the last fighters cleaning up their areas, I caught Olivia coming out of an empty side room. Her eyes widened when I crossed in front of her path. "Walker."

My eyes narrowed as she looked back at the door closing behind her, then back to me. "Olivia. Have you seen Blue?"

"No, I haven't. Sorry."

I waited a beat, noticing a little nervousness to be read from her body language alone. "Who's in there?" I asked, lifting my chin at the room behind her, itching to move my feet. "Is it Blue? As I stepped forward, she moved in front of the door handle, so I was unable to force my way through. "Olivia," I grit. "She's in there, isn't she?"

She moved from one foot to the other as she reached up to tuck some hair behind her ear. "No," she drew out slowly. Too slowly.

"You're on a very thin line with me right now. If you want to keep your job, I suggest you move out of my way."

"I promise you; she's not in there."

My attention moved to the door handle as someone from the other side pushed down. And as Hudson stepped out, I drew my gaze back to Olivia. Her face scrunched up, followed by her eyes closing tight. And then Hudson spoke, "Blue's definitely not in there."

"Jesus, Hudson. Are you fucking serious? You're due to walk out any minute."

"Chill," he said.

It was one word. One word that only made my blood run

hotter because in spite of not wanting everything to go tits up on one of the most important events in The Lagoon's history, everything seemed to be much fucking worse.

"I can't be doing this right now. If anyone sees Blue, ring me. It's urgent."

With that, I carried on down the corridor and out the back exit of The Lagoon. There was a dampness to the air, daylight drawing out as the night darkened. I heaved in a lungful of air, mouthed a "Fuck," and palmed my face so hard I felt the burn of the friction against my skin. In order to gather my thoughts, I tilted my eyes to the ground as my hands fell to my hips.

I heard the door open and close behind me, feeling her before seeing her. Except it wasn't her I was looking for. It wasn't her I wanted. It wasn't her I needed. I was no longer concerned for her. In fact, I was confident I no longer cared for her in any way whatsoever. She'd fucked what little respect I had left for her the moment I found out who it was she'd been fucking.

"There you are," she cooed.

"If you as so much as step any closer to me, Sophia, I swear I'll ruin your whole fucking life." My eyes opened, and I pinned them on her as she held her hands up in mock surrender.

"Don't be so dramatic."

I turned around to face her. "Where's Blue?"

"How should I know?"

"Don't fucking play. Where is she?"

She pouted. "I don't know. She ran off once I explained that you make a habit of cheating on me. And then there was the text…"

I frowned. "What text?"

"Oh, you know." She tipped her shoulder as she seized her phone from her clutch bag. "Incoming."

In the next second, my phone chimed with a text, and I slipped it from my pocket. Though I needn't have bothered because Sophia was already reading aloud what she'd forwarded me. "I've told you time and again, Soph, there's only ever been you." She pouted. "Yeah, she didn't take it too well. Surprising, considering you said yourself she was no more than a job."

"You took that text completely out of context."

"Did I? So you didn't cheat on me with James Sterling's teenage daughter?"

"You know what? Fuck you," I said, looking from her to my phone as it chimed with another text. **Blue's back at the penthouse.** A message from Finley and my only saving grace.

Those five words were all I needed.

Two weeks ago, I'd never imagined fucking off fight night. Two weeks ago, I'd never imagined my life the way it was in the next moment.

I began to take off in the direction of the underground staff parking lot, not sparing Sophia any more of my attention.

"Wait, where are you going?"

She didn't deserve an explanation. She didn't deserve any more of my time. But even so, I still gave her some parting words.

"James knows everything, Soph." At least as much as he needed to. "It's time to move on."

The moment I reached my G-Wagon, I knew what I had to do. And I owed Blue answers, if nothing else.

CHAPTER TWENTY-THREE

Walker

IT WAS like deja vu as I stepped foot into the penthouse and heard Blue's crying in the distance. Only this time, I didn't hesitate to get to her. And maybe it was wrong, and perhaps it wasn't fair of me, but I wrapped my hand around the handle of her bedroom door and went to push it open, only to discover she'd locked herself inside.

"Blue." My eyes closed as I leant my forehead against the hardwood. "Open the door."

"You lied to me," she accused. "About everything."

Apparently, I did have a heart, because the sound of her voice was breaking it.

I swallowed, pushing my head against the door as I tried to force my way through one more time. "Come on, open the door. Let's talk properly. Please, not like this. I can't fix it like this."

"Talk?"

I could hear she was crying.

Just the sound of it tortured me.

"We have nothing to talk about. Your *wife*, she told me everything, Walker. I had begun to fall for you. I began to fall for you, only to discover you're nothing but a fucking fraud."

I shook my head against the wood, knowing Sophia had filled her head with inconsolable bullshit.

"You should have told me."

Fuck.

"I know," I admitted, feeling my chest tighten while trying to breathe through the reality of my betrayal. The feeling of regret was relatively new to me, and I wasn't entirely sure how to tame it.

"About everything."

"I know. You're right."

"About Sophia," her tone choked. "About the accident."

"Blue, baby, I know. I fucking know. Please, just... open the door." I took hold of the handle again, resisting the urge to break the door down. Because all I wanted to do, all I fucking wanted to do, was take her in my arms, hold her and tell her I was sorry.

I was so sorry, but I wasn't going to apologise to a fucking door.

"I'm... not ready."

My hand shook against the handle, and I inhaled a deep breath before exhaling it back through my nose and dropping my arm. "I'm not going anywhere. Either open the door so we can talk, or stay right where you are, but you'll hear me out if it's the last thing you do before you leave."

"What?"

I turned around, sliding down the door until my ass hit the floor. "You're going home tomorrow. You're going to go back to Miami, and you'll forget about us." I bent my legs, dropped my head back against the door, and relaxed my forearms over my knees. "I don't know what lies Sophia fed you, but we're in the process of getting a divorce. What you saw in my office... shit, I know what it looked like, but nothing happened. I wouldn't do that to you. Not after what happened between us this morning. Sophia wants a baby–she thought–fuck knows what she thought, but she's nothing to me, Blue. You hear me?"

Her crying lessened, but her breathing was ragged. "I don't know how I'm supposed to grasp all of this." I heard her back hit the door, and I was sure she mimicked my position from the other side as her voice moved with her. Ignoring everything I mentioned of Sophia, it seemed she only held on to the most crucial factor. "I'm going home?"

She was strong, even through her sadness. And I admired that.

I admired her.

Everything about her was worth admiring from the moment she sat beside me on the plane. And if I wanted her to be happy, the only thing that made sense now was for me to admire her from afar. The thought made me sick to my stomach, but despite me wanting to be selfish, of fighting the battle for her to stay, it was the right thing to do. The only thing to do. Because look at what I'd done to her in the small amount of time we'd had together. What was I if not stuck between a rock and a hard place?

I closed my eyes. "Your father... he doesn't believe it's healthy for you to stay in London. Not after everything you've discovered. If it's what you want, you can protest, but I can imagine it won't end well if you do."

My muscles tensed. I wanted her to protest as much as I didn't.

"Does he know about us?"

"No, and it's probably in your best interests that we don't

complicate things further by telling him." I pinched the bridge of my nose and cursed under my breath, aware I was being cold, but knowing my intentions came from a good place.

"My best interests?" She scoffed. "By complicate, you mean you don't want him to pull out of the buyout? Sophia told me," she stated, and I had to bite my tongue. "Do I mean that little? Was anything we shared real? I don't even know who you really are."

I was conflicted.

Completely conflicted.

I only had to transfer the funds, and The Lagoon would be mine. What was in the way of keeping Blue too? Perhaps we had something worth fighting for.

There was a possibility I was fucking deluded, because what thirty-four-year-old man fell in love with an eighteen-year-old girl and lived happily ever after?

When I reopened my eyes, I realised they were wet. Admitting to myself I'd fallen in love was, in fact, fucking painful.

And I was crying?

Honestly, what the fuck?

"In just two weeks, you've probably gotten to know more of me than anyone else," I said solemnly.

Her voice trembled, but I heard the defiance. "I don't believe that for a second."

I knew I couldn't have it both ways–I had to choose.

Did I open up? Destroy the remainder of the relationship between her and her father? Between her father and me? Did I fight for her? Did I let her go?

Stay.

Be with me.

Go, live your fucking life.

"Don't waste your youth on me, baby," I whispered the words

into thin air. She wouldn't hear them–they were louder in my head than they were leaving my mouth.

I sighed. "You have every right to be mad. But you have to understand it was never my decision to keep the past from you. I have to live with the guilt for the rest of my life. How could I have known that running that red light would have had your mother do the same? If I could have saved her, Blue, I would have. But it was too late. She was gone the moment the cars collided."

"It should have been you," she murmured. "The other car should have killed *you*."

I rubbed the pads of my fingers over my eyes, revisiting the memory as it came to the forefront of my mind and feeling the guilt as it held me hostage. When people hurt, they often said shit they didn't mean. Though I knew she didn't mean what she said, it didn't make it any less true.

"It should've," I agreed, my voice thick.

It should've been me.

WITH EVERY DROP *of rain that hit the windshield, the window wipers in the shitty rust bucket I was driving fought to clear my view. But with the rain falling hard, my visibility of the road was limited. And with Noah in the backseat, constantly sprouting question after question about where we were going and if I was going to get into trouble for stealing my father's car, the rain against the windshield felt like the least of my fucking problems.*

"Are we there yet?"

"How do I know if we're there yet, if I don't know where we're going?" I replied.

"We've been driving for hours."

"Four," I deadpanned. "I've been driving for four hours, and if I

hadn't had to stop for you to piss every thirty minutes, we might have been somewhere by now."

"How do you know we would be somewhere if you don't know where we're going?"

"Fuck, for a ten-year-old, I don't know if you're smart or stupid."

"Maybe I take after you."

I smirked. "Maybe."

"Are you gonna miss them?"

Them.

As in our parents.

Though even calling them our parents felt like a push. Parents were supposed to care, love, and provide. Noah's father was nowhere to be found, and pushing aside my mother, my father was a drunk. A drunk who took his anger out on Noah–an innocent child, and yet, to him, nothing but a reminder of our mother's infidelity. I'm not quite sure my little brother understood the risk I was taking, running away with him like I was.

I shuffled in my seat, rolling my head over my shoulder to get a quick glimpse of him in the backseat before attempting to refocus on the road. "Are you?" My hands clenched around the cracked leather of the steering wheel. And again, I swung my head back to him for the second time. "Are you going to miss them?"

He looked out the window, unable to answer me.

"Noah."

Silence.

"Lil bro."

When I refaced the front window, I caught a glimpse of a red flash through the rain covered windshield. It only took me a second to realise I ran a red light. With that, panic ignited me, and I pressed my foot down on the accelerator. It was only when I reached the clearing that I glanced at my rearview mirror. And as the back wiper cleared the rain from my view, two sets of headlights collided behind me with a crash.

Blue

I WAS grateful for the invention of waterproof make-up, as Walker revisited the night he saved me. Despite the tears free-falling down my cheeks, I managed to apologise for what I said before I knew his side of the story. And as much as it hurt to relive the past, I realised now it truly was a freak accident. He didn't reply, and a part of me couldn't blame him. Before he told me his version of events, I'd all but wished him dead, and though I hadn't heard him leave, I wasn't entirely sure he was still on the other side of my door.

With my back against the hardwood, still fully dressed for the event I never got to experience, I found myself staring through the window and up at the stars as life in the city carried on as usual below. It seemed I was going through the motions. One by one. Two by two. Nothing but bloodshot eyes and a heavy heart as I pondered whether there was a point to all of this... hurt.

It appeared I was all cried out, and now I was left with a hollowness in the pit of my stomach.

My cheek pressed against the wood as I spoke to the man I somewhat hoped was still on the other side, even if I gave him no reason to be. "Are you still there?"

"Yeah." His voice was all rough and lazy. I forced a deep breath, waited for a beat, and then stood to unlock the door. We seemed to have discussed the accident, but what about the rest?

"Do you still love her?" I asked, opening the door and asking the question before he had the chance to stand.

"Sophia?" he questioned as he placed his palms on the floor and pushed up to face me.

I hated the way he said her name.

He rolled his lips as his gaze travelled the length of me. He only settled his glare when he met my face, no doubt puffy from all my crying. His own eyes were bloodshot, his hair a mess like he'd been running his hands through it. And like me, he wore the same clothes he had on earlier.

"No," he said sternly, holding my eyes. "I could never love her. Not the way a husband should love his wife, at least."

"Right," I said, my gaze drawn to the faint red of his wife's lipstick still on his neck.

He drew his fingers to the skin and began rubbing, as if I'd just reminded him it was there. "You're too young to understand."

"Nate," I huffed. "Don't do that. You know I hate it when you treat me like some damn stupid kid."

He released a pent-up breath. "After the accident, Noah went into foster care–"

"My father told me this," I interrupted. "But what has Noah going into care got to do with you and your *wife*?"

"Blue," he all but growled, stepping towards me. "Quit being a brat, yeah? If you want to ask me questions, you need to let me speak."

His tone was as tempting as it was demanding. I lifted my chin, looking up into his eyes, and he stared down at me, gnawing on the inside of his cheeks.

"I married Sophia because the courts wouldn't allow me to adopt my brother without providing a stable family unit. That's it. That's all it fucking was. And trust me, I tried everything I could until I was forced otherwise. Sophia knew the arrangement, and she knew what she signed up for. She'd always known I was never with her out of love. Fuck, I had a vasectomy because I never wanted anything more with her. I didn't love her, Blue. I couldn't."

He had to be fucking with me.

"Eleven years, Walker. It's a long time to be married to someone you 'couldn't' love."

His nostrils flared. "I realise that to anyone on the outside looking in, it seems unusual. But it worked for us. It worked for the things we wanted and for the life we lived. I don't believe in love. I've witnessed enough loss in my life to rid myself of the grief that leeches on to it."

His words winded me. "Even now, you don't believe in love?"

I waited for his response, only to receive silence.

"Wrong answer," I told him. Except it was the only one I needed to help make my choice. And yet I felt his silence wrap around my heart and squeeze so hard, the only thing I wished it would do was burst. And then I stepped back and slammed the door in his face.

He'd warned me we wouldn't ever grow roots and flourish. I was the fool who didn't listen.

CHAPTER TWENTY-FOUR

Walker

I REMAINED sat on the floor outside her bedroom until morning finally broke. When she finally opened the door, I climbed to my feet.

Again.

Only when I stepped into her, she blanched back. We stood like that as I took in her eyes, red-rimmed from the pain I caused her. And without speaking, she shouldered past me and walked away. I followed her tentatively to the main bathroom, only for her to close the door in my face like I wasn't there. But one thing I'd noticed was she hadn't slammed it this time.

She hadn't slammed it–so that must've counted for something.

While she showered, I used that time to shower in my en-suite. I'd left my phone in the pocket of my trousers all night, only texting Noah to say I wouldn't be at Hudson's fight before turning it off. He was concerned, but he didn't press when I explained I had to stay with Blue. I plugged in my phone to charge while I showered, and since turning it back on, I'd received a bunch more texts. The most important read: **He fucking did it.**

Noah, on Hudson.

The kid's life was about to change.

Really fucking change.

I half-smiled as I placed down my phone and picked up my watch. It wasn't the happiness or excitement I expected to feel. Perhaps that was all down to what'd unfolded in the last however many hours. The lack of sleep. The lack of alcohol in my system which only made my head pound and made thinking more difficult. What Blue said last night. The thoughts of her leaving–

Typically, my phone rang from the bedside table as I finished fastening my watch, disrupting my thoughts and feelings. Though weren't they two of the same?

One hand gripped the towel at my waist, while I answered my phone with the other. "James."

"Morning, Walker. How is she?"

I cleared my throat. "Quiet," I offered. "Upset with me."

He was silent a beat, unable to offer a response before changing the subject, which only had me tightening my hold on the phone in my hand. Why did he do that? Why did he often come across like he didn't give a shit about anything? Except even as I contemplated it, I realised the same could be said for myself.

And I cared.

Fuck, quite often I cared a whole lot more than I let on.

"You missed the fight. Hudson took Killian down in the third round. Killian was leading up until the second. Seemed Hudson got a second wind and smashed it right out of the fucking park. You should be proud, Walker. Fantastic night. You did a remarkable fucking job."

I may have made it all happen, but our fighters were the ones to entertain. Hudson, he deserved more praise than me. He'd put in all the work, though I didn't say as much. Besides, I wanted to watch a replay of the fight with my own eyes and not have someone give me a play-by-play.

It would have to wait when other things were demanding my attention.

Like his daughter, and the fact she was leaving.

"What time is your flight?" I responded, glancing at the time.

"Twelve 'o'clock."

"Twelve?" That didn't give me and Blue much time to say goodbye. I thought we'd have the day at least.

"Is that a problem?"

"No."

"Will you have Finley drive her to the airport?"

I considered taking her myself–clam up as much time with her as I could before she left me. Even if that time was in silence. But as I was undecided, the only response I could offer was, "She'll be there."

With that, I hung up the phone and placed it down on my bedside table. When I turned, I noticed Blue hovering in my doorway, a towel around her body as I had around mine. I didn't expect her to say a word, but she asked, "Was that my father?"

I nodded. "Your flight's at twelve."

"Then I guess I should pack."

"I'm sorry for everything," I said as I moved towards her, only for her to frown and step back.

"Don't."

"Blue," I pleaded. "I just..." *want to fucking hold you.*

"You just what?"

My heart palpitated, but my mouth refused to voice everything it wanted to say. I'd spent the whole night convincing myself that all this was for the best.

I swallowed hard as thoughts like, "What do I do?" and "What should I do?" drove through my head on a loop. But fuck, what did they matter? This wasn't about me; it was about her. London wasn't good for her, and neither was I.

"Nothing," I replied, exasperated. What the hell would my apology fix anyway? It couldn't change anything. It was actions that spoke louder than words, and I was failing at both. "You're right," I grit, angry at myself. Maybe even a little angry at her for not giving me what I wanted in return, even if she had no idea what that was. Even if I didn't. And for not telling me what I wanted to hear, even if she couldn't stay. Even if I shut her down.

I was a dumb cunt who couldn't communicate his feelings because I didn't fucking understand them. I cemented that when I told her, "You should go and pack."

NOW DRESSED in my comfy sweats, I leant against the doorjamb of Blue's bedroom, overlooking her walk in and out of the closet as she packed the two suitcases she had sprawled across her bed.

"When will the rest of my things be sent back?"

"I'll have them shipped as soon as possible."

One by one, she folded an item of clothing, placing each one inside her suitcase neatly. When she finished filling both, she zipped them up and pivoted to face me with her hands on her hips. Even with the circumstance we found ourselves in, I couldn't force my eyes away from the hem of her tiny skirt as I remembered how, just yesterday, I took her virginity and claimed she was mine.

But that was before.

And this was now.

"I've been thinking," she mused.

"About...?"

"I don't have to go," she suggested.

I frowned. I might have been thinking it. Wishing it. But I never said so out loud, which meant... she didn't know how much I wanted that to happen. And it wasn't going to happen because, for one, it wasn't possible for her to stay and things to be as they were. Not after everything.

"You're looking at me like I've grown two heads," she went on to say. And then she grew defensive. "When I say stay, I don't mean here, with *you*. I could get an apartment, and I could continue my apprenticeship at the club."

No chance could I have her working in my club, knowing I could never have her. I couldn't sit back and watch wankers closer to her age pine after her. Though that's not what I said.

"Your future isn't over just because you're moving back home, Blue–there're options to continue your education in Miami too."

I'd make sure of it.

She didn't have a reply to that, so I found myself walking into her bedroom and standing in front of her. I took her chin between my forefinger and thumb and raised it, so her eyes met mine. The touch was minor when I compared it to visions of how I really wanted to comfort her. How I really wanted to say goodbye.

"You're going home." Still, even as I said the words, I found my gaze dropping to her lips, desperate for one final kiss.

"I'm going home," she reiterated in a whisper. Three little words that sliced my chest right open, and still, I denied bleeding out at her feet. I watched as the blue in her eyes morphed into a green hue, and then she drew her face away from my hold. "You're right," she mocked. "Thank you for reminding me."

And so, I backed away with my hands in my pockets, leaving her alone to do whatever she had left to do.

———

NOT LONG LATER, I heard her walk out of her room with her suitcases in tow, the wheels spinning down the hall until she reached the living area. A lot like the wheels in my head as I sat on the couch, my head slouched back and my gaze set on the ceiling. "You have to be at the airport within the hour. Finley's waiting outside; he's ready to go whenever you are."

It all felt very final.

A lot like the beginning, but in reverse.

Behind me, the wheels stopped, and I figured she'd left her suitcases beside the kitchen island. A moment later, she took a seat beside me, and I turned my head only slightly to acknowledge her. I chose not to speak first, worried I might say the wrong thing and scare her away.

She licked her lips. I could only assume she was tired of fighting and accepted everything for what it was when she said, "I'm sorry for cutting you off when you were trying to apologise earlier."

I released a pent-up breath, about to tell her she needn't apologise, but she continued. "And I'm really sorry you missed the main event. I know how hard you worked and–"

I interrupted her, not having it in me to give a fuck about work. "I'm sorry you learned everything the way you did."

There was no point in wasting our last however many minutes together. There was no part of me that wanted to fight with her. Zero part of me that wanted to go around in circles when time wasn't on our side.

She ignored me though, shaking her head. "I'm sorry for what I said last night."

My brows pinched. "I'm sorry for what I didn't."

That got her attention.

Noticeably, she took a deep breath. "Do you think we'll still be friends?" she asked.

"Friends?" I repeated. My cheeks quirked, but the word rolled from my tongue uncomfortably. I wasn't sure whether I found it funny because it was so left-field, or completely ridiculous for all the reasons it shouldn't be.

"Pen pals?" She smiled. A smile that was completely cute as fuck, in spite of the sadness in her eyes. "You can text me. Or email. I'm easy."

I threw her a look that said both, "You've got to be kidding me?" and "How can we ever be friends?" but I avoided the words.

Friendship wasn't on my agenda, nor was it possible.

She dropped her head to the sofa, either reading into my thoughts or deep down, feeling the same way. "I didn't think so."

I nudged her knee with mine, trying to be friendly and ignoring the buzz she set off under my skin. But it felt fucking weird. It felt like we were never meant to be friends. It felt better to imagine us as strangers who, I don't know, knew each other in another lifetime. Who locked eyes across a crowded room and reminisced on our once upon a time from a distance.

"You have that faraway look in your eyes," she spoke softly. "The same one you had when we were on the roof."

I pulled my bottom lip into my mouth, deep in thought.

Brazenly, she slid onto my lap, her knees on either side of my hips. I had to clench my fists to stop my hands from roaming.

"What are you thinking about?" she whispered.

My throat was suddenly dry, clogged with emotion as I swallowed. I couldn't tell her what I was thinking about. I couldn't tell her that the night of her birthday was the happiest I'd felt with someone in a long while. That there wasn't nowt I would do for her if it meant doing the right thing.

I lifted my chin and forced a smile. "Just thinking about how if you don't hurry up, you might miss your flight."

She gave me a sad smile in return, and then, taking me off guard, she leant forward and placed a kiss on each of my eyelids. The touch of her lips was so tender, so soft. A total contradiction to the way I viewed the world.

I went to speak again, not even sure what I was about to say, but she placed her finger against my lips, silencing me. The warmth of my breath hit her finger before I closed my mouth, and as she slowly retreated, she wrapped both her arms around my neck.

She made it difficult for me to hold back.

My fists unclenched without permission, and my hands went to her waist.

Knowing the inevitable was right around the corner, I dropped my head to her neck and inhaled, absorbing what little I had left of her.

Because she was leaving.

And I wasn't going to stop her.

The same way I hadn't stopped her from turning her head and slanting her mouth against mine in a goodbye kiss. My fingers dug into her waist, but I knew no amount of hold would let me keep her. Fuck, I'd never been good with words, with vocalising how I felt, but this? I could express myself like this. I could say goodbye like this and still have it mean something.

I'm not sure who instigated tongue first, but they tangled, slow and soft, until our kiss became heated. Sparks flew. They flew like we were free-falling from a burning building as she writhed against me. The heat hit my cock, and I hardened beneath her within seconds.

My brain told me to pull back, but every other part of my being was fighting to push. The truth was, I just wanted to be as close to her as possible before she was half the world away. But there was a part of me that believed I could say goodbye in spite of not wanting to let go. And when she began to move against me, jerking against the outline of my cock, I realised she was just as eager and needy for me as I was for her. Even if I wanted to stop this, I couldn't. And suddenly, I was no longer thinking about her leaving, but how much I wanted to be deep inside her warmth.

My hands moved under her skirt, and then I spread her cheeks, encouraging her back and forth along the hard ridge inside my sweats. I didn't want to take more than she was willing to give, but as she moved, I looked down at the mess she was making all over me and in between kisses, I murmured, "Stand up. Take off your underwear."

She was already so wet for me, and shit, she was perfect.

So fucking perfect.

She slipped off my lap, stood in front of me, and quickly lowered her lace underwear down her legs and away from her ankles like we'd done this a handful of times. Though I knew better, because it was just yesterday when I impaled her with my cock for the first time, only for everything to fall to shit hours later. Regardless of how it all played out, I couldn't find it in me to regret it.

She climbed back onto my lap, reaching into the waistband of my sweats to palm me. Her hand was warm and soft against my hard cock. She moved upwards from the base to my crown, spreading pre-cum around my tip. Once. Twice. Three times. I kissed her repeatedly, practically tongue fucking her mouth. Swallowing the symphonies from her throat as she touched me.

When it got too much and I felt like I was going to explode in her hand, I helped her remove my cock from the restraint of my sweats. She watched with heat in her eyes as I took myself in my fist and rubbed myself over her slit, bathing in her wetness. I directed my cock at her opening, but before I buried myself inside of her, I wrapped my free hand around the side of her neck and leant forward, breathing her in as she breathed me out.

"Fuck, Blue." My tone was equal parts pleasure and equal parts pain as she sank down on my cock like the good girl she was. As was her moan when our eyes locked, and she felt me fill her.

Her eyelashes fluttered as I shoved in, pushing myself to the hilt and making her lips part against mine in a gasp. We started slowly at first, with long, slow, teasing thrusts. Thrusts that said, "I'm sorry" and "I'm going to miss you." But as her pussy clenched around my cock and we found a rhythm, it was only fitting that our tempo increased. Again and again, I pushed upwards as she came down. Again and again, I bottomed out inside of her until the two of us were sweating and breathing fast. It was everything we weren't saying. We were broken, whole, damaged, and perfect in every way which we weren't.

"Remember how you asked me if it always felt like this?" I gripped her hips and raised her up before forcing her back down, my eyes dancing between where I entered her and the look on her face. "The answer's no, baby. It's never felt like this. You were never meant to make me feel like this."

She was too lost in her pleasure to find the words to speak, or the energy to fuck me back as hard as before. So I took the reins, giving her time to get some energy as I thrust in and out of her nice and slow. She moaned repeatedly, encasing her top half around me as best as possible. Holding on to me like I was a lifeline. It was probably the closest I'd ever came to making love with a woman. And in that moment, I understood I'd never find this again.

I'd never find another Blue.

The sudden urgency I had to feel her come all over my cock began to creep up on me, and I knew, I just knew, I was close to spilling inside of her. I wanted to fill her up until her veins were full of me. I wanted her to be so full that when she cried, she cried me. I wanted her to live, breathe, and fucking sweat me. Wherever she went, I wanted her to feel me. But most of all, I wanted her to never forget the way I made her feel, no matter where in the world she ended up.

No matter who in the world she ended up with.

"Nate," she breathed. Over and over.

With our bodies stuck together in the web of us, I reached around to her ass and began spreading her wetness over her puckered hole.

Apparently, before she left, I was taking that too.

She whimpered, needily. "Oh God, Nate, that feels–"

She didn't get the rest of her words out before my little finger was creeping into her ass. The remnants of whatever was left in her throat morphed into a glorious toe-curling moan. And her nails drew blood from my back as they bit into my skin.

Because she was high.

So fucking high on me and us, and–

"Jesus fuck," I grunted, feeling her pussy tighten around my length. "You're so nice and warm, baby. You fit me like a fucking glove." Her legs began to shake as I continued thrusting up inside her, angling her forward so her clit rubbed against me. I continued to finger her ass, knowing we were both about ready to come. "Jesus, Blue. How the fuck am I going to live without you? How the fuck am I going to live knowing someone else gets this?"

I don't know if she heard me above her moans. I don't even know if I said the words aloud. The only answer she gave was in the form of a mewl as she stepped over the edge with me, milking my cock within an inch of its life.

This girl was my devotion.

Only I realised it too little, too late.

Entirely worn, I slipped my finger from her ass, leaning back to memorise every inch of her pretty face. She collapsed onto me, her head against my chest as our hearts and our minds regained their clarity.

And then I realised something, like a stab to my stomach.

This was it.

Our goodbye.

CHAPTER TWENTY-FIVE

Blue

WITH NO TIME TO shower before I was due at the airport, I cleaned up as best I could, knowing I had a ten-hour journey ahead of me. It seemed Walker had gone to do the same because when I re-entered the living area, he was nowhere to be found. I used that time to go back to my room, grab my bag, write what I wanted to say on a sticky note, and return to the kitchen, where I placed the same note inside the cupboard. I heard Walker's footsteps down the hall as I closed it, so I made my way over to my luggage, only for him to reach it first. It seemed he'd changed into clean sweats.

"I got it, brat."

I smiled, hiking my bag up onto my shoulder. "You know, I might even miss you calling me that."

The corner of his mouth tipped up in response, but it wasn't quite a smile. "You got everything?" he murmured. There was still a slight blush on his sharp cheekbones, a reminder of what happened between us not so many minutes ago.

"I have everything I came with," I said. Only it felt like I was leaving with a lot less, because everything I came here to do, I didn't. And everything I wanted didn't quite work out the way I'd planned.

He nodded, but he worked that jaw of his hard. I wondered what he was thinking, but this time, I refused to press. I was leaving, and he wasn't stopping me, despite chance after chance.

We entered the elevator and rode downstairs in silence. Over my shoulder, I glanced at him, but he refused to look at me. He was shutting down and closing me out. Whether it was to make it easier on me, or easier on him, I wasn't entirely sure. He had to know as well as I did neither would work.

The elevator lights highlighted the sharp features of his face, the glimmer of his unique eyes, and the tick in his jaw that continued to work overtime. And still... nothing.

I guess we'd already said everything we needed to say.

We walked through the lobby, the same girl on the desk as the day I arrived. Only this time, he didn't bother to greet her. It wasn't just me suffering in his silence; he'd put up a wall. The atmosphere in the lobby was awkward, if not calm. At least until we stepped through the doors and out into the city. The Saturday sun, despite the cold, shone down on us, and I pulled my sunglasses from my bag to place them over my eyes.

Now it seemed, we were both hiding.

It wasn't just us in the world.

It was us and everybody else.

Finley rolled the car closer when he spotted us. When he stepped out of the car to help Walker with my luggage, Walker held out a hand to halt him. "I got this," he said dryly.

Finley nodded, popping the lid on the trunk, and then

returned to the car as Walker loaded my suitcases inside the vehicle.

"You know," he said, pulling on the lobe of his ear. "Finley told me you were a pearl."

My lips pulled into an awkward smile as he rounded the car and met me beside the car door.

I glanced between him and Finley in the front seat. "Finley said that? A pearl?"

He nodded. "He said if I break you, there'd be no way to repair the damage. Because that's the thing about pearls... once they're broke–"

I frowned. "Stop it, Walker."

His eyes narrowed, focused hard on me. "I just need to know before you go, Blue. Back then... Did I break you?" He barricaded me against the car, his fists on either side of me. "Am I the reason you thought of yourself as broken? Because of what I took away?"

I looked down between us to reflect, forcing air into my lungs through my nose. I didn't want to talk about that night, but it seemed he did. At the most inconvenient time to bring it up again, why did he choose now?

"I couldn't save her. If I could, don't you think I would've?" he said quietly, his tone pleading.

When I looked back up, I pushed my sunglasses to the top of my head and gave him as much eye contact as I could muster. "You did break me," I admitted. "But that was before I knew it wasn't all your fault. Growing up, remembering the tragedy in parts, I couldn't comprehend why I couldn't just be like everybody else. Why I couldn't be normal like *everybody else.*"

I placed my hand against his heart, and though my words felt hoarse, I forced them from my throat. "You didn't break me, Nate. Meeting you like this, I think it may have even fixed me a little bit." I shook my head. "I'm not a pearl."

He dropped his forehead to mine, aiming his head down, his breath fanning over my face. Then he straightened, dropping one last kiss on my temple before stepping back and opening the car door for me with the movement.

He said one last thing to me in a quiet whisper. So quiet it barely touched my ears.

"You could never be like everybody else."

My heart beat harder with every step he took further away, and then, as quick as my car door closed behind me, he was gone, and the car was already in motion.

CHAPTER TWENTY-SIX

Walker

MY HANDS BALLED into fists as I shoved them in my pockets and made my way back to my floor. There seemed to be a bottomless pit in my stomach full of all the things I wanted to say, yet didn't. As soon as I re-entered my penthouse, it felt like something was missing. It was probably because I knew she was gone. And I knew there wasn't any chance of her coming back.

As I made my way to my bedroom, her scent seemed to pollinate all my air, which only irritated my eyes and throat. I removed my hands from my pockets and fisted my eyelids, but it seemed all that did was blur my vision. "Fuck," I cursed. Why was saying goodbye to Blue after just two weeks harder to handle than a goodbye to my wife of eleven years?

Ignoring the discomfort taking over every molecule of my

body, I stepped into my bedroom and collected my phone. After typing in my four-digit passcode, I dialled Noah.

The moment I considered hanging up, he answered.

"Nate."

"Lil bro," I mumbled. "You sound like you're still in bed."

"I am," he grunted. "Heavy night."

"Are you home?"

"Nah, I'm at Hudson's. We brought the party back with us. He was a little knocked up, but not so bad he couldn't celebrate."

I swiped a hand across my jaw. "I'm gutted I missed it."

"Have you watched the replay?"

"I haven't had a chance."

"No?" I heard a scuffle of his duvet and then movement through the line before he spoke again. "Why not?" A door closed, and then I listened to the sound of his piss as it hit the bottom of the toilet.

"Blue's gone home," I said. It didn't explain anything, but speaking the words into the universe rather than dealing with them on my own released whatever it was I'd pent up.

"Home?"

"Yeah. Finley's just taken her to the airport," I carried on. "James insisted she went back to Miami. He didn't think the apprenticeship... or this place, was good for her."

"That the reason you missed the fight?" he asked.

"Yeah, I guess. Sort of. That and the past."

"That explains it," he mumbled.

"What?"

"You're weird as shit."

The fuck?

"I'm weird?"

He sighed. "Yeah, Nate. Why are you ringing me to tell me she's gone home instead of going after her?"

I frowned, choosing to speak my thoughts aloud. "The fuck are you on about?"

"No reason to be coy with me, man. I saw you."

"Saw me?"

"Yeah, I saw the both of you."

"No idea what you think you saw, Noah... but I doubt it was anything." I shook my head. What the hell could he have seen?

"Wednesday," he stated, flushing the toilet as he spoke. "I realised you left your phone on your desk the night you were rushing outta work, and when I went back into the office again later that evening to double-check everything was ready for fight night, I realised it'd gone. So I checked the CCTV–"

"You checked the CCTV?"

"–and that's when I saw the two of you on the roof."

"The roof?" I grunted.

"Yeah, the two of you looked like you were having fun, man."

I rubbed at my forehead. "You didn't think to mention it?"

"Who was I to say anything? I didn't think much about it until the next day. The way you looked at her at the weigh in. Shit, the both of you couldn't have made it any more fucking obvious. And when Sophia showed up, fuck me, Blue looked at Sophia like she was the other woman, and she was your girl."

I didn't have a response to that. How had I not realised it myself? In fact, how had I not realised that Noah had?

"You want me to continue?" He yawned, like this whole conversation was tiresome or irrelevant. "James showed up, mentioned Blue's birthday dinner... and well, guess I figured you'd tell me when you were ready. And if you didn't, then I wasn't gonna bring it up. Until last night, when you got aggy and went looking for her."

"I don't know what to say," I mumbled.

"Say nothing, brother. I don't know how many times I need to tell you that you deserve to be happy."

"She's eighteen, Noah." My mouth went dry. "There's still so much shit to settle with Sophia, I–"

He interrupted me. "Who gives a shit? Fuck Sophia. You wanna know something else?" Huffing a breath, he went on. "Sophia cornered me last night and told me how you only married her because you wanted to provide a home for me." My mouth opened to respond, but he spoke again. "I've no idea what the fuck she expected me to say. Whether she wanted me to take sides in whatever warfare you two have going on, but like I said to her, I already figured that shit out long ago. The two of you fought so loud it was hard not to pay attention."

"I'm sorry, Noah, I... shit." I pinched my fingers against the bridge of my nose. "Not sure how I feel about you knowing that," I admitted. Sophia not leaving things alone after I'd left her outside The Lagoon pissed me off, but it didn't shock me. "You were just a kid," I mumbled. "She had no right to drag you into our mess."

"Yeah, well... don't apologise," he grunted. "Sophia's just... Sophia. I couldn't have asked for a better brother. And I'm being sappy as fuck, so that's my cue to hang up."

"Wait," I said, leaning into my phone. "Blue... do you think–"

"For fuck's sake. You're my big brother. Ain't I meant to be getting advice from you? If you want your girl to stay, then you oughta get a hold of yourself, you daft prick. If you don't... well, if you don't, then let her fly home and move the hell on."

Even if I'd wanted to, I didn't have the chance to respond, because the next thing I heard was a feminine voice and a "Gotta go," before he hung up.

I wasn't sure what to make of what he knew, or what to do when it came to chasing after 'my girl.' Just because Noah was cool with it didn't mean society would be. Just because I wanted to wake up every day next to her didn't mean she felt the same way. And then there was James... which, wasn't worth thinking about.

Because I was absolutely not going after 'my girl.'

Because she was not my fucking girl.

In a fret, I threw my phone to the bed and took off towards the kitchen. I set my eyes on the top cupboard as I entered, knowing the only thing to fix my frustration was behind the door that housed it. And then I was there, reaching up for my antidote, only to find something else in its place.

I pulled off the sticky note attached to the bottle, my eyebrows pinching as I read the words aloud. *"Think twice."*

My stomach rolled, and I slammed the cupboard closed with a curse.

Then I grabbed my car keys.

Blue

ONCE I SAID my goodbyes to Finley, I entered the airport and went in search of my father. He'd texted me to tell me he would be waiting for me at the check-in desk inside terminal three.

I followed the signs, and as I turned the corner, I spotted him ready and waiting at the front of the queue. He waved me over when he noticed me, but no more than that. It probably had something to do with his phone glued to his ear. Pulling my luggage along, I held my chin high so my sunglasses didn't fall from my face. I didn't need my father asking me why my eyes were red and bloodshot. I was too tired to talk, never mind fight. A queue had begun to form behind him by the time I reached him. He didn't seem to care, preoccupied with whatever he'd yet to handle through the phone.

He continued his conversation as he lifted his suitcase onto the conveyor belt and handed the man at the desk his passport. In response, the man stuck a luggage tag onto the handle of his luggage and handed him back his passport before repeating the action with mine. Embarrassed by my father's lack of manners, I apologised on his behalf.

"What were you apologising for?" my father asked me once he'd hung up his phone.

"You were rude," I stated. "What was so important that you couldn't have handled it later?"

He side-eyed me. "Business."

"Figures."

He wrapped his arm around my shoulder as we made our way to security. "Count yourself lucky you won't ever have to deal with any."

There was that word again.

Lucky.

We reached security, and I placed my bag onto the conveyor belt to be checked for any dangerous items. Then I stepped through the metal detector. As I waited for my father from the other side, I wondered what the hell I was doing.

I collected my bag, and even as I placed it back onto my arm, I couldn't stop thinking why I was going back home to Miami when Miami had nothing to offer me.

Still, I didn't say anything, and when they cleared father through security behind me, we proceeded to walk to our boarding gate.

"We have an hour," I stated as I sat on one of the airport's long line of chairs.

"What are you doing sitting there? We have the comfort of a private lobby." He pointed towards a double door.

I didn't want the comfort of a private lobby. I didn't want to be here at all.

With a scratch of his chin, he settled down beside me on a chair, and we both stared ahead.

After a few minutes of preening his suit, he asked, "You want to come home, don't you?"

"Whatever gave you that impression?"

"You didn't fight me."

"Do you really care about what I want, dad?"

He scoffed. "What a silly question. You're my daughter; of course, I care."

I'm not sure where I found my courage, but the next words to leave my mouth didn't just shake him–they shook me.

"Do you miss her? *Mum*."

In my peripheral, I watched as he smoothed over the ink of my mother's initials on his ring finger. And then, barely loud enough for me to hear, he said, "All the time."

"Why do you do it, dad? The countless women, the parties, the–"

"That's enough, Blue." He looked around, seemingly embarrassed that we were having this conversation in public.

My lips locked, and under the frame of my glasses, my eyes closed. He wouldn't talk about it, and I had no idea why I'd expected him to. It was probably another fifteen minutes before he spoke again. I hadn't expected him to continue where we'd left off, but that's precisely what happened.

"Your mother was my soulmate. A love like ours doesn't come around twice."

Something in my stomach clenched and squeezed. "How do you know for sure?"

"I've had my fair share of women, as you know... but not one of them could compare to the way I felt when I was in the presence of your mother. It didn't matter what we were doing. It didn't matter where we were; we connected like either end of a rope. If you ever find a love like that, you hold on to it. No matter how tangled the rope gets or how many knots form. You work to unravel them, one by one. You ever find a love like mine and your mother's, you tie yourself to it, and for the fucking life of you, princess, you don't let it go."

It was the first time my father had truly opened up to me. It didn't explain everything–it didn't explain why he was the way he was–why he'd coddled me my whole life–but the advice he gave me was invaluable.

I realised then that I wasn't just afraid of living, or scared of dying.

I was afraid I'd already lost that once in a lifetime kind of love.

Scared that it had slipped through my fingers.

But most of all, I was terrified of getting on that plane and wondering what if.

I slid my sunglasses from my head and placed them into my tote bag, and then I startled myself by wrapping my arms around my father and telling him, "I think I'm making a mistake."

Because maybe mine and Walker's rope wasn't tethered, just tangled. And if I didn't stay–if we didn't try–we'd never know.

Did I really want to spend the rest of my life wondering what if?

Did I really want to look back on my life in ten, twenty years' time, and wonder what we could've been?

Who I could've been?

The two of us stood from the chair, and he opened and closed his mouth. "Walker?" he said, his eyes bouncing from mine to some place over my shoulder.

My brows creased.

"Walker." He brushed past me, and I swivelled on my feet, confused, only to see Walker walking towards us.

He grew closer with every powered step, and my heart struck harder every time his feet touched the floor. I half expected him to stop when he reached my father, because there was no way the man who refused to believe in happy ever afters was about to have the same conversation with me as I'd just had with myself.

I was completely taken off guard when he didn't. And I barely had time to blink before he stopped short in front of me.

There was a small space between our chests, and as he pulled our invisible string, I fell forward, eradicating it completely. His arm threaded around my back, and his fingers caught hold of my neck. His breath fanned the side of my face, and though his lips touched my ear, his words—somehow before he even spoke them—rushed to the centre of my chest.

"I want you to stay."

"Stay?" I murmured.

"*Stay,* Blue. Let me hold you when it thunders."

I tilted my head back to look at him, my stomach rushing with butterflies as his eyes captured mine. He was waiting for me to respond, but I couldn't seem to find my voice. Maybe he thought I didn't hear him, maybe he thought I didn't want him. That I didn't want to stay—that I didn't even consider a future with him in it.

"Please," he said, pleading for me to hear him. "If you let me, I'll repaint the sky for you."

I wanted to say yes.

I wanted to speak.

But my father was right behind him, and my words were lost.

I took a breath to slow my heart rate, and though I felt eyes on us, Walker shielded me from everyone else.

It was just us.

Us and… "My dad–"

He shook his head before trailing his gaze all over my face. "Let me worry about it." He squeezed my neck, forcing my attention his way. "I can't promise you the world, Blue Sterling. I can't promise you children, or the happiness you spoke about that first night on my sofa. I can't even promise you a month from now. I don't know if I can love you as we grow old, but I know I fell in love with you like a zephyr." *A soft breeze.* His lips brushed against mine. "Slowly, then all at once."

My father's hand clutched Walker's shoulder in a bid to pull him away. Walker flinched, but he continued to fight for me.

"Stay, Blue. And if you don't want to stay for me, then how about you think twice? Think twice about everything you want. Don't let anyone stop you. Don't let me."

"You read my note?" I murmured. "Did you… did you drink?"

"Yeah–no," he said, shaking his head. "I didn't drink." His fingers lost their grip on my neck as he stared at me apologetically. As if he was disappointed in himself, reaching for the bottle before deciding to reach for me.

"If you asked me to give it up for you, I would," he said as his fingers pressed into the middle of my back. "If it meant you'd stay."

I shook my head. "That's a lot, Nate, you can't use that–"

He interrupted me. "Shit. I know, I know. I'm not good at this," he admitted. "What I meant to say is, I think you're worth it, Blue Sterling. I think you're worth every goddamn side effect."

He unthreaded his arm from my back, and though his line of sight didn't waver from me, I glanced between him and my father, who stood blindsided, shifting his gaze from me to the man standing in front of me. I'd never seen the look my father wore on his face. And I wasn't sure if he could hear every quiet word between me and Walker. I wasn't sure what was about to go down–if anything. And I don't know what he saw in my eyes, but he removed his hand from Walker's shoulder and scrubbed it down his face with force, muttering something under his breath I couldn't make out.

For a brief moment, I wondered why he wasn't reacting. I wondered why he wasn't kicking off. But then I remembered our conversation. The one we were having before Walker showed up.

He'd been the one to tell me if I ever encountered a love like this, I should never let it go. I wasn't sure if he was going to, but he knew full well he'd be a hypocrite if he stood in my way.

"Last call for passengers. Please proceed urgently to gate five."

The three of us seemed to divide our attention as the announcement through the speaker sounded. But Walker's eyes came back to mine as he whispered words only meant for my ears. "Are you going to make me beg, baby? You want me on my knees?"

The image of him on his knees for me made my lips spread, even if it wasn't the same way he insinuated. This man, with his cold heart and brooding frown, didn't believe in fairy tales. Still, I dropped my bag to the floor and hauled myself into his arms. His hands slid under my thighs as my legs wrapped around his waist, and just as I broke out into a full-blown smile, he did something that surprised us both. He was looking at me when he said it, but his words were meant for my father still standing behind him.

"I'm in love with your daughter, James."

My father grunted. "I heard that."

"Consider this my hard turn," he said, and I frowned, not understanding. "I'm putting trust into your opinion of me."

I went to speak, but Walker silenced me. "Don't ask questions," he said in a breath against my lips.

"Okay," I replied.

"Okay." He smirked, pressing his forehead against mine. "I think I might hate that word." And without giving me another chance to speak, he asked me again, "Will you stay?"

"I'll stay," I whispered. I felt him exhale and physically felt the tension flood from his body as he held me. The words on the tip of my tongue were basic compared to the way he confessed his love for me, but I spoke them anyway. "I'll stay because I fell in love with you too," I murmured. "I think I might have fallen in love with you before I knew what it meant."

His eyes lit up in a way I'd never seen them shine before, and he pressed a kiss against my temple as I glided down his body like a ballerina and landed on my feet. Silently, I wondered what happened next. I wondered what our future looked like.

He brought his hands up to skate across my cheeks, and as if he knew what I was thinking, he said, "We'll figure it out together." And then, taking a deep breath, he turned to face my father.

My father had minutes–minutes until the departure gate was closed–though I knew he'd be able to pull strings if he missed it the same way I had the day I left Miami.

"I can't be sorry for the way I feel," Walker told him, sliding his hands into his pockets as he looked down at my father's clenched fists.

"Walker," he remarked. But even as he said his name, I didn't hear anything out of the ordinary in his tone. He looked from Walker to me, and with a quick shake of his head, he unclenched his fist and held out his hand to the man who just admitted he was in love with me.

Two weeks was barely enough time to make a dent. To fall in love with a person. But what was time, if not for the moments that made it up? Every intention. Every choice. How every action someone made always bled into the next.

As my father shook Walker's hand, I mulled over all those times he'd told me Walker was a good man.

How he came in clutch every time.

The way he'd trusted him to take care of me above anyone else.

And then, I thought, not for the first time, nothing in my life ever happened by coincidence.

"I have to catch my flight," my father said. "But we'll discuss this... later." I'm sure his words were meant for the both of us, but he directed them at Walker. I knew he meant them. "I know you'll take care of her," he went on to say. And I knew he meant that too.

It seemed my father had already heard, if not seen enough, to leave without a fight.

Walked nodded as their hands retreated, and then stepped away so I could say my goodbyes.

"Like a rope," I explained as my father embraced me.

He exhaled a pent-up breath as the final warning came through the airport speakers, and then with one final look between me and Walker he said, "Then you don't let him go, princess."

Epilogue

SITTING cross-legged with my laptop over my knees, I glimpsed at Walker who lay beside me, asleep in our bed. The sun was just beginning to rise, peeking through the curtained voiles that weren't quite closed. A smile spread across my face at the sight of him, his naked chest on display, his muscled bicep thrown over his face so the minimal sunshine didn't aggravate his eyes.

I'd never seen him so relaxed.

I was still smiling as I turned my attention away from him and my gaze refocused on the paper aeroplane he'd created, sat on the floor of our bedroom. I'd noticed the heavy weight immediately falling from his shoulders as he'd read aloud the words inked on the page, before he'd shaped the paper and flown it across the room, barely missing the bin.

An aeroplane of ink and paper that told us he was divorced–officially.

I liked the way he made light of it. I liked how he didn't place the letter to the side of our bed, or leave it out in the open for us to make a big deal from. It felt like a metaphor in a sense–how my flight to London was inbound, whereas this was out and non-returning.

We climbed into bed after that, locked in an embrace with nothing but an "I love you" passed between us, his lips to my temple, and his fingers in my hair.

The two of us had a late night at The Lagoon, so we hadn't had a chance to soak up what it meant for us, or speak about how much longer we were going to wait before we stepped up our relationship status. That's not to say things weren't already in motion, because they were.

I shook my head, clearing my thoughts as I turned back to my laptop and uploaded my final assessment of the year to Duke.

Things were good.

Really good.

So good that I'd done two years' worth of work in one.

My phone pinged from my bedside table, and I cringed, realising I'd forgotten to put it on silent. Seeing Ebony's name on the screen, I went to grab it, but my attention fell away from my phone and to Walker as he shuffled in bed.

"Get back in here," Walker groaned, peering at me and lifting his arm from the bed to shut down the head of my laptop.

For a second, I didn't move. I just focused on him. On the colour of his eyes, to the sharp panes of his face, to the stubble on his jaw. I was so grateful for everything he was. For everything he'd done for me. For the way he continued to love me and put me first.

"What are you waiting for?" he asked with his usual morning rasp.

My smile didn't waver as I pushed the laptop from my legs and climbed back under the covers. And then, with a mischievous twinkle in his eye, he took hold of my hand and directed it onto the thick bulge over the top of his boxer shorts. His cheeks rose with a small grin of his own, but I couldn't stop the frown forming across my forehead.

"Nate," I mouthed.

"What?" he replied sincerely, pushing the weight of our hands against his morning wood.

My lips parted in a soundless gasp, but he seemed to be observing my eyes for more of a reaction—one that told him I was hot for him. Still, I couldn't stop my brain from going *there*.

And by there, I didn't mean to his divorce. But there, as in, we hadn't been intimate in seven days. Not while he was recovering from his operation.

"Are you sure you're ready?" I whispered, raising my hand as he stretched the material of his underwear from his hips and pushed them down his legs.

"Does it feel like I'm sure?" He took my hand back in his and guided it onto his hard length. "It was a reversal, baby. What are you worried about?"

What *was* I worried about?

I licked my lips and his gaze fell to my mouth.

"Actually, I think my cock might need a little kissing better," he murmured, his mouth pulling up at the corners.

My lashes fluttered and my eyes rolled simultaneously. "That's not entirely what I meant. I'm glad you're okay... but are you, you know? Are you still sure?"

He didn't say anything as my fist tightened around his smooth girth, but with his hand over mine, he encouraged me to stroke him up and down. Within seconds, we reached a steady rhythm, and then he removed his hand, nestling back into the sheets and throwing an arm behind his head, all while watching me touch him.

If I considered him relaxed before, he was even more so now.

I slowed my strokes, not because I didn't want to touch him, because I did. My underwear was wet already, and if that wasn't enough proof of my arousal, I don't know what was. I was just... nervous. Yeah, I wasn't worried. I was nervous. There was a difference.

He lifted an eyebrow as my cheeks stained with heat. I was too embarrassed to look at him, so I looked down at my fist wrapped around his length. "Are you sure this is what you want?" I blurted, and then mentally slapped myself because it seemed like I was asking his cock the question, and not him.

He chuckled and leant forward to grab me by the hips, tugging me over top of him in one swift movement. My knees hit the bed on either side of his hips, and his cock settled against my slit as he pulled my thong to the side. "How about you rub up on me, baby? Then you can feel how sure I am."

A smirk lined his lips as I swatted at his chest, and then he dipped forward, taking my lips for a heated kiss. Naturally, I moved against his cock, feeling myself grow wetter.

When he pulled back, he said, "I've never been so sure about anything in my whole life. I'm going to marry you, baby. I'm going to make love to you every day until we know for sure I'm back in full working order, and when my seed is finally fucking planted, I'm going to watch your stomach grow with our child. I'm going to hold your hair back when you're sick. I'm going to hold your hand when you're screaming blue fucking murder in that hospital room, and there's no doubt in my mind I won't stop loving you until I'm forced to stop." He bit at my neck, angling his cock into my opening as he lifted me by the hips. "So don't ask me again if I'm sure," he murmured as he thrust into me. "But if you're not sure... if you've got doubts"—he looked into my eyes as he pulled back out—"then I'll wait until you're certain this is everything you want. If it's not–"

His words hung in the air, but I knew what he was going to say.

If it's not, we don't have to.

But I didn't need to think about it.

I sank back down onto him, and that frown of his I loved so much marred his forehead as I took his cock to the hilt, burrowing myself down on every inch of him.

"That your answer?" he rasped, looking at where our bodies joined.

"Yeah," I said, bobbing my head as the two of us worked our bodies in sync. "No doubts."

He groaned, low in his throat, and thrust into me hard. "Seven days was way too long to be without your warmth, baby."

I fell forward as he penetrated me, not sparing a moment inside me, before he pulled out again and repeated the motion. His mouth pulled down the top of my pyjama top, and as my breasts floated across his face, he used his mouth to divide his attention between each of them.

"Seven days was too long without your cock." My words were a mixture of moans and whispers as he continued to move in and out of me, fucking me like he'd been without me too long.

When it felt like too much, I wrapped my hands around his head, needing him to take control. And then, taking me by surprise, his palm collided with my ass cheek hard and fast.

"Fuck," I cursed, feeling my orgasm pending. "Do it again."

I needn't have asked him, because his palm was already hitting my ass cheek for the second time before I'd even finished my sentence.

"Such a needy brat. You want me to put a baby in you?" he rasped, rubbing the sting of his slap away.

My pussy clenched around him, and my fingers tugged on his dishevelled hair as I moaned an incoherent "Yeah."

I felt the vibration of his chest as he chuckled, but in spite of that, both his hands went to my ass and his palms spread my cheeks as his cock hit a spot deep inside of me.

"Say it."

I captured his eyes with mine. "I want you to put a baby in me."

"Fuck." He grinned, seizing my lips in a kiss.

He shifted his hips, filling me to the brink, and my clit sought friction against him with every thrust. A ripple started in my toes, making its way up my body, and the moment it reached between my thighs, my legs began to shake.

All I felt was him.

All I could taste was us.

All I could see was our future.

I felt the moment he came, the moment his cum spilled into me and filled me up. But unlike any time before, this time it held purpose. My body burned as I came with him, and when it was all over, I collapsed against his chest.

Our foreheads stuck together with perspiration, our eyes dancing as they glazed across one another's with emotion.

His hand reached up to cup my cheek. "You good?"

"I'm more than good," I whispered.

"More than good, huh?" he replied, his lips pulling into a smile.

I nodded gently, teasing his lips with mine. "So much *more* than good."

His smile widened, and then he breathed whispered words of "I fucking love you" across my lips before sealing them with a kiss.

Now I'm lucky, I thought.

Lucky to love someone so much, and be loved so much in return.

Acknowledgements

First and for always, my husband, Adie. I wouldn't want to live in a world without you in it. Our children, for your patience and understanding, even as young as you are. I hope by pursuing my dreams it will encourage you to pursue yours. Joey, for being a total girl boss, for never having ill intentions, and for being there throughout every chapter of my life. Jess, for never failing to hold my hand from two hundred and thirty-eight miles away, not just through the process–but through this crazy thing we call life. Katie, for keeping me back from that ledge I'm forever hanging from with your noodle arms (there's nothing noodle-sized in your heart). Dad, for always being supportive and never judgemental. Mum, for being with me in spirit–I can only hope I've made you proud. My beta readers, Rachel, Brianna, and Holly. My street team, for hyping me up and sharing my excitement for this release. My cover designer, Kirsty from The Pretty Little Design Co. for bringing Blue and Walker to life. My editor, Mackenzie, for being nothing but absolutely wonderful throughout the editing process. And you, my readers, for taking time out of your day to read my book. You make every keyboard banging, document deleting, and every fuck, shit and "I'm going to quit" day worth it enough to do it all again.

About the Author

www.jessicagraceauthor.com

Jessica Grace is a British author of New Adult Romance. She lives in a rural town in Wales with her husband and three young children. When she's not adulting, you'll usually find her one of two ways. That's with her head in a book—nursing a cuppa tea, or procrastinating to songs from her youth, thinking of all the stories she wants to write but is yet to put on paper.